**Doranna Durgin** spent her childhood filling notebooks first with stories and art, and then with novels. She now has over fifteen novels spanning an array of eclectic genres, including paranormal romance, on the shelves. When she's not writing, Doranna builds web pages, enjoys photography, and works with horses and dogs. You can find a complete list of her titles at doranna.net.

## Books by Doranna Durgin

### Harlequin Nocturne

#### *Sentinels*

*Sentinels: Leopard Enchanted*
*Sentinels: Alpha Rising*
*Sentinels: Lynx Destiny*
*Sentinels: Kodiak Chained*
*Sentinels: Tiger Bound*
*Sentinels: Wolf Hunt*
*Sentinels: Lion Heart*
*Sentinels: Jaguar Night*

*Claimed by the Demon*
*Taming the Demon*

Visit the Author Profile page
at Harlequin.com for more titles.

Doranna Durgin
and
Denise Lynn

# SENTINELS:
# LEOPARD ENCHANTED
# AND
# DRAGON'S PROMISE

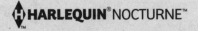
HARLEQUIN® NOCTURNE™

Recycling programs
for this product may
not exist in your area.

ISBN-13: 978-0-373-60177-6

Sentinels: Leopard Enchanted and Dragon's Promise

Copyright © 2015 by Harlequin Books S.A.

The publisher acknowledges the copyright holders
of the individual works as follows:

Sentinels: Leopard Enchanted
Copyright © 2015 by Doranna Durgin

Dragon's Promise
Copyright © 2015 by Denise L. Koch

**Printed in U.S.A.**

www.Harlequin.com

# CONTENTS

# SENTINELS: LEOPARD ENCHANTED

## Doranna Durgin

## The Sentinels

Long ago and far away, in Roman/Gaulish days, one woman had a tumultuous life—she fell in love with a druid, by whom she had a son. The man was killed by Romans. She was subsequently taken into the household of a Roman, who fathered her second son. The druid's son turned out to be a man of many talents, including the occasional ability to shapeshift into a wild boar, albeit at great cost.

The woman's younger son, who considered himself superior in all ways, had none of these earthly powers and went hunting to find ways to be impressive and acquire power. He justified his various activities by claiming he needed to protect the area from his brother, who had too much power to go unchecked…but in the end, it was his brother's family who grew into the Vigilia, now known as the Sentinels, while the younger son founded what turned into the vile Atrum Core…

# *Prologue*

Ana Dikau saw him before anyone else did.

The rest of the Atrum Core team crouched behind a camo blind in the pines uphill of the narrow, rocky trail, watching the camera feeds on a laptop encased in a rugged military shell. The wireless cameras pointed down along the trail, one of the less popular tracts of New Mexico's high, looming Sangre de Cristo mountains.

But Ana watched the trail itself, and she saw Ian Scott first—a shock of bright silvered hair, long and spiky and pretty much unreal in the perfection of its fall across his forehead. Crazy lean features and cheekbones to match his jaw, a rangy body to match his face, and a way of moving that made her feel quiet and small and very much like prey—a flush of warmth and awareness.

Then again, she had practice at feeling like prey. And she was far too aware of this man's Sentinel nature. The fact that he was so much more than human.

*Snow leopard.*

Walking into an Atrum Core trap.

Not to capture him—they knew better than that. There were far too many strictures between the Core septs prince and the Sentinel consul, between their factions as a whole. Direct action meant trouble. Even indirect action such as that they were about to undertake…

It was risky.

So they were hedging their bets. Filming this staged encounter to justify their need for action.

*Ana's new assignment.*

She'd long begged for this opportunity, a mission that would prove her worthy of more than her usual personal assistant work for Hollender Lerche, her supervisor since she'd been transferred to active Core duty at the tender age of thirteen.

Ian Scott bounded a few effortless steps uphill to clear a scattering of hard-edged rocks embedded in the trail, and she drew a deep, sharp breath—holding it, all unaware, until her lungs ached. He was beautiful in an uncivilized way, muscle and lean form perfectly evident under a casual shirt and the dark gray cargo pants riding low on his hips, shaping the strong curve of his bottom.

He was the enemy.

The team leader murmured into his field mike, "You're on." She didn't know his name. It didn't matter; she hadn't expected the courtesy of an introduction. All that mattered was what came next.

The mountain lion, barely caged just down the trail from their position.

The animal had been caged for days, starved and prodded into a frenzy. The hiker was one of their own, a man familiar to Ana who was working off a disgraceful failure—and he was already scented with blood and mountain lion urine.

Ana wasn't sure he knew it, though.

The mountain lion knew.

Freed, the beast didn't hesitate. It charged onto the trail in a snarling blur of tawny motion, claws already reaching to bat the man down.

The big cat screamed and the man screamed with it—a bloodcurdling thing with all the authenticity the team could have wanted. Convincing, because the man hadn't known these details of his work.

"Here we go," murmured the team leader. "Watch the bastard."

Ana watched, all right. Scott didn't hesitate. He sprinted forward as man, all coiled strength and energy, and then leaped— a dive, as if he intended to take cover in the scrub of the pine-shaded mountainside.

Instead he dove into a blinding roil of lightning and sharded energy, and when he emerged from the thick of it he landed on the two massive front paws of a snow leopard. Lush white fur splashed with black spots, staggering blue eyes, a thick length of tail—Ana held her breath again. He leaped forward almost before he'd fully found his feet in that form—smaller than the mountain lion but never hesitating.

Ana's handlers had said that the Sentinels looked for any excuse to unleash their violent natures.

He blindsided the mountain lion, latching on with claws and teeth so the two animals rolled off the hiker and right down the steep slope, spitting and snarling and breaking brush along the way. Fierce growls rose from below, and the mountain lion's angry scream split the air.

Ana strained forward as if she'd be able to see; the team leader's hand closed around her arm in a harsh and warning grip. She wanted to tell him she wasn't so stupid as to risk their cover, but she bit her lip and kept her words inside. She couldn't afford to be blamed for anything that went wrong, even an errant whisper—no matter that this man had already broken their silence.

The hiker rolled to his feet, stunned and unsteady—

and marked with fresh blood, but remarkably unharmed in the wake of Scott's swift reaction. He staggered on up the trail to rendezvous with the other half of the Core team, where they'd dig in out of sight until Ian Scott had moved on, protected with the same silent amulets that hid this camo blind.

The conflict below broke away into a few hissing spits, and then the sound of running retreat—and the quieter sounds of one of the animals returning, his footfalls more deliberate and almost silent. Ana watched the trail, waiting to see which of the big cats would emerge.

Not that there was any doubt. The mountain lion had been weakened, and Ian Scott was more than animal and more than human. Utterly beast, too dangerous to live unfettered.

The leader's hand closed more tightly around Ana's arm. "The team will finish recording. He'll be looking for trouble when he gets back up here."

She resisted his pull. "This is why I'm here," she said. "To see this. To see *him*. So I know what I'm up against." It was, in fact, the purpose behind this entire operation, although the footage would also be used to study the enemy in a way they'd never accomplished before. "I'm safe, as long as we're quiet." None of the Sentinels could detect the perfected silent amulets—not even Ian Scott, the Sentinel bane of many an amulet working.

The man made no effort to soften his derision—at her, at the Sentinel. "You've seen enough to know he's not human—he's nowhere near human. And we can't risk you. We don't have the time to start over with this op."

Because they didn't have another woman in place to fill her role. Not because she mattered, personally. It shouldn't still sting, after all these years.

But it did.

So Ana allowed herself to be led away, doglegging back to pick up the trail in the direction from which the Sentinel had come. Eventually the team leader released her arm, and she forbore to rub away the marks his fingers had made.

She'd wanted to see Ian Scott again. She'd wanted to see more closely the look in his eye when he took himself back to human—to get a glimpse of what lay beneath. Without it, her mind's eye showed only his instant understanding of the mountain lion's attack, and his instant response to it. *Efficient ferocity.* And somehow, she could think only of the warm flush of her reaction, and the fact that if she'd been that hiker, she would have wanted someone coming to her rescue, too.

But then the team took her back to the Santa Fe mansion that served as the local Core installation, and she learned that Ian Scott had returned to the trail and bounded after the Core hiker with only one thing in mind.

To finish what the mountain lion had started.

# Chapter 1

"'*Take a vacation,*' he said," Ian Scott grumbled, lifting free weights as he sat out in the gorgeous landscaping of the gorgeous Santa Fe property under the gorgeous blue skies in the gorgeous fall weather. "'*You'll like it,*' he said."

"You *could* like it." The woman's voice from the patio sounded anything but repentant for her eavesdropping.

Ian found her standing on the porch with her arms folded over her motherly shape, her expression a mix of affection and exasperation.

His own face held nothing but exasperation, he was certain of it. "He took away my team. My *computer*. My *tablet*. My *lab*!"

"Pfft." She made the noise with no sympathy at all. Her name was Fernie, and she ruled this retreat with nothing so overt as an iron fist. An iron spoon, perhaps. With cookie batter on it. "That's what happens when you work yourself sick."

Ian's grumble grew closer to a growl. "Field Sentinels," he said distinctly, "don't get sick. And I wasn't." He hefted the dumbbell for a quick set of curls, proving the point.

"You," she said, just as pointedly, "were injured. And

Nick Carter knows better than to let his people wear themselves down."

"Right," Ian said, switching the weights to his other arm. "Can't have that. Can't have people getting *tired* when there are lives to be saved."

His angry sarcasm was meant to drive her away. Instead she came down the three porch steps, past the towering, bloom-heavy hollyhocks and into the yard, her body language neither aggressive nor submissive—a woman with an extra touch of empathy who well knew the full-blooded Sentinels with whom she often worked.

Especially the cranky ones.

"Ian," she said, and the soft lines of her face held understanding, "you can't do it all. Maybe you can do most of it, but not *all*."

Something in his temper snapped; he felt the hard coil of it in his chest. "I don't have to do it *all*. I just have to do this one thing! *One* thing, to keep my friends safe!"

The best amulet tech in Brevis Southwest, and he still hadn't devised a defense against the Atrum Core's rarely detectable silent amulets—a failure that had cost them all dearly. Repeatedly. And which had given the Core time to devise other new deadly workings—while also leaving them vulnerable to new third-party interlopers, as of yet undefined in spite of their recent activity in the Southwest.

Fernie stood her ground. "That working is a fearful thing, no doubt. But the man who made it is dead now. You have time. And you've only been here a week."

He glared. "They have stockpiles of silent blanks. Sooner or later, they'll reproduce his work. And then the rest of us will die."

"Let it go for this moment," she said, quite steadily. "Don't you think that's why you're here?"

That hard spring coiled tighter. Ian left the weights on the ground and gave way to his leopard, letting the prowl of it come out in his movement—pacing away to the tall latilla coyote fence and back again, feeling the strength of four legs and solid big cat muscle lurking beneath his skin. Out and back again, thinking that although he could detect any normal amulet within a mile, identify its nature, even *trigger* it if he wanted, he still didn't have a thing on the silents.

Until Fernie said, in understanding admonishment, "Ian."

He snapped a look at her. Her eyes widened; she took a sharp breath. But she held her ground, because that's what she was here for. *"Ian."*

His snarl was as much acquiescence as temper. He paced onward…but tucked the leopard away.

Mostly.

"All right, Fernanda," he said, pausing by the fence. He found his fingers tapping against the rough, pinto bean bark of the hand-peeled latillas; he stilled them.

*Maybe a run.* Better than a hike up in the Sangre de Cristo trails, at least until he was certain the previous week's activity hadn't roused any interest. Strange that an aggressive mountain lion hadn't been reported.

The narrow Santa Fe River Park ran east-west before them, a riverbed greenway full of cottonwoods and trails. He drifted to the front of the compact yard, through the groomed pines to the thick old adobe wall— four feet near the open gate, stepped up to five feet and then six to meet the tall latilla poles at the corner; another group of stout blooming hollyhocks festooned the transition from adobe to the old fashioned poles. The rest of the fencing was just as idiosyncratic, done in stages to include a high adobe corner in the back and token rail fencing along the property line. Typical of these old Santa Fe properties, where bits and pieces had been added over time.

A dirt road stretched out before them, defining this barely developed privacy in the middle of Santa Fe. The Sangre de Cristo mountains loomed to the east, marching northward to Taos and Colorado—over fourteen thousand feet high, full of bear and cougar and pristine air, tall pines and craggy outcrops. Perfect for a snow leopard.

That had pretty much been the whole point. Nick Carter, Southwest Brevis Consul and definitely the boss of Ian, could have sent him to any one of the Sentinel retreats, from oceanside to low desert scrub. Instead he'd sent Ian from their Tucson base of operations into the high cool mountains for his snow leopard to love.

Ian had simply been too preoccupied with what he'd left behind to truly walk away from it.

*Atrum Core bastards.*

Two thousand years earlier, the strictures of their cold war with the Core hadn't been so important—not when druids held sway and Romans were trying to beat them down. Then, the Sentinels hadn't tried too terribly hard to hide their developing nature, their mandate to protect the Earth—and the Core hadn't even considered hiding their intent to gather power, ostensibly to make sure the Sentinels didn't get out of hand.

Mostly it had been seen as a power struggle between two half brothers—and maybe, mostly at the start it was.

But the Core turned to dark ways and corrupted energies to achieve its goal, and the Sentinels honed their skills—and the world changed around them until both factions were in agreement over the need to remain undetected. Their conflict went underground, a worldwide détente with certain understandings: no direct offensives, no breaking cover. Theirs would be a cold war.

Until the Core's most recent Southwest *drozhar* had gone rogue. Thanks to his silent amulets, too many Sentinels had been killed or wounded—especially the full-blooded field Sentinels. Those who took the shape of the other within.

Like Ian.

*Atrum Core* bastards.

"Go take a run," Fernie said, startling him. "You think I can't tell that you've gone off inside your head again?"

He growled at her.

She waved it away. "Go," she said. "Run. Think about something else." And she left him in the yard, returning to tend the cause of the yeasty sweetness wafting out into the yard.

What good was it to have a great growl when people ignored it? Ian propped his foot against the wall and retied his laces. *All right, Fernie. A run.*

But if he was distracted, he wasn't oblivious. He saw well enough that he was no longer quite alone. Never mind the male cyclist at the end of the road...the woman coming his way deserved plenty of attention.

She walked along the edge of the dirt and gravel with a green cloth shopping bag tucked over one shoulder and a small leather shoulder bag over the other, wearing a lightweight blazer over a creamy shirt that shimmered with her movement and set off the olive tones of her skin. Her tidy jeans were more smart than casual, and they highlighted her every move. Even from here, he found his gaze drawn to the delicate set of Eurasian features, from the distinct tilt of her eyes to the defined elegance of her nose.

She hesitated several properties away, eyeing the typical adobe wall, gravel driveway and gate—and then, rejecting it, looked ahead to the next property. And finally to this one, where Ian leaned against the wall, watching her. She picked up her pace, walking with more purpose—no longer looking at house numbers, but at him.

*All right, Fernie. First* her, *then a run.*

Ana knew better than to assume anything about this man. She'd seen what he could do. She'd heard what he'd *done.*

The Core soldier playing the part of a hapless hiker on the mountain hadn't deserved to die. She'd known him. He'd been only moderately skilled and not as hard-edged as most, taking his punishments without complaint. He hadn't been nice to her, but he hadn't been cruel, either.

She approached Ian Scott with one hand hooked into the grocery bag strap and the other in her purse and on her pepper spray—and even so, she hesitated.

She thought she'd known what to expect. Not just from the week before, but because she'd seen head shots—the faintly lengthened nature of his canines in that often rueful smile, the pale and unruly nature of his hair, silver by nature and smudged with faint streaks of black. She should have been prepared for the impact of those pale gray eyes rimmed with black, and for the striking contrast of dark brows and dark lashes. *The snow leopard, coming through.* Not all of the Sentinels showed their other so strongly, but this man...

Even standing there, he had a physical grace. Even not as tall as some of the Core posse members, even not as brawny.

She thought she'd known.

But she hadn't been this close to him on the trail. So she hadn't really known at all.

It took everything she had to offer him a steady smile. "Hi," she said, taking advantage of an opportunity she hadn't expected when she'd set out to survey this Sentinel retreat in person. "I'm so embarrassed, but when I left my rental this morning I didn't realize how similar these yards are—"

"And they aren't well numbered," he finished for her, as polite as any man should be, but his eyes...never to be mistaken for anything but a predator's eyes. His muscles ran strong and well-defined beneath a bright red sport shirt, his shoulders wide and body lean. Just as it had the week before, her body flushed with the awareness of what he was.

She swallowed her reaction, nodding to the drive beyond this one. "It might be that one. I'd recognize it if I went back for a look. But I don't want to intrude."

"I'll come with you, if you'd like," he said. "As long as you don't taze me." Those eyes flicked to her purse.

She lifted her hand from it. "Pepper spray," she said without apology.

"Of course, pepper spray." He said it amiably enough. "I wouldn't worry too much about intruding. That driveway goes to a cluster of rentals. You won't be the first person to look around."

It was, she realized with surprise, his way of politely

giving her space to move along on her own. For that instant, it flummoxed her; she was unused to such courtesy. Something fluttered in her chest, and she thought it might have been regret.

But in the next moment she jerked back, stumbling as his expression changed entirely—turning feral and predatory and triggering the fear that not only came of knowing what he was, but of *seeing* it in him. *Oh, God he's going to—*

And he did, planting his hands on the wall to leap over it in one smooth—

The blow came from behind, so suddenly she had no warning—just the impact, the wrenching twist of her shoulder, and her instinctive grab at her purse. She scraped against the adobe, losing the purse after all—and only then seeing the cyclist behind her.

Ian came over the wall feet first. The cyclist went flying, the bike went flying, the purse went flying...

Ian landed on his feet.

The cyclist scrambled up and away and somehow thought he would make it. Even Ana knew better, dazed and clinging to the wall—and stunned all over again by Ian's speed as he pounced. She winced in anticipation as he landed on the man, poised for a fierce blow—and then slowly relaxed as he drew himself up short, one knee on the man's chest, his knuckles resting at the man's throat in an aborted strike that would have been fatal.

"Bad move," he told the man. If he was breathing hard, Ana couldn't see it.

But she could see the man's face. And she knew him.

The shock of it piled on to the shock of the attack and kept her pinned to the wall, struggling to understand.

He was Core, she was sure of it. She couldn't fathom

it. Why would Lerche seek to sabotage the assignment he'd given her?

She came back to her wits as Ian Scott scooped her purse from the ground. Her attacker pedaled wildly away, not quite steady on the bike.

"What—?" she said, far too nonsensically.

"You okay?" Ian said, and held out the purse.

"Yes, I—" She rubbed her arm, taking the purse to fumble for her phone. "I should call the police—" Not because she truly thought it best, but because she thought it was the thing to say.

He sidestepped the matter—no surprise. Sentinels eschewed official notice as much as the Core. "I'd rather offer to see you home again. You have any idea why that guy would be targeting you?"

For the moment, she forgot her script. "What do you mean, *targeting* me?"

"He's been lurking at the end of the street, watching you."

*Ah.* She understood now. Someone hadn't trusted her to get this job done on her own…and then hadn't trusted her enough to let her in on the plan. She groped for words that would ring true. "I can't imagine it was personal."

"Didn't smell like coincidence," he said, his fingers tapping lightly against the wall. Surely the man sat still every once in a while. "It smelled like—" He stopped himself.

She had the sudden understanding that he spoke literally, and she remembered again who this man was—no matter his charismatic presence or his beautiful eyes. He was Sentinel, and he was the Southwest's best amulet specialist. If the Core had sent out a posse member who carried amulets…

Even Ana could sometimes perceive the regular amulets, like a stain in the air. Many Core members couldn't, and it wasn't considered a necessary skill. But of course he'd know, and far better than she would. And of course he'd want to avoid the cops. The Sentinels and the Core kept their encounters off the books.

"You're probably right," he said, making an obvious choice to relinquish control of the conversation. "Coincidence." He bent to pick up her groceries, scattered as they were from the encounter, and appropriated the bag so he could reload them. "You're all scraped up. Come on inside, we'll get you fixed up."

She hesitated a moment too long. He added, "Fernie is inside, too. She'll slap my hands if I do anything you don't want me to."

For that moment, she froze. She heard the unspoken message there—the potential that there were things she might *want* him to do. His eyes told her as much, seeing her absorb the meaning, confirming it—smiling just there at the corner of his mouth.

*Run away. Run fast.*

Run to safety, where the flush of her awareness wouldn't expand into a flush of wanting—of wondering what it would be like to be touched by such strength and consideration. As if this man might just give back as much as he received.

She took a sharp breath, using it to slap herself back to reality. There would be no running, no matter how smart it would be. Because getting inside the house had been part of her assignment all along.

*Get inside the house. Plant the silent amulet.*

And maybe, finally, she would gain not only the respect and belonging she longed for, but also the safety that came with it.

# Chapter 2

Hollender Lerche hated adobe.

He hated flat roofs and stucco and chunky viga pine columns and pretentious entry arches, and he hated a high altitude climate that thought it could be desert and yet still had far too much snow in the winter.

Still, he should be grateful. Many from Tucson had died during the illicit attack on the Sentinels; others had acted too publicly and paid the price at the hands of the worldwide septs prince.

In the wake of that attack, Lerche had merely been assigned to this small city—an annoyingly artsy place that had persistently remained the region's capital city. He didn't have to be told that his future rested on his quiet success. The septs prince would turn a blind eye to certain events as long as they brought results—but not for an instant if they brought more embarrassment.

For now, results meant taking out Ian Scott.

A man who had so conveniently ambled into Lerche's new territory, leading him straight to the quaint little retreat property—and to opportunity.

Lerche looked out onto the rolling piñon and juniper foothills of the Sangre de Cristo mountains and narrowed his eyes as if that spearing glare could blast the high grasslands into something more palatable. When someone rapped politely on the sliding glass door behind him, he ignored them. This second-story patio was his *Do Not Disturb* zone.

But eventually he left the squintingly bright sunshine of the morning and returned to the oppressive gloom of thick textured walls. The man inside greeted him with an unusual combination of resentment and defiance.

"Mr. Budian," Lerche said, which meant many things at once—a greeting, a demand for a report...a demand for explanation.

David Budian stood before him not in the neat suit of an active posse member or the dark slacks and shirt also allowed those working strenuous field positions. Nor was he the usual stature of such field agents—the classic deep olive skin and black hair, set off by silver studs and rings. Budian was a man of middling complexion, middling height, middling features.

None of that came as a surprise—the man's appearance was why Lerche assigned him to particular activities with particular anonymity. Even Ana, as naive as she was, would spot a man of brawn and classic full-blooded complexion.

But it surprised him to see Budian in torn clothes and bruises.

Lerche said, "Have you compromised us, Mr. Budian?"

Budian looked as alarmed as he should. *"Drozhar—"*

"Don't suck up." *Drozhar* was a term held by regional princes, as well as the world septs Prince. Not a posse leader. Not even when the posse was as large as the one Lerche now commanded here in Santa Fe. "I want to know what's happened!"

"I observed Ana as ordered. She was dawdling,

so I provided an opportunity for her." Budian's self-satisfaction made it to his face in a way he likely didn't realize. "You know how those Sentinels are, sir. If they see a chance to meddle, they'll take it."

Lerche sat at his massive desk, relaxing into the padded chair. He brushed his hand across the black gleam of the surface, displacing invisible dust motes. "True enough. Did you achieve results?"

"I gave him a chance to play the hero and he took it. If that little dirt-bred bitch can't make something of it, then she's as hopeless as I think she is."

"Mind your tongue, Mr. Budian." Lerche's words held no heat; it went against everyone's instincts to use a woman in an important field operation. But Ana was everything they needed—petite, beautiful with an elegant delicacy and utterly determined to prove her worth to them…without the faintest idea that she never could. "She knows nothing of that thin Sentinel heritage, and I want it to stay that way."

"Until it's too late, you mean," Budian suggested.

Lerche smiled. "Exactly so, Mr. Budian." And then he would be free of her. "Just exactly so."

Ana found herself sitting in cool Santa Fe comfort—saltillo floors and kitchen counters, hand-painted Talavera tiles set in the walls around the light switches and along the counter backsplash, gauzy curtains under shaded windows. The air was redolent of spices and oils and the scent of something baking. Something *good*.

Ian had introduced himself, and Fernie—Fernanda—and had handed her a damp washcloth, disappearing with "Be right back."

Ana waited on a spindle-backed stool at the breakfast bar and patted the cool cloth against the road rash beneath her elbow, near to dizzy with the conflicting experiences of being in such a homey welcoming atmosphere while within the grasp of the enemy.

Especially an enemy who kept her on edge in every way.

Ian—the enemy—returned to the kitchen in a billow of what seemed to be his usual energy, dropping a tub of salve on the counter. "This stuff will speed the healing."

Fernie put a hot tray of muffins on the sideboard and sent Ian a disapproving frown. "A gentleman would help her take care of such awkward injuries."

"Oh," Ana protested. "You can hardly call them *injuries*. A few scrapes and bruises—fewer than that cyclist had, I'm sure."

Ian stepped back. "A gentleman respects the boundaries a lady sets." But his gaze met hers with amusement, as if they were somehow in this together.

She understood why. Fernie obviously ruled this house—a so-called *corporate retreat*—with an iron pot holder. Of medium stature, with a plump figure and shining strands of gray in her black hair, Fernie's Latina and Native heritage came through in both her features and the gentle roll of her words. Given Fernie's position here in the house, Ana guessed that she wasn't a full-blooded field Sentinel—one of those with roots deep enough to reach to their lurking *other* within.

Looking at Ian, Ana would never doubt it of him. Even if she hadn't actually seen his snow leopard the week before.

But field Sentinel or not, Fernie was obviously formidable and just as obviously possessed of an uncanny ability to read beneath the emotional surface of those around her. She cleared her throat at Ian as she tapped the previous tray of muffins loose from the cups.

Ana pressed her lips together in a smile. "Well," she said, and offered Ian the washcloth, "maybe under the circumstances..."

"All right, then." He stopped tapping to whatever rhythm ran in his head to take the cloth. The same hands that had taken down the cyclist became surprisingly gentle as he turned her arm to see the scrape.

"Don't you ever sit still?" she asked, not truly having meant to say it.

Fernie laughed, placing a selection of muffins on a plate and sliding it within reach along with butter, a knife and napkins. "Not that anyone's observed so far. What brings you to Santa Fe, Ana?"

*Oh, nothing of importance. Just spying on you.*

"A quiet vacation," she said, in spite of the fact that she'd lived here for months now, along with the rest of Lerche's posse. They'd had no idea the retreat existed until Lerche had tracked Ian to it. "The Georgia O'Keeffe museum, the plaza, the pueblos, the Indian Market... I meant to come with a friend, but family issues cropped up." She shrugged, comfortable with the amiable cover story Lerche had given her. "It's a little strange to be here without a travel companion, I admit."

Fernie sent Ian a pointed glance. "You see? You *could* be doing something other than fretting. See the sights with this woman!"

Ian glared at Fernie, not Ana. "I do not *fret*," he said, even as he dabbed her arm. "And I don't need mothering."

Fernie ran a trickle of water into the sink, briskly rinsing dishes before stashing them in the dishwasher.

Ana only got a glimpse, but she was pretty sure the other woman smiled behind her noncommittal noise of response. And Ian, with his mix of annoyance and affection...

He wasn't what she'd expected. Even beyond what she'd seen and what she'd read.

She knew he'd been badly hurt in early spring but had healed well and quickly, as Sentinels did. She knew he'd had several skirmishes with the Core before that. She knew, most of all, that the Sentinels counted on him to solve the mystery of the silent amulets, and the Core therefore needed to find out everything they could about his progress—here, away from protected Southwest Brevis headquarters.

That was her job. To plant the spy amulet—to connect with him and absorb what she could of him in person.

"You're staring," he said, keeping his voice low—although Fernie had left to clatter around in the dining room, laying out silverware and dishes. He held her arm as he dipped into the herbal unguent and spread it lightly over her skin.

She shivered at the touch, bemused at her own sensitivity—at her sudden extreme awareness of his fingers against her skin. "I was thinking," she said—but stopped, caught by his eyes—the contrast of those pale irises with the dark rims, the dark lashes and glinting silver hair, mussed with the casual authority of a bad boy model even though she doubted he paid much attention to it at all. "Your eyes—"

His brows shot up; she looked away, profoundly embarrassed. She wasn't cut out for deception. *The Core should have known better.*

She'd never understood why they'd chosen her for

this—she knew only that she was desperate for acceptance and that this had seemed like her chance. She decided on the truth, after all. For the moment. "They're striking," she said. "I'm sorry. I didn't mean to embarrass you. Or me. Maybe I hit that wall harder than I thought."

"Maybe," he said, applying a transparent film bandage of a size that few households would carry as a matter of course. "Or maybe it would just be nice to see this city with a companion." He smoothed the bandage into place, stroking her arm with a confident touch.

*Maybe I* should *run.*

She was in so far over her head.

She should plant the amulet under the counter edge, make her excuses and run. She should tell Lerche that Ian was so much more than she'd expected—much more than she could handle, a Sentinel force of nature. They expected her to fail; they'd always expected her to fail. It would come as no surprise to them if she did. She'd simply be sent back to the personal assistant work she found so very stifling.

But she hesitated there at the breakfast bar with his hand still closed over her arm, full of warmth and a very personal touch—and she noticed, to her surprise, that he stood perfectly still. He didn't vibrate; he didn't shift his weight or bump his knuckles against the granite counter.

He only watched her.

And she didn't want to run from that.

He grinned, an unrepentant expression on an irrepressible face. "Georgia O'Keeffe. Tomorrow, if you'd like. Now. How about we go figure out where you're staying?"

Ana smiled back at him. And when he turned away

to toss the bandage wrappings and rinse the washcloth, she pressed the tiny silent spy amulet into place, activated it with the faintest twist of will, and told herself she was only doing what she had to do.

Ian paced the yard perimeter, rubbing a restless thumb across the sample amulet in his hand—a simple thing of rough making, and a thing with which he was already deeply familiar, even if he hadn't cracked the secrets of its silence.

That breakthrough wasn't likely to happen now, with his thoughts so scattered. Ana might have left the retreat the day before, but she'd definitely lingered in his thoughts.

*Soft skin beneath his fingers, the gleam of honey beneath the brown of her eyes when she'd been caught staring, the faintest of blushes over cheek and neck when she'd realized it. The way she'd owned up to it, seeming surprised at herself while she was at it.*

There was something about her matter-of-fact acceptance of her injuries that bothered him; he hadn't quite put his finger on it. They weren't serious, but they must have stung like the dickens. A little *ow!* wouldn't have been out of place.

Ian glanced down the road and decided he wasn't *quite* as bad as a kid with a schoolyard crush, no matter what Fernie had said. He'd dressed in the best of the casual clothes he'd brought, been glad for the lightweight hiking boots, and wandered out to the yard thirty minutes early for his meeting with Ana.

He'd figured it would take that long to settle his mind over the working he thought he'd detected that morning.

Now he knew himself to have been optimistic, and he paced the yard perimeter with impatience.

Just as well that he wasn't one of those Sentinels who could reach out to mind-tap Annorah, their brevis-wide communication hub. Or to anyone, for that matter, though he could hear well enough if someone else initiated a tap on his shoulder. No doubt he'd be driving her just as crazy as he was driving himself, checking in to see how things were going with his AmTech assistants— if they had what they needed, if they'd stumbled over any faint clue he might build on...

No doubt she'd be ignoring him by now.

The working on this crude amulet was innocuous enough—easily identified as such by the lanyard. Simple identifying knots, rough leather...nothing worth the silence that had been stamped on it. But this particular amulet had been recovered at Fabron Gausto's evil little hideout in Tucson, where Nick Carter had almost died in the attempt to stop *Core D'oíche*.

The thing's value lay not in its function but in its silent nature. Only the rare Sentinel tracker had any chance of perceiving this one.

Ian couldn't. In spite of his expertise, his ability to find and identify amulets at a distance, it was nothing but a disk of crudely inscribed bronze. No matter how tightly he focused his attention, nor how finely he sliced the bands of his perception.

He prowled back over into the shade. This morning in the house he'd thought he'd felt something from this amulet, but he wasn't the only one in occupancy, and that meant interruptions and noise. He shared the retreat and its half-dozen cozy little rooms with a light-blood couple from Kachina Valley, Arizona, a strong-blood courier from Senoita who quite obviously took the cheetah, a tech of some sort from Tucson Brevis and a mid-teen youth who couldn't more obviously be in retreat from the mundane world while he grew accustomed to his burgeoning Sentinel gifts.

The accumulated effect left him far, far from the buffered and isolated conditions of his lab. Trying to pin down the subtleties of what he'd felt had only served to trigger a headache, driving him outside to wait while he ignored Fernie's reminder that the whole point of his presence here was to take a break from such things.

The faintest sound of a footfall on sandy grit lifted his head from those inner thoughts. When Ana appeared over the wall some moments later, he was waiting, his mood lifted by an anticipation he hadn't expected. She caught sight of him and turned to rest her elbows on the wall. "Surely I'm not that late?"

"Not late at all," he told her, resolutely stuffing the amulet away. "But I'm not much good at sitting still."

"I got that impression." Her smile softened those dry words, lighting features that had seemed just a little too somber before she'd seen him. A delicately angular jaw, a sweet curve of a mouth, dark eyes that dominated her face…they lent her an air of mystery, the impression of strength and vulnerability that wasn't the least offset by the way the breeze teased her hair—short enough to reveal the peek of earlobe and the graceful sweep of her neck, long enough to tousle and beguile.

But he'd looked too long, for the smile faltered. Not so much uncertain as just a little too serious. "You know, I never asked. I thought at first this place was your home, and Fernie your housekeeper. But as I was leaving yesterday—"

"Jack came out." Lured by Fernie's muffins, no doubt, given how much the kid could eat.

"And I heard laughter from the lower level, so I gather you're not alone. Family?"

"In a manner of speaking." Ian told her the truth easily enough, if not the entirety of it. "This place is a retreat. Sometimes it's a think tank, and sometimes it's just a place our people come when they want the same thing you're here for—a quiet vacation."

She looked at the house a moment longer, a faint furrow between her brows. "Your people?"

"The group I work for." It was close enough. He laced his fingers between hers over the top of the wall and his thoughts stumbled, his equilibrium lost. For an instant he knew the stunning peace of having one focus and one focus only. *Ana.*

"Are you all right?" She let him keep her hand, but not without concern. "You look…distracted. Something's wrong?"

"The opposite," he told her, and captured that hand, too—did it without second thought, as though he had every right. Even the headache had lifted. "You ready to take in some Georgia O'Keeffe? It's a twenty-minute walk from here."

She didn't hide her bemusement. "Something tells me you'll enjoy that twenty minutes of motion more than the museum itself."

"I'll enjoy the company," he said, surprising himself by just how much he meant it. And she surprised him back, squeezing his hands in an unspoken response.

She might just have surprised herself, to judge by the look on her face—a little bit uncertain, a little bit amused. She glanced down the greenway path. "Would you like to just...walk?"

"I've got a better idea." He looked east toward the mountains—not thinking of the trail where he'd encountered the mountain lion, but a little south of it, where the scenic byway wound upward to Vista Grande through splashes of aspen gold. "If you don't mind a motorcycle, that is."

Her eyes widened faintly, pleasure behind them. Ian grinned at her, for the moment, not thinking of the silent amulets at all.

"I've never been on one," she warned him.

"It's a touring bike," he assured her, and then laughed when she only looked blankly in response. "It's comfortable. You'll feel secure. Though the retreat has a car—we can take that, if you'd prefer."

She lifted a brow. "What kind of car?"

He nodded at the side of the house, where the bright blue Smart car just barely peeked out. She eyed it and then leaned over the wall to also ostentatiously eye the length of his leg. "Maybe not."

Ian laughed. "Maybe not," he agreed. "Come on around. We've got a jacket you can use. It'll be cool up on the mountain."

The retreat had plenty of such little extras, and if the leather jacket was a little big on her, the sleeves shoved back well enough—and the biking gloves fit perfectly. He showed her how to secure the motorcycle helmet, threading the double-D rings and snapping the trailing strap, then stowed her purse in the saddlebags. A quick primer on mounting, the foot pegs, the muffler placement and how to be a neutral passenger, and they were ready to go.

By then Fernie had emerged from the kitchen, an unusual flush to her features and her smile looking a bit determined. She proffered a packed lunch, and while Ian tucked it away and grabbed his own jacket, all black leather and zippers and snaps, Fernie leaned close to Ana as if Ian didn't have the ears of a Sentinel to hear every word. "You hang on tight, now."

Ana laughed—a faint uncertainty to it, but a low musical note, too, and one that tickled his ears.

Only once, after he'd mounted the bike and held it steady for her to settle in behind him, did she hesitate—and then, only just for a moment. Long enough to touch the pocket of her dark slacks, and he guessed she had her phone there—although reception on the mountain road would be touch and go at best. Then she climbed on, placing herself precisely on the seat and her feet on the passenger pegs, her legs barely brushing the outside of his hips and her hands resting loosely just above them.

"The trick is not to think too hard about it," he told her, briefly resting a hand on the side of her lower leg. "And just nudge my shoulder if you need anything. I'll pull over."

"What are you waiting for?" she demanded.

He laughed and started the bike—and if she clutched tightly at him on the first turn and made him fight to keep the bike on line at the second turn, by the time they eased out of town and through the expensive foothills real estate, she'd started to relax. By the time they'd climbed through the piñon-juniper to the ponderosa, swooping gently through the curves and ever climbing upward, her hands rested around his waist as though they'd always been there, her knees snug at his hips without tension.

She shifted only slightly, never interfering with their balance, as he pointed out the things he spotted along the ride—the ferruginous hawk perched off the side of the road, the amazing tower of an ancient pine. He slowed down for the scatter of elk in the trees, giving her a good look and grinning when her hands tightened in the thrill of spotting them.

And along the way, he found himself just as relaxed as she was—just as willing to go along with the moment, without the constant nag of activity in his mind.

*Huh.*

Sixteen miles later he pulled over at the Vista Grande overlook, bracing the bike while she dismounted, her hands suddenly self-conscious as she steadied herself on his shoulder. He felt the distance like a cold chill, the descent of cares and the weighty awareness of...

*Everything.*

She fumbled at the helmet strap but managed it, pulling the helmet off to fluff up her hair. Then she got a good look at the view and faltered, her eyes widening.

"The Jemez Mountains," he said, hooking his helmet over a handlebar as he dismounted and moving up behind her to point out the distant range, his arm over her shoulder where it felt like it belonged. "The Rio Grande Valley. Albuquerque, if you squint." Not to mention the swatches of golden aspen against the dark green of the predominant ponderosa pines, Sangre de Cristo fall drama in all its glory.

She leaned back into him; maybe she didn't even realize it.

Ian realized it. Boy, did he realize it. He cleared his throat. "There are a handful of trails leading out from this overlook—including one that goes into the Pecos wilderness." He nodded eastward, and her hair tick-led his chin. "If you'd like—if you have some hiking shoes—we can come again, and hike out into the as-pens."

A car drove past, slowing for the overlook...not stopping. When the sound of its motor no longer hummed among the trees, Ana pulled away from him—turning to face him, her hand touching her pocket as if it steadied her...her expression a little wary.

"Why?" she said.

He grew still inside, understanding the danger of taking this question lightly. "Because it's beautiful, and I'd like to share it with you."

She turned away, looking out over the sprawling vista of forest and valley and distant ranges rising anew.

Ian tapped a pattern against his thigh. "Hey," he said, resisting the impulse to close the space between them. "If I misread the situation, no worries. We drive back down the mountain, you head off to the rest of your va-cation, and we still had a good ride together in amaz-ing country."

He could hardly believe himself. Not when he wanted to—

Except it didn't matter what he wanted, if she *didn't*. And it wasn't as if he didn't have work to do, no matter his orders and Fernie looking over his shoulder. Until he cracked the secret of the silents, they were all at risk. *High* risk.

He hadn't come near to convincing himself when she said it again. *"Why?"*

This time, he realized what she was asking—but not before she turned to look at him, searching his expres-sion as she added, "You don't even know me."

He suddenly felt off balance. "That's how it usually starts," he said. "By meeting. And liking. And wanting more." Who could *not*? And not just because of her delicate beauty, or the natural color of her lips against the glow of her complexion, or the way she wore that ill-fitting jacket that made it perfectly clear what curves lurked beneath—although his body responded to those things readily enough.

No, it was more about the complexity waiting behind her eyes, calling out the puzzle lover in Ian. One moment laughing, the next turned inward, and always—always—a shine of vulnerability. As if she simply waited for someone who could figure her out.

It was the way she made him feel. Moments of peace and inner quiet.

She must have seen something on his face. Her expression turned suddenly fierce. "I don't need saving from being alone, if that's what you think."

Ian made an impatient sound. "That's not what this is about." He closed the distance between them then, reaching out to cradle her head and thread his fingers through her hair—holding but not constraining, and watching her eyes go wide while her body stiffened inside the ridiculously large jacket.

But then she relaxed, those eyes still huge and not so much wary as uncertain—waiting. *Learning*, he would have said, as he leaned down to her. Her hands rose to brush against his forearms as if they didn't know what else to do, but her mouth...it rose to meet his. And when he kissed her, she kissed him back—a gentle thing, as uncertain as the rest of her could be.

He wooed her with that kiss, making it light and teasing, just a touch of tongue along her lips and a touch of nibbling tooth. Keeping it light in spite of the instant fire licking along his skin and settling heavily in his groin.

Maybe he trembled faintly—maybe it was just the breeze stirring her hair. Either way, Ian knew his limits, no matter how it surprised him to hit them so soon. He stroked the fine line of her cheekbones with his thumbs and lifted his mouth from hers, unbending himself into his full height.

Another car drove past, slowing dramatically until it moved past the vista. Ana closed her hands around his wrists, holding his hands where they cupped her head, and lifted her gaze to his—luminescent brown eyes that caught him as securely as the warmth of her fingers. "But how do you know this is what you want?"

He instantly sensed this wasn't about fishing for compliments. He hunted for truth.

"For sure?" he said. "You don't. You just believe. You feel, and you follow it. The rest either comes or it doesn't." He slid one hand around to the back of her neck and lifted slightly, changing her balance just enough so she stepped forward, bringing them together in the most unmistakable way. His other hand slid down to the small of her back, absorbing every inch of the curves along the way and stopping just above the round swell of her bottom.

No way would she miss all the evidence of his response to her, from the tension in his body to the distinct erection so uncomfortably trapped by his jeans.

She drew a sharp breath, and her hands tightened on his arms—at least until he laughed, just a short huff of amusement. "Breathe," he advised her, and brushed his cheek against hers. "If you faint, I'll never figure this out."

At that, she stepped back, brushing her hand over the pocket he'd decided held her phone. "Figure what out?"

"Whether you want me, too," he said as matter-of-factly as anyone could. "Because I don't want *yes*. I want *hell, yes*."

Finally, she laughed. "Either way, we're not getting back on that motorcycle until you're a little more *relaxed*, are we?"

"No," he said, and grinned. "We certainly are not."

She scraped windblown hair from her face. "You don't doubt yourself much, do you?"

He shrugged, his peripheral vision catching yet another car on approach. "All the time," he told her. "But I don't fear the doubt."

Failure was another story. He could sell her nightmares about failure.

"You know," she said, "you're right. You knew it, didn't you? Meeting. Liking. Wanting more. Yes, I'd love to go on a hike with you while I'm here. Yes, I *feel*...and I want to follow it."

This grin came along with a slow burn of warmth—a spot inside himself that made itself quiet long enough for him to feel the simple pleasure of the moment.

But damn, it didn't do a thing for his ability to hop back on that bike.

The approaching car slowed enough so he thought it might stop, then moved on. Gawkers, he decided, fully aware of the moment they'd interrupted.

At least, he thought it right up until he felt the unmistakable taint of a Core working. He turned sharply from Ana, eyes narrowing, body readying—for attack, for defense, for the challenge of identifying the working just as quickly as he could even if he had very little means to protect from it. His shields were only moderate and, without laboratory conditions and warding to enhance them, of only minimal use against a direct working.

Ana whirled to follow his attention, cuing from his body language—shrinking back, but also readying herself—a shift of balance, a grab for the jacket pocket where he'd be damned if she hadn't probably stashed that pepper spray. "What—?"

*Late model midsize SUV, a dark metallic green. Driver, passenger and enough tint to the windows so he couldn't say anything else of them.*

And then it was gone, and the car accelerated away just as any other sightseer might have done.

"Ian?"

He tried to stand down; he tried to convince himself he hadn't felt the working—a thing that had passed too quickly to identify it as anything other than a detection amulet. His fingers drummed a pattern against the side of his leg. He hadn't quite found the right words, his mind too full of their vulnerable position here on the mountainside, the ramifications of Core presence, the phone calls he should be making—when she rested a hand on his arm.

*Silence.*

He turned to her, startled by it—not quite able to respond to it.

"Are you all right?" Nothing uncertain in those brown eyes now, just concern, her arching eyebrows raised in question.

"I'm—" he said, and shook his head. "It's nothing." And maybe it wasn't. Maybe it was just as simple as sightseeing posse members with an alert working— one that would warn against Sentinel presence simply because some Core members were no more prepared to deal with Sentinels than a light-blood support tech wanted to deal directly with Core.

No wonder they had sped away, if that had been the case.

"Nothing," he told her again. "And I've got an idea. You, me, takeout of your choice and a movie at your place tonight." Not that he wouldn't gladly spend the whole day with her, hitting the Railyard artisans or Old Town or even the O'Keeffe museum—but he had the sudden impulse to check in with the lab and see if they'd made any progress without him, and to check in on Fernie, who in spite of her cheerful send-off, hadn't seemed quite herself today.

"Me, you, takeout and a movie at my place," she agreed. "And then... I guess we see."

Dammit. It was going to take forever before he could get on that motorcycle again.

# Chapter 3

Ana closed the door behind Ian Scott and leaned against it with a sigh, still fully feeling the movement of his mouth over hers and the way it woke everything inside her. Pounding heart, warmth pooling in intimate places, the frisson of those faintly pointed canine teeth on her skin, her breath coming just a little bit fast.

Until reality hit, a blow that momentarily took her breath away altogether.

She wasn't here to *feel*. She was here to plant two amulets and gather information. Tonight, when he came back with takeout and his unsuspecting, habitually wry hint of a smile.

*He is snow leopard, Ana Dikau. He is* beast.

She slipped a hand into her front pocket, running her fingers over the tiny listening amulet she hadn't yet planted.

*Because I'm doing well so far. Because I don't want to risk blowing the operation if he finds it. Because he's more sensitive to such things than his dossier indicated he would be.* The amulet-tainted car along the overlook road had told her that much.

It was all true. But she didn't know if such reasons would convince Hollender Lerche, a man with little patience for underperformance. And she *did* know that

this was her one and only chance to prove herself to the
organization that had never quite found her of value.
Certainly never treated her as though she was of value.

If she could just do this one thing for them...

"Ana."

She jerked her hand out of her pocket with a guilty
start. "Mr. Lerche! What are you doing here? Ian might
have come inside—"

He emerged not from the great room of this modest
vacation rental, but from her bedroom—dressed in his
usual suit, heavy silver flashing at his ear and wrist and
fingers, his skin a darker shade than hers and his features heavier. She flushed, a furious heat on her cheeks,
but the look on his face silenced her, and then so did his
words. "Surely not into the bedroom, Ana. *Woo* him,
dearest. Don't *fuck* him."

She knew better than to respond. He didn't want her;
he wanted only to claim and control her. To distress her,
because it made him feel more than he was.

The problem was, knowing those things didn't change
his status with regard to hers—and it didn't change his
effect on her. The dread in her stomach, cold and hard
and a little bit sick. The way she felt smaller and weaker.
And the way just *once*, she wanted to feel as though she
belonged in this society to which she'd been born.

Maybe if she tried harder. Maybe if she was stronger.
Maybe if she didn't let her sentimental tendencies get
in the way, as they always had. Then again, few women
rose in the ranks, preferring the anonymity and protection of an early marriage. No man in the Atrum Core
would touch another's spouse.

Now and then it occurred to Ana that it should be

enough that a woman simply didn't want to be touched. But experience proved otherwise.

Certainly Hollender Lerche felt free enough to touch her—as he did now, grasping her jaw in a hard grip and then tightening his blunt fingers even further, bringing a sting of involuntary tears to Ana's eyes. "We need to talk, Ana."

"He'll be back in this evening for dinner." Desperate words, barely intelligible. And that's all she said, because suggesting that he not leave a mark would only invite him to hurt her in ways that wouldn't.

His grip didn't ease. "I'm not concerned about an hour from now. I'm concerned about *now*. And why you haven't activated the second amulet. The one that should be planted on your friend Ian Scott."

"How—" But Ana didn't finish the question. She squeezed her eyes closed in understanding. "The car. The working Ian felt. That was someone checking up on me?"

"An entirely necessary precaution, it would seem," he said, and gave her a little shake before releasing her with a disdainful flick of his fingers. He turned away, withdrawing a folded handkerchief from his pocket to wipe his fingers.

"But he's an AmTech. He *felt* it. He knows we're here—"

"That was always a risk." Lerche snapped the words. The modicum of security she'd gained at his distance evaporated. "Entirely on your shoulders, Ana dear. If you were trustworthy, we wouldn't have risked exposure. As it is, it seems we had good reason."

"I just need a little more time!" she cried, trying and failing to soften the resentment threading her plea. She scrambled to find the right words, hoping to distract him. "He's more sensitive about amulets than we thought—and besides, if I plant it on the wrong item of clothing, the amulet could sit in a closet for *days*."

"You're cozy enough with him," Lerche said, tucking the handkerchief away and squaring the lapels of his suit. "Carry the activated amulet on your person until you can make that decision."

*But I—*

This time she managed to keep the words to herself—a protest at her loss of privacy would not be well received. It might even make him realize that such concern had caused her to delay in the first place.

She'd wanted to talk to Ian Scott without being overheard. She'd wanted to connect with him her own way.

Although she'd never expected to *connect* with him at all. Or to relax behind him on the motorcycle, clasping his hips as if such closeness was a familiar thing, or to respond so strongly to his presence.

To his touch.

*Snow leopard.*

Surely she should have been frightened. More than just nervous and unfamiliar, but downright terrified of what he was and of what she'd seen him do.

*Snow leopard.*

And yet he'd been gentle with her. He'd been respectful. He'd been *careful*. And he'd allowed every decision to be hers.

Not that she'd truly had a choice. The Core demanded of her to do this thing—to get close to him, to plant spy amulets on him, to learn of him what she could.

*You could have said no.* In her heart, she knew that. *No, don't kiss me. No, don't touch me that way.*

If she'd wanted.

Lerche's voice was a silky thing, all the more dangerous for it. "What are you thinking, my little Ana?"

"About the best way to do what you've asked." As if there was any other answer.

His hand flashed out to pat her cheek—nigh on close to a slap, and enough to rock her head, jarring her vision. "You betray yourself, Ana. I haven't *asked* you to do anything. I've *told* you what you'll do."

She covered her burning cheek. "Of course," she said, and hated that her voice wasn't quite steady. "I misspoke."

He eyed her coldly enough so she knew she wouldn't be forgiven that easily. "It's fortunate for you that we don't have the time to bring someone else up to speed on this operation. See that you do better this evening. Wear the amulet yourself until you have the opportunity to plant it to our advantage."

"Yes," she said, forcing herself to drop her hand and stand straight but not facing him directly. Not a hint of confrontational body language. "Of course I will."

He smiled in tight satisfaction. The kind of smile that said he knew he was better than she was, that he was entitled to more respect than she was, that he was in control of his own destiny in ways she would never be. "I'll be watching."

Only after he'd gone did she allow herself to explore her hot cheek and tender jaw, and wonder whether he'd gone so far that bruises would bloom beyond what she could hide with casual makeup.

First step, an ice pack. She dumped ice into a zipper storage bag and wrapped it in a thin towel, curling up on the couch while she did the things that would calm her—thinking only of the cool relief of the ice and soft cushions of the couch and the quiet of this place. Reminding herself what the Sentinels were and why she did this—and of how much of that Sentinel *other* she could see in Ian at any given time.

Of how easily he'd killed a man the week before.

But somehow, as she dozed off, her thoughts wandered back to the forest that week earlier when Ian had heard the hiker's peril. The way he'd bounded forward without hesitation. The way he'd flowed from one form to another, surrounded by a cloud of stunningly beautiful energies. How he'd done it for a *stranger*—and what would he do for one of his own?

What would it be like to be with someone who cared that much?

She didn't heed Lerche's voice in her head, so scornful that she'd already forgotten Ian's true reasons for what hadn't been a rescue at all—the excuse to turn loose his beast, a thing so fearsome that it had turned on the man he should have been saving.

She thought instead of being allowed choices, and of respect, and of how deeply he'd responded to her without the hint of a harsh touch.

She didn't mean to fall so completely asleep with Ian on her thoughts, but she did. She woke an hour later with her jaw stiff and her body humming in memory of gentle hands and skillful mouth. She froze, making sure of herself—*am I still alone?*

Silence. A clock ticking. A brief flurry of birds outside.

No, Lerche hadn't returned. Nor had anyone else made themselves at home here. Slowly, she unwound from her dreams, from the sensations.

From the fantasy of being loved.

And then she drew herself up and headed to the kitchen, dumping the bag of melted ice in the sink and heading to the bathroom to freshen up. Her cheek was no longer red, and she thought it wouldn't bruise at all. Her jaw was a different story—pale impressions from Lerche's fingers with the bruising coming up between them.

She pulled out her makeup bag.

Ana had an hour before Ian arrived. It was long enough to ply her skills with powder and brush, and to dim the bright reflected sunshine of a late afternoon in the fall—angling the blinds, drawing the shades. She set the table so the remaining light would fall on his face and not hers, placing a half-full glass of iced tea as a casual claim to the correct seat.

She might not have worried at all. When she opened the door to him, take-out bags in hand, she found an entirely different man than the one with whom she'd spent the morning. This one looked worn and pale and pained, and just a little bit baffled. She instantly forgot her concerns about hiding her bruises. She even forgot her mixed feelings about putting herself in the hands of a Sentinel for the evening—one who had been perfectly appropriate during their very public afternoon ride, but who might now reveal another side of himself.

"Ian!" she said. "You look—" and then stopped herself. She'd learned that mentioning someone else's condition tended to draw scrutiny to herself, and she didn't want that.

Besides, "You look terrible" didn't seem like a great opening for the evening.

But Ian just laughed, low as it was. "I do look terrible," he said. "I'm not one for headaches, but—" He shook his head, most gingerly.

She relieved him of the sandwiches. "Are you sure you want to do this? We can do lunch tomorrow, if you'd like. Or dinner tomorrow evening."

"You're kidding, right?" Distracted as he was, his gaze still pinned her—an intense stare peering out from beneath a civilized veneer. "I can forget about the headache if you can."

She gestured him into the little rental house. "I'll draw the blinds—maybe we can find an old movie."

"Bogart?" Ian said, head tipped with interest. Even not at the top of his game, he exuded intelligent energy and restlessness—at least until he tripped over the threshold as he entered the house. "Whoa," he said. "Smooth."

"You're sure—"

"I'm sure," he told her. "Let's eat that food while it's fresh."

She took the bag to the table, pulling out cartons and filling the room with the yeasty scent of fresh bread and savory herbals. He wandered in after her as she set ice water before his place and closed the blinds a bit more, feeling more secure about her ability to hide the bruises as they settled in for the meal, full of the small talk of such moments. Plain old normal small talk from a man who wasn't quite normal at all, while Ana thought about the amulet in her pocket. The one she'd been commanded to invoke.

Ian clearly wasn't quite focused. He fumbled his fork in the salad, nearly knocked over the salad dressing, and seemed to find his thick, layered deli sandwich as much by feel as by sight.

"Have you considered seeing a doctor?" Only in retrospect did she realize that of course he wouldn't, because Sentinels never did go to mundane doctors—not the strong-blooded Sentinels, at any rate. They wouldn't be able to hide enough of their true nature.

"If things don't get better." Ian ran a thumb up and down the ice water as if, even now, he couldn't find a way to be still. "I don't get sick often. I'm probably not much of a patient."

Compared to the Core posse members who demanded that she wait on their every need even when they weren't sick, she thought he was doing just fine. But it interested her to see how close he skirted to telling her the full truth of his nature—that, in fact, he'd not come right out and lied to her. Of course a strong-blooded Sentinel wasn't used to being sick. Given the unnatural rate at which they healed, it would be a wonder if they ever were.

Ana herself had been blessed with a naturally quick rate of healing—or cursed with it, rather. It was one reason Lerche felt free to leave his mark on her. But she got sick as often as anyone else, with the same clusters of cold and flu and a stomach that could be touchy. She made sure she was always a very good patient, requiring as little from the Core physicians as she could. But she said merely, "If things don't get better, you probably should."

Ian caught himself rubbing his temple and gave a rueful laugh, if not much of one. "It's probably something going around." He didn't look convinced, and she wasn't surprised. Field Sentinels like Ian Scott didn't catch such things, even if the light-bloods did. "Fernie wasn't looking well this afternoon, either. I spent the afternoon in the kitchen, helping her clean up after one of her bake-fests."

Her fork hovered in midair as she tried to imagine it…and found that she could. Found that she could easily see this sharp-edged man putting aside his work to help the retreat manager on a tough afternoon.

She couldn't say the same for Hollender Lerche.

"Maybe I shouldn't have come," he said, mistaking her hesitation. "If it's catching—"

She laughed and speared the fork into her salad. If he noticed how carefully she'd been chewing, he didn't mention it. "If it's catching, then I think I've already got it, don't you?"

He grinned. "There's something to that." And then they talked quietly of favorite old movies while she pulled her laptop open and rented them a Bogart flick— *Key Largo*, of course—and Ian demonstrated that whatever the state of his headache, his casual mastery of tech also included hooking a laptop up to the house TV so they could watch on the larger screen. By the time they finished the last forkful of their cheesecake dessert, they shared the couch as if they'd always done so.

Only when Ana was fully nestled in under Ian's arm, her legs curled beneath her while he stretched the length of his out on to the kitchen chair he'd appropriated for that purpose, did she realize she hadn't yet invoked the second amulet—and that she didn't dare do it now, for fear he would sense it, no matter its silent nature.

It didn't matter. Surely Hollander Lerche wasn't interested in murmured chitchat over a classic movie. Surely he couldn't expect her to delve into a conversation of more substance until Ian was more comfortable with her—more confident with her.

Although he was, most obviously, comfortable and confident enough to fall asleep on her couch.

She realized it as the film credits began to roll. She drew back from beneath his arm to consider him in the flickering light of the television, pulling her feet up on the couch to wrap her arms around her legs and rest her chin on her knees. Knowing that she ought to be curled up on the other end of this couch, trembling in fear. And that she ought to trigger the amulet, shortening the time she was exposed to Ian and his entitled, arrogant ways.

He was, after all, a man who represented everything about a race of people who considered themselves *more than* and *better than* and quite evidently above the law altogether.

But Ian's touch had given her choice. Brought her pleasure. Inspired her napping dreams. Protected her from a mugger.

It startled her to realize that Lerche's man had known Ian would leap to her side when the cyclist grabbed at her—that he'd counted on it. She frowned, thinking that one through—or trying to. Instead, she found herself distracted by the way dark lashes swept a shadow across Ian's high, strong cheek. And by the way his mouth, in repose, relaxed to show the definition of lips that pleased her—their shape, the little hint of a curve at one side that revealed his habitual dry humor. The faint cleft in his chin, the unlikely perfection of the way silvered bangs scattered across his forehead, the equally unlikely short, dark hairs that defined his hairline at sideburns, nape and even buried beneath the lighter strands.

The movie credits ended and the sudden silence

alerted him; she saw the glimmer of his awakening gaze and smiled. She felt the promise of that look and of his interest in her. She felt her body warming to awareness—not of the Sentinel, but of the man.

Then again, the Core had always considered her to be weak of heart and mind, hadn't they?

"Hey," she said, and even her quiet voice seemed loud in the house. "Feel better?"

He stretched—an indulgent thing, right down to his fingers—and relaxed utterly again. "Hey," he said. "Much better." But then his eyes narrowed, and for an instant she felt pinned by his gaze—she felt all the fluttering uncertainty she'd told herself she ought to. "Ana... are those bruises?"

"Bruises?" she said, sounding as stupid as she felt. How could he...darkness had fallen, and she hadn't turned on any lights. Only what came from the TV, where the bubbles from her laptop screen saver drifted over the surface. Between the makeup and the darkness, she should have been safe from questions about the marks Lerche had left.

"You didn't have those this morning." He no longer reclined, relaxed, but now sat straighter, tension filling his shoulders. He tapped a quick pattern against his leg and nodded at her jaw. "I should have seen them earlier, but that headache..."

Of course. Right. Because Sentinels had that vaunted night vision—a spillover from the beast they carried within. What had Lerche been thinking?

But Ana knew the answer to that question. He hadn't cared.

"Are they that bad?" She touched her jaw, and a wince gave her the answer. Still, she addressed the bigger elephant in the room. "I can't believe you can see them in this light."

"Just one of those things," he said, making no attempt to explain it—but not making anything up, either. "Ana, *who*—"

"I'm here alone," she told him, and realized with those words that she was the one who lied to him, who had lied to him from the moment they'd crossed paths. "It was just one of those stupid things."

He searched her face as if he might find the truth there.

Well, it *was* one of those stupid things. She knew better than to show disrespect to Hollender Lerche. That was on her, that she'd done so. But she also knew that sometimes Lerche's mood meant there was no avoiding his temper. That was on him.

Ian let it pass, in a way she thought meant he wasn't actually going to forget it. He rose to his feet, so fluidly she couldn't believe he'd been deeply ensconced in the couch an instant earlier, and prowled to the window—looking out into the darkness and seeing who knew what.

"You *are* feeling better," she said. "And I guess I have the answer to my question."

He turned his head just enough to offer a puzzled frown. "Which question is that?"

"The one where I wondered if you ever sat still," she said drily.

He laughed, short as it was. "No," he said. "Not often. When I sleep. And…" He gave her a thoughtful look, and quite obviously didn't finish the sentence.

"Oh, come on," she said, unclasping her hands from around her legs and letting her feet slide to the floor.

"Now you've got to tell me. Even if it's embarrassing. *Especially* if."

He padded back to the couch; somewhere along the way he'd lost his shoes, and the barefoot movement only added to the prowl in his walk.

*He killed a man. I should be frightened.*

But she wasn't.

She was *alive*.

Her fingers tingled as he reached down to offer his hand. She took it; her body pulsed as he drew her to her feet. Warmth suffused her, instilling just a hint of weakness in her knees—a delightfully liquid sensation.

"And now," he said, pulling her closer—not with so much strength she couldn't hold her own, but with enough ease to demonstrate the strength still lurking. He touched her face; he skimmed his fingers along her jaw so lightly that she felt only their presence and not the pain of the bruises beneath. "Now," he said, and kissed one eyelid, and then the next. *"Now,"* he added, and brought his mouth down on hers, kissing her with a gentle assertion—and kissing her, and *kissing* her, until she threaded her fingers through his hair and stood on her tiptoes to kiss him back, so caught up in the firm sensation of his lips, the tease of tongue and teeth, the impression of being...not taken, but *worshiped*.

He bent over her and she trusted. He dipped her as if they were in a dance, and she gave herself up to his strength. He settled her perfectly over the cushions of the couch, and she never stopped reaching for him.

She had no idea how much time passed before he groaned and drew back—and said, with no little wonder, *"Now.* I can't explain it... I never—"

She silenced him with boldness, slipping her hand

inside his shirt to caress skin and feel it flutter beneath her fingertips, a sensitive flinch that came with a grin. She suggested, "Just feel…and follow it?"

He searched her eyes. For once she didn't feel like the vulnerable one—not with the uncertainty she saw there, or his eyes gone so dark with what she'd done to him. Or *for* him. Definitely not with the hard tremble of his arms and body—a tremble that in no way came from weakness. "Is that what you want?"

*Yes.* Because what she felt right now was safe and enclosed and *accepted.* As if, in that moment, she was everything she needed to be.

How could she do anything other than follow that feeling?

"Yes," she said, surprised by the husky sound of her own voice. "Yes, please. Let's."

"Let's," he agreed, and laughed just a little—in relief, she thought. Not that she had much time to think about it. He lowered himself over her only enough so she could wrap her legs around him, ruing the impediment of clothing—and then surprised her when he slipped his hands more firmly beneath her and pivoted to sit, putting her squarely in his lap. Squarely against him and his quite obviously already straining erection.

Pleasure speared through her, startling her into a cry—one she'd not heard herself make before. And then when he moved against her, another, this one echoed by the faint snarl of Ian's expression—just as surprised as she was, his fingers clamping down on her hips.

Such a pure, hot lightning, striking so deeply within… Her fingers dug into his shoulders, gathering the material of his shirt—but only briefly, because the more she *felt*, the more she wanted to touch him. Fumbling at buttons, pushing the shirt back to expose the planes of his chest—a lean man's muscled body, layered in strength without bulk, crisp pale hair scattered to tease her fingers and fade across his abs to reappear in a narrow line above his belt.

As it had before, his skin twitched, more sensitive than she'd imagined. When she spread her fingers across his belly and went seeking beneath the belt, he made a disbelieving sort of sound, half laugh and half gasp, and rolled them over again. The soft couch cushions enveloped her just as he found her mouth. He kissed her with fiercely thorough attention, his fingers at her blouse buttons and then tangling with hers. He moved his mouth to her neck, nipping, as she reached for his belt, and he reached for her slacks button. She tugged his pants over his hips; he deftly yanked hers out from beneath her, his mouth still on her neck, on her collarbones, dipping lower to ignore her bra and find one nipple right through the soft material.

She bucked up against him and reveled in it—reveled in watching herself and her response to him. No man had evoked such response in her...no man had ever tried.

Ian laughed again, this time with a growl in the background. He lifted his head to capture her gaze, and she stilled under the impact of it—bright intensity, heated desire...

"Please," she told him, understanding the question behind that look. "Yes. Most definitely *yes*."

He drew a sharp breath—relief or fettered passion, she wasn't sure. But then she didn't want to wait any longer. She kicked her pants aside, shoving her panties off with them, and then went after his boxers. In a moment they were both free, both already warm and wet with the wanting, and she didn't think twice. She wrapped her legs around his hips and reveled in his unrestrained grunt of pleasure as flesh met flesh.

And then Ian surprised her all over again, flattening himself on her, muttering—grasping for his pants while the couch all but swallowed them both. He made a sound of triumph and emerged with a condom. She shared his breathless victory with a grin, and between the two of them they got the thing unwrapped and in place, and then *he* was in place again, and with a single nudge of adjustment, they slipped together.

Ana stopping thinking. She stopped being able to think. She barely realized it when Ian swung her upright again, thrusting upward as her knees sank into the couch cushions. *Pure hot lightning...* Ana reached for more of it, finding a rhythm with him, barely aware of her own cries. She shot straight through that pleasure to sensations she'd never even imagined, and found herself with a sudden new awareness.

His response to her. His gasps and his expression, cords of muscle straining in his neck and his face flushed, his eyes widening with the same sort of startled recognition that suffused her own body. An utter vulnerability that he seemed to fight against and lose to with every thrust, with every breath.

"Ian," she breathed, and it was a kind of plea, an understanding that she was in an unfamiliar place and didn't know where to go from there. His hand slid from her waist to cover her pubic hair, thumb sliding downward to touch her *just so.*

Lightning struck. She cried out in abandon and lost herself to it, a flood of sensation that tugged at her toes and filled her from the inside out, every muscle clenched or throbbing in the best possible way. She dimly heard Ian's shout, feeling the pulse of his release in a way that had never mattered before but now suddenly did. She opened her eyes just soon enough to see it on his face—ecstasy ripping right through him, laying him as bare as it had laid her.

That's when she understood, even as the final throb of pleasure ebbed through her body, leaving her limp in its wake.

Being with Ian wasn't just about seeing where things went or following along in an adventure or *feeling*, even pulling the most possible pleasure from it all.

It was about doing those things *together*.

# *Chapter 4*

Ian gulped for air, reveling in the sensation of Ana's body draped over his. Not to mention the pulses of lingering pleasure and the distinct memory of her expression as orgasm had washed over her. His breathing steadied; his mind steadied.

Quiet. Replete.

A completely unfamiliar inner silence.

He floundered in it, uncertain—looking for some mental handhold, even if it brought him back to the plague of internal noise he couldn't remember being without.

She stirred, pushing off his chest to look at him with her face still flushed and now blushing on top of it, her hair a delightful disarray. "Oh, my God," she said, putting a hand over her mouth. "I... I *screamed*."

He smiled, finding his anchor in her expression. "Yeah," he said. "You did."

"I never—" She stopped herself. "I...*never*..."

It caught his attention. There was more here than the aftermath of great sex. *Stupendously great sex*. Even he knew that much, still floating in the physical satisfaction and silence. "What?"

"No, I—" She shook her head, looking around—bringing herself back to the details of what had happened. He knew what she'd see—scattered clothes, scattered couch cushions and a man she hadn't known all that long still lying beneath her.

He stopped her just before she would have removed herself from it all, his hands over her thighs—enough to encompass, not enough to force compliance—and asked it again. "What?"

She covered her face, only briefly, and then flipped her hair back. "I've never come with anyone before."

He frowned. "At the same time? Because technically, you beat me to that finish line."

She laughed, but it sounded sad. "No, I mean...when I've been *with* someone. Ever." She took a breath as he tried to absorb this. "I'm 'too hard to please.'"

He half sat, his hold on her legs keeping them just as together as they'd been. "*Who* said that? Because—" Then he stopped, suddenly aware of the depth of his reaction, his protective response. "Never mind. That's not what I want to say. But just so you know, whoever said that is obviously fucking nuts. Pardon me."

She laughed again, this time sounding as if, just possibly, she'd been freed from something. But she quickly turned uncertain. "Ian," she said. "Seriously. Is this how it should always be?"

"Babe," he told her, still awash in the aftermath of silence within himself, "*this* is how we always *wish* it would be. But it should always be good. A man makes certain of that."

*Blessed, blessed silence...*

She said, "I'll have to think about that."

"Don't," he said, and was a little hard pressed to explain when she raised a brow at him. "Think, I mean. Just stay here with me a little while longer. *Not thinking.*"

"Look who's talking. I got the impression that you never actually do stop thinking. I bet you run calculations in your sleep." But she smiled, relaxing the fraction that told him she'd stay. She made another attempt to tame her hair back and gave up on it, instead turning her attention to his chest—chasing whorls of hair with her fingertips and the edges of short, practical nails painted something faintly pink. His skin pebbled in response, all the way down to his balls; he twitched faintly inside her. She laughed, disbelief at the edge of it.

"Hey," he said, though he couldn't help but grin back at her. "It is what it is." Then, as she scraped the outside edge of a nipple, he shifted with a less lighthearted purpose. "But be merciful, if you would. I only brought the one condom."

She withdrew her hands entirely. "Oh. Well. In that case—" and then she laughed again at his dramatic groan. "Not everything requires a condom, I hear. And there are some things I've always wanted to try—"

Of course his body fairly leaped to attention, squirming here and stiffening there, and this time she laughed right out loud—and then laughed again at his ruefully self-aware expression. "That felt to me like you might just be interested."

"C'mere, babe," he growled, an exaggerated version of manly prowess. "I'll show you *interested*."

And she had the audacity to *stretch*—right there, still sitting on top of him and surrounding him, the faint light painting the lines and curves of her body, all beauty and delicate grace. "Okay," she said, and her tone had changed. More than confident. *Eager.*

He could do eager. With this woman? God, yes, he

could do eager. And in that moment, and in the next, and the one to follow, he barely even noticed the silence in his mind at all.

Morning brought bright sunshine and the faintest taste of a hangover.

Or what Ian thought a hangover might be. Given the speed at which a strong-blooded Sentinel metabolized alcohol, it took a concerted effort to feel the effects— both during and after. Ian had done the usual youthful experiment and then ceased to bother.

But he was pretty sure this would be it. The underlying throb encompassing his eyes, the uncertainty in his stomach. Leftovers from whatever had struck him the day before.

And that deserved some thought. Ian wasn't good at being sick because Sentinels generally *weren't*. So what had he gotten into, or what had gotten into him?

He stared at the back of his eyelids a moment longer, taking in the unfamiliar sounds and scents of his surroundings, and especially the unfamiliar light. A different window, east-facing, than the one he'd taken here at the retreat. And Fernie's kitchen smelled of sausage and egg in the morning, not just tea and toast.

*Because this is Ana's place.*

Whoa.

Since when did he fall asleep so soundly in a strange place? Since when did he actually sleep the night through in *any* place? He finished waking in a burst of motion, rolling up to his knees, tangling in covers, and altogether ready for anything.

A cup of tea awaited him by the side of the bed, still steaming. He scowled at it, instantly aware of the significance—that Ana had not only left without waking him, she'd come and gone again with the tea.

And here she was again—padding out from the bathroom in a minuscule robe, scrubbing a towel over her hair. Damp and fresh and smelling... He inhaled deeply in spite of himself. *Smelling like woman. Smelling like...* His.

"Not a morning person?" she asked, draping the towel over one shoulder. Her hair was mussed in a way he wished he'd done, her cheeks flushed with the shower and her eyes bright with...amusement?

He realized he'd frozen in that ready-to-pounce yet totally hungover fashion, and looked down at himself. Wearing his boxers, tangled in her sheets, thoroughly unable to get his thoughts together. Nothing to do but shrug. "Generally I'm an everything person," he said. "Clearly that doesn't apply to today." With effort, he clambered out of the bed, straightening himself joint by joint, and reached for the tea. *Irish black, oh, thank you.*

The first sip finished waking him. When he lifted his head and caught a glimpse of the bathrobe hitting the floor, he went beyond awake and straight to alert. *Attentive.*

Ana reached into a drawer to extract a bra—faintly pink, like her nails, an underwire thing that would support the beauty he'd seen the night before. Modest in size but perfectly shaped, just ready for his hand or mouth. She gave a meaningful glance at his groin, where the boxers hid nothing. "I'd wondered if I wore you out, but I'm not sure that's possible."

"Not when I'm with you," he said, somewhat fervently. Another Sentinel blessing, that recovery time—

but he couldn't talk to her about Sentinels. Only the think tank aspect of his work.

"Leftovers from whatever got into you last night, then," she suggested, stepping into panties with faint pink stripes.

Oh, hell. Yes. Exactly so. And not just him. No one had been feeling quite right at the retreat when he'd left. Ian floundered, caught completely behind in his own thoughts. Thoughts he would normally have worked on in pieces through the night, rising to wakefulness long enough to chew on them and then, if he was lucky, falling back to sleep. Either way, awakening in the morning with his thoughts spread out before him, ready for the day.

Not *this* day.

"I've got to go," he said, gulping half the remaining tea in one swallow and setting the mug aside. His pants must be here somewhere, right? "I need to check on Fernie. And the others."

She cocked her head, a stretchy bit of ribbed camisole in hand and her expression gone careful. Very, very careful. "Is this you running away?"

Because of course, he could call the retreat. Or he could assume that a house full of adults could manage minor illness without panic. She had no way of knowing that these particular adults were, like him, not used to managing illness at all. Or that anyone with even modestly strong blood did better with a Sentinel healer than they ever would with the average urgent care clinic.

"This is me taking care of my people," he assured her, spotting the neat stack of his shirt and pants where she'd smoothed and folded them. He scooped them up, pulling them on in record time—and then stopped to regard her, scrubbing one hand through his thoroughly disheveled hair, across the scrape of his beard.

She'd tugged the camisole into place and now looked back at him with evident doubt, and he had to face the brutal truth of his off-balance morning. "Yeah," he said. "I can use some space while I'm at it. But not because I'm running away. Because…"

*Because I wasn't expecting this. To be affected.*

*Oh, face it. To be reeling in the wake of her.*

She'd put on a mask—the same face she'd worn when he'd first seen her. Unapproachable. Distant.

And, he now understood, self-protective.

She held her ground when he stepped up to her, and when he put a finger under her chin—lifting it slightly so the bruises along her jaw were beyond evident, and careful of them—careful of her. Biting back on fury to see them and knowing he'd find out what they were about when all was said and done, but that this moment wasn't the right one.

"Because," he said, "sometimes when you follow the feeling, you get far more than you ever expected. And if you want to do right by that, it takes a little space."

Something in that stiff expression eased, allowing him back in. "Yes," she said. "Okay. I can see that. I guess I can even feel some of it, this morning." She caught his gaze, held it—a hint of honey in the brown of her eye. "Just promise this—when it's time for you to walk away from us, be straight with me. Tell me you're going. Don't leave me wondering. Don't leave me *hopeful.*"

The anger bubbled up again on her behalf. "Someone, somewhere, has done very badly by you." He rested his hands on her shoulders. "Look, I may not always know what I'm doing. I might mess up. But I'll do it *honestly*. And we'll figure this out. By which I mean—" and he couldn't help but grin as he bent to kiss her *"—this."*

Her mouth was just as soft as it had been the night before, just as responsive. And so was he, immediately slipping into a possessive, claiming frame of mind, the strength of which only swelled once he noticed it.

She put a hand on his chest—not pushing, but enough to remind him what they'd been about. What *he'd* been about. When he pulled back, she'd regained the hint of a smile he'd already learned to look for. "Okay," she said. "Check in with your mother ship. And today, the museum."

"Come at noon and I'll feed you first." Ian held her chin a moment longer, bringing his thumb up to run along her lower lip where it shone damp with the attention he'd just given it.

*Feed you, and find out who put their hands on you, and make sure it never happens again.*

But first he had to make sure his people were all right.

Hollender Lerche found himself annoyingly aware of intrusion. He barely needed to glance at his office doorway to know that David Budian hesitated—no, *hovered*, in a most irritating way—outside his domain. But glance he did, looking up from the two receiver amulets on the otherwise empty desk, his very attention a demand for explanation.

This day, Budian dressed in natty slacks and short-sleeved dress shirt, a touring cap on his head and glasses he didn't need over his nose. From this Lerche surmised that the man intended to again trail Ana Dikau. It was a precaution made necessary because she had only recently invoked the second amulet—and it, unlike the first, remained silent.

Not that the first had provided any useful information—although the primary working was as successful as they could have hoped, and the occupants of the house had definitely sickened.

Unfortunately, Ian Scott didn't seem to be one of them.

Budian asked, "Anything?"

"Not of import," Lerche told him. "The feeble-blooded Sentinels at the retreat are sickening, but Scott didn't spend the night there." Anger flickered to life at Ana's defiance—her delay in invoking the second amulet, her whorish behavior with the Sentinel.

"So my man reported," Budian said. "Scott left her rental a few moments ago—she wore him out, no doubt about that. I'll pick her up if she leaves—or let you know if he returns. I've also planted a tracker on his motorcycle." He took a breath on new words, hesitating there.

"What is it?" Lerche snapped.

Budian found the necessary mix of cautious respect. "Her face," he said. "She came outside to say her good-byes, and the bruises were visible. I must counsel caution when it comes to disciplining her, no matter that she deserves it."

The anger flickered higher. "She should take better care with her makeup."

"Agreed. But these Sentinels are notoriously possessive—that's been the problem with them all along, hasn't it? Possessive of the earth, possessive of whatever they deem to be theirs. It will complicate our task if this one goes looking for whoever left those bruises."

"She knows better than to talk. And she heals more

quickly than most." Not that she knew it, or had any understanding of the taint her blood carried. She puzzled over her lack of acceptance within the Core ranks, but that was her problem. Lerche shook his head. "She is mine to discipline as necessary. But I'll take your words into consideration."

"Thank you," Budian said, as well he might. "I'll keep you apprised."

Lerche nodded in dismissal, turning his attention back to the spy amulets. One still offered a mutter of occasional conversation and clattering kitchen noises, and the other briefly provided a muffled and unidentified sound.

Ana Dikau was a problem. Had always *been* a problem. Too eager for acceptance, never seeing that she wasn't worthy, never understanding why—and yet constantly defying even the simplest edict. Never understanding that how little her value to him, she was still *his*.

*She'd slept with the Sentinel.*

Anger surged—and then slowly ebbed into satisfaction.

After all, she *had* invoked the amulet. She *was* spending time with Scott. He might sicken first, but ultimately she faced death right along with him. And she had no idea it would come at her own hand.

"Aspirin, yes. Ibuprofen or acetaminophen, no." Ruger's deep voice rumbled over Ian's phone. Southwest Brevis's skilled, no-nonsense healer was a man who took the bear in his other form—bigger than most, rumblier than most. "Keep 'em drinking—and put a drop of lemon oil in their water. *Not* the stuff under the sink for the furniture."

"Not the furniture polish," Ian repeated, amused in spite of the circumstances. He rounded the breakfast bar where he'd been taking notes, and opened Fernie's remedy cabinet.

"You'd be surprised," Ruger muttered. "Look, every once in a while something like this comes along—it sweeps through a bunch of us and goes on its way, showing up mainly in the light-bloods. Stick with common sense, and in a few days it'll be history. Besides, it'll take your mind off those silent amulets."

"Does *everyone* know I've been sent up here to turn my brain off?"

Ruger made a rumbling noise of amusement. "Who do you suppose talked to Nick about prying you out of that laboratory for a while, little leopard?"

Ian made his own throat noise, and it wasn't amusement.

Ruger laughed outright. "Never mind. We'll talk about that later. Meanwhile, you're not affected by this thing?"

Ian hesitated, thinking of the previous evening, not quite ready to admit vulnerability when he'd spent so much effort of late telling everyone he was *fine, dammit.* But then he'd hesitated too long, so he shrugged as he reached into the cabinet for the lemon oil. "Last night," he said, tapping the little bottle against the counter in a clinking percussive accompaniment. "Helluva headache. Today, a little…yeah, hungover. Nothing more."

"Sounds about right," Ruger said. "Take the aspirin. Drink the fluids. Don't get in over your head with activities."

Ian snorted. "Now you sound like Fernie."

*"And,"* Ruger said as if Ian hadn't spoken, "call me if things don't get better over the next day."

Ian heard the serious note behind that directive. "Got it."

"In fact, just call me. Tomorrow. I want to know how this thing is going, in case you're not the only ones." When Ian hesitated again, Ruger offered no leeway. "You're not up there to get distracted by your work. *Call me.*"

Ian didn't quite mean to mutter, "It's not *work* that's distracting me."

Ruger laughed again. "Well, then," he said. "Tell her hello, and look no further for the source of your little virus."

"I only met her two days ago," Ian grumbled. "Hardly even that."

"That's all it takes, with the right virus." Ruger sounded altogether too cheerful. "It happens, you know. Even with us." He gave Ian a quick list of other remedies they might find useful and that Fernie was likely to have on hand, including a recent batch of Ruger's own tonic. "But don't pull that one out unless things are getting bad. You'll have the whole house bouncing off the walls. Of course," he added, humor back in his voice, "you do that as a matter of course, so who's to tell the difference."

"Ha," Ian said. "And *ha.*" And managed to mutter a promise to make that update call before he hung up.

But when he turned to face the kitchen, he couldn't be quite as sanguine as Ruger—a man who had good reason to be cheerful, with his love Mariska newly pregnant. Another reason not to draw him up here. Mariska was also bear, small and fierce, and floundering a little in her new role as pending mother.

But Ian had arrived to find the place cluttered with an unprecedented number of dishes and no other evidence of the other retreat residents. A quick look around had revealed them all to be sleeping, and he'd left them that way, choosing to clean up and call Ruger before he disturbed Fernie.

Now he brewed her a quick cup of her favorite soother tea and added the lemon to it…and then hesitated and made one for himself, gulping an aspirin before he rummaged up one of yesterday's muffins to add to her tray.

Unlike Ian's room—a bedroom off the back of this quirky, open air home with its half-basement warren of little rooms and its common spaces—Fernie lived in a tiny little casita attached to the home but separate of it, just barely within the enclosed courtyard. Her own tiny kitchen, bathroom and bedroom—and a place into which Ian had never ventured, because it was quite obviously Fernie's territory. Full of Southwest color and wrought iron and photos of a family grown and scattered across three brevis regions.

But he'd stood in the doorway, and that's what he did now—knocking on the door until he heard the rustle of sheets and a sound of quiet dismay through a window that habitually remained cracked during the cold nights and warming days.

"It's me, Fernie," he said, cracking the door open. "I brought some tea. And one of your muffins. And I've talked to Ruger. So that means either I come in there with this tea or you come out, because…you know. Ruger said."

"Come in," she said, her voice a little ragged but perfectly alert. And then, practically before he'd crossed the threshold, "How are you? What about the others?"

He entered the bedroom bearing the tray like an offering, relieved to see that although he'd clearly woken her, her gaze was sharp enough and her expression alert. "I haven't checked yet. I'm triaging, and you're the important one."

"And you?" she said, tucking the covers around her plump waist so he could settle the tray into place. Her graying hair hung over her shoulder in a long, simple braid, and age had settled into her plain, welcoming features overnight. "You didn't look good last night, and you don't look good now—and of all of us, you must stay well."

"I'm—" He started to say he was fine, but didn't finish. He wasn't. The headache had returned, settling in behind his eyes. "Ruger says this should pass quickly— just some atypical virus. He didn't sound concerned. I took notes about the remedies that might help."

She'd taken a sip of her tea, and nodded. "The lemon is always good. But I need to know that you heard me. We're counting on you."

A stab of pain caught him behind one eye, and he winced, rubbing it. Fernie didn't fail to note it. "And if this isn't *just some virus*?"

He stared at her as if he'd suddenly forgotten how to think. Maybe he had.

"Ian," she said, buttering her muffin with quick, impatient movement, "I've been managing this retreat since my Manny passed. He had no Sentinel blood at all, you know. So I know what a virus looks like, and I also know what it looks like when we light-bloods get hit with one. You think this would be the first time?"

Ian pulled her robe off the back of a wooden chair and draped it over her footboard so he could flip the chair around and straddle it. "And this doesn't look right to you?"

She lifted one shoulder, sipping tea. "It doesn't look familiar. Even here, we don't take things for granted."

He thought about the working he'd felt at the overlook, the mere ripple of corruption in the air. It hadn't been a thing of significance—a passive detection spell, unless he missed his mark, and he wasn't *that* far off his game. And members of the Core were everywhere, just as the Sentinels were. Clustered, yes, but always with plenty of individuals moving freely between.

"I see I've got you considering it, at least."

"I'll take a look around," he said, tapping absently on the back of the chair. Slowly, to reflect the speed of his thoughts. "Once I've checked on the rest of us."

"Leave that to me." She pushed a strand of graying hair from her face. "I feel much better. If the others are anything like me, they simply went to bed last night and decided against getting up. It's more of a tiresome thing than anything else."

Ian rubbed the spot between his eyes. "Damned headache," he said. But the aspirin must have been kicking in, because it seemed to be easing. "Okay. I'll check outside. If I find anything…well, I don't have my gear, but we can improvise. A kitchen isn't so much different from a lab, when all is said and done." He gave her a meaningful look. "But you'll call me if you need help."

"If it makes you feel better about going out there, then, yes." She reached for another piece of the muffin. "But you, Ian—I hope you felt well enough to enjoy your time with Ana yesterday evening."

He grinned. "Now you're just prying," he said, standing back from the chair. "Let's just say I felt better when

I was with her. And," he added, before she could ask, "she's coming over around lunchtime."

"Because if this is a virus, she's been well and exposed to it." Fernie looked decidedly better now, that twinkle back in her eye.

"Now you *are* prying," Ian said. He put the chair back where it had been and bent over to kiss her cheek, ignoring her surprise. "You're right. We won't take it for granted. I'll check in after I take a quick look around, and then go back out for a second sweep."

"Good," she said. "Thank you."

But what Ian didn't say, and what they both knew, was that if the Core had targeted the grounds with a silent amulet working, Ian had no more chance of finding it than any of them—and that was no chance at all.

# Chapter 5

Ana arrived at the retreat to find Ian prowling the grounds—a lean, sunlit figure in constant motion. He'd clearly showered and shaved, and now wore a pale, lightweight shirt over faded jeans. The jeans fit perfectly, hanging off his hips and snug over the strong curve of his butt, but the shirt had only received haphazard attention to the buttons—as if he'd been interrupted when he'd barely just started.

She had the feeling that the interruption had come in the form of his restless nature, but a second glance at the intensity of his expression made her think twice.

He wasn't just prowling. He was *searching*.

She stood back and watched for a long moment. Considering him. Still able to feel his hands on her skin, to see the care in his eyes. And to see so clearly his expression when she'd touched him back, and how it had affected her.

It had made her realize that until Ian, she'd never made love. She'd made sex. She'd had sex made with her...and to her. Her previous partners, limited as they were, had been Core. Had been expected of her. And after so many similar experiences, she'd thought the fault, if there was one, to be hers. Or she'd thought simply *this is the way it is*.

She'd been wrong. Ian had shown her that. He'd given her more of himself in one evening than all of her previous partners put together. And he'd shown her that it wasn't about what one could take…it was about what one could give.

Surely, if this man—who offered such clear care to her, and to the woman named Fernie, and even to Ana when she'd still been only a stranger under attack by a mugger—was a Sentinel, then it should be possible for the Core and the Sentinels to find common ground. To work together. No matter what she'd always been told.

But she'd need time to prove that. She'd need Ian's trust. And she'd need space from Lerche's interference.

*He won't bother me if I'm with Ian.*

The thought came out of nowhere, striking her as true as anything could. Lerche wouldn't bother her if she was with Ian—he wouldn't bruise her or intimidate her or push her. Because he knew as well as Ana that Ian wouldn't allow any of that.

Ian hadn't seen her yet, which startled her—it seemed to her as if he generally saw everything in his world. But this intensity, she suspected, was also uniquely Ian. So focused, so immersed in his work that he'd closed out everything else.

Though what *was* he doing?

*Prowling.*

And doing it with an expression that should have alarmed her, dark brows drawn over piercing eyes—shadowing them. Utter concentration on his face as he paced the latilla fencing, gaze sweeping every inch of uneven vertical poles. Once he crouched, a stunningly simple display of the graceful leopard hidden within, and Ana found herself holding her breath—appreciating not just the beauty of it, but anticipating the outcome.

After a moment he merely stood and went on, his head cocked slightly as if he was listening for some inner voice.

Ana resumed breathing, her pulse still rocketing. How well she understood this man after only two days. How well she understood what his presence could do to her.

She swallowed hard against sudden fear in her throat, caught in fragile crystalline understanding. *Lerche would kill her.*

He would call her weak and corrupted and traitorous; he would call her a failure. And wouldn't tolerate those things, on top of years of barely accepting her in the first place. *He would eliminate them.*

But Lerche wasn't here. And he wasn't the entire Core. If Ana could prove to them that Ian's respectful nature was representative of the Sentinels, if she could broker a breakthrough in communication…

She'd be more than accepted. She'd be safe.

She released a deep and steady breath, settling her mind to it all. Putting herself back in the moment, where reaching her goal and simply spending time with Ian amounted to the same thing. Especially now that she'd put the second spy amulet into the pocket of her light blazer…and activated it.

That time, he heard her. Lifted his head and saw her. For an instant, he looked stunned—and she immediately understood.

He'd forgotten all about their date.

She ought to feel hurt. She ought to feel resentful. Instead she blurted out, "What's wrong?"

Relief crossed his features, but only briefly. "Fernie," he said. "The others...not so much. But Fernie."

"Hey," she said. "I'm outside your brain. I need more words."

At that, he laughed and seemed to shake something off. "I think I should be frightened," he said, and stretched in a way that made her ache to touch him. "Do you know how long it takes some people to deal when I get stuck inside my head?"

"Then they aren't paying attention." She said it haughtily, deliberately lightening the moment. "But seriously, Ian. What's going on?"

He glanced back at the house. "Probably just a weird virus. The others aren't doing too badly—they stayed in bed—but Fernie is pretty sick." He frowned. "She seemed better this morning, but it didn't last."

She put hands on hips, tapped her foot a couple of times. "So Fernie is sick and you're worried, but you're not taking her to a clinic...you're out combing the yard?"

"Ah," he said, straightening a little. "Right. Actually, the company has a medic on call, so we've talked. This is just a precaution. Sometimes people throw things over fences."

It took her a moment, and then she understood. *"Poison?"*

He shrugged. "People get frustrated with the neighborhood cats."

She nearly laughed out loud, full of the double meaning of that sentence. But Ian had no idea she knew he was actually one of the neighborhood cats, so instead she said, "That's awful. Do you want some help looking? Do you need any help inside? We don't have to do the museum today—"

He shook his head—looking down at himself as if to check for dirt or grass stains. "We'll go. If our guy thought there was a real problem, he'd have come up to check things out himself." He rotated his shoulders, stretching again—completely unselfconscious, and completely unaware of the impressive display of lithe strength. "Besides, I'm doing okay. You?"

"A bit of a headache," she admitted, realizing it for the first time. "If you have an aspirin, I'd take it. And then we can be on our way, if you really still want to go." She glanced in the direction of the museum without thinking about it and caught sight of a figure hovering at the tree line of the greenway. Lingering.

Ian followed her gaze.

If the man hadn't frozen—hadn't so visibly thought about ducking to hide—nothing would have come of it.

But he did.

And Ian muttered, "What the hell—?" and hopped over the fence, striding toward the man.

Who took off.

*Posse.* It had to be. And Ana wanted to kick the man. What was he thinking, to lurk where a Sentinel could see? What was Lerche thinking, to send him out to watch after he'd already put Ian on alert with that drive-by at the overlook? He'd blow her cover if he wasn't more careful, and she knew exactly who'd get the blame for that.

There was no way Ian wasn't going to catch the guy. He ran full out, his strides long and swift, his movement effortless—

Except even as he closed in on the man, he stumbled. His movement grew choppy, his strides uneven. The man pulled cleanly away as Ian came to an abrupt stop, his hands braced on his knees. Staggering.

Ana ran to him, feeling not relief that the posse member had gotten away, but concern for Ian. Knowing exactly how lucky the fugitive had been. "Ian!" she said, reaching him just lightly out of breath, because the Core made sure she was as fit as anyone could be. "Are you all right?"

He straightened, his expression full of puzzlement—and something more. A wounded look, as though his body had betrayed him. "I'm okay," he said—and at her sound of disbelief, flashed her a wry look. "I guess I'm not quite back to myself."

"No kidding. And just what did you plan to do if you caught that guy?"

"Ask him questions," Ian said, more grimly than he probably meant to.

"What? Like why he thought he could get away with relieving himself on that tree?" Another lie, another misdirection. But she couldn't afford for him to suspect the man as Core. She *couldn't*.

"He was what?" Ian said in surprise, looking off after the man—long gone now. Ana held her silence, letting him work it through. "I'm sorry. I thought—" He shook his head. "I guess I'm on edge." He bounced on his toes a time or two, recovered from whatever instant of weakness had caught him—more like the man she'd seen upon her very first glimpse of him. "I'm still working out this *relaxation* thing."

"So I see." She offered her hand. "Let's grab an aspirin and a snack, and see what the walk to the museum does for you. We can take the greenway almost all the way there."

He took her hand, but the faint gathering frown at his brows didn't fade as they returned to the retreat porch, both of them warm in the wake of exertion and the beat of the midday sun. She pulled off her blazer when he went inside to grab them some water, dropping the coat over the back of a wrought-iron porch chair without a second thought—at least, not until they were walking away.

Only then did she realize that the second amulet had been left behind in her blazer and how Lerche would respond to her error. But amazingly, with her hand back in the warm and careful grip of the Sentinel who had trusted his body to her the night before, she couldn't bring herself to care.

She was, at the moment, right where she needed to be.

Ian's feet moved of their own accord, taking him through the beautifully spare hallways of the O'Keeffe museum; he only vaguely heard Ana's voice. His eyes were full of beauty under the museum spotlights in this stark adobe hallway, gaze drawn by paintings of sublime and subtle color and sweeping lines. And his mind was full of...

*Frustration.*

Ana moved in beside him, nudging his shoulder. "Where are you?" she asked. "I'm not sure you're quite here."

He pulled himself out of his thoughts to look down at her—there, where she'd so expertly covered the evidence of someone's damned fingers.

He was well aware that her whole story hadn't been told. Not with the not-so-random mugging, or the man he'd scared off that morning. But he was beginning to fill in the blanks.

This was not, he thought, so much of a vacation as it was an escape.

He'd find out. But not now—here, in this museum, with her concern looking up at him. So he told her the truth, without much thinking about it. "I can't make sense of it."

"Your people? Are you still worried?" She took his hand—just enough hesitation to let him know she wasn't used to reaching out, and just enough confidence to reflect the startling nature of their fast-solidifying connection.

Quiet floated over his thoughts like a blanket, leaving him room to think. "More than that." He hesitated over just how much to say, O'Keeffe's winter cottonwoods drawing his eye back to the hazy brown sweep of branches emerging from misty beige and muted ochre. "The pattern of things just doesn't make sense. We feel fine…we feel terrible. And then we're fine again."

"Like you last night," she observed, rubbing a thumb lightly across his knuckles in a fashion that focused his thoughts in an entirely different way, thank you very much.

"And Fernie this morning." He didn't mention how badly he'd felt before he'd gone to the yard to hunt amulets; he didn't mention that it seemed to be harder to shake the illness off today than it had been yesterday. To clear his thoughts, which had blundered around in their usual overactive state—only now they seemed just as blurred as O'Keeffe's winter trees.

Abruptly, he turned away from the painting, moving along the stark adobe hallway to the exit and out from under the track lighting to the tight, unpretentious grounds where the building rose like an assortment of adobe blocks behind them.

She kept her hold on his hand, following without hurry. "Are you all right now?"

"When you touch me?" he said. "Never better." He made a quick, wry face, without explanation. "You give me a peace I haven't felt before."

She presented him with a dubious look, and he laughed. "That wasn't supposed to sound corny. It was supposed to sound..." He hesitated. *"Real."*

She looked away, her face dappled by the shade of the trees lining the street and sidewalk, groomed landscaping sand and gravel crunching under their feet. "There's a lot going on with me. You should know that."

"I already know it."

She flicked a glance at him and then away. As if she couldn't quite deal with meeting his gaze. "It's not anything I expected to get into with such a short time together. It's not anything I *want* to get into."

"Then, don't. You don't owe me anything." Why that brought a sheen of tears to her eyes, he didn't know. "Look. I came here because I was ordered to. Things at work have been intense, and I don't know how to slow down at the best of times."

Now she did look at him, intrigued—and guessing. "And it hasn't been the best of times."

Understatement. So many dead, so many attacks barely thwarted. Unless the Sentinels could detect the silent amulets, their field agents would continue to die, and their families would always be under the threat of another *Core D'oíche*.

Unless *Ian* could detect the silent amulets.

"No," he said. "It hasn't been the best of times. The only time I've been able to take a mental breath…" *Is with you.* He didn't say the words out loud but wrapped his arms around her, resting his cheek on the sun-warmed tousle of her hair.

His mind settled. His thoughts quieted. He took a deep breath and absorbed her—how she felt sturdy and delicate at the same time, how her breathing synced with his, how she enveloped him not with strength but with caring. The warmth of his response rose not like the previous evening's lightning but as a gentler thing. A more lasting thing.

In that quiet clarity of his mind, his thoughts settled—a brilliant clarity of overlapping understandings.

Like the fact that he had no intention of letting this woman just *go*. Of walking away from this week—of walking away from *him*. That he wanted to scoop her up right here, let her wrap her legs around his waist as he carried her back to the retreat, back to his bed—to claim her, and let himself be claimed.

He stepped back from her just enough to tip her head up and hesitate the instant it took to see permission in her eyes. More than permission—request for the kiss he wanted to share. And he would have kissed her longer and deeper but he felt himself falling into her and knew better. Not here.

Even so, they made a mutual sound of regret when they parted, and Ana's face was flushed, her eyes bright. At least, until she stiffened, looking past him—

Ian jerked around, seeing nothing but the back of a well-dressed man as he walked away. He'd barely turned back to Ana before she grabbed his hand, tugging slightly as she angled in the direction of the retreat.

"Let's go check on your friends," she said, taking a step or two before Ian responded, when it was clear she meant to drop his hand and keep walking.

He stopped her, closing his fingers around hers so she swung around to face him. "Look," he said. "We all have our secrets. And there's a lot we don't know about each other. But you should know that I want to follow the hell out of what's happening with us. And you should also know that if you need help—" he glanced back to where the man had disappeared around the corner "—*any* kind of help…then I'm here for that."

Her expression softened, not in the least hiding the distress in her eyes. "I knew that," she said. "I think I knew it from the moment we met." She gave his hand a gentle squeeze. "Let's go check on your friends."

The house greeted Ian with quiet…everyone sleeping again, with another round of dishes in the sink. Ian gave Ana a quick tour of the retreat's common areas, from the sunny sitting room to the courtyard, an area of flagstone, fountains and tasteful native plantings enclosed in the front with a privacy fence and the back with tall wrought iron, leaving a full view of the mountains rising up behind them. Afterward Ana pulled out the dish soap while Ian went to peek in on everyone and left a voice mail with Ruger that amounted to *call me*.

And then they tumbled into bed, where they didn't talk about illness or enemies or bruises, but explored each other with a thoroughness that left them both limp and panting. She had a mole in the dimple over her left butt cheek. Her voice grew breathless when he kissed the hollow of collarbone and neck, and she giggled when he licked the outside curve of her ear. And from him she evoked new sensations—her tongue down his spine, the clamp of her thighs around his hips, the way she could move herself just so and just when and wring yet another shout from his throat.

For a while they lay together, listening to the quiet of the house. No sound effects from the game room, no clinking from the kitchen, no laughter from the covered open-air dining area—not even to Sentinel ears. Then Ana rolled over to trap Ian's leg under hers, brushing a hand over his brow. "It's back, isn't it?"

The underlying ache in his head, the muddle of his mind. He didn't have to nod to confirm it; he felt the tension of it in his face and knew she'd seen it just as clearly.

"Me, too. Just a little." She scraped her fingers lightly through the disarray of his hair, massaging his scalp until he wanted to groan. Or purr. Or both. "But maybe we just got dehydrated—it's a warm day, and a dry one. Or maybe these things just come and go because that's the way illness is."

"Maybe," he said, not pretending to be convinced but fully immersed in her touch. Wanting not just to purr, but to show her the rest of himself.

Because she wouldn't run screaming to find a snow leopard in her bed, oh, no.

She touched his mouth, tracing a fingertip along his lower lip. "What's so funny?"

"I am," he said. "Because I don't think a couple days of this will be nearly enough."

Her breath caught; her fingers stilled. "It's not the real world, Ian. It's vacation. It's *indulgence*." But she sounded wistful.

He rolled over quite suddenly, pinning her, kissing

her soundly, and rolling right off her again. "Doesn't mean it's *not* real."

She lay silent—tangled in his sheets, her hand trembling where it touched her mouth—so very well kissed, that mouth, even before his impulsive attention.

*Delicate.* In more than one way. *Don't push.*

"Tomorrow," he said, changing the subject just as abruptly as he ever did, "how about those trails?"

"Which ones?" She still sounded a little breathless and maybe a little reticent. "Are they even open, after that man was killed last week?"

Ian stilled. "After what?"

She didn't respond immediately, and when she spoke he heard an unexpected caution. "That man on the trails. They said he got between two mountain lions in a territory spat—one of those ended up dead, too."

He held his silence a moment, then rolled out of bed. Too unsettled to pretend he wasn't, with the snow leopard so close to the surface—remembering that day, that fight.

Remembering that he'd gone looking for the man without much success—but that he hadn't looked all that hard. There hadn't been any blood on the ground, or the heavy scent of it in the air. At the time he'd chalked it up to the fact that he'd been pretty much on top of the attack when it happened—he'd stopped it short, and the man had quite wisely fled. There had been others approaching by then, their conversation rising uphill through the trees from a lower switchback—and Ian hadn't wanted to be found in the area.

But surely he hadn't left a man to die.

He paced over to his laptop, reached to flip it open... and didn't, resting his hand on the case instead. Realizing that his eyes weren't quite ready to focus, and not willing to let it show. "You're sure? The hiker died?"

She sat up and crossed her legs, as intent as he was. "That's what I heard." She watched him with a searching gaze. "I thought you'd know about it. You seemed so at home up there yesterday."

*Left a man to die.* Ian scrubbed his hands through his hair, the heels of his palms coming to rest over his eyes…pressing just a little too hard where the headache lurked. A dull throb of a thing, interlaced through his mind like a foggy lattice…making it hard to manage the duality of thinking he needed in this moment.

She wouldn't understand his upset. And he couldn't explain it. He needed to distance himself from the being he'd been on that mountain, feeling the surge of power in leaping muscle, the power behind flashing claws and the crunch of sharp teeth clamping down. He needed to be Ian Scott, think tank employee on retreat who simply enjoyed hiking in the high beauty of the Sangre de Cristo mountains.

Too late, of course. She asked, "Are you all right?" The question seemed to encompass all the things whirling around in his head, and seemed to do it with a perceptiveness he couldn't quite reconcile.

But then, he couldn't quite reconcile anything about this day—other than the time he'd spent with Ana.

"Headache," he told her, willing to let it take the blame for all. Rather than a glance at his watch, he checked out his window—easy enough to see the last rays of the sun creeping up the side of the mountain range. "I need to check on Fernie. On everyone." He scrounged for his jeans, foregoing the underwear…snagging a T-shirt from the back of the small desk chair. "You want anything? Ginger tea or aspirin? That's about all we have around here."

"Can I help?" She patted the bed in search of her underwear.

He found her bra on the floor and dropped it on the bed on his way past. "Not that everyone won't be able to tell exactly what we've been up to—" Ian coughed, a meaningful sound.

"Right," she said. "They know anyway, don't they?"

"They don't care," he said. Sentinel culture was quite necessarily an earthy one, full of people who reveled in their senses and in their ability to enjoy one another. "They'll like you. Fernie already likes you."

"I like her, too," Ana said. "Let's see if she's feeling any better."

As it turned out, Fernie was—but she was taking a lesson from the ups and downs of the past day and keeping herself to quiet, restful activities in her tiny cottage. She'd advised the others to do the same, so Ian found them grateful for a snack but not yet ready to emerge.

"We should do the same," Ana said, returning to the kitchen with a tray now emptied of food. "And let's look at the trail map. I think a short hike in the fresh air might help us both, and there must be some trails that aren't anywhere near the spot where they found that man." She rustled in the food—pulling out a couple of croissants, slicing them for lunch meat and dabbing on some mayo. She plated them on the tray while Ian rummaged in the remedies cupboard to add a careful dollop of Ruger's herbal tonic to his tea mug. "Oh," she added, an odd reluctance in her voice. "My blazer. Fernie must have brought it inside."

He followed her gaze through the open archway of

the kitchen to the coat rack inside the door, found the blazer hanging there. "I'll grab it if you're worried about losing track of it. I've got room in my closet."

"Yes," she said, tucking the sandwich makings away and appropriating the steaming tea for the tray before she picked it up to head for the back of the house. "Thanks. I guess that's best."

Her lack of enthusiasm seemed like another layer of something Ian should have been able to unravel on this day of amazing moments mixed with confusion. But he was starting to get used to the muddle, so he simply finished tidying the kitchen, flicked off the lights and detoured to grab up the light linen blazer, rearranging his grip to avoid the heavy little object in one pocket.

And then he went to be with Ana.

# *Chapter 6*

Ana woke to a throbbing head and cool, rumpled sheets beside her.

No Ian. No sound of Ian. No sight of him. His clothes were gone; his phone sat on the dresser.

She sat, ran her hands through her hair, and very nearly flopped back down on to the pillow. Only the fact that it would jar her aching head and a glance at the bedside clock stopped her. *Past nine!*

There were aspirin on the little desk, beside the food tray. And a half-full glass of water. They beckoned her.

She slipped out of bed, realizing then that she wore one of Ian's colorful T-shirts and nothing else. Remembering that they'd returned to this room the evening before, eaten the light dinner and watched a sensationalist nature documentary that amused Ian more than not.

She'd been so aware of herself, cuddled beside him. As if every inch of skin knew of his presence and responded to it, her mouth pleasantly bruised from his kisses and every sensitive part of her body remembering his touch. She couldn't have been more comfortable beneath the weight of his arm, her head propped on his chest to catch the beat of his heart and the gentle rise and fall of his breath.

She hadn't been surprised when he'd flicked off the

show and curled up around her, spooning snugly enough so she'd felt encompassed in a new way. *Safe* in a new way.

Able to sleep in perfect confidence.

So where was he now?

She squelched a little spear of hurt. Ian was a complicated man—a *busy* man. The surprise wasn't that he'd slipped out to do something around the retreat—it was that he'd spent so much time with her already.

Ana tossed back two aspirin and gulped down the rest of the water, ignoring the faint unease in her stomach. Her underwear was around here somewhere; she flipped the sheets over without finding it, then twitched them back into place, smoothing and folding the knitted spread at the base of the bed. Perhaps underneath…

Her ringtone gave a muted peal, buried somewhere and set to low. She glanced around the room and finally spotted her blazer, pushing it aside to find her purse beneath.

Of course it was Lerche. Her few friends didn't have this particular number. She accepted the call just in time.

"Can you talk?" he demanded without preamble. "If not, get somewhere that you can."

"I'm fine here," she said, but kept her voice to a murmur. Sentinels, she knew, had keener hearing than most. Than *all*.

"Report!" And then he didn't give her a chance. "What's happening with the second amulet? The first is giving us nothing but kitchen noises. The second is giving us little at all. If you've failed in planting them properly, you'll need to relocate—"

She took a bold chance, interrupting him. "It's in his private room," she said, looking at the blazer and failing to add that the spy amulet was completely muffled within her pocket, not to mention that it had only arrived here after their conversation—and lovemaking—had made way for the ridiculous documentary.

"Oh?" The single word sounded startled but also surprisingly pleased—given how little the location had yielded so far. And surprisingly neutral when he added, "I suppose you're still whoring yourself to him there."

She said, as steadily as she could, "I'm doing my best to fulfill the needs of this mission."

"And going above and beyond in ways I never imagined of you." His voice regained some of its cutting edge, but still held that hint of satisfaction.

"It would help if the posse kept its distance," she told him, dredging up the courage for it. If he took it as implied criticism of his management, he wouldn't forget it. "Ian isn't dulled by his time in his lab, whatever they think—he's got Sentinel instincts, and he trusts them. A lot more than he's going to trust me if this keeps up."

"It won't take much longer," Lerche said, cryptically enough. "You just play your role. And in the end, remember that you chose it."

He hung up on her, leaving her staring at the phone and trying to make sense of him—his moods, his implications, his underlying threat.

A gentle knock on the door startled her far out of proportion to the moment; she fumbled the phone and jammed it into her purse, although there wasn't a thing wrong with making a personal call. "Ian?" she asked, even as she realized he wouldn't knock on his own door.

"It's Fernie. I brought you some breakfast."

Ana looked down at herself, glancing around the room as if a robe might magically manifest itself, and finally snatching the light throw from the end of the bed to drape over her shoulders as she opened the door.

Fernie stood with a serving tray in hand, a smile in place. She wore a fresh housedress but hadn't put her hair up or applied any daily makeup; her face looked tired, but her eyes were bright enough. She let herself in, nudging the evening's tray aside to place the breakfast—bowls of homemade granola, fruit and two cups of steaming tea.

When she looked up, her smile faded. "Where's Ian?"

"I thought—" Ana stalled out on bafflement. "I thought he was out in the house. Helping."

"I haven't seen him," Fernie said, gathering up the used tray. "I didn't get up until nearly eight, myself." She shook her head at this. "We're a sorry excuse for a retreat right now, all of us!"

"Are you feeling better this morning?" Ana crossed her arms over the throw, letting it enfold her. If Ian wasn't in this house, she shouldn't be here, either. Just let the aspirin kick in…

Fernie shook her head. "Such a strange thing. I rest, I feel better, I get up to do some chores and feed some people and bam! I'm right back in bed. I'm beginning to think we picked up a mold with the summer rains." She gave Ana a sharp eye. "You don't look so good this morning, either, Ian's girl."

*Ian's girl.* Ana swallowed the guilt of the phone call. "I don't feel so well. But that's not surprising. I've been with Ian on and off for days, and I've been here, too."

"You've been good for him," Fernie said, giving her a closer look—an unabashed one. Ana keenly felt the absence of her underwear. "I hope he's been good for you, too. I hope he's told you that no woman deserves whoever put those bruises on your face."

Ana gasped, realizing she'd been caught without makeup over the bruises, one hand clutching the knitted throw even more tightly and one flying to her jaw. It was much less sore today, and she'd hoped the bruises would be gone.

Fernie offered her a tight smile. "It's the reason they gave me this job," she said. "I meddle. Now have something to eat and get yourself dressed, and I'll see if I can't scare up Ian."

But Fernie couldn't scare up Ian—and a call to his phone revealed it to be on the desk beside his laptop. By the time Ana had shaken out her clothes and climbed back into her pants, appropriating another of Ian's T-shirts, Fernie was on her way back down the hall. Ana hesitated with the blazer in hand and then quickly flipped it out, doubled it and folded it tightly with the listening device in the center, tucking it against the wall behind the door.

She met Fernie at the door, tray in hand and headache somewhat ameliorated by the aspirin. Fernie didn't wait for her query. "This isn't like him," she said. "This isn't *anything* like him. Did something happen yesterday?"

Ana floundered, frowning and unable to think of a thing. "He's worried about you...he doesn't seem to feel as though he's done enough to help."

"Typical." Fernie frowned, giving Ana the most direct look. "This doesn't have anything to do with that phone call I overheard, does it? *Could* it?"

Ana froze, instantly trying to recall what she'd said—knowing it was certainly enough to indict her as far as Fernie was concerned, but reasonably certain she'd said nothing to reveal her Core affiliation. With utmost care, she said, "Not as far as I know."

Fernie said, "We'll talk about that later, then." She tipped her head at Ana, her expression somehow reminiscent of a satisfied mother bear. "Like I said, I meddle. But first, we need to find Ian."

"All right," Ana said faintly. "What can I do to help?"

Fernie didn't hesitate. "If this illness stays to pattern, we don't have much time before it's hard to be smart about this. I have some people to call. You check around the grounds—don't forget the fountain courtyard or the garden area outside the walls. And don't assume he'll be on his feet." Fernie shook her head, making a sound of disapproving dismay. "That boy is always putting his hands on things he shouldn't."

*Amulets*, Ana wanted to say—but didn't. She couldn't give that much of herself away, even if Fernie had already overheard her compromising words. "He has a keen curiosity," she agreed, and headed out of the room…but then couldn't stop herself. She turned, finding Fernie scowling around the room with a stern eye— one that stayed stern as it found Ana. "Why aren't you angry with me? Or showing me the door?"

Fernie snorted faintly. "That could come. But right now, whatever's going on, you're still Ian's girl and you've still been good for him. I'll let him make his own decisions."

Ana wanted to lift her chin, wanted to be proud and to be confident in herself and what she'd done. If the Sentinels didn't want Core attention, they needed to practice self-control, and to quit taking advantage of their abilities at the expense of others.

Instead she could only stand in confusion, wondering

at the sensations of acceptance even from this woman who so clearly knew Ana was more than she'd begun to say. Floundering in this nurturing atmosphere, where Ian had set aside his personal needs to take care of those beneath him in Sentinel hierarchy, and where Fernie's affection for her guests permeated this place like a physical embrace.

In the end Ana simply said, "Thank you," and went on, out into the yard to look for Ian.

At first Lerche had resented the number of silent amulets necessary to manage this endeavor—from the simplest tracking amulet used on Ana and on Scott's motorcycle to the complex layering in the amulets she had planted.

There'd been no choice—not with Ian Scott as their target. Intel on Southwest Brevis had identified the man as the only one capable of breaking the silence of those amulets, and he would most certainly detect anything not completely silenced, just as he'd detected the faint whisper from the feeble working used to discern whether Ana had triggered the second amulet.

But the expense was paying off. Even if Lerche hadn't gathered much information—the foolish woman had planted the first amulet in the retreat kitchen, of all places, and the second was full of so many muffled noises that it must have malfunctioned in that respect— Ian Scott was clearly sick. Clearly not thinking quite right any longer.

Not to have taken the motorcycle out into the mountains so early in the day, leaving Ana behind and leaving the Sentinel light-bloods worried and looking for him. Or so Budian reported, his phone pickup muffled with what must have been gloves. The man had moved in upon Scott's departure, confirming that the Sentinel had gone alone.

"Excellent work," he told Budian, thinking of Ian Scott—alone, sick and vulnerable. The one man who could bring them down—and the one man who could tell them how close he'd already come. "We'll take advantage of this opportunity. Find Scott on the trails and bring him to me."

Budian sounded cold—as well he might, after a stakeout in one of these stupidly cold desert mountain nights. "On the trails? He could be in his beast form."

Lerche dismissed the possibility with the ease of a man who wouldn't actually be on those trails. "Not with the amulet working on him to this extent. Ana said it was in his bedroom. Such concentrated exposure on a full field Sentinel will have resulted in profound effects by now."

"I'll send men to look for him," Budian said. "But it's a big mountain."

"Don't *look*," Lerche told him. *"Find."*

He cut Budian's response short with a swipe at his phone, and tossed the device onto his desk. Soon Ian Scott would be his—and then dead—and the only threat to the silent amulets would be eliminated.

It would be a good day.

Ana found no sign of Ian at the retreat, but the cool morning air refreshed her—clearing her thoughts, invigorating her body. The aspirin kicked in, and the granola sat well in her stomach.

She returned to the house to find that Fernie hadn't been as lucky. The older woman stood at the dining room table, a large map spread out before her and her own breakfast untouched to the side.

"Come out to the porch," Ana said. "It's a beautiful day, and you've been stuck inside since I met Ian."

Fernie regarded her for a moment, then nodded. "There's truth to that," she allowed, and gathered up the map. Ana picked up the cereal bowl and muffin, just in case, and brought it along.

Fernie sat in the porch chair with an undisguised weariness, opening the map on her lap. "Oh, Ian," she said, looking at it. "What are you up to?"

Ana set the bowl on a tiny round patio table, glancing at the map in belated recognition. "That's a trail map."

"Indeed it is." Fernie smoothed it. "Ian's not *here*, where he should be. And he's not himself—he's done well with this bug of ours, but you've seen it—when it hits him, it hits hard."

"It seems to," Ana agreed.

Fernie gave her the most perceptive of looks. "Ian is special, as you likely well know."

Ana gave her a surprised look, wondering if this was a direct allusion to Ian's field Sentinel nature. To his *other*. And if it was some sort of test to see how Ana reacted—if she *knew*.

The best she could do was not react at all. After a moment, Fernie said, "Things affect him differently—illnesses, medicines, even something as simple as caffeine. We can't assume he's thinking clearly right now. But when he's troubled…" She tapped the map. "This is where he goes."

Ana touched the map. "We were planning to hike today."

"Were you?" Fernie gave her a sharp look. "He was going to share this with you?"

"I didn't think of it like that," Ana admitted.

"You should have."

Fernie's short words sat on silence for a moment, and then Ana admitted, "I was worried, though, because of that mountain lion attack last week. The man who died." Worried because it reminded her that Ian had killed someone, she meant, even if Fernie didn't know it.

"What?" Fernie sat up straighter. Her eyes had brightened, and her expression looked livelier. "When? Where?"

Ana tapped the map. "Right here. Just over a week ago."

"No," Fernie said with some assertion. "I would have heard. Someone misspoke. Or they were telling tales."

"No, I—" Ana hesitated, her finger lingering on the map. The trail where she'd first seen Ian. The trail where she'd seen him *change*. It occurred to her that she'd never seen any news stories of the attack, no headlines in the paper.

Fernie saw her uncertainty. "Honey, when there's a lion attack around here, *everyone* knows. I don't know who told you that, but they were telling stories."

Ana couldn't quite fathom it. *Why* would Lerche tell her such a thing if it wasn't true? Why even bother, when it would have been so easy to double-check?

Except he'd known she wouldn't question him. That she'd believe him utterly, as she always had—and that in believing, she would not only be wary of Ian, she'd believe even more deeply in the task to which he'd set her.

*What other lies has he told?*

She pressed her fingers over her closed lids, searching

for a way out of the confusion—in the end, she found nothing but the need to focus on Ian. *His safety.* "Okay," she said, releasing the rest of it for the moment. "Never mind that, then. What do we do about Ian?"

"I'm waiting for a call back from our company," Fernie said. "I want some help up here. It's one thing for us to get a passing virus, but this thing is holding on. And if Ian is reacting so strongly to it, it could mean there's something else going on." She didn't make any offer to explain her thinking. "Meanwhile, either he's gone out to clear his head and he'll be back, or he's too sick to get back and we should look for him."

"Me," Ana said. "*I* should look for him."

Fernie gave her a look. A reminder that she'd overheard too much of that last phone call from Lerche, even if there'd been nothing directly incriminating said. A reminder that Ana wasn't one of them, even if she wasn't truly supposed to know the significance of that fact.

Ana made a noise of frustration. "At least point out his favorite trails, if you know them—I can check the trailheads for his motorcycle. If we do need to go looking—or to send someone—then we'll know where to start."

Fernie took the deepest of breaths, glancing back into the house...quite visibly considering her options. At last, she nodded. "There's sense to that," she said, and shifted the map so Ana could see it more easily. "Here. Check this one. If he's not here, check the overlook parking—there are a handful of trailheads there, and some go directly to a wilderness area." Then she tapped the first spot, an assertive gesture. "But this is his favorite."

Of course it was. It was the trail where she'd first seen him. The one where her own people had first set him up for an encounter to reveal the depth of his true nature to her.

The one where he might or might not have killed an innocent man.

Ian wasn't sure how he'd made it to the trail. He had only an impression of those early morning hours—his vision bleary, his head a muddle, and his entire being driven by a singular need to find surcease in the wilds of the mountain.

Given that his lab wasn't available. Or the basement in the echoingly empty bachelor pad of his house, surrounded by earth and as deeply calm as his complicated world ever got. *His den.*

But here he'd found himself—not as the snow leopard, which surprised him. As plain old human, crouched by the side of the trail.

Only after he'd blinked a few times and oriented himself did he realize where he'd taken himself in that muddle. And only then did he realize he was growling softly in the back of his very human throat, a rolling commentary on his situation as a whole.

Now he still crouched here, not quite warm enough, accepting the fact that he wouldn't figure out his exact location until he found familiar features along the trail. For now he knew only that he faced west. And that he'd gone high.

Ian stood, hopping down to the trail—a single-footing thing that wound along the side of the slope, uphill on one side and downhill on the other. Little room for misstep there. He placed his feet carefully, drawing on his snow leopard—or trying to. That part of himself was obscured and hard to reach.

It was an unfamiliar feeling. The snow leopard was always there.

Always filling the heart of him.

But now his feet felt leaden...his senses dull. The part of him that seemed ever imminent—ready to burst right through his skin, full of energy and loud with life—

It simply wasn't.

The lack of it made him place his steps with extra care, as if they belonged to someone else. It made the world seem dull and distant around him, not quite as vibrant. As if he walked through it but not *in* it.

The moments passed, one step after the other, a painstaking effort to navigate a mountain he'd all but owned until this point. Until suddenly he stopped, a rebellion of sorts. He took a deep breath, then another a deeper breath and closed his eyes to inhale the pine-sharp air, the cool hints of juniper and the distinct scent of fall—oak leaves browning, the ground cover still faintly damp from the most recent of the area's brief but intense fall rains.

Inside, the snow leopard roused into clarity—irritable, demanding and tail twitching.

Ian released a gusting sigh, settling back into his skin. Not fully himself, but able to see it from where he was.

Just that quickly, he knew his exact location—which trail and which section of the trail. His favorite. And the very same trail on which he'd saved a man from a mountain lion, only to find him gone upon return.

The man had then supposedly been killed, although Ian had heard nothing of it—and no lion kill would go un-sensationalized by the local media. *Make sense of that, why don't you?*

Another fifteen minutes of walking brought him to

that very spot, as his mind grew increasingly clearer, and the hint of a bounce returned to his step. As if the very act of hiking in this place had pushed back the virus.

Or the *not*-virus.

For the illness gripping the retreat had *seemed* like a virus, but now—today, waking up in this place—Ian thought there was very little chance of it.

He'd seen Fernie recover and fade not in the natural wax and wane of such things, but just the same as he'd seen himself recover and fade.

Depending on where he was.

The first headache had faded after a few hours at Ana's. The next surge of malaise came the following morning after he'd cleaned up the retreat and taken trays to the others, and it had faded after he'd gone out to search the grounds—and faded even more thoroughly after an afternoon at the museum, leaving him alone until after he and Ana had quite thoroughly made love. After which it had descended again harder than ever— this time to include Ana.

In other words, as he spent time inside the retreat.

And there was Fernie, recovering inside her little casita and but fading each time she came out to tend the others—none of whom who seemed as affected as either he or Fernie, but who had more consistently sequestered themselves under the direction of Fernie and Ruger.

None of the others at the retreat were as strong-blooded as Ian, or as affected as he was when he did go down. For them, malaise. For Ian, blinding headaches, muffled thoughts and a delirious blackout that had brought him to this place, only to clear once he'd spent time here.

Not illness.

*Amulet.*

But if it was a silent one, he'd never find it—not by prowling the yard, and not by searching the house. And if it wasn't silent, he would have found it already. *Frigging silents.*

The only way to find the things was to solve the very riddle he'd been sent here to forget.

And he needed to do it without his lab—the place where he could isolate and deconstruct amulet elements.

Ian jammed his hands in his jacket pockets, searching...

*Finding.* The silent amulet he'd been carrying around. He crouched there, in the middle of the trail in the middle of the day, no one else within sight or earshot, and focused on the thing—for what must have been the millionth time—willing himself to be able to perceive it. Shifting up and down the long scale of energies he'd long ago learned to visualize and target, hunting any small sign of—

His head jerked up, eyes narrowed, nostrils flaring. *Core corruption.*

But not from the amulet in his hand. And not fresh. Not even particularly strong—just an afterthought of presence. The big cat in him flared whiskers, rising to interest—responding to a beckoning call he hadn't had a chance to notice the last time he'd been here, simply because he'd never gotten quite this far.

Not just a call, but a challenge.

He felt the solid undertone of a growl in his chest before he even realized his response to that call. *Territory. Invasion. Defend!*

With effort, he shook off the urge to take his *other*,

to bound along this trail until he found an interloper—a leap and pounce and satisfying crush of jaw—

"Down, boy," he muttered at himself.

It was time for a different kind of hunt.

He rose to pace the trail, a slow and careful progress—hunting overturned ground matter, disturbed needles…exposed dirt.

Finding the solid trace of an amulet working. Following it. And then finding the small overlook, well-hidden, with the three equidistant gouges that could only be a tripod of some sort. There, he picked up a snagged section of someone's gillie suit. And, leaving that spot, he backtracked to the exact spot where he'd seen the mountain lion attack what had seemed to be a hapless hiker.

*Had seemed to be.*

Here, even though still muted by illness, his snow leopard bristled so strongly that Ian backed swiftly away.

It didn't matter. He didn't need to be on top of the site to see the lingering gouges in the earth.

And he didn't need to stick his AmTech nose in it to understand the setup. The lion had been a plant, lured here and excited into attack. And someone from the Core had watched—perhaps even filmed it, to judge by those tripod marks. Probably filmed his response to it.

If anyone had killed that man, it had been the Core.

*What the hell?*

What sense did this even make?

"None," he decided out loud. "Absolutely no sense at all."

*Okay, Scott. Yours is not to wonder why. Yours is to figure out the whole damned silent amulet thing.*

So he'd take this information back to brevis, fully aware that he'd never have found it at all if he hadn't been searching out Core energies—hunting any hint of the silent amulet right there in his hand. If he hadn't been so...

*Receptive.*

He stumbled over the thought.

*Receptive.*

Because a receiver was a passive thing. A thing that waited for energy to come to *it*.

His thoughts scattered, reminding him just how recently he'd not been particularly lucid at all. Warning him not to take any of it for granted. Unsettling him enough so he hunkered down beside the disturbed trail, getting closer to the earth...hunting balance. Finding it elusive—and finding himself, the man with the overactive mind and the endless energy, without the means to work through it.

*Ana.*

Ana had quieted his mind. Had calmed it, when he'd thought it might just hit terminal velocity. He closed his eyes, settling down to sit cross-legged on a carpet of pine needles and tiny broken branches and plant detritus. For that moment, he thought only of Ana and of the unexpected peace at her touch. He thought of her courage these past days, reaching out to him in spite of her obvious trepidation—and responding to him in a way that revealed her heart, her receptive and sensitive soul. From the way her breath hitched when she caught his eye to the unfettered nature of her cries in pleasure, the flush of her face as her body strained for and tumbled into completion.

The warmth of those thoughts suffused his body and settled his mind. For a moment he luxuriated in them, wrapping himself in them—along with the vague discomfort of rising desire that had nowhere to go. But the discomfort was of little consequence, coming as it did with the certain understanding that when he made it back to the city—when he found his balance—he and Ana would have a discussion about exactly where following his feelings for her had led.

*To more than just a carefree vacation fling.*

When he opened his eyes he found the world clear around him. His thoughts, still hazy, no longer cascaded so quickly from one to another that he couldn't follow them at all. He picked his way through them to find the spot where he'd fallen into chaos.

The part where he'd for the first time characterized the entire Sentinel history of detecting Core amulets and workings. *Listening. Hunting.*

Active listening, to be sure, and listening by some incredibly skilled sensitives along the way. Always, in the past, a perfectly viable technique. Definitely the technique Ian had attempted to refine in his efforts.

But what if he'd been thinking like the wrong animal? Not a big cat listening for the rustle of prey or inhaling a drifting scent, but something equally elegant. *Dolphins and whales and sonar...*

Send energy out. *See if it comes back.*

And most importantly, see if it comes back *changed.*

He'd never done it. He'd never had to. He was snow leopard, stalking and bounding pounce. He was laboratory finesse and amulet study and deconstruction.

But he'd been in the field. He knew how to shield—and shielding was, in its modest way, a manipulation of energy.

Ian dug into his pocket for the test amulet, the one from which he'd never perceived any energetic signal at all. He tossed it aside—fifteen easy feet along into the ground cover.

Then he pushed through the hazy elements in his thinking and formed for himself a light shield—close to himself, good for protection against equally light workings. Nothing a light-blood or mundane human would notice at all.

But every field Sentinel knew how to protect others—how to push the shielding outward, even if only a little. He did that, enlarging his space…and then gave the concentrated shielding energies a quick, hard shove—expanding outward in all directions, and just about as much focused energy work as he had in him on this particular day.

And *then* he listened.

Then, the energy came back to him.

His heartbeat kicked up into overdrive. His hands, resting on his thighs, closed into fists—an alternative to releasing his burgeoning shout of triumph into the forest, where it would ring without understanding.

*Ana.*

Ana had done this. Ana and her calm, Ana and the distraction of her smile, Ana and the honesty of what she'd given him these past days.

For the silence was broken.

## Chapter 7

Ian grabbed the silent amulet up from the dirt, jamming it into his pocket and hitting the trail at a jog. His mind already whirled off in a dozen different directions—wondering if, with experience and experiments, he'd be able to teach others to not only find the amulets, but identify their nature. He was eager to get back to the lab and try it—and eager to get back to the retreat and search it. Not to mention he wished he'd been smart enough to bring his damned phone when he'd wandered away from the retreat in the first place.

He'd have no reception up here. But down at the trailhead, maybe. Out on the road, definitely.

Beneath all that, he worried. He'd left Ana alone at the retreat; he'd left Fernie and the others sick.

And he had no idea how long he'd been gone.

He slowed to navigate a narrow section of rock-cobbled trail, then struck out again, a little faster this time. *Driven.* Running familiar ground now, and knowing when he could stretch his legs and when to gear down for rocks and single-foot sections. One mile… three… The trail finally widened as it looped back toward the trailhead, and he loosed a little more speed, freeing the power of the snow leopard that so often simply lurked beneath.

He rounded a final curve, breaking free of the trees to spot the trailhead lot—finding himself relieved that he'd actually parked the bike here instead of jamming it into some out-of-the-way niche during an insensible delirium.

It sat up close to the trailhead, but it wasn't the only vehicle in the tiny area in this early morning. At first he was simply relieved that he hadn't run into the SUV's driver out on the trail while he was so busy being Sentinel.

But then the occupants of the car disembarked, and a second car pulled in—a familiar-looking little city car.

*Ana.* He'd seen the car in her driveway, a little rental that she didn't seem to use much. Of course she'd come looking.

But as he approached, his pace steady, he realized that the men from the SUV weren't preparing to hike out on the trail.

They were waiting.

They were waiting for *him.*

He eased back, seeing Ana's reaction as she, too, exited her car, her initial wave faltering as she got a look at the men. His mind went back to a million miles an hour, wondering if these men had had anything to do with the bruises on Ana's jaw...or if they had anything to do with the sedan that had passed them two days earlier, the reek of a Core working trailing behind them.

He found himself running again as one of them snapped something to Ana. She stepped away, clearly fearful—but then stood up to them, a petite figure gesturing at them to leave, one hand clutching her blazer closed against a chill that looked as though it came from within.

The snow leopard surged at him, wanting to bound fully free—ready to leap between Ana and the men, and ready to take them down. *Ready—*

He didn't. He slowed, his breath coming hard now. His fatigue catching up with him. Realization catching up with him. For these men were Core if anyone was— the unofficial muscle uniform of a snug black T-shirt and black slacks beneath black jackets, dark hair pulled back into stubby clubbed ponytails, heavy silver glinting at ear and throat.

*Threatening Ana.*

Or were they? He hadn't felt any workings; he still didn't feel any workings. But he no longer took such things for granted. Clumsy as he was with the newfound amulet detection, he still pulled a shield into place... steadied it...*pushed* it at them.

And staggered to a stop when a silent amulet pinged back.

Not from the two men.

Not from their car.

*From Ana.*

Ana held herself as still as she could, caught between two worlds.

*What has Lerche done?*

She couldn't warn Ian without giving herself away— not to Ian, and not to the two giants who stood in her way.

Ian hadn't hesitated. He moved with the grace of a wild thing and the power of a predator, his strides full of purpose and intent. Even a week ago on this very mountain, the snow leopard hadn't ridden him so clearly, painted him as *other* so distinctly. It wouldn't take knowing his nature to see it—to make way for him on this trail and to yield to the temptation of simply standing openmouthed to watch him move.

Ana felt the tug of that temptation, the lure of knowing she saw the extraordinary—and the realization that she'd not only been with that man, but that he'd chosen to be with her.

That until she'd felt his embrace, she'd never known what it felt to be safe. To be revered. To be *respected*.

And here she was, standing beside his enemy. *Being* his enemy.

"Stay out of the way," one of the posse goons growled at her. She didn't know him—didn't know the other one. They were enforcers, far too noticeable to manage everyday surveillance and public chores. They were muscle and force and proud of it, and she had no idea what they were doing here.

"Leave him alone," she told them, knowing it pointless. "This is my operation!"

The biggest of them glanced at her. Bigger than Ian, who, for all his power, packed leaner muscle on a more graceful frame. "Things change," he said, and she would have bet anything that he had no idea of her role in the situation and no concern about it one way or the other. He paid her no more attention.

That, she could understand. Because Ian had pulled up only fifty feet from them, standing loose and ready, his breath coming fast. And his expression...

Ana wanted to cry—and discovered that she was, tears dampening her cheeks.

He'd recognized the goons as Core, no doubt about that. But his initially cautious expression turned startled as his gaze jerked to Ana. He took a step—as if he might come to her, torn between a demand for explanation and the need to gather her up in his arms.

*He knows.*

Not just guessing, not just hoping it wasn't so. Somehow, he *knew*.

Because of who and what he was, and how strongly it shone from him now. Oh, he definitely knew.

She lifted a hand in supplication; he shook his head ever so slightly, taking a step back again—the recognition of her betrayal coloring his eyes, painting his face with shadow.

"No," she said—not loudly, but knowing he'd hear. "It's not like that."

"Shut up," the biggest goon said, stepping out in front of her. "And stay out of the way."

But Ian was already poised for flight, glancing at the distance to the motorcycle.

*Too far.* She knew it, he knew it…and the goons knew it. And still…

"Run!" she cried at him. "Ian, *run!*"

Ian broke for the motorcycle, an astonishing sprint of speed. Ana ripped her blazer off as both goons leaped to follow, their movement slow and clumsy, compared to Ian's, but far more inexorable. She threw herself at the smaller one from behind, wrapping her blazer around his head and yanking the sleeves tight, falling away almost in time to miss the sharp backhand blow of response.

She tumbled away from the impact, losing her bearings for that instant. When she oriented again, her shoulder throbbing, Ian had flung himself on the bike, jamming the keys in for a quick start and barely settling in the saddle as the bike came alive beneath him, spitting dirt and gravel and finally grabbing traction. It leaped away—not over the barely paved lot, but cross-country over cactus and scrub.

One goon threw himself into a hopeless effort to take Ian off the side of the bike, missing to land in scrub. The other pulled himself up short—and Ana pushed herself away from the ground, daring to come up where she could see the heavy bike wallow and spurt across the ground, cutting across to the curving drive where he could gun it and *run*—

But he didn't. She didn't believe it at first, scrambling to her feet as he targeted not freedom, but the lot just behind her car—letting the bike slew to a stop while he beckoned to her.

He'd come back for her.

He'd known of her betrayal, and he'd come back for her.

*Why?*

She stared at him, stupified. Because he'd seen the goon hit her? Because he wanted to question her? Because he...

*Cared?*

Cared *enough?*

"Ana!" he shouted, glancing over his shoulder because *yes, they were coming.* She broke her stasis and ran for him. Not swift, not powerful, but small and determined, her hands clenched into fists and with not the faintest idea how she could ever make her actions right with either Ian or the Core.

*"Ana!"* But this time his shout was a warning, as he came off the bike saddle in alarm. She barely had a glimpse of motion from the side, shooting out from behind her little rental and then slamming into her with smashing force—hurling her into Ian, who twisted aside

to free himself from the bike and still went down beneath her.

But not for long, because he'd quite clearly had enough of playing fair. Preternatural light flared around him as goon hands grabbed at Ana, lifting her...tossing her *through* the sudden play of light and energy and into the thorny scrub.

By the time she landed, a snow leopard crouched by her side—so close that the pale splendor of its pelt brushed against her, its long tail slapping against her leg—altogether not quite as big as she'd expected, but every bit as magnificent. Only for an instant before it leaped, broad paws spread wide and claws unsheathed, a wild snarl of warning in the air.

The first goon went down before him, and went down screaming—legs flailing, fists beating against the big cat's head and deterring him not at all. A whiskered muzzle closed around the man's thick neck, flesh giving way with a grisly crunch—

The second goon had grabbed a tire iron on his way, and he came in swinging. Metal thumped against feline ribs, and the cat—*Ian*—tumbled away, his teeth tearing free. He landed in a crouch beside Ana, already prepared for another leap.

But the goon had also brought out a gun. And he yanked Ana to her feet and jammed the muzzle of it to her temple, grinding metal into tender flesh. He snapped, "Your choice!" and gave Ana a little shake as if that would make his point more clear.

Ana gasped, knowing all too clearly that Ian understood her betrayal. She was the enemy; the Sentinels gave no quarter to the Core. He'd come for her on the bike, but he'd surely never intended to give himself up for her.

The goon wrenched her arm, jamming the gun against Ana hard enough to torque her head aside. She cried out, twisting in that grip—feeling small and insignificant and helpless and yet unable to ask Ian to do this thing.

And yet Ian did it.

With a final snarl, he disappeared into that blinding fog of energy and light, and when it cleared he still crouched there—blood smeared on his face, one arm clamping protectively against his ribs...bright blue eyes locked to Ana's.

"Ian," she whispered. "Ian, no..."

The goon shoved her aside and slapped the gun across Ian's face, and it turned out that was enough to take even a Sentinel down.

The stench of Core workings permeated Ian's head, throbbing along in time with the pain of his cheek and brow. His side radiated with stabbing pain against a lumpy excuse of a mattress. He absorbed the faint surprise of finding himself alone and unbound, and pondered opening his eyes.

And remembered, then, exactly how he'd gotten here.

Trusting Ana.

Trusting her right up until the moment he'd found her carrying the silent amulet—and even then, he hadn't been able to leave her to the fate her Core compatriots would have dealt her.

Or *might* have dealt her. Hard to know for sure. She might well have orchestrated the whole standoff. The Core was rarely kind or respectful to its women, and those who made it out of low-level support roles tended to be both the best of them and the worst of them.

Either way, she'd played him like a pro.

Thanks to his delirious midnight departure from the retreat, the Sentinels had no idea where he'd gone—and no idea that he'd been taken. Worst of all, he had no way of telling them what he'd learned. That finally— *finally*—he had a way to detect the silent amulets. One that with refinement, might even allow the Sentinels to identify the amulets as they detected them. Right now the technique was nothing but a clumsy thing, baby steps that could at least alert them...

If they knew.

*They needed to know.*

He'd bet anything that his illness, Fernie's illness... *everyone's* illness there at the retreat—had come from one of those silent amulets. Although Ana had seemed to feel the faint effects of that illness, as well...

*Nothing that couldn't be easily faked.*

He took a steadying breath, full of a new pain he hadn't expected—a hard twist in his chest, radiating up the back of his throat to mingle with the effects of the blow he'd taken.

*Probably broken.*

The thought made him snort in faint laughter, figuring *broken* in more ways than one, and in turn the faint laughter sent bright shards of pain lancing along his ribs, wringing a gasp from him.

The tire iron. Right.

Eventually he opened his eyes, expecting a cell or some crude containment, and blinked at the sight of a textured paint ceiling. A careful turn of his aching head revealed similar walls done up in a classic Southwestern taupe, and a small window with tasteful decorative bars. A closet door, an opening at the corner he was fairly certain led to a tiny bathroom, and a bedside table and chair completed the furnishings. The table held a glass of water and what looked like two aspirin.

All the comforts of home.

With much care and several false starts, he eased off the bed. Healing swiftly wasn't the same as healing instantly, no doubt about it. A quick tour of the bare space revealed a small desk and nail holes in the wall where someone had been smart enough to take down the pictures. If it had occurred to them to rip up the comfortable carpet underfoot, they could have removed the tacking strips, too. As it was, he kept them in mind.

The bathroom was indeed tiny, tile floor and a corner shower, plus a securely locked second door to another room. The mirror was just big enough to give him a glimpse of his face—blood streaked and swollen over the angle of his cheek, a split over his brow—and, when he pulled up his shirt, his ribs. Just about what he expected there—bruises blooming purple unto black, the worst of them gone white in the center.

Dammit.

He availed himself of the facilities and went back to the bed. Whatever this particular Core mastermind had planned for him, Ian would meet it as well-rested—and recovered—as he could. Napping in relative comfort seemed like a fine idea when his painful ribs meant he wasn't going anywhere anyway.

Except that his fingers twitched against the covers, drumming to a silent song. There was no nap waiting here, only the tangle of his thoughts.

His mind whirled with *Ana*. His heart whirled with

*Ana*. His body ached with mingled hurt and remembered touch, and his mind's eye gave him Ana laughing and Ana uncertain, and Ana's face lighting up in response to him.

He had no idea how to reconcile what he knew of her. What he felt of her. What she'd done to him.

In the end, with the most ultimate irony, the memory of the peace she'd given him allowed him to fall back into a meditative quiet. Relative rest, his body burning with the attempt to heal.

By the time quiet footsteps sounded outside his door, he'd had time to settle into himself. To resist taking the form of the snow leopard, no matter how close to the surface it lurked. The leopard was a hunter—it knew how to wait. How to persist.

So did Ian.

And Ian wanted answers.

But he hadn't expected Ana.

To judge by her uncertainty as she slipped through the door—as it locked behind her—she hadn't quite expected to be here, either.

She pressed her back to the door and regarded him, biting her lip. Definitely uncertain.

Or pretending to be.

He didn't rise to greet her. She'd changed to slacks that fit her petite, rounded form perfectly, and a stretchy shirt that molded to her slender body. Her face held a new bruise—from the morning's struggle or something fresher, he couldn't tell.

He tried to tell himself he didn't care, but that was a lie.

"Ian…" she said, and stalled out.

"Ana," he said, much more flatly. A lie of disinterest,

as his heart rate kicked into gear and his fingers gave him away, twitching against the plain green bed blanket.

Her eyes flicked to the corner of the room and he saw what he'd missed before—the tiny dark spot of a camera lens. Well, that only made sense. Of course they'd keep an eye on him.

"They must think they can get in here pretty fast," Ian said, making his voice hard. "Or else they don't care what I do to you."

She flinched. "This wasn't supposed to happen."

"No? What in particular? The part where I end up with broken bones? The part where you make wild passionate love with me? Or just the part where your cover gets blown?"

"We both had secrets," she said, but her voice held a note of desperation.

Ian shook his head. "My secrets were my own. Yours were there to hurt me."

"No!" She moved forward from the door, just a step, her entire body tensed, her fists clenching—and then releasing in defeat as she retreated, turning away. Her voice came strained. "I guess maybe that's turned out to be true. But not like *this*." She looked up, but he didn't think the glare was meant for him. "*This* wasn't part of the plan. Not that I knew."

"So no broken bones, no incredible intimacy and no ever knowing who you really are." He gave no quarter. "What *were* you supposed to do?"

Her mouth twisted in some emotion he couldn't quite read. "Get inside your retreat. Plant a listening device. Spend time with you—get a sense of you. Fill out our dossier on you. And I thought… I *hoped*—I could start some sort of dialogue between your people and mine."

Ian couldn't help but bark a laugh, one that ended in a grunt of pain. He stiffened against the lash of his damaged ribs. "Is that what they call it where you come from? *Dialogue?*"

She glared at him. "These bruises?" She pointed at her jaw, where she'd either done a better job than usual of covering them or they'd faded faster than he'd expected—maybe they'd never been that bad after all. "I got these because I was only ever supposed to *talk* to you. I wasn't supposed to get—" she swallowed hard, looking away "—close to you."

"You *weren't*," Ian said, hard words to match the hard sensation in his chest. "You have no idea what *close* even means. Nice try, though. You had me fooled."

"That's not fair!" She rose to that, pushing away from the door and this time holding her ground. "I had nothing to do with this! You *saw*—" She stopped herself, visibly gathering up her thoughts and something of her emotions. "You saw what happened at that trail. I had no idea they'd be there. I came looking for *you*. I was worried. Your friends were worried."

"Awesome," Ian said. "I guess they'll be even more worried now."

She held her silence for a long moment. "There's not going to be any talking to you, is there?"

Ian felt the finality of that to his bones. "Not for a while."

Not for a long while.

Defeat enervated Ana, leaving her with nothing else to say.

But then, she'd known this wouldn't be something

she could fix. She'd known it from the moment Ian rec-ognized her as Core.

That the muscle goons had threatened her along the way made no difference—it hadn't surprised Ana, and it likely hadn't surprised Ian. The men who worked enforcement for the Core were trained to accomplish their task regardless, and Ana would have been a fair enough trade for Ian.

She stepped away from the door to look up at the camera. It was enough. She heard movement from the other side—a long, curving hallway that ran along the wing of this luxurious house, only ever meant to be a Santa Fe mansion and now altered by interior locks and latches and camera feeds so it could serve as Hollender Lerche's little posse hideaway—and Ana's home—since their flight from Tucson after *Core D'oíche*.

After only a few moments of silence—she couldn't bring herself to look at Ian, as aware as she was of his painfully uneven breathing. She'd barely been able to look at his face in the first place—the ugly puff of his cheekbone, the angry split at the edge of his brow. She certainly hadn't been able to ask how he felt beneath it all—if he still carried the headache and illness that had driven him away from the house to start all this.

She rubbed the side of her head, perfectly well aware of the lingering headache and trying not to think too much of it. She carried her own bruises, both physical and emotional; she'd been just as ambushed as Ian on that trail, if in a totally different way.

The room locks disengaged; the knob turned. Ana moved away from the door, tucking herself into the corner beneath the camera—barely making way for Lerche and the remaining posse goon.

Ian didn't move as they entered—not really. But something about him changed, his gaze going from Ana to Lerche, his eyes narrowing to shadow the bright blue. Lerche might not see the anger there—he was far too busy gloating over the coup of capturing Ian—but Ana did.

Anger for her. In spite of what she'd done. For she knew, seeing that expression, that Ian had instantly identified Lerche as the man who'd dealt her those earlier bruises.

It left her naked. Vulnerable and revealed and naked.

She swiped desperately at welling tears, swallowing against the barely controllable sob in her throat and perversely glad for the blur that kept her from seeing that look on Ian's face.

But humbled, too.

By Ian.

By a man who cared more for what had been done to her than for his own grudges and hurts.

"I want to thank you," Lerche said to Ian, characteristically unaware of the subtle byplay. "For you to have stumbled out of your safe little retreat and onto the mountain while we happened to be paying such close attention to you…for you to have done so while so clearly out of your head…it was a tremendous opportunity. I know you'll forgive me for taking advantage of it."

So many things Ian could have said in response. He was brilliant; he was never without words and never without dark humor and never without attitude. But as Ana regained control over her emotions, she found him silent, regarding Lerche with such a simmering anger that she couldn't imagine how he restrained himself at all.

"Well, perhaps not," Lerche acknowledged. "But I'm sure you'll see that I couldn't waste the chance." He shot one cuff, adjusting it with a twitch. "In any event, here we are. Do I need to mention that the more cooperative you are, the easier these days will be?"

"How about if I'm not cooperative at all, and you cut to the chase and kill me so you can see how I tick inside?"

Ana startled at Ian's words. Lerche didn't. He assumed a thoughtful expression. "But that would deprive you of the chance to pretend to cooperate while you look for ways to escape."

Ian barely lifted one shoulder. "True."

Lerche waited a moment for Ian to say more, and made a brief disappointed moue when Ian did nothing but watch him. "Well, then. Let me make your circumstances clear. Not only does no one know you're here, once your motorcycle is discovered, they'll think that you met your demise on the mountain. No one will look beyond that convenient little parking lot. I own you, Mr. Scott."

"You've captured me." Ian didn't look captured, sitting against the headboard with an aplomb Ana couldn't begin to muster. "It's not the same thing."

Lerche tipped his head, a casual *point-to-you* gesture. "Not yet." He left the obvious promise implicit. "You'll have a day to recover from your illness—I'm afraid I need you thinking straight for my purposes, at least to start with. By then your broken ribs should be tolerable, from what I understand of your healing proclivities. Future persuasion will be more exacting." He smiled unpleasantly. "You do intend to need persuasion, don't you?"

"Probably," Ian said.

"Excellent. You expand my opportunities by the moment."

Ana couldn't stop herself. "Ian—" *Don't play with him,* she wanted to say. *Don't doubt him.*

Lerche offered up a cruel laugh. "Ana, dear, he knows what he's up against. That's more than I could ever say for you." He gestured to the walking wall of a posse bodyguard.

The man reached for the doorknob, opening it just enough to indicate he'd done the job and then waiting for further sign from Lerche—one eye very much on Ian. "As you can imagine, at that point I'll be asking you a certain number of questions, as well as using the opportunity to test some of our new workings on you. Nothing mortal, of course—that would be wasteful. But I wouldn't look forward to it if I were you."

At his nod, the bodyguard pulled the door open and stepped back so Lerche could precede him. Ana held her breath on a sigh of relief, prepared to make her own escape.

From what she'd done. And from what she was no doubt about to do.

She should have known better. *Lerche.*

He gestured at her. "Since it causes you such discomfort to be here, Ana, I'm happy to strengthen you with a new assignment—you will be the liaison for our prisoner. You'll see to his every need, and keep a log of his meals and other requests. You'll report to me on the schedule I provide. Of course, someone will make sure your records correlate with the camera footage."

Humiliation washed across her face, heating it. She couldn't help but glance at Ian—preparing herself for his annoyance, and for the rejection she expected to see there.

But the anger was directed at Lerche, not at her. When he did meet her gaze, she found an expression she couldn't quite fathom—something with compassion behind it.

For the merest instant, she didn't feel quite so alone.

And then his expression shuttered and he looked away, his eyes gone cold and his body quiet, and she tumbled back into the realm of the utterly bereft.

# Chapter 8

Lerche left the Sentinel alone for the rest of the day—not so much as a mercy, but to provide him with time to think about his situation. To let his resentment toward Ana build, and his worry about his little friends at the retreat.

Not to mention the reality of his capture at Lerche's hands—the inevitable unpleasantries and ultimate death.

And, yes, the man needed time to heal. Not that much time, being what he was, but Lerche wanted to start with someone who was robust enough to take the process. He hadn't wanted the Sentinel damaged at all, but he supposed it had been inevitable—he'd had too much recovery time away from the retreat amulet to be taken easily.

Those at the retreat continued to sicken in a satisfying manner. No doubt they had help coming—perhaps even as soon as today, to judge by what the spy working had relayed—but Lerche expected it to be deliciously too late. Even if the healer guessed there was a working in play, he'd never find it in time.

In another several days the amulet would slowly disintegrate, destroying all evidence it had ever existed. That, too, was a skill that the Sentinels had not yet discovered.

Lerche smiled to himself, heading toward the small amulet workshop housed in what had, most incongruously, been a baby's nursery. Now the bright windows illuminated specialized sorting cabinets and wooden work tables alongside the man who called this place his domain. Budian waited for him here as well, no longer taking pains to hide himself from Ana.

Lerche gave them no preamble. "Which amulets have you chosen?"

The specialist, a man named Peter, glanced up from his work and gestured to a wooden tray of samples, each labeled with a neat, hand-printed card. "Experimental inducers," he said without ever turning away from the notes he was making. "Having primary feedback on the efficacy of these would be most helpful."

Lerche looked them over, only skimming the identifying cards. The amulets themselves were a variety of shapes, each with its own meaning, and each was also incised with precise, delicate glyphs—an ancient language known only to the specialists. That the glyphs were formed with such precision told Lerche all he needed to know—only complex, upper level amulets received such exacting attention.

Peter pushed two amulets across the table with one finger each and withdrew to his notes again, a disrespect that inspired Budian to look at him askance but which Lerche had learned to accept as part of the man's brilliance.

In truth, at this level of craft, the only specialists left were the brilliant ones. The others didn't survive.

Peter said, "Get this one into his room today. It should lower his resistance. He'll detect it, of course, but I assume you can overcome that."

"It won't be a problem."

Peter grunted as if he'd expected it to be just so. "The second of these will tell you whether his shields are still up. Don't waste any of these amulets until you've broken through."

"No," Lerche said, amused at Budian's stiffening posture. "I have no intention of wasting this opportunity."

Peter nodded to himself, as if checking that point off a list. "I've arranged the amulets in order. The first ones will be quite subtle in effect, and I'd appreciate careful monitoring—pulse, respiration and a camera on his face. Once you reach the red dot amulets, the effects should be perfectly clear—but of course you'll continue with the notes."

"Ana will," Lerche said, and smiled when Peter glanced at him. "As I've said, this is an opportunity not to be missed."

Peter only shook his head slightly and went back to work. Lerche chose to interpret the gesture as admiration, and left Peter to his work. It was time, he thought, to put Ana through her paces...and to remind her of her place.

Breakfast was good, and Ian ate it without reservation. If Hollender Lerche wanted to drug him or poison him, he'd do it either way—he'd already planted amulets to keep him isolated from other Sentinels, to chip away at his shields. Meanwhile Ian was healing—healing fast, in those dark restful hours of the night, and in need of fuel to keep doing it.

When lunch came, he asked for seconds.

Ana brought them, duly noting the fact in on her clipboard page for the day—along with the readings from the glorified fitness band he now wore around his wrist. She'd readily shown him the notes—had even taken his suggestion in a spot or two.

But now, as she brought the second tray, she also sat in the room's single chair for the first time, tucking it back in the corner under the camera. "I think he'll be in to talk to you soon," she said, her hands folded on the clipboard in a way that might have seemed casual if it hadn't been for the whitened knuckles. "I don't know what'll happen then."

"He'll torture me somehow," Ian said, so casually, dipping a forkful of grilled steak into barbecue sauce. "And he'll probably ask me a lot of questions while he's at it. Because, as we know, your Hollender Lerche isn't one to let opportunity pass by."

"He's not *my*—" But Ana stopped herself, openly gripping the clipboard now.

Ian shot her a look, not inclined to be charitable. "Ana, I get it. However you got tangled with this guy, he's got power over you. Easy for me to say you should have walked away before things came to this. So, yeah, I get it. It's complicated."

She gave him a wary look. "I *got tangled* with him by being born," she said. "And because I believe in what I do."

Born Core, just as he had been born Sentinel. No telling what she thought she knew of Sentinels. "Right," he said. "You believe what you did was justified, then?"

Her mouth flattened. "I believe what I *thought* I was doing was justified. That I'd be helping the Core to learn more about you. And after I met you—after I *knew* you—I believed that I could bring a new perspective to the Core's understanding of Sentinels. I thought… if the Sentinels are like you, at least some of them, then why can't the Core and the Sentinels come to some sort of understanding?"

He laughed shortly, pressing his hand against ribs still stiff and sore if not nearly as bad as the day before. "Did you think you could undo a couple thousand years of trouble with one short assignment?"

She flushed. "I thought I could try!"

"Yeah? How's that working out for you?"

She looked away, her expression troubled. "It's confusing," she said, taking his sarcasm and turning it into truth. "How things are for me in the Core…it's never been easy. My family isn't favored, and it's only right that I should have to prove myself more than others—"

Ian snorted, reaching for the glass of milk beside his plate. "Bullshit."

She blinked. "But—"

"Bullshit," he said again, and drained half the glass with a few big swallows before setting it aside. "That's just another way they control you. Keeps you useful. Keeps you from asking too many questions."

"What are you talking about? I *want* to be useful. I want to be—" She stopped, took a hard breath and struggled to control her voice. "Accepted."

"Only because they've made so damned sure that you aren't," Ian told her. He tossed his napkin on the tray, his appetite gone. "*I* accepted you, Ana. Remember that."

She blinked again, this time rapidly, with the glisten of tears on her lashes. "That's not fair."

"It's true." Ian would have scrubbed a hand over his face, had it not been still bruised and aching.

She sat a little straighter. "Your people have taken advantage of your abilities from the start!" But she couldn't hold her gaze on his; she looked down at the clipboard. "Mine have simply made sure you don't get out of hand. It's a thankless task, and it takes hard choices."

Ian sucked in a breath to snap back at her—and then let it ease away, making room for the ache that filled his soul as much as his body. She'd been conditioned since childhood, no doubt about that. Accepting the way her own people treated her and yet condemning him. His heart pounded—a peculiar thing, not racing with effort, but each beat deep and strong, as if these seconds mattered so much more than any others.

After a moment during which she kept her gaze fixed to the clipboard, he finally said, "Okay, you believe that. Nothing I can do about it, right? But I should warn you—I won't be answering their questions. And it's not going to be pretty." She jerked her gaze up, her eyes widening at his meaning, and he gave her no quarter. Not with his eyes, as hard as they ever got. Or his voice, dark with warning. "So be prepared, Ana."

"Ian...*no*. They'll break you!"

No kidding. If Lerche was right, then his choices were between a slow and lingering death or a quick and merciful one.

But if someone at brevis thought to send a skilled tracker up here, they'd know. And they'd come looking.

So he'd bide his time as best he could.

And meanwhile he regarded Ana with something akin to pity. "Listen to yourself. Are those the words of a woman who believes in how her people are acting?"

"Hard choices," she whispered. "Sacrifices..."

"Right. They've sacrificed you from the start, bullying you into compliance." He wanted to get out of the bed and take her into his arms and hold her until she understood just how badly the Core had done by her. Instead he only glanced up at the camera, knowing it a lost cause and knowing the price, at the moment, to be too high. "Ana, the big difference between your people and mine isn't what we can do. It's how we do it."

She made a stricken sound—part denial, part distress. And then, at the sound of a faint digital alarm, she pulled herself together and lifted her phone, checking the fitness band app and dutifully noting the readings in her neat, tiny print—no doubt understanding, as Ian did, that if Lerche wanted those readings he need only check the download himself. Forcing Ana to chart them was just another way to exert control over her.

Ian picked up his fork again, resolute.

The hardest choices for both of them still lay ahead.

Darkness fell before Lerche returned. Another meal gone by, another several visits for Ana—during which Ian held his silence and Ana tried and failed to hold her detached demeanor, the tip of her nose gone red with emotion.

Now she trailed behind Lerche, who had brought an assistant—a man he introduced as David Budian, which Ana took to mean he'd be here as often as not. Budian wasn't one of the bodyguards, which spoke of Lerche's confidence, but was a smaller man whose features looked faintly familiar and not terribly reflective of the Core.

As Ana's hadn't been. Too delicate of nature, her skin tones not quite as deep, her hair not quite as dark, her eyes too close to a honey glow.

Budian placed a soft-sided briefcase on the small desk and unzipped it, flipping it open to reveal neat rows of secured amulets and closed partitions. Then he wrestled a restraint chair into the small room, leaving little remaining space and relegating Ana back into the corner beneath the camera.

"First things, first," Lerche said. "As much as I'd love

to goad you into changing into your beast form so you can discover we've made it impossible, I have more important things to deal with and don't want to risk damaging you in a way that would delay us."

Ian hadn't intended to respond to Lerche at all, but hadn't counted on that little revelation. *Not possible?* He reached within himself, brushing against the leopard... looking to rouse it just enough to reassure himself, and only then realizing that he hadn't felt the leopard stir since he'd woken here.

It must have shown. Lerche smiled. "You feel it, don't you? Excellent. We can move forward with efficiency. Because, as you've surely guessed, our Ana did more than plant a simple spy amulet in your pathetic little retreat. She also planted a working we've been developing—a clever idea, if I say so myself."

*You might as well. No one else will.*

"It interferes with the manifestation of the Sentinel *other*, among other things," Lerche said. "It made you all quite satisfactorily ill."

Ian stiffened, his gaze shooting to Ana. She gasped, clamping her mouth closed too late.

"Yes, dearest," Lerche told her, his smile far too close to a smirk. "You made that household sick. If you weren't so reliably problematic with such details, you would have been informed ahead of time. As it is, you performed admirably. The kitchen was too noisy to yield much in the way of information, but the location worked nicely for our other purposes."

*Ana.*

*Ana had planted a spy amulet.*

She'd planted the very thing that had made them all ill—from Fernie to the kid who'd barely manifested his full potential.

Ian understood it all in one dizzying swoop of horror. The pattern of his illness, and Fernie's. The way he'd been so badly affected—but recovered so quickly, only to falter again.

The strength of his *other* dictated both his weakness and his strength.

*Ana had done this.* Ian speared another look her way, hot and furious—only to see how pale she'd turned. How clearly she'd believed the amulet to be of no harm. *To understand you all better*, she'd said of her role.

Just as manipulated as he'd been, in her way. And yet—

*Ana had done this. To him. To his people.*

And he'd never seen it coming. She'd been the perfect operative—nothing of the Core about her appearance, her presentation, her actions...

Or the way she'd touched him.

But Lerche wasn't done making the moment about Lerche. "Eventually we believe it will kill a field Sentinel such as yourself, but for the moment...the related amulet currently residing in this room is of a more refined nature, if just as effective. So if you were counting on being able to shield yourself from the consequences of declining to participate in our conversations...well, I'm assured that isn't possible, either."

*Blah-blah-blah.* Ian got it. The evil overlord, strutting his stuff.

And he got the underlying message well enough.

They'd rendered him defenseless against their tricks. No resistance, no delays.

If his people were going to find him, they'd have to do it quickly.

* * *

Ana sank into the chair in the corner, too stunned to do anything else.

This was her fault. All of it.

Not *fault*.

*Accomplishment*.

That's what Lerche would say. What any of her early teachers and remedial tutors would say. What any of her low-level coworkers would have said. *This is your break. Don't blow it.*

But inside, it wasn't what she felt. Instead she felt a flush of shame, a cold, heavy guilt…a sickness in her stomach. She hadn't ever wanted to do things *to* others. She'd only wanted to further the Core cause of controlling the Sentincls.

*Controlling the Sentinels…*

Just as she'd been controlled.

What she'd done suddenly didn't seem at all the same as understanding the enemy, or finding ways to communicate with them, to allow them to understand how dangerous their ways were. How potentially disastrous.

*Understanding* was what she thought she'd had with Ian, during those moments she'd allowed herself to forget why she was there with him in the first place. Understanding and respect and a response that she couldn't even quantify at all. The one that had kept her at his side, yearning for more of his touch, for yet one more dry snap of humor, for the glimpse of vulnerable truth in his eyes when he moved beneath her.

*In his bedroom.*

Where she'd taken her blazer. Muffled the amulet, thinking to secure privacy…and never knowing that she poisoned him all the more.

No wonder he'd stumbled away in the middle of the night, out of his head.

She'd sent him out into the mountain, creating the circumstances under which Lerche couldn't help but come after him. She'd made it possible for Lerche's men to accost him...to capture him.

Not the same as *understanding him better* at all.

So much for her lofty goals of creating better communication between the Core and the Sentinels. Could she have been any more naive?

She spared Lerche a quick, blurry-eyed glare. *I trusted you.* She'd known herself to be bullied and controlled, and she'd known it to be because she hadn't yet proved herself.

Now she wondered who she was trying to prove herself *to*.

And if Lerche had lied to her about all these things, then what else?

Ian sat against the headboard, his expression unreadable behind the healing bruises—or nearly so. Ana saw the understanding in his eyes, and the mixture of resignation and determination.

He knew what was coming. He'd known from the moment he'd seen the posse musclemen in the parking lot.

She thought that, just maybe, he'd understood better than she had all along.

Lerche gestured at the restraint chair. "If you would be so kind."

"Yeahhh," Ian said, drawing it out. "I don't think so."

"I'd prefer not to damage you."

"Much as I hate to inconvenience you..." Ian let it trail off into a shrug. The corner of his mouth crooked into something wry. "The way I figure, the sooner I get this over with, the better."

Ana didn't follow his meaning, but Lerche understood well enough—and was displeased by it, his mouth thinning in a way that Ana had learned to dread. He rapped lightly on the door without turning away from Ian, stepping aside to admit two of the posse—the big man from the parking lot and another who could be his twin, both of them wearing full posse getup of black slacks and polo shirts and heavy silver and arrogance. Not men that Ana knew—except she knew their nature.

*Ian*, she thought, suppressing a shudder. *Don't do this. He's not bluffing.*

But she saw the gleam in Ian's eye as Budian withdrew into the bathroom with the chair, getting himself out of the way with no apparent need to prove himself equal to this task. The men approached one on either side of the bed and Ana knew with a certain horror that this was what Ian had wanted. What he'd intended. He understood Lerche's nature and had used it, even as Lerche had thought to use him.

*You can't possibly be healed enough...*

They were bigger than he was, and they were professional. And Ian sat quietly on a sickbed—

Except then he didn't.

He rolled off and came up from beneath the man on the left, driving a fist into his groin and rolling aside, sweeping a leg alongside to bring the man down in that small space, awkward and clutching himself. Ian rolled up not to his feet but in a crouch, barely a hesitation. He launched, briefly airborne, adding momentum to the knee that jammed down on the side of the man's neck.

Ana gasped—to see again Ian's speed, his precision—

the sharp strength behind his movement. To know she saw the leopard within him, the very thing that made him such a danger.

This man had touched her. Had loved her. Had brought her more pleasure than any man before him, and never once made her fear for pain.

Bone cracked, and still Ian brought the rest of his motion into play, slamming the edge of his hand along the man's throat.

The man's partner gave an inarticulate cry of rage, but he was hampered by size and the bed between them, and he launched himself over it far too late to do the first man any good. Ian met him on his way, jamming the heel of his hand upward, stiff-armed and precise and into the man's face. Another crack of bone and blood spurted, and Ian drove farther upward, driving his forehead into the nose he'd just broken.

The man went limp, stunned past the scream that had bubbled on his lips. Ian ducked aside but went down under that limp bulk anyway, his grunt of pain barely audible.

*Silence.*

And then Ian crawled out from beneath the vanquished guards and straightened to face Lerche—or nearly straightened, bent over his damaged side, his arm clamped tight to it. "Sorry," he said, and the calmness of his voice belied the look in his eye—dark and wild and barely controlled. "I hope you brought more."

Lerche's mouth had thinned to near invisibility; his sharp rap on the door brought the pounding feet of reinforcements. "I had hoped you'd be sensible about this."

"Hollender," Ana whispered, using that first name exactly for the sharp glance it got her. "Please. Stop this."

*Leave him alone*, she meant. And *let him go. Just let him go*.

Lerche held up a hand to forestall the two men who reached the door. They stopped short, looming beyond it. "Perhaps you're right, my dear. Clearly I failed to strike the balance between keeping him whole and keeping him controlled. An expensive learning experience." But he left the door open, and Ana knew it for the taunt it was.

"Yeahhh," Ian said, drawing it out as he had before. He stood apart from the two men on the floor behind him—standing still and protecting his side, and yet his whole being filled with a sense of imminent action. The fallen men filled the space between the bed and the wall, and only one of them moved, groaning over the ruin of his face. "But I've got my own plans."

*It's not going to be pretty*, he'd said. Ana had thought he'd meant what would be done to him. Now she knew he'd also meant what she'd see him do in return.

Lerche saw it, as well. This was no rebellion—this was Ian, taking his fate into his own hands. Escaping, either way. Lerche's hand darted into his jacket, and Ian snarled a laugh and *moved*—moved so fast Ana hardly saw his intent.

But Budian did. The restraint chair shot out from the bathroom and into Ian's path, bringing the chair down and Ian with it—but only for the instant it took before he sprang up again.

By then Lerche had drawn his streamlined weapon, jamming it into Ian as they collided with a force that drove Lerche back into his men.

Ana flinched in anticipation of gunshot and instead heard the arc of electricity. Ian stiffened with an involuntary shout, and Lerche, full of disdain, shoved him

away. Ian fell, a clumsy caricature of his normal movement in collapse.

"No," Ana said, barely out loud. *No, don't do this.
Don't hurt him. Don't break what he is.*

Lerche straightened, distancing himself from the supporting hands of his men and brushing a hand down the
front of his suit. He tossed the Taser to Budian with a jerk
of his chin, and Budian bent to apply another shock. Ian's
eyes rolled up; his grunt was purely involuntary, all the
air pressed from his lungs with the force of his reaction.

"No," Ana whispered again, tears spilling over once
more—more tears in this past day than she'd allowed
herself for years. *Don't break what he is. Can't you see
the wonder of it?*

Lerche stepped aside so his men could finally enter.
With cold indifference, they hauled Ian into the heavy-
duty chair and strapped him down, and then helped—
and carried—the fallen men away. Within moments,
Ian was right where Lerche had wanted him all along,
already stirring—blinking, jerking his head to shake
off the effects of the stun, his hands in an involuntary
tremble that quickly faded.

"Recovering already," Lerche said. "That *is* interesting. I see I'm going to learn a lot from you, my friend."

*My friend.* Just as he'd always called Ana by various pet names. Never meaning it…meaning only the
opposite.

But as Ian came back to true awareness, jerking
against the restraints with an instant of obvious panic—
*the leopard, a wild thing, caught and bound*—Lerche
reached over to the soft-sided briefcase and withdrew
several amulets, sorting through the knotted lanyards
with swift efficiency and making a sound of satisfac-

tion as he found the one he wanted. He briefly closed his hand around it, his face blanking with an instant of concentration.

The unpleasant taste of an invoked working flooded Ana's palate, making her blink and swallow hard. Ian made a sound she'd never heard before, an involuntary gasp filled with pain—she found him rigid, his fists clenched and every inch of his body straining against his bonds, as if some invisible force flooded him with nothing but pain.

"No," she said again, a little more loudly this time. "Hollender, you've won. You've got him. But he can't tell you anything like this!"

Lerche laughed. "My dear," he said. "I'm not doing this to get information. That will come. I'm doing this because I *can*. And because I want to." He spared her a meaningful glance, and she saw he was more affected than he'd let on by his close call, his face flushed and his expression not nearly as controlled as he probably thought. "And, Ana, dear—I very much hope you're making notes."

Ana swallowed a sound of despair, her hands clenched around the clipboard as her pen and smartphone tumbled to the floor. As she bent to retrieve them, Ian moved his head just enough to catch her eye. His struggle to draw breath was a palpable thing.

She understood that glance perfectly—the pain of it, the meaning of it and the intent still lurking behind it.

*It's not going to be pretty.*

# Chapter 9

Ana hadn't done him any favors.

If she hadn't interfered, Ian would be that much closer to useless as far as Lerche was concerned. That much closer to one escape or the other. Or that much closer to the point where Lerche would have to leave him to heal. *Buying time.*

Sitting in this chair, bound at ankle and wrist and across his chest, Ian knew where things would lead now. He was helpless—damaged just as much as Lerche wanted and no more—as Lerche had so amply demonstrated by leaving him here to recover.

No matter Ian's intention, there would come a point where he would betray his people simply because he no longer had the control over his mind to prevent it. He would become weakened and befuddled and confused, and he'd mutter something important without even knowing it.

He had to put an end to this before things reached that point, one way or the other. That meant pushing Lerche harder and faster…making him go too far.

So Ana hadn't done him any favors at all. But Ana still didn't understand—not the way Ian had understood all too well from the moment he'd opened his eyes in this room.

"Ian," she whispered—not that there was anyone here to listen, or that he cared if they heard anything he might say to her.

She might still think they had secrets, though. Or that they *could* have them.

Her clothes rustled; the clipboard made a subtle sound as she set it on the small wooden desk. "I think you're awake."

More than awake. Awake and still throbbing with pain, a gripping lattice of pressure around his bones and trickling along nerves. A low-impact working as far as the Core was concerned—one chosen purely to punish him and restore Lerche's authority.

He reached for his leopard with caution, found...
*Nothing.*

Frigging effective, that particular working.

But it hadn't stopped the healing. Slowed it, he thought. But not stopped it.

"Ian, I'm sorry." She reached him, soothing his nose with her scent and a tentative brush of her fingers in his hair. "I'm in so far over my head right now... I don't know how to help."

"That's a start," he said tightly without opening his eyes. "Knowing this is complete fuckery."

She drew in a breath, holding it only an instant before acceding, releasing it with a sad sound. "It shouldn't be like this."

He couldn't restrain a snort, much as it pained him in all ways. "Babe," he said, "It's *always* like this."

She continued as if he hadn't spoken, determination in her voice. Determination to be heard, if nothing else. "Maybe I can't undo it, but I need you to know that I *want* to. If I could only turn this into what I thought I was doing—what I *wanted* to be doing..."

"You never had that power." He had no energy for anything other than blunt truth—barely that, as another shudder of the fading amulet effect gripped him tightly, scraping along rebroken ribs and forcing a desperate gust of air from his lungs.

"I'm sorry," she said again, and this time she rested the back of her hand just beneath his jaw, the touch of a lover.

The rush of quiet took him by surprise—his mind calming, the churning excess making way for peace. It hastened the retreat of the lingering pain, such a sudden surcease that he choked on it, struggling for composure.

She seemed to understand. She gave him the time he needed. And when he finally opened his eyes, she gave him an uncertain smile. "Better?"

He shook his head, not only unable to respond, but simply unable to fathom. The understanding of what they'd been together, what they somehow still *were*...

*Heartbreak.*

She seemed lost in her own thoughts. "I'm grateful that you aren't...taking this out on me. I wouldn't blame you."

"Hey," he said, making no attempt to soften his harsh voice. "Don't get me any kind of wrong. I'm mad as hell, and what you've done..." He shook his head. *Carefully.* "But I'm more than just *Sentinel.* I'm a whole person. With layers. I'm as complicated as anyone. So don't go making assumptions about what I'm going to feel."

She bit her lip, blanching tender skin. "I really thought I was doing the right thing. A good thing."

It wasn't a conversation he could have right now

and stay sane. *Ana, his lover, versus Ana, Atrum Core pawn.* He forced himself to more practical matters. "It doesn't make any difference. As soon as Lerche thinks I'm ready, he'll be back for more. And I'm going to give it to him."

She sat on the side of the bed in this tight space, still able to let her hand linger—this time on his thigh. The long muscles tensed involuntarily under her touch, but then relaxed into the bliss of it. She said, "I don't understand. Or I hope I don't."

He forced himself to relax his grip on the chair arms, flexing his fingers. "I mean that I'm not going to be a very good guest."

She gave the chair a meaningful look; he shrugged in response. Tied, he was. Utterly helpless, he wasn't.

She must have decided to let it go. "I'm to feed you," she said. "And to stay here with you—*observing*—although I'm allowed to return to my own room to freshen up after you've eaten. Are you up to that now?"

He was nowhere near *up to it*. But the better he ate, the stronger he was…and now, more than ever, he had to stay physically strong. So he said, "Go for it."

She fussed with the monitor on his wrist, straightening it. "When I get back, I can feed you." She glanced up at him with some uncertainty. "Or I can release one hand so you can do it yourself. But—"

Right. He'd just pledged to be a bad guest. And even if she'd always obviously known, deep down, the precarious nature of her position with the Core, now she was in the process of recognizing it out loud. "Ana," he said, "I won't ever do anything to make your situation worse." But in all honesty, he had to amend those words. "Not directly."

She gave him a faint smile, the tension around her mouth relaxing. "Okay, then," she said. "Let me go get a tray. And, Ian..." She faltered, glancing up at the camera as if reminding herself how closely they were watched. "If I find a way to help..."

His words came out harder than he meant them to. "You want to help? Fine. Then promise me this— whatever happens here, once this is over, you break from these people. You don't belong here, and you know it. *They* know it. Just get out of here and into the rest of the world where you can live your life the way it should be lived."

It startled her. She opened her mouth for a protest, and he shook his head sharply. *"Promise."*

She glanced at the camera again, doubt and fear evident. Of course she wouldn't believe that she *could*; she'd been conditioned against it. Whether she believed that she *should* was something Ian couldn't glean. She lowered her voice to near silence when she said, "I'll think about it."

He hadn't expected that much. It was a start. And convincing her of it might, in the end, be the only thing he had left to accomplish.


Ana made it back to her room with the neutral expression she'd learned to cultivate from childhood— never disapproving of anything she'd seen and never showing weakness.

But once she closed the door, leaning against it as if that would ensure privacy, she tipped her head back and allowed the emotion to release—her mouth trembling, her face quivering out of control, and again, those tears. Silent tears, but tears nonetheless.

For herself. For Ian. For what could have been, and for what she'd always thought had been.

Because she wasn't what she thought she was. The Core wasn't what she'd thought it to be. The Sentinels...

She had no idea.

After a long moment and a gulping breath, she decided against trying to sort those things out. There was too much, and she had too little information to go on. She began to think she'd always had too little information to go on.

But she'd been lucky earlier, when Lerche had been too busy to take true notice of her pleas to stop hurting Ian. She'd never seen him taken off guard so thoroughly—his authority challenged, his dignity lost. He wouldn't like it when he had the time to realize her quiet witness from the corner.

But that, too, she would face at another time.

For the now, she simply had to get through the moments. She rubbed a circle on her temple, massaging the dull ache there, and pushed away from the door—headed for the shower with her mind's eye full of the past hour.

Never mind that Ian was Sentinel. She'd believed his promise not to give her trouble in a way she never would have believed one of Lerche's posse members. She'd released one arm from the restraints and positioned the tray on his lap, eating her own meal beside him while lending him a hand as necessary—but allowing him to feed himself.

The small things, she knew, made a difference. A grasp at the illusion of control.

And now, with the weak shower sluicing water down her sides, she let her hands linger on her body—not pleasuring herself, but recalling the sensation of Ian's touch, and how it had felt so natural. How she had felt so safe.

Once out of the shower, the contrast struck her hard.

She wasn't truly safe in Lerche's posse. She'd never been. Not since she'd arrived here in adolescence. Not truly before then, in the hands of tutors and a communal Core household where she somehow quite naturally ended up as the one to blame for whatever happened while her father took no strong stand for her and her mother remained absent.

It was something she'd grown used to, until she'd felt Ian's touch.

She blotted her wet hair with a towel, rubbing her temple again. The ache had grown. In fact, when she took the time to think about it, it had never quite left.

It made her think of Fernie with that weary look in her eyes, and of the others at the retreat, hiding in their rooms without ever realizing they truly had something to hide from. That the amulet Ana had planted was making them ill when they spent time in the kitchen.

She faltered, looking around her room—a space no larger than Ian's prison but more comfortably appointed, if with little in the way of personal touches. Her eyes fell on the closet door, and she tossed the damp towel onto the bed and crossed the room to open it.

Because, of course, her blazer hung here—along with the clothes someone had already recovered from the vacation rental home. She slipped her hand into its pocket without removing it from the hanger, her fingers closing on the small button of cool metal she'd never bothered to remove.

She pulled it out, turning it over in her fingers. The sleek, barely marked object had once struck her as elegant in design, unfettered by any lanyard with its braided or knotted cord. Easy to invoke and endowed with the ability to cling if pressed against a surface at the moment it was activated.

But it was poison. It had poisoned Fernie, and it had made Ian deathly ill. And that, she knew now, had been the point. To kill Ian. His capture here had been a change of plan, a moment when Lerche had seized opportunity. If Ana had a headache now, it was only just—even if this amulet couldn't possibly be affecting her.

The polished brass button evoked sudden revulsion in her—the impulse to fling it across the room and as far from her as possible. Instead she closed her hand around it and before she could think twice, strode back into the bathroom and dropped the thing into the toilet, flushing not once but twice.

Sudden trepidation trembled through her as the empty toilet stared back at her. There were always consequences for such small rebellions and misbehaviors. One day soon, Lerche would ask about the location of the amulet, and she'd have to say she lost it.

She made herself breathe slowly, lifting her shoulders back to completely fill her lungs. Then she snagged her robe from the door and slipped into it, wrapping it snugly to ward off the sudden chill chasing goose bumps along her arms.

Footsteps outside the room door gave warning—a man's footsteps, the tread slowing at the last moment. She pushed the uncombed hair from her face and made it to the bathroom doorway before Lerche entered.

He never knocked.

At some point during the afternoon, he'd taken a minor blow to the side of his mouth—as likely from his collision with his bodyguards as anything else. Ana found the sight of that insignificant abrasion gave her some small, mean satisfaction. It was enough to provide her the strength to stand here before Lerche in a short, light robe that offered not nearly as much coverage as she'd felt when she'd slipped it on.

He said, "Tomorrow you'll return to the Sentinel retreat and retrieve the amulet you planted."

It was the last thing she expected. The last thing she *wanted*.

She wanted to be here with Ian—if not able to stop what was happening to him, at least *knowing*. At least *here*, so if opportunity arose...

She'd learned to think like Lerche in that, at least.

But she knew better than to challenge him, so she did what she so often did, and offered confusion. "I don't understand. I thought it served a purpose there."

He scowled at her, his eyes raking over the vulnerability of her exposed neck, the easy handhold of her tangled hair. "Ana, I begin to despair that you will ever understand." He didn't sound despairing. He sounded disgusted.

He sounded as if he believed her and as if he'd always believed her—never understanding just how much she'd always managed him.

Maybe that, too, would be opportunity.

But now he only looked at her with his patronizing, disapproving mien. "On the whole, it isn't necessary that you do understand. You will simply carry out my orders. But in this case, it happens that I'm removing evidence. It wouldn't serve me for you to be caught, so be forewarned—Sentinel reinforcements have arrived at the retreat. Field Sentinels in truth, unlike the laboratory squint you were able to fool. Do not play with them."

"No," she said, fervently enough to convince anyone. "I would never."

"They're looking for our guest, of course—they won't find him, although they've already found his motorcycle. We spread obfuscation workings all over that trailhead, and we're fully surrounded by them here."

She nodded, struggling with the understanding that he'd been ready for this—this completely forbidden direct move against the Sentinels.

Because the Core, as a matter of course, didn't take action against the Sentinels. Not directly. They worked only to prevent their egregious use of the Sentinel power that no one else had.

So she'd been taught.

Lerche evinced no sign of noticing the whirl of her thoughts. "Get in on the pretext of looking for Ian—tell them you, too, have been ill."

"Misdirection," she said. "So they won't think it's a working aimed at them." As well as explaining her absence after she and Ian had connected so strongly, so quickly.

He gave her a sharp look. "Exactly so." His gaze scraped her up and down. "In truth, you aren't quite looking yourself."

She stopped herself from narrowing her eyes at him. He wasn't one to notice the subtleties of her disposition unless it suited him somehow. "I have a headache," she said, and didn't miss the satisfaction in his eyes. "I'm sure I'm just unused to the intensity of this day."

"No doubt." He dismissed her well-being with a flick of his hand—and then closed the distance between them with swift purpose, grabbing her jaw as he so often did, pushing her up against the bathroom door frame. "I am not pleased with your interference at the trailhead," he said, grinding the back of her head into wood. "You would have no doubt of this if it wasn't necessary to leave you unmarked for tomorrow."

Ana gasped at the brute ugliness of his grip, and the escalation of his threat. Never had he handled her so much before, so cruelly—so frequently. Bruises on her arms, yes; the red welt of a slap on her cheek, the hot, puffy feel of an inside lip bruised against teeth. Rarely something she found so hard to cover. His hold muffled her words, but she managed them anyway. "I understand."

No excuses. No explanations. No crying out that he'd lied to her and taken her by surprise, and how could he expect her to be a team player that way?

No spitting back the words of accusation that on this day he'd been everything he'd ever accused the Sentinels of being. Or everything she'd learned from childhood that the Sentinels were.

While Ian had never been any of it.

"Good," he said, and thrust her away from him, leaving her to grasp at the gaping edges of her robe, her mind spinning. "I might have left a mark at that. No matter. You've always healed so conveniently fast."

He spun on his heel and left before she could ask what he'd meant by that, not bothering to close the door and thus leaving her exposed to the sneering curiosity of the posse member who passed by.

No matter. She pushed the door closed without haste, too stunned by events for her thoughts to do more than hover and clash.

After a lifetime of wanting to be part of something—
to do *more*, to be involved in *more*, it seemed that now
she very much was. Just not nearly in the way she'd
imagined it.

And now she had to decide what to do about it.

The Sentinels' compound was the last place Ana
wanted to be. And the last people she wanted to be with.

But morning found her here anyway, searching—and
failing to find—the confidence to approach Ian's friends.
Knowing she'd been the cause of their illness and that
even now she remained complicit in his captivity.

Uncertainty left her just down the block from the retreat where the odious David Budian had dropped her
off, and where he would pick her up again at her call.

"Don't dawdle," he'd told her, his voice bored and
bossy as she disembarked from the nondescript sedan
he'd chosen.

"I'll take as long as I take," she'd told him, no longer finding herself so automatically respectful of those
in Lerche's chosen posse—even if she'd once aspired
to join it.

Budian had merely grunted and waited for her to
close the door before he pulled away from the dirt and
gravel lane.

Leaving Ana to gather herself and move forward.

Each time she steeled herself to walk confidently
to the door and innocuously inquire after Ian, she also
thought of Ian himself—restless in the chair restraints,
his body stiffening in leftover waves of pain while Ana
pretended to sleep in the bed beside him.

She'd wanted to kneel beside that chair and unbuckle
every single restraint, kissing away the marks of them.

She'd wanted to brush his hair from his eyes and take away his pain.

Instead she'd done what she could, slipping a hand from beneath her light blanket and letting it rest on his wrist through the night. Giving him the peace he craved, and seeing the visible signs of how much more easily he rested.

Come dawn she'd fed him and managed his needs, knowing he wouldn't betray her even though she'd betrayed him, and knowing her presence here was Lerche's way of reestablishing his control over her. She would pay for giving herself to Ian; she would pay trying to protect him.

And Ian would pay, too. Lerche had never wanted her as a woman, and he'd never bothered to notice her brief, obligatory encounters with the Core members who'd shown any interest. But her intimacy with Ian had triggered something in the man.

It was the first weakness she'd seen in him.

The thought startled her. It meant that in her own way, she'd had control over Lerche—that his reaction made her important in a way she'd never understood.

She didn't truly understand it yet. But she'd use it, if she could. If only to bolster her confidence.

She drew the deepest of breaths, shook her hands out and moved out down the lane with a confident stride. Armed with purpose and carrying only the one small protective amulet she'd slipped out of the amulet room.

Ian's motorcycle sat not in the barely visible driveway, but off to the side—out of the way of the two cream-colored SUVs in the driveway and the several economy cars behind them.

The Sentinels were here, all right.

One man sat on the porch, brown hair and bright eyes and jeans beneath a pale plaid button-up shirt. Not a large man, but a lanky one who lounged with what Ana considered remarkably alert insouciance. He lifted his chin in greeting as she hesitated, as if quite certain she meant to come into the yard.

She did.

"Mornin'," he said. His eyes were brown and she thought they might just see right through her. "Ana."

She raised a brow at him in question.

"We've been hoping you'd stop by. Fernie'll be out in a moment." He seemed to reconsider this. "Probably Lyn and Jet, too. Maybe Ruger."

Sentinels all, no doubt. But unless they'd already figured out who she was—*what* she was—why come out at all?

"We've been worried about you," he said—and she had the sense that he didn't read her mind, no matter what horror stories she'd heard, but that he'd simply read her face, seen her confusion. Those eyes were too alert to miss much.

Like Ian's.

They were *all* that way, she discovered, as two women pushed their way out of the house, followed by Fernie at a more sedate pace and by a looming form that remained just inside.

"Fernie!" Ana said, relief spilling out. "You look better!"

Fernie nodded back at the house, her gaze on Ana openly assessing. "Ruger has his ways. We worried about you, Ana. We're worried about Ian, too. What can you tell us?"

Ana looked at the other two women—one no larger

than she was, graceful and petite and tidy, and the other a tall, lithe form with a dancer's movement and wild whiskey eyes, her dark hair cropped short and mussed, her body clad in leather from snug black pants to a black vest and her bare arms strong with muscle.

The shorter woman eyed her without any friendliness. "Where is Ian?"

Ana's heart kicked up a notch. She had no chance of fooling these people—field Sentinels, all of them. If they couldn't read her mind, they'd read her body. And they obviously weren't taking anything for granted.

"She is already frightened," the dark-haired woman observed. "You just made it worse."

"Stop it," Fernie told them. "This woman is important to Ian. She's our guest." She came down the porch steps to take Ana's hand and give it a comforting pat. Today she wore her hair in a bun again, and her square features looked more relaxed. "Are you well, Ana? And yes, we need to know—have you seen Ian?"

Ana was supposed to say *I've been ill. I left early yesterday to look for him and had to go home to bed. Haven't you found him yet?* She was supposed to make her way into the kitchen—not so hard to ask for a glass of water in this climate—and quietly reacquire the amulet.

But when her mouth opened, the words wouldn't come out.

And the words that wanted to come out would probably get her killed. By these people, or—

She thought suddenly of the man on the trail—the one who'd been bait for the amulet-enraged mountain lion, and for Ian. The one who'd died without garnering any attention from local authorities.

Because the lion hadn't killed him and Ian hadn't killed him. But Lerche's posse...

They could have done it. They no doubt *had*. Because, no doubt, it had served Lerche to convince Ana of Ian's perfidy.

That man had been assigned his role as a consequence of his failure in the field. If Lerche had discarded him for failure, what would Lerche do to Ana if she...

*Betrayed him?*

Even if he had betrayed her first. In so many ways. Controlling her, lying to her, *shaping* her...

She couldn't think. She took a step back. Another. Her hand fell from Fernie's, and only then did she realize how long the Sentinels had watched her—silent, waiting.

"You see," the leather-clad woman said, her whiskey eyes wise and wild. "She is prey."

"Jet!" the other woman said, and the man on the porch smothered a laugh. "That's not appropriate. And she's more than prey. She's..." The woman trailed off, taking a step forward—which Ana mirrored by taking a step back. The woman wrinkled her nose, held up a finger...and sneezed.

From the giant shadow behind the screen door, a voice rumbled. "She's Core."

Ana froze. Jet's whiskey eyes narrowed. Fernie made a sound of dismay. But the woman only looked thoughtful. "She's certainly been exposed to their workings," she said. "But there's nothing active here."

Ana's knees went to water. She stiffened them, bracing herself—readying herself. She would never outrun them, but surely it was better than not even trying—

But she didn't run. And no one pounced on her.

*They didn't have to.* They could afford to bide their time when she had no chance of escape in the first place.

But the smaller woman circled to the side, frowning— and then quite surprisingly closed her eyes, while the others just as surprisingly—and obviously—waited on her.

Finally the screen door opened, and the man who stepped through was every bit as big as his shadow had suggested. Tall and rugged and full of shoulders and a hint of pure brawn. "Lyn?"

The smaller woman shook her head, opening her eyes. "Don't ask me to explain it. There's Sentinel blood here."

*No. No there wasn't.*

The woman Lyn gave Ana what seemed to be a sympathetic look. "Not much," she said, glancing back to her friends. "But it's there."

Ana took yet another step back. She couldn't think. She couldn't begin to understand, and yet so many things suddenly made sense. The outcast nature of her parents; the way she'd been taken from them just a little bit early—and the way no one had ever expected her to amount to much anyway. The way Lerche treated her.

The way Ian had responded to her.

*Lerche had known.*

She touched trembling fingers to the side of her head, where the ache still lingered. *The amulets.* The ones that were only supposed to be spy amulets, and yet were so much more.

He'd known they'd sicken her. Maybe he'd even looked forward to it—taking the *opportunity* to assess how strongly her Sentinel blood ran.

"Ana," Fernie said, reaching out to her with a look that warned Lyn back. "Let us help."

"No!" Ana said, not rejecting Fernie so much as the entire situation, the overwhelming waves of understanding—her life rewritten in whole. She took a step back, and another. "Stay away from me! All of you!"

# Chapter 10

Ian sat silent before the camera, waiting with the patience of the big cat.

Even aching and battered from the inside out, he heard things they probably hadn't meant him to hear, drew conclusions they likely hadn't meant him to draw.

They were packing up. Preparing to withdraw and relocate.

It meant that brevis was coming. Was maybe even here.

It meant Lerche wouldn't have as much time as he probably wanted—and the man would cut his losses rather than risk moving Ian.

But not until he'd wrung as much as he possibly could from the situation.

In the midst of the bumping and thumping of the packing, Ian easily heard when Lerche approached—knew there were three of them altogether and that Ana wasn't with them.

She'd been gone for hours.

The door opened to reveal Lerche and his soft-sided amulet case. He put it aside on the creaky little desk and faced Ian with some satisfaction. "It's time for a little blunt conversation."

"I hadn't noticed any particular niceties so far." Ian

flexed his wrists against the restraints, finding them as snug as ever. He didn't waste energy on shields. His had never been profound, and Lerche had already demonstrated he could dispense with them at will.

"Nonetheless," Lerche said, "Ana has a propensity to interrupt, as you've seen."

Ian looked not at Lerche but at the two walking walls he'd brought for backup. Not a bad thing, perhaps, to have the man so wary of him that he brought muscle even under these circumstances. "What is it about her, Lerche? Why keep her so close, when you don't think much of her at all?"

"I see she did this particular job well, if nothing else." Lerche smiled in a way that made Ian want to hit him. Hard. Nothing of the leopard behind it, and everything of the man. "She betrayed you in the worst possible way—she continues to betray you—and still you care. One of your Sentinel weaknesses."

"I consider it a strength." Ian spoke as evenly as he could. He didn't defend Ana. No matter how impossible her situation, or his belief that she'd been misled and used...

Her choices had been hard, but she'd still had choices. She was still responsible for them. And the ones she'd made still hurt like hell.

"As you will." Lerche unzipped the case, flipping it open. Amulets gleamed more brightly than the limited window light should have allowed; a sickening ochre taste oozing out into the room. "Although the truth about Ana might amuse you."

Ian doubted it. He flexed his fingers, his ankles... tensing and relaxing the long muscles of his legs as he'd done all morning. Tied he might be; willing to let himself stiffen, he wasn't.

"Once upon a generation or two ago," Lerche said, running his fingers over the amulets with appreciation, "one of our *drozhars* met one of your Sentinel bitches and found he had a point to make. The incident resulted in a child. Naturally, he couldn't allow such a child to remain in Sentinel hands, so he took it, and kept its mother on hand until the child was raised far enough along to be interesting." He glanced at Ian. "If you had a chance to check, you'd find your records back this up."

"If," Ian said. Not believing, not disbelieving. Just filing away the words for another time. Trying to keep the impact of them from rousing emotion. *Anger. Desperation.*

"As happens from time to time, we found it convenient to have Sentinel blood for experimentation," Lerche said. "We allowed the child to breed, in a limited fashion—and we kept the bloodline ignorant of its heritage."

"To control the experiment," Ian said, finding in Lerche's satisfaction a convincing truth. One that churned inside his chest as he understood, all over again, how deeply and perversely the Core had continued to work against them. Generations earlier, the Sentinels had thought the detente successful and had focused on protecting their world from the burgeoning environmental costs of industrialization.

"Ana is the end of that line," Lerche said. "The blood has become too thin to remain interesting, while still thick enough to render her deeply flawed for our purposes." His face flickered with annoyance. "I had hoped the spy amulet would deal with her, but her blood is apparently too thin for that. A shame she hesitated on triggering the second working."

"Bummer for you," Ian said, trying to still the clamor of his pounding heart.

"Still, it gives me the chance to play with her a while longer." Lerche seemed genuinely cheered by the thought. "Make no mistake, Ian Scott. You might have temporarily had her body, but she remains mine."

"Can't argue with that." And he couldn't. Not when Ana had been the one to snug his restraints back to the tightest setting. Whatever the pain on her face as she'd done it, her regret didn't begin to echo what that decision had done to *him*. "As long as we're gloating, you want to tell me where we're going with this? Because my people are coming, and I'm guessing you won't leave me behind as a welcome gift."

Lerche made a noise that Ian couldn't quite read. Derisive, perhaps. Amused, maybe. "As you wish." He patted the soft briefcase as if it were a pet. "Fabron Gausto once thought he could create a working that would eliminate your various bestial advantages."

"Right. As I recall, he simply turned himself into a monster. And then he died."

Lerche made a dismissive gesture. "He wasn't looking at the situation from the correct perspective. Why change us, if we can change *you*?"

Of course. All of the recent amulet developments had focused on destroying the Sentinel *other*, from the bullets that had poisoned Kai Faulkes over the summer to the very working that now held Ian's leopard at bay.

He hadn't meant to clench his fists against the restraints, but of course Lerche noticed it. "You," he said, lifting a shoulder that in no way offset his smug expression, "were an opportunity I couldn't pass up. I had hoped to wrest more information from you—you're really quite the prize—but..." Lerche shrugged. "As it is, I'll simply focus on permanently peeling you away from the beast you call your *other*. Being the first to accomplish that will be equally as rewarding."

Ian fought for composure through throbbing head and aching ribs and fury. "I don't suppose it's occurred to you that after those interlopers crashed our party outside Ruidoso this summer, we'd be better off working together? Because they're after us both, and I can tell you right now we don't know crap about whoever was behind that."

"I'm sure we have people working that situation," Lerche said. He nudged the amulet case into the exact center of the desk. "In any event, Ana will be back soon. I care little whether you tell her any of this. Her fate is sealed regardless."

"I'm not sure why you even bothered to tell *me*."

Lerche smiled. "You're smarter than that, Ian. Obviously, I knew it would distress you."

Ian grit his jaw on the snarl rising to break free, the tension of it aching down his spine.

Lerche only laughed. "I have things to do," he said. "When Ana returns, I'll be back to play." He gestured at the open case, laughed again, and swept out the door with an exit worthy of an evil overlord. Ian glared after his back, then glared at the muscle who had never deigned to notice him in the first place—and then found himself glaring at the closed door.

Alone. And waiting. And, just as Lerche had intended, anticipating. Not only his own fate, but Ana's—

spread out there before him in the open case and its sickly gleam of metal.

*Spread right out before him.*

None of these amulets were silent; there was no need for it.

Lerche, perhaps, didn't understand the intuitive nature of Ian's work with amulets. Didn't understand that his strength, the thing he did better than any other, was combining that intuition with the logical process of deconstructing the things in the same layered, rote fashion of their construction.

Didn't understand, perhaps, that while even a Core expert required the cords, knots and braids to identify an amulet at a glance, Ian found them convenient but needed none of it—not so long as he'd encountered the basic elements of any given amulet in the past.

Ian rolled his shoulders within the confines of the chair, and began to explore the amulets.

The big man facing Ana from the porch made a harrumphing sound. "If we want you," he said, quite matter-of-factly, "you're ours. You must know that."

She glanced from one to the other of them, utterly unable to think. The lanky man on the porch bench gave her a modest little shrug, confirming the big man's words. Jet waited in readiness and Lyn stood back slightly as if leaving it to the others, now that her job was done.

Fernie said, "Don't you dare push her. We just turned her whole life inside out…and I don't think she ever meant to hurt anyone in the first place."

The lanky man snorted. "If you say so, Fernie. That's your thing, isn't it?"

"Yes, Shea," Fernie snapped at him, "it is. So have

some respect. And remember that Ian—" She didn't finish that sentence, glancing at Ana as she started another instead. "Remember that Ian thinks much of her. He's no fool, our Ian."

But he'd been a fool to trust Ana, no matter that she hadn't meant for any of this to happen.

Fernie reached out to her again, palm up and fingers gently beckoning. "Ana. Let us help. We can keep you safe here—and you can help *us* help Ian. I know that's what you want."

True enough. But a single clear line of thought broke through her confusion, and she grasped at it. She couldn't stay here. Lerche would know something had gone wrong. He might well shut down the house, cut his losses and relocate.

He wouldn't leave Ian alive.

"Start over," Lyn said, very practically. "I'm Lyn Maines. I take the ocelot, and I'm a tracker."

"*The* tracker, you mean," the lanky man said. "You don't want to be a Sentinel on the run if Lyn is on your track."

Ana looked more closely at him, then, floundering in her assumption that Lyn tracked not those from the Atrum Core, but Sentinels.

Lyn caught her expression well enough. "We do police our own," she said drily. "As well as get them out of trouble."

The lanky man made a noise that Ana couldn't quite interpret and said, "I'm Shea. I take the coyote and handle shielding." Ana glanced around them somewhat warily, and Shea nodded. "Right. This whole place is shielded now. Including you."

"Jet," said the wildest of them. "I am wolf." She frowned, glancing at Fernie.

"Yes, that's a good way to say it," Fernie agreed. To Ana, she said, "Jet was born wolf. One of yours got hold of her."

"Gausto." Ana winced. She'd heard things—the Southwest *drozhar* gone rogue. And she knew how quickly Lerche had dissociated himself from the Southwest *drozhar* when things went bad—but also that he secretly admired the man. She'd never known details.

"I'm Ruger," said the big guy on the porch. "I'm the reason Fernie is up and walking around when she shouldn't be."

"The healer," Fernie interposed, more drily than was her wont. "And a very bossy one, too. Not in the best of moods, with Mariska newly brooding back home."

"Bear," Ana guessed, looking at him—though she hadn't quite meant to say it out loud.

Ruger showed his teeth in a laugh. "Kodiak."

Ana said with some hesitation, "My name is Ana Dikau. I'm not anyone important to the Core. I guess... now I know why."

"You're important to *us*," Lyn said. "You can help us with this illness. Maybe help us find Ian."

The illness. The amulet. She glanced at Ruger.

"It's all I can do to stay ahead of it," he said. "We're all feeling it. It's silent, isn't it? And you know where it is."

She took a breath. A deep one, not caring how visibly it revealed her nerves and her lack of inborn courage. "I do," she said. "I'll get it. But not until everyone comes away from the porch."

Of all of them, Jet seemed to understand most readily.

She moved off the porch and over toward the driveway, and seemed surprised when no one else did. "Come," she said. "She is prey. She will not go past us to enter. And she will not enter if she thinks we'll be waiting outside the door for her to come out."

*Prey.* Exactly so, in far too many ways and for far too many years. Ana crossed her arms and looked at those who hadn't yet moved. Ruger made a sound deep in his chest, and she thought it might have been amusement. He followed Jet, and Lyn and Shea moved more reluctantly but still ended up beside the cars.

Fernie held out her hand to Ana—most assertively this time, nodding at it. "We're vulnerable, too," she said. "We go together, you and me." When Ana hesitated, she said, "Ana, I take no other shape. My blood probably isn't all that much thicker than yours. At some point, we must trust."

"Follow the feeling," Ana murmured. Ian, she trusted. Fernie had less reason to trust her than Ana had to return it, making her continued understanding a gift.

She took Fernie's hand.

But when they entered the house and reached the kitchen together, Ana pulled away. "You should stay away, now."

"My kitchen," Fernie said in dismay. "Of course, the kitchen. This is where you were, that first day."

"I didn't know," Ana said, unexpected bite in those words. "Not *any* of what I thought I did." *I didn't know the amulet would hurt anyone, I didn't know I would find good people here, I didn't know I would follow one of them right into love.*

Fernie said nothing, her mouth flattened, the strong

morning light and her recent illness making her face severe.

Ana knew the feeling of being unforgiven. A familiar thing, now that she knew she could pin it on the way Lerche had never forgiven her murky heritage.

Somehow, that feeling mattered more with Fernie. It mattered deeply with Ian.

Maybe because this time, she deserved it. She hadn't known what she was doing...but she'd done it. She'd deceived them all, and she'd deceived Ian, and she'd hurt them.

And Ian was captive. *Captive.* In what world did that even make sense?

"It's a lot to take in," Fernie said—and if she was upset, she was still understanding. At Ana's sharp look, she said, "Oh, yes. That's what I do. Empathy of a sort. Who else would manage a retreat for overworked, damaged and recovering Sentinels?"

Ana hesitated beside the counter, suddenly panicked all over again. "If you could read my mind, you'd have known about this from the start."

Fernie laughed. "No, *hija.* I've known you to be troubled, and I've certainly known you were mistreated. But I have only the sense of your reactions. And Ian's. Or did you think my defense of you was simply blind faith?"

"I didn't have much time to think about it at all," Ana told her, and ran her hand along the underside of the counter overhang until she found the smooth button of the amulet. A simple twist of thought released the working that held it there, and it dropped into her hand. She held it out to Fernie. "I'm supposed to return with this, but I can cover that if you need it."

Fernie wrinkled her nose in distaste. "Leave it there. Shea brought one of Ian's warded isolation cases."

Ana gladly dropped it to the counter, wiping her hand along the side of her jeans. Jeans and minimalist cross-trainers and a waffle-weave shirt that would allow her to move.

She'd come ready to run. Now she said, "Please. Make sure they're still back from the door."

Fernie gave her a look that might have been pity. "Child, if they want you, they'll take you."

She knew. But she held Fernie's dark gaze anyway, and Fernie shook her head and went to clear the way. Once Ana left the house—cautiously, finding them all still clustered by their vehicles—she kept right on walking until she'd made most of the distance to the lane.

"Wait," Lyn said—a little closer than Ana wanted now, but not threatening. "Don't go. We can protect you. We can *help*."

"A whole lot more now that we won't be fighting that amulet," Shea said, tipping his head at her—eyes narrowed, as if trying to figure her out. "And we need your help to find Ian. We know that matters to you."

"I've stayed too long," she said. It was truth. "And I'm already returning without the amulet. Lerche will suspect something, if he doesn't already. He's had someone watching this place all along."

Shea coughed into his hand and nodded at Jet.

Jet said, "The wolf likes to run in the greenway. It was a good chase."

Ana's eyes widened. "You didn't—"

Ruger interrupted her with a snort. "He's downstairs, nice and tidy. And you should stay. Help us find Ian. We know him best from his lab and his work. You know him best *here*. Now. With what the illness has done to him."

She found it hard to breathe, facing reality all over again. "I can't," she said, struggling to say the words. "Lerche... Lerche has Ian." The pronouncement brought the Sentinels to a tightly strung alert, and Ana shrank away. "If I don't return, he'll shut down the house. He'll hurt Ian—he'll *kill* him, if he can't control him."

"He can't begin to control a field Sentinel," Ruger said tightly. "Not Ian."

"Where is he?" Lyn moved closer—too close. She might be no bigger than Ana, but she was Sentinel, faster and stronger and dangerous. "Where's the base?"

"It's got to be a big house," Shea said. "They always are."

Ana shook her head, a quick and nervous gesture. "No," she said. "You don't *know him*. You don't know what he'll do. I don't think *I* knew what he was capable of until these past few days."

"We know he's cruel," Lyn said, and tipped her chin at Ana.

Ana clapped a hand over bruises old and new. *You've always healed fast*, Lerche had said. Now she knew why, and how he had taken advantage of it. "Yes. He's cruel. He's been cruel to Ian. And I think he had a man killed just to convince me that Ian was as awful as I was supposed to think he was. That you *all* are. You have to believe me—if you push him, he won't hesitate to make Ian pay."

"Ana," Ruger said, and that deep voice of his, that size of his, that unassuming lurking *strength* of his as he, too, moved closer—

It was too much. Too big, too close, too *Sentinel*.

Ana fled. She wasn't as strong as they were or as fast, but she was fit and ready to run, ready to take the chance she could reach the end of the lane and witnesses before they caught her.

Lyn's sharp command followed her out. "Let her go! I can follow her anywhere, now that I have her—"

*No*, Ana thought, sprinting hard—driven by the need to return to Ian, no matter how little control she had over Lerche. She made it to the corner, turned sharply north to cross the bridge over the greenway canal and plunged abruptly into the pedestrian population of Santa Fe. *No, you won't.*

She found the silent shielding amulet in her pocket and gave the necessary twist of will to invoke it.

*I'm sorry, but you won't.*

Because if Lerche saw them coming, Ian would be dead.

# Chapter 11

Lerche ignored the bustle of packing to focus on the security camera feeds on display in the mansion's dining room. Half a dozen views showed on the large-screen monitor, but only one was enlarged. *Ian Scott.*

The man seemed to doze, impressing Lerche in spite of himself. Conserving energy was indeed the smart thing to do, but Lerche hadn't thought the man had it in himself to tame his own restlessness.

It wouldn't do to give the Sentinel too much recovery time. Especially since Lerche had decided to use another, possibly more effective weapon against the Sentinel's silence.

*Ana.*

Lerche couldn't countenance the loyalty Ian Scott had shown to the woman. She'd thoroughly betrayed the Sentinels, and quite specifically betrayed Ian Scott himself. And Lerche had no sense that Scott had taken that betrayal lightly.

But he knew, without qualm, that Scott would be more affected by threats to Ana than he would to the ones aimed at his own person.

Stupid Sentinels. They could never, ever be trusted to use their powers properly. Far too emotional, all of them.

Activity at the house entrance caught his eye, and

he discovered Ana on approach—not with Budian, who had escorted her to the retreat, but emerging from a taxi, after which she hurried up the long ornamental walk to the house. As she grew closer, her harried expression and disheveled state became evident. She stopped at the door and attempted to finger-comb her tousled hair back into place, straightening her colorful tank top. One of his favorites, the way it exposed the delicate sweep of her collarbones and the graceful rise of her neck.

She had always been a pretty little thing. Too bad she couldn't have been more useful in other ways.

An interior camera caught her slipping through the entryway, avoiding several of his posse on the way—shrinking away from them, as she well might. They thought no more of her now than they ever had.

He assumed she'd look for him—coming to report. It took him a moment longer than it should have to comprehend that she was heading toward the opposite wing of the house.

*Ian Scott.*

He watched with rising anger as she entered Scott's comfortable little jail, her back to the camera, her expression hidden from Lerche. She glanced over her shoulder, a moment of trepidation that told Lerche she knew someone watched, and then knelt beside the restraint chair, her hands folding over one of Scott's.

It took the Sentinel a moment to rouse. She reached up to stroke the side of his face, a visage no longer satisfactorily covered with bruises, once-deep cuts healing. Scott's eyes fluttered open—Lerche was pleased to see that groggy response, at least.

She spoke urgently to Scott, as aware of his state as

Lerche was, and sent another, more urgent, glance back at the camera.

She had, somehow, surmised that she and Scott had little time left. She had, somehow, actually learned something on her little mission to retrieve the amulet.

That she rushed to Ian Scott's side to give him this news first only sealed her fate.

Righteous anger suffused Lerche's body, stiffening his back and bringing warmth to his face. Lerche pushed the chair back from the security desk, full of intention to show her just how gravely she'd erred—and then stopped himself.

He was not, after all, a man to pass up opportunity.

These moments she spent with Ian Scott would be a bittersweet final reminder of what she'd come to mean to the Sentinel, no matter how she'd betrayed him in the end.

And *then* Lerche would interrupt them. He'd learn what Ana had discovered, and more.

After which they could die together.

Lerche stood, straightened his suit and strode toward his office with great purpose. Budian was still out in the field, and Lerche hadn't sent him unprepared. Now that Ana had removed the evidence of his illicit Core strike, Lerche could buy that time.

Not with the subtle amulets that Ana had used, but with those that Budian had been planting along the retreat perimeter.

Silent, strong and just waiting to be triggered.

Ian sank deeply into meditation—giving his body a chance to heal itself, such as it could. Preventing the endless and exhausting spin of his mind.

Hunkering down to wait.

He was slow to come back to the surface, floundering off balance as the effort of maintaining his quiet gave way to an effortless silence of internal clamor.

"Ian." Ana's voice came in a whisper. "Wake up. We need to talk—quickly, before Lerche sends someone to join us."

"I'm awake," he said, making it so and opening his eyes to her concern, to her brows drawn, her lip caught between her teeth. "I'm good and awake. Means I remember very well what's happened between us." *Love and betrayal. Loss.*

"I know." Her features took on an intensity of determination he hadn't seen before. "I get it—you can't truly trust me. But you know what else I know? I've been a pawn all along the way. Around here, truth seems to be a moving target. So I figure I'll forgive myself if I miss it now and then."

She had his attention. Not so much her words, but her manner. Anxious, yes. Definitely aware of the precarious nature of her words here deep in Lerche's private little lair. But no longer a woman waiting to see what might happen.

Just maybe a woman who was about to *make* things happen.

He worked his jaw a little, getting moisture to his mouth. "What's going on?"

"Lerche sent me to retrieve the amulet I planted at the retreat. I ran into your friends."

"Who?" he said, shifting in the chair as if he could sit more upright—but he was too restrained to do any such thing.

"Ruger. Shea. Lyn. Jet. And Fernie and the others are doing well." She saw his intensity and shook her head.

"I got away from them, Ian. They're not coming after us. *You.*"

*They let you go.* If they hadn't, she wouldn't be here. And they were looking. With Lyn on the track, they'd find him.

She shook her head again. "Believe me, Ian. They're not coming. I know Lyn thought she could follow me, but I used a working to cover my tracks."

The reality of it hit harder than he'd expected. He struggled to breathe past the hard, cold disappointment. *"Why?"*

She scowled. "Why do you *think*? Lerche is already preparing to run. If he sees them coming, he'll cut his losses—he'll kill you outright and be gone."

He tried to absorb her words and ended up absorbing only the sincerity of them—the realization that the courage he saw in her face, the determination, had come from her need to protect him.

Or to try.

"You could have stayed." He couldn't help the bemused tone in his voice. "You would have been free."

"Ian Scott." She said it firmly, her hands closing around his wrists and holding tight. With meaning. Her face uplifted to reveal the honey depths of her brown eyes, and he saw the truth there, absorbing the impact of it. "You're here because of me. Because of the way I feel about you. What makes you think I could have walked away, and ever truly been free again?"

Ian Scott, rendered speechless.

She was the enemy. She had betrayed him. But she had always been sincere. She had given him everything of herself that she'd been able to give—and now she'd gone beyond. Now both of them were captive.

He opened his hand, turning it over, and she slipped her own into its grasp. Ignoring, for the moment, the cameras. "Ian, I—" But she stopped on a gasp when he tightened his hand around hers, a grip too firm.

"Not here, Ana." He hadn't meant for his voice to have so much grit. "Not under Lerche's terms."

Even if it meant saying those words never.

She didn't respond immediately—and then her hand gave his the faintest squeeze in return. She sat back on her heels, her demeanor nothing but practical. "Then let me see what I can do for you before he gets here." This time she did glance at the camera, if only with a flick of her eyes. "I'm sure he's on his way."

She poured him a glass of water, unstrapped one hand so he could drink, and sat on the side of the bed while he downed it in a series of deep gulps. Then she exchanged the glass for the container he could use from the chair and turned her back to stand between him and the camera, giving him what privacy she could.

Not that Ian cared. If Lerche wanted to watch him pee into a bottle, that was his problem.

The necessities finished, Ana fetched a damped washcloth from the bathroom and allowed Ian to wash his face around the healing areas, even to wipe down his arms and chest.

The big cat in him appreciated it.

But in the end she returned his wrist to the restraints. "I have to," she said, though she didn't tighten the strap nearly as snug as before—and she took a quick moment to loosen the other one, very nearly loose enough for his hand to simply slip free. "For the same reason I always have. If he sees you unrestrained—"

"I get it," he told her. Their interactions had become

remarkably tacit, a quiet teamwork in an untenable situation. "He'll come down all over both of us. It takes things out of our hands."

Not that things were very much in their hands to start with, especially not with distant footsteps on approach, perfectly clear to Sentinel ears. Ian let a piece of his attention slide away, returning to the amulets that had been left to intimidate him. Feeling their various natures, the sick taste of them on the back of his tongue and the slick feel of them beneath the touch of his mind. Amulets of pain and persuasion. Amulets of sickness and power. And a number of amulets that served no purpose in this context—a noisemaker, a spy-eye, even an amulet of pleasure.

She lifted her head as she finally recognized the approaching footfalls as headed for this room. Her calm deserted her in a blurt of words. "Try to hold on," she said. "You know your people are looking—and I think they'll find us. This place stinks of Core. I just needed some time to be ready for them. And to let you know, so together...somehow...we can try to last that long."

*That's the plan.* But it didn't mean he didn't have a backup. Because Lerche had his friends surrounded by silent amulets, and Ian was the only one who knew how to find them.

"Ana, listen." Ian pulled on reserves to bring the room into sharp clarity, his thoughts with them. "Listen," he said again, enough urgency to it that he pulled her attention from Lerche's approach. "Lyn had every reason to believe she would be able to follow you. If there's Sentinel energy out there, she can find it—along with almost anything Core. *Sentinel* energy, Ana."

"Oh," she said, and flushed, her hand over her mouth. "I can't believe I forgot…so much to say—"

He understood in an instant. "They told you."

Her eyes shone in a way he hadn't expected. "It explains everything," she said. "It explains my *life*."

"Then you know she can find you. You just have to hang in there."

"She should be able to find *you*, too," Ana said, a certain stubborn note coming into her voice.

"Yeah, yeah. Here's the thing." Ian didn't hesitate. He should have told her this first thing, before the personal stuff, before the wash up. But he'd been groggy and hurting, and, without those very personal moments, he simply hadn't been willing to trust. *And now Lerche was at the door.* "My team needs to know I can locate the silent amulets."

Ana gave him a startled look, freezing as the doorknob turned. "That's not possible."

"There's a reason Lerche was so happy to get his hands on me. I've been working on this for over a year—and I got the last piece while I was out on that mountain." Ian lowered his voice, drawing her in closer even as Lerche entered the room, his musclemen behind him. Noisy and self-assured. *"Tell them to use sonar."*

But he saw from her expression that she absorbed only the implication that Ian wouldn't be able to tell them himself. "Ian, no—"

He clamped his hand around her wrist. "Tell them to quit listening and—"

Ana cried out as a huge hand landed on her shoulder, another on her arm—tearing her away from Ian and sending her sprawling into the corner to collide with the chair. A growl burst from Ian's chest; he jerked against the restraints, leather scraping skin, freedom only an inch away—

But already the posse muscleman returned, his hands clamping down over Ian's wrists, his weight grinding bone against the thin padding of the chair arm. The second man entered to tighten the straps hard—looking back at Lerche for approval.

"Not so tight that his hands fall off," Lerche said. "I need him able to answer questions."

Together the men loosened the straps by a single notch, retreating to stand outside the door of the small room and relieving it of their bulk.

Ana pulled herself upright, steadying herself with the chair and pinning Lerche with the wariest of looks, sparing only a glance of apology to Ian. Apology and a quick scowl of demand. *Survive, Ian Scott.*

Well, that was the plan.

It just wasn't a very *good* plan.

"I expect you to pay attention when I enter a room, Ana dear." Lerche's mild tone belied the look on his face. "Sit, please. I'm quite sure you'll want to take notes for this."

Slowly, Ana sat, bending to pick up the clipboard and its disarrayed papers but never taking her eyes off Lerche.

"Ian Scott," Lerche said, playing to his tiny audience. "Southwest Brevis AmTech." And then smiled, as if just thinking of the words that followed. "And former snow leopard."

Ian let the leopard show, lifting a lip to expose the canine tooth that wasn't quite human.

"Excellent," Lerche said. "Bravado. Let's see how far it gets you."

* * *

Lerche had changed.

Or maybe he'd just revealed himself.

Ana stared at him from the chair, shocked by the rough handling—her arm stinging from impact, a myriad of small pains pricking at her mind. Pains she would normally have tended, but which suddenly seemed insignificant.

For Lerche had lost his classically condescending mien and now displayed a harder expression. A meaner one.

He wasn't holding back any longer. He was looking *forward*.

*They'd run out of time.*

Ana cast a frantic look at Ian, and found that he already knew.

Lerche ran a caressing hand over the amulets, plucking one up along the way. "You're familiar with this class of amulet, I'm sure." He let it dangle from one outstretched hand, spinning quietly at the end of its cord.

Ian gave it a glance. "Targeted," he said. "Point and shoot, so to speak. And if I'm not wrong, it's a series working. Turn it on, turn it off, rinse, lather, repeat." He shrugged, but Ana saw a faint tension on his face and knew there was more to it than just that.

Whatever this amulet did, it would be ugly.

"Excellent," Lerche said. "Then you see this coming."

Cloying bitterness from the invoked working flooded the back of Ana's tongue, pushing a sound of dismay from her throat. Ian's eyes widened ever so slightly— and then his body stiffened and his head jerked back. His features contorted, a grim, involuntary sound harsh in his throat.

"Stop it!" Ana screamed at Lerche. "He can't tell you anything like this!"

Lerche dropped the amulet into his waiting hand, closing fingers around it with satisfaction. Ian slumped forward, sucking in air. And Ana scrambled not only to make sense of it all, but to understand where it was going next.

She flinched when Lerche reached into his suit coat pocket, and then again when he extended an object in her direction—only to wilt in relief when she recognized his fancy phone. "You don't seem to have yours active," he told her, a patently gentle tone that felt more like a lash. "Use the app to monitor him, please."

Gingerly, she took the phone, fumbling it—risking a glance at Ian, who lifted a face wet with involuntary tears and drew the deepest of breaths.

Preparing himself.

"Excellent," Lerche said once more. "Please keep notes, Ana."

Ana dutifully scribbled a line of unintelligible nonsense—knowing she had to pull herself together or she'd be of no use to either of them.

She'd known Lerche to be cruel. She hadn't known him to be a monster.

A monster nurtured by the organization in which she'd been so eager to excel.

Lerche dangled the amulet again, letting the cord slip through his fingers with appreciation. "Ian Scott," he said, clearly relishing the moment—his glance at Ana told her as much. "Would you care to share your progress regarding detection of the silent amulets? And while we're at it, who else has been working that project with you?"

Ian showed his teeth, as clear a threat as Ana had ever seen.

"You see, my dear," Lerche said. "He has no intention of answering questions. Not yet." He smiled, raising the amulet in an entirely unnecessary fashion. Ian's head snapped back, his hands splayed and body jerking within the restraints.

Ana knew better than to cry out this time. She pressed her mouth closed and breathed through her nose in careful, even rhythm, refusing to acknowledge the hot and steady tears that ran down her face and dripped from her chin.

And she made herself watch. Because this was *her* fault. *Her* responsibility. She'd drawn Ian in, and she'd never seen this coming. Seeing his agony was her penance. Watching him slump in the restraints as Lerche released the amulet—seeing that this time his eyes fluttered open to a dazed expression, and blood trickled from a bitten lip, and from his nose.

At that she couldn't help but whisper, "What are you *doing* to him?"

Lerche affected a modest expression. "Hurting him, mostly. But yes, there will be cumulative damage. To the small vessels...and then to the large. It's always a question of which will go first—the heart or the brain. Won't it be a shame to see your brilliant friend turn into a vegetable?"

Ian's gaze sharpened with obvious effort, even as Ana drew a sharp breath—understanding better than she would have, days earlier, the depth of that threat.

"I'd wanted to experiment with the new workings, of course," Lerche said. "To see how carefully I could peel the layers of his Sentinel *other* away." He glanced at her.

"It's a shame *you* couldn't serve me in that capacity, Ana dear. Once again, a failure."

Ana stiffened at this blatant reference to the Sentinel blood he'd not mentioned to her directly. Her mouth felt clumsy in response. "I don't understand—"

"Of course you do." Lerche shot her a look of false patience. "They told you, didn't they? They're like that, and since they're looking for your friend here, they surely sent someone who could easily sniff out your insipid nature." He smiled. "I'm honestly surprised you returned to me, Ana."

"You shouldn't be." She snapped the words at him, the fervency not coming at her bidding, but simply welling up from inside. "I've always been loyal, Lerche. And now I have reason to be. It's just not to *you* any longer."

Ian managed to shake his head. Barely. His voice came ragged. "Ana, no. Don't."

Lerche laughed right out loud, short but delighted. "Excellent," he said. "You're still with us. The truth is, I don't want your mind destroyed before I have the chance to sift through it—and although we're dealing with your Sentinel friends at the retreat, I'm sure more will be along quite promptly. So I have very little time." He set the amulet aside, quickly plucking out another—a smaller thing, with less complicated knotting and rough, scribed surface. He sent Ian a meaningful glance. "I've warmed you up nicely. Now let's see how you feel about watching Ana suffer."

Ana sprang to her feet. The clipboard fell from clumsy fingers; the chair toppled backward. Protest sprang to her tongue and she swallowed it—terrified, knowing herself not strong, not brave and nowhere near as well-trained as Ian.

But she would not give Lerche her terror.

At least, not yet.

"Don't do this," Ian said, and his voice was gravel. Not desperate...not pleading. *Warning*.

Lerche's expression shifted to the one that frightened Ana the most—his response to defiance. The one that meant he would reassert control. Swiftly. Decisively.

The one that had always left marks on Ana.

He lifted the amulet, the subconscious little *tell* of his triggering effort. Ana drew breath, bracing herself—knowing she was defenseless even as her senses flooded with the ugly stench of the amulet invoked.

One of the men behind Lerche made a startling sound of surprise, lifting to his toes as though by some invisible force as he staggered backward and bent over himself. In the stunned silence that followed, he straightened with extreme effort—his deep olive skin tones gone pale, his expression still stunned.

Lerche scowled, pinning Ana with a scowl—focusing on her with deliberate effort and lifting the amulet—

The second bodyguard jerked, his arms flailing as he fell back from a faintly audible pop of impact, as though the very air before him had exploded in directed force.

The amulet steamed, used up and darkening into tarnish. Lerche eyed it with an expression Ana might have called baffled if she'd seen it in him often enough to be sure. She sought Ian, looking for answers, but he met her gaze only briefly before resting his head against the high chair back.

Lerche dropped the amulet onto the table as his men recovered themselves, looking both sheepish and still a little startled. "Not a great loss," he said, but frowned nonetheless.

Ana could well understand their confusion. Directing an amulet to a specific target took practice and a certain focus, but someone like Lerche took the ability for granted.

With less ceremony than before, Lerche selected another amulet from the case. "I do hope you're not awash in relief, Ana dear. I still want my answers."

He displayed the amulet to Ian, smiling as Ian's jaw tightened. Ana wasn't close enough to see the details of the thick metal disk, only that it was more complex than the last. Lerche said, "Nerve pain can be a terrible thing."

"I know what the amulet does," Ian said, his voice still stuck in that gravel register, his throat working.

Lerche tipped his head at Ana. "She didn't. And now she can anticipate. Are you ready, Ana? Or perhaps your *friend* would like to discuss his progress on the silents, or share the name of the colleague most likely to pick up on that work."

Ian rolled his eyes at that prospect, and Ana wanted to cry *no*! Because here came that look on Lerche's face, fury lighting his eyes into something not quite sane. Ana found herself backed up hard into the corner, bracing herself.

But it was Ian the working struck, stiffening his body, forcing a choked cry of what sounded so very much like *laughter* that Ana stopped breathing for an instant, too torn by threat and fear and horror to take in the moment.

Lerche clutched the amulet hard, his fury at the misfire giving way to satisfaction as Ian made another sound, a more primal thing of unendurable pain, and Ana covered her face with her hands, dropping to a crouch and rocking slightly in the awfulness of it all—as if she could simply wish it all away.

"Stop it!" she cried. She lost her balance, dropping to one knee. Something hard ground into her kneecap, a trivial pain. "What kind of man *are* you? Just *stop it*! He's not going to tell you anything, and the Sentinels will surely be here any moment—just pack up your things and *go*!"

Ian fell free of the working, his gasping groan holding that same edge of dark laughter. "Ohhh, yeah," he said. "*That* hurt."

"What kind of man am I?" Lerche said, and his voice held a cruel edge that seemed all too sharp to Ana after years of pretending it wasn't that bad, or that she deserved it when it was. He laughed just as darkly as Ian had. "Of all people, you should know that." He took two swift steps in the small room and crouched before her, taking her jaw in that cruel grip over bruises still tender to the bone.

"Leave her," Ian said, words that scraped in his throat. "Leave her *alone*!"

Lerche paid him no mind, giving Ana's face a little shake. "And you *would* know, if you weren't so unrelentingly dense about the bold tactics needed to manage these beasts. Your mother was allowed to have you for far too long, little Ana. She damaged your thinking beyond what I could repair."

"Lerche," Ian said, his voice louder. "I am about *done* with you—"

The bodyguards shared a laugh over that one. Lerche smiled, fingers grinding into Ana's jaw. Her knee slipped over the object beneath it and she suddenly knew—*the pen*. She felt herself break from terror to anger to *I. Have. Had.* Enough!

She groped for the pen, found it, fisted it and jammed

it into Lerche's thigh, years of defiance crammed into a single instant and driving the sleek metal deep.

Lerche roared with surprise and fell back from her, the pen embedded halfway up the barrel. He scrabbled at it as the bodyguards swooped in, snatching Ana up one on each arm and yanking Ana to her feet. Ian made an inarticulate sound of frustration, jerking within his restraints, and Lerche scraped his fingers across the floor to sweep up the amulet, glaring at Ana with an intent so clear he might as well have spoken it.

"—Goddam sonnuva *bitch*—" Ian snarled, fighting with an animal intent, and she wanted to cry out *no, don't wear yourself down* but there was Lerche, thrusting the amulet right into her face while she lifted herself up in the grip of the bodyguards, kicking out at him—

Only delaying the inevitable, the first electric slice of pain down her arms, down her legs and scattering into branches of lightning through her limbs. And the last thing she saw before her vision flashed into white and red and stark bright bursts of light was the satisfaction on Lerche's contorted face, and the last thing she heard was Ian's rising shout of demand, his chair crashing over—

And the screams in her own throat.

# *Chapter 12*

Ian's shouts rang impotent to his own ears, eclipsed by
the sight of Ana strung between the two bodyguards—
her body taut, her screams strangling in her throat.

As if Lerche hadn't done enough to her already.

The restraint chair lay on its side, trapping him just
as thoroughly. He'd missed his chance to divert the amulet from Ana—he'd underestimated Lerche's cruelty,
had been too stunned at Ana's explosion of defiance.

The lower restraint shifted against the floor, grabbing his attention. The stiff buckle jabbed against the
carpet, pushing back at the buckle tongue. He grabbed
the hint of room it gave him, twisting his wrist and jamming the thing down again—doing it again and again,
gaining space until a final twist and his wrist slipped
free, his fingers stiff and clumsy.

A quick glance showed him no one had noticed—
showed him, too, that Ana no longer strained against
the working but dangled limply. And still Lerche plied
the amulet, the bitter, broken taste of it a thick corruption of the very air around them.

*Dammit.* He plucked at the stout leather around his
other wrist, stiff fingers slipping and making no head-
way. *Dammit it to—*

His gaze fell on the amulet case. The amulets he'd so

carefully explored the evening before, learning of the tools Lerche would ply against them.

*Do it. Take them.*

Lerche hadn't expected that Ian could redirect the amulets; he hadn't yet figured it the cause of those failures.

Or realized that Ian could trigger them, as well.

*Do it.*

But triggering them from a distance wasn't easy— even Lerche needed them up close and personal. And triggering them from a distance and then directing them with any precision...

*Do it.*

If he didn't do it right, he'd kill them all. He'd send every bit of power raging through his body and through Ana's, including the workings that would shred his very nature.

But what a grand bright beacon it would create for Lyn, for any Sentinel within the region. What an unmistakable warning, and a neon-bright cry for help.

And if he didn't do it, Ana would die. If she wasn't already—

Lerche stepped into her, taking her jaw in that favorite grip of his, shaking himself out of his own satisfied reverie to check in with Ian—to revel, too, in that.

"Yeah?" Ian said, his upper lip stiff with dried blood and his body tensed with the understanding of what he was about to do and what it was about to do *to* him. "You think that's impressive? Suck on *this*, why don't you?"

He couldn't shield; Lerche had seen to that. Hell, he could barely think. He just *knew*. And he followed the moment to the only conclusion left, wrapping the amulet case in his awareness, touching each and every one of those cold metal disks, the buttons, the miniature tablets...

*Twisting.*

The room flooded with the thick taste of ichor. Lerche flung him a look of astonishment—an utter awareness of what Ian had done, his expression giving away his instant understanding of Ian's earlier interference. "You *imbecile*—!"

Ian lifted a lip in what was left of his snarl—and braced himself.

The bodyguard farthest from Ian cried out, his face twisting horribly and his skin sagging, squirming as if a colony of bees swarmed beneath it. He threw himself away from Ana to writhe on the carpet, his flailing legs tangling with Lerche's so the amulet went flying and Lerche staggered away, hands slapping at his body one moment, then twisting terribly, unnaturally, in the next. The crack of bone came at the same time the second bodyguard cried out, and someone else in the house shouted in surprise and then screamed in agony, and the wall across from the open door split from top to bottom while dust sifted down from the joints and seams above them and—

And Ian saw nothing more, because not all the workings took direction. Some of them simply sought targets.

*Sentinels.*

The leopard twisted within him, robbing him of sight and sound and pouring chaos into his mind. Dark agony ripped along his limbs, filling his ears with an insensate yowl. He felt claws ripping through carpet and tail lashing, teeth bared and whiskers bristling.

Screaming filled what was left of his mind and he had no idea from whose throat it came. He lost track of the world and of himself in it. Just a swirl of motion, sensations sweeping over him, most of them scraping through with jagged edges and stinging hints of insanity.

A blink of reality swam before him—*Ana at his side, tugging on his hand, urging him into blinding sunlight, the mansion creaking into a new tilt behind them.* Gone, and he stumbled, but at least felt himself do it before he fell away into bright darkness again. Another blink and *he slammed up against a tree, the rough bark a familiar comfort and the scent of pine strong in his nose. The ground rose steeply before him, unmarked by any trail. Fingers closed around his arm and he jerked himself to freedom, turning on the perpetrator with a snarl. Striking out and hearing a woman's cry and then falling away...*

His mind tumbled. It grasped at the clarity and brilliance he once knew to be his, seeing just enough of it to know it had been there but now was not. Reality turned *shivering in darkness, still moving, still climbing. The night should be awash with the scent and color of moonlight, a Sentinel's unique vision of the world after sunset—*

But it wasn't, and it continued to tug and roil and snap at him until it used him up. Until he heard nothing but a steady groaning that came with each exhalation, and each inhalation sounded like a forced thing, a thing to be endured instead of a thing that came as naturally as life. Endless running, endless movement, endless pain and confusion.

*Endless...*

A twig snapped, echoing unnaturally in his mind. A hand touched his shoulder, and he felt it to the bone. A whisper of comfort scraped against his ears. The air felt stifling against his face, scented heavily with sap and musty old needles.

*This is real.*

The groans were his. The whispers were hers. The night belonged to the mountain, cold and crisp and alive around them.

"Ian?" she said as if she somehow knew he'd emerged.

"For now," he managed, and fell asleep.


Ana jerked awake with the dawn—not that she'd ever truly slept.

She barely remembered escaping that horrible house she'd once called home. She'd come to her senses to find the bodyguards dead and Lerche moaning into the carpet, and her own body barely responsive to her demands.

She'd thought Ian dead at first, too. He'd sagged limp in the chair, on his side—one hand free and still clenched around the restraint for the other, his wrists and ankles chafed into ragged, bloody abrasions and blood at his mouth and fresh from his nose.

*My God, Ian, what did you do?*

She had no idea. Her senses rang, her body echoed with pain and trembled with weakness. She'd not given any thought to her actions—she'd only done them. She'd pulled herself over the strangely squishy body of one of the men beside her, reaching Ian to tug and scrabble at the remaining restraints—freeing him and rousing him and tugging on him until they made their way out of the house, quite instinctively heading for high, wild ground.

Their progress had been more of a mutual tumble than flight. Ian had struck out at her without warning, connecting more than once. He'd snarled at nothingness, and he'd fallen into trees. There'd been no sanity in his eyes. No sign that he'd seen Ana, no sign that he knew her. And still they ran, because she'd rather be with Ian in this state than anywhere near the organization to which she'd once been so loyal.

To which she'd subsumed herself and for which she'd doubted her sense of right and wrong, allowing others to devalue her for simply being who she was and burying the small, still lessons of her early years.

At least now she knew where those values came from. And why.

Ana shivered in the brisk fall air. She'd had the sense to snatch a blanket from the bed, wrapping it around her shoulders. Still, a blanket was no match for high country fall, and even the warmth pouring off Ian—an unnatural warmth, as though his body fevered itself with healing—had been unable to hold the cold at bay.

She had no idea where they were, only that this mountain was plenty big enough to get lost in. The sun gilded the slope across from them, painting the thick forest a glimmering tint of gold over green, the shadows still deep. She and Ian had tumbled beneath an overhang; a giant tree had lost its grip on the earth to slant above and beside them.

For the moment, Ian slept on. His silvered hair stuck out in disarray. Dried blood smeared across his face and down his chin, and she remembered what Lerche had said about the first working—the one that weakened all the small vessels and thinned the blood.

*Please, not his mind.* Not the brilliance and compassion and essential *Ian*.

Or maybe he'd just run headlong into a tree during their flight. He'd certainly had the opportunity.

Ana shivered again, tucking herself back in beside

Ian. When he woke, when they could move, they would find some sunshine and let it blaze against them.

But they also needed water. Dehydration came quickly on a desert mountain no matter the green around them, and free-flowing water was a scarcity. She and Ian needed such things as civilization could offer—and Ana had no idea which direction would lead them home.

Or if they were safe to go.

Lerche had not been dead, after all. Hurt, most certainly—but still alive enough to cry out threats as she'd fled.

Another shiver, one that rattled her bones. She ached right down to the heart of herself, and couldn't tell what of that discomfort came from her treatment at Lerche's hands and what simply came of being so cold.

Ian moved not at all. He breathed lightly but not quite steadily, with an occasional exhalation that verged on a groan.

"I'm sorry," she whispered to him with nothing to offer but her presence and a ragged blanket. She wrapped herself around him, soaking up his unnatural heat and letting herself fall into memory. In memory he'd lost his breath in pleasure, not pain, and the lines of his body had been hers to explore. Muscle layered tightly over ribs, all long lines and grace and that sense that he could, at any moment, put his body exactly where he meant it to be. Precision and brilliance wrapped in power and masculine beauty.

He had been the one to grin at her, as irreverent as a man could be, and talk about following the attraction between them—faster and further than she'd ever expected. He'd been the one to treat her so tenderly, so respectfully, that she'd let herself go, taking chances with her heart and with her fate.

*If I could do it over again...*

Who was she even fooling? She'd do it just the same. She didn't have the courage to give up the things he'd offered her—the look in his eye as he made himself vulnerable to her touch. The hint of surprise at her effect on him, and the deep gasps of his response. And there, too—the way his expression grew just a little bit fierce when he offered the same back to her, drinking her cries with a greed she found as arousing as his touch.

*Ian.*

She pulled the blanket more tightly around them both, resting her head on his shoulder while his body heat radiated into the chilled lump of her torso, warming her from the outside while memories warmed her from the inside.

But they couldn't stay this way forever. If he didn't wake soon, she'd have to find some way to mark this spot—and then she'd have to find her way out of these mountains, with no idea what awaited her once she did.

Or she would die here, and Ian would die here, and the Sentinels at the retreat would die under renewed attack, never knowing Ian's secret to finding the silent amulets.

And Lerche would have just what he'd wanted all along.

One broken arm. One dislocated shoulder. Three badly wrenched fingers, and one badly bruised kidney.

Those things had come from the mass release of the amulets—but his ferocious headache came from the intrusion into his space. From the loss of so many of his posse, and the rebuilding to come.

But opportunity remained. In the wake of his report—

the "unwarranted attack by Ian Scott gone rogue"—there were Core reinforcements on the way. An investigation of the Sentinels to come. And plenty of work to do so they all got the story straight.

*Ana, a low-level support admin, had a chance meeting with Ian Scott, and none of the wiles to recognize how he used her. He wooed her. He conquered her. He discerned the location of Lerche's safe house, and somewhere along the way his mind snapped—he was, after all, in the area for enforced R & R due to the strain he'd been under.*

*No one had realized how far gone he was, however, and it allowed him to launch an attack the likes of which no one had realized was possible—triggering amulets in bulk from afar. Ana had then tried to stop him the only way she knew how, by seeding amulets at the retreat.*

*Such a shame the rest of the Sentinels would die before anyone realized what she'd done. Or that Ian had given way to his beast, taking Ana deep into the mountains to kill her.*

With the few men he had left—with the final card he'd already put into play—Lerche would make certain of that. And if his story had some weak spots, there would be no one around to naysay it.

He'd already ascertained that the retreat amulets—one at each corner of the property—had done their work well. The Sentinels at the retreat had quickly fallen ill. The tracker, Lyn Maines, had finally given up on locating Ana and returned to the unnatural silence of the house—wary, he'd been told, but not wary enough to save herself.

No doubt there were reinforcements on the way—this time, in likelihood, a team that would make no bones about its presence. There would be no *playing nice* from the Sentinels at this point.

But they'd have no means to contradict his story.

Because they'd be too late.

Ian burned.

He burned hot and then he burned cold, and the jumbled sensations of his escape and his journey to this rough shelter had faded into a dully overwhelming throb of pain that silenced all else.

"Ian." That was Ana's whisper in his ear.

Come to think of it, that was her body pressed up against his, soft where it should be soft, yielding where it should yield—but nonetheless shivering with the cold.

It was a cold that hadn't penetrated further than Ian's fingertips, held at bay by the burning.

"Ian," she whispered again, this time her hand closing over his shoulder. Agonizing spikes of fire spread from that touch. He didn't mean to groan, or to curse, but he apparently wasn't in control of such things just yet.

"I'm sorry!" But she still whispered. "I won't do that again. But, Ian, you have to wake. They've come for us."

"Killed the bastards," he muttered.

She released what might have been a sob of relief, touching her forehead to his back. "Not all of them," she said. "Not Lerche, I don't think. And there were others—men who weren't in the house when you did... whatever you did."

She wouldn't know, of course. She'd been insensible when he'd triggered all those amulets.

Pretty much like Ian was right now.

"They might not find us here—but they shouldn't have found us at all. How could they track us so quickly?" She released a breath he felt along the back of his neck. "I only saw them because I had to, you know, find a bush. They're down in the gully between these two rises."

The words should have made sense; they didn't. They floated away along with his grasp on the immediate situation, leaving him only the understanding that he was missing something. It eluded him no matter how he swam though his thoughts, grasping at threads of reality.

A firm but careful hand turned his head. Cool lips found his, molding to his mouth and moving in a gentle rhythm that grabbed every bit of his attention. Her teeth nibbled; her tongue teased him, a touch and then gone.

Complete and utter clarity folded around him, cutting through inner chaos to present him only with Ana. Ana's scent, Ana's mouth, Ana's hands on his shoulders and slipping into his shirt.

Ana's cold, cold hands.

Ian gasped something between a laugh and a protest, grabbing those hands and enfolding them in his, chafing them slightly. She shivered and he went one better, pulling her to curl up in his lap and wrapping his arms and the blanket around them.

There they sat, with the morning settling in and the sky brightening ever so subtly as the sun's angle changed, starting to fill in the gaps and shadows of the folded mountainside. A faint mutter of male voices reached Ian's ears, rising from below as sound was wont to do in the mountains. He caught no words but heard a tone of frustration.

They were looking, she'd said. And Ian would guess they had good reason to expect their fugitives to be here—or they wouldn't have arrived so promptly in the first place.

The woman in his arms held the answer to that. She held any number of answers.

Ian could fill in some of the empty spots on his own. His memory held pieces of crystalline detail—moments of agony, the awareness of his body bruising inside and out. The look on Ana's face when the two bodyguards took hold of her. Deep fear as he'd reached for not one amulet but all of them, doing that which might save them or might kill them. Trying to direct them away, still knowing that the ones meant specifically for Sentinels would find him.

After that...

They'd gotten out, he knew that much. Must have been Ana's doing. And they'd run—farther and faster than he would have countenanced under the circumstances.

*Ana's doing.*

"You betrayed me," he said, and heard the surprise in his own low voice. Not that he hadn't known it before... just realizing it all over again. Especially in the wake of the world's sweetest kiss, his salvation through inner chaos.

It hadn't fixed the internal bruising or the lingering ache in his face, or the angry burn of his body healing just as fast as it could. Sentinel advantage, not without its costs. If he didn't get food soon, the whole process would collapse on itself. If he didn't get water, it would be a moot point.

Ana lifted her head from his chest, drawing back enough so she could meet his eyes. Cold air drifted between them, wringing another shiver from her. She didn't seem to notice. "Yes," she said, murmuring the words to keep them here inside this scant shelter of theirs. Her restraint somehow only leant them more meaning. "I did betray you. And then I betrayed my own people *for* you. And then they betrayed me. It's a horrible, confusing mess, and right now all I know is no matter how crazy it is, I love you and I think you know it."

He had no response for her, no matter how it felt to hear the words in the moment. Couldn't turn his feelings for her off; couldn't turn his trust for her back on. Not just like that.

She dove into his silence, still barely audible in her intensity. "Let's just get through the mess, Ian. Just feel what you feel right now and so will I, and let's get out of this and we'll see how we feel *then*."

He let the words sink in. *Feel what you feel right now.* "Yes," he told her, seeing relief in the faint sheen of the tears she blinked away. "Let's do that."

"Good," she said, nonsensical words with a tremble that told him she wasn't nearly as certain of herself as she'd seemed. She breathed deeply. "Yes. Okay."

He took a breath, scrubbing his hand over his aching face. They needed food and water, and to get off this mountain past Lerche's men…two of whom had tracked them with unlikely certainty. "Okay," he echoed her. "First things, first. How are you?"

She hesitated to answer, lifting her head to listen to the movement of the two men still significantly below them. "Cold," she murmured. "But that's probably obvious. Thirsty. And I'm afraid I pretty much used myself up last night. You?"

He tucked the blanket around her shoulders and answered only with another question. "And from the working Lerche used on you?"

"Ah," she said. "*That*. If there are aftereffects, I can't feel them." Her low voice took on a bitter note. "I think it was all about the pain."

In that bitter note, he heard all kinds of self-recrimination. "Ana, look at me." When her startled gaze met his in the shadows of the slanting tree trunk, the surrounding scrub oak and jut of rock, he shook his head. "Be grateful you didn't truly understand the man before now. That you couldn't says more about you than it does about him."

"Naive?" she suggested. "Malleable? Downright stu—"

He growled, finding himself suddenly closer to the big cat than he'd thought he was, the human veneer scraped away by the events of the past days. She startled into silence, a flicker of fear on her face—but it quickly passed, replaced by a wondering openness as he found the words to say, "Don't talk about yourself like that. It's no shame to have a fundamentally good nature. Or to be taken in by a man like Lerche when he's had so much control over you for so long. But *now*—" he tightened his hold on the blanket "—*now* you know better. Now you move forward, as you said. Now *we* move forward."

She blinked. "Okay," she said, and her whisper this time came from emotion and not from their precarious situation. She swallowed quite visibly, took a deep breath and said, "Well, that's it. Nothing from the amulet. I'm hungry and tired and cold, and I don't feel as if I can be of much help when it comes to these men, but I'll try."

Relief swept through him. Maybe she'd been affected

by his mass amulet release, maybe not. But not so much that it dogged her.

"*We'll* try," he said, and followed sudden impulse—kissing her forehead, her cheeks and then lingering a moment on her mouth. But not long, because they didn't have long.

The men had started to quarter the slope beneath them, no longer traveling up the easy gully bottom.

Ana's cold hand closed around his arm, above the deep abrasions left by the restraint. Under other circumstances, that wound and the others like it would have been well on the way to healing by now. But too much other damage had been done, and they were far from life threatening, and his overwhelmed body hadn't even tried. Ana said, "But you, Ian? What *happened*?"

Of course she had no idea. She'd been unconscious. And even if not, she'd have had a difficult time deciphering the abrupt chaos he'd unleashed. The targeted workings had no doubt been drawn directly to Ian himself. Not just Sentinel, but full field Sentinel.

Juicy target, at that.

"Lerche underestimated a few things," he said. "You. Me. And how familiar a Sentinel AmTech could be with all his precious amulets."

She just looked at him, a frown starting at her brow.

"I triggered all his toys," Ian said. "Aimed what I could at them and deflected what I could from us."

The frown turned to horror. "And absorbed the rest? *Ian!*" That last came in a furious whisper that threatened to break free of their little respite.

Ian shrugged, not a little abashed. "Hey," he said. "I knew what was in that case before I did it."

For a moment, it appeased her. And then the frown returned. "So you could have done that at any time?"

A random spike of pain shot through Ian's head; he winced, and wished their hunters would hurry it up. He needed the element of surprise that leaping from this hidey-hole would produce, and he needed it to happen before this spate of functionality faded.

For he had the distinct feeling it would fade. *Was fading.*

"Lerche didn't leave the amulet case in the room until that morning," he said, briefly splitting his attention— making a tentative foray outward with his inner awareness—brushing against the men below. Brushing against the amulets they so foolishly carried. "It was supposed to intimidate me or something. I doubt he realized I could identify them *or* trigger them from that chair."

"But after that," she said, persisting, "you could have done it?"

Suddenly he understood. "Ana," he said. "I am so sorry Lerche hurt you. I'm damned sorry he hurt *me*. But triggering those amulets…it was a last stand kind of thing. It could have gone wrong in so many ways." He hesitated. "Do you remember the first time he tried to aim the amulet at you? The way it went wrong?"

She worried her lip, her gaze gone inward. "Vaguely. Yes. It hit his men. And then it hit…" She looked at him, startled. "You. It hit *you*."

"Just stalling for time," he said, drawing breath at another stab of pain, closing his eyes against it. "Took him a while to catch on. I don't think even then that he had any notion I could trigger them all. He might not have figured it out yet."

She stroked cold fingers across his brow and down

the side of the cheek that hadn't been broken. Soothing. "So you waited…"

He tipped his head into her touch. "For all sorts of reasons. But mostly… I didn't know what it would do to you. Or to me." He opened his eyes to pin her with that gaze. "If not for you, Ana, I would have died in that room."

"If not for me," she said bitterly, "you wouldn't have been in that room in the first place." But she quickly shook her head. "No, I'm not going there. We have other things to do."

As became ever more obvious, with the men quartering upward, the tension in their voices making it clear they knew they were closing in.

Ana dropped her voice so the words barely had sound at all. "What can I do?"

Ian swept another feathery touch over the men—men who would be invisible to that touch had they been without amulets. But they weren't, and they were closer than he'd thought. Close enough to recognize the tracker they carried, and close enough to find the far-from-silent offensive amulets—pure energy of the sort that would release with concussive violence. He smiled darkly, only to be struck with another shaft of sharp pain, a thing that shot from one temple down the side of his face and radiated out along the nerves of his arms, spreading to encompass damaged ribs. He couldn't help his grunt of response, the snarl against his awareness of the blanketing fog that closed in on his mind in the wake of it.

"Ian," she said, desperation giving her murmur a new intensity. "Please, tell me how to help!"

"Come here," he managed to tell her, although there was hardly any distance between them to start with.

"Hold me, and put yourself back in your mind to how you felt when you kissed me. When you *woke* me."

He was asking the impossible, and he knew it. *Trust me enough to make yourself just that vulnerable while death creeps ever closer.*

But she didn't argue. She didn't ask how that could possibly help, wasting what little time they had. She twined a leg over his, slipping her hand beneath his shirt to avoid his ribs and hold him low over his belly. Her head tucked into the hollow of his shoulder and neck, her breath the only warm thing about her.

Except for the warmth that came from within, seeping into him like a balm. Clearing him. Giving him the focus to reach out one more time, keeping the sense of those approaching amulets until they came within the range he could manage without risking misdirection.

One final effort, reaching out to embrace the acrid sense of the repulsive things, twisting them awake as the taste of them washed across his senses, making Ana flinch—

The sound of the workings rang across the mountainside like twin gunshots, echoing away into silence.

Ian shuddered in the wake of them and let the fog wash him away.

# Chapter 13

Somehow the lingering sensation of the amulet working felt even uglier this time. Ana swallowed hard against a dry throat and managed a raspy whisper. "Are we safe?"

She couldn't quite bring herself to ask the real question. *Are they dead?*

By way of response, the tension drained from Ian's body; he sagged against her, his head lolling down to rest against hers.

"Ian!" She ducked out from beneath him, and then knew it for a mistake as he continued to fall and she struggled to control his descent. In the end all she could do was cradle his face from the impact. For all his lean grace, he was heavy with muscle—she didn't imagine she could do much to move him.

Though she was almost certain that if she put herself in the calm, open state of mind that seemed to most affect him, she could bring him around. She just didn't know if she *should*. His cheek still burned against her hand; his breath stuttered against pain. She had no way to know how much damage had been done—by Lerche, or by the explosion of workings Ian had triggered himself.

Best let him sleep. And heal.

Besides, there wasn't anything to be done here that she couldn't do herself. Not if the men were disabled.

If they weren't, then she was in over her head to start with.

Ana pulled the ragged blanket more tightly around her shoulders with one hand and lifted the drag of it with the other, stepping out from their scant shelter to scan the hillside below—a view of tree trunks and scattered underbrush, everything scrubby and stunted and dry. Only as she shivered in renewing panic did she finally locate the three men—a little cluster of lumpy forms that slowly resolved into awkward bodies in awkward poses, each equipped in camouflage outfits and equipment packs and what looked from here to be holstered pistols.

To her shame, her first thoughts were utterly selfish. Instead of regretting their deaths—for they surely looked to be dead—she found herself relieved. Not just because they so likely carried the supplies that she and Ian so badly needed, but because Lerche had sent three of them.

With those three now down and so many others affected by Ian's amulet explosion, Lerche would have fewer yet to send after them again. Hard to imagine herself so callous.

Then again, hard to imagine herself taking up against the Core.

*It doesn't mean they're wrong. It doesn't mean the Sentinels aren't out of control. It just means that Lerche is an awful human being.*

After all, he'd been in control of her life since those preteen days when she'd arrived, grieving and confused. He'd kept her so isolated that she had no idea how other major Core posses functioned.

*Take your own advice, Ana Dikau.* Now was not the time to worry about such things. It was much better to scurry on down the hill, grasping at tree trunks for support and losing the blanket along the way as it snagged in a prickly scrub oak.

Didn't matter. The men had coats.

She reached the three of them and looked back up the hill, only then realizing how close she and Ian had come to disaster. From here, the fallen tree that canted over their tiny hollow of a shelter was clearly visible. From here, since she knew what to look for, she could see glimpses of Ian's shirt.

They'd been close enough to unleash these workings, if they'd but known it. But she put that, too, aside, and went to each man in turn, ascertaining that they were, in fact, dead—or close enough to it that she couldn't tell the difference, cold fingers against the cooling skin of their necks.

It came as a relief, in the end. It meant she could rob them without compunction. And she did.

Each man had water—bottles at their waists, water bladders and tubing in their packs. She snagged a bottle that was almost empty and forced herself to a single swallow, then put it aside to wrestle away the man's pack, and then, with more difficulty, his coat.

Not so easy to handle the dead weight of a large man, after all.

The coat swallowed her, instantly trapping warmth. It was activewear, thinly insulated and full of zippers, toggles and pockets, but it made all the difference in the world. She luxuriated in it for a long moment, and then jostled herself into motion—adjusting it at the waist and tightening it in all places so she could continue her plundering.

By the time she was done, she'd emptied the water bottle and gathered two more, along with three packs, two more jackets and a vest—not to mention the gloves and hats. It took two trips to get everything up the hill, after which she no longer felt cold at all.

She sat beside Ian to riffle the packs, finding a gold mine of energy bars, a trail map marked with the men's progress and several precious heatable MRE packets. She tore into one right away, heating the stroganoff bag and dipping the spoon inside to hold near Ian's nose.

His face twitched; she ate that portion before it cooled and then presented another. As the third spoon approached, he opened his eyes. "What?" he said, and sounded annoyed while he was at it. "Seriously?"

Ana grinned, as out of place as it seemed. "I know, right? Not quite manna from heaven, but…pull yourself together, Ian. Eat up. We've got decisions to make." She reclaimed the spoon to swallow its contents and kept it in her mouth as she helped him straighten up, settling one of the jackets across his shoulders. He still frowned, expression bleary, but she decided first things, first and thrust the food at him, relinquishing the utensil. "Eat that," she reiterated, and unwrapped an energy bar, breaking it in half. "And then eat this."

He gave her a halfhearted disgruntlement of a growl, and she waved him off. "Whatever. I'm warm, I've got food and water, and I've got a *map*. You just go ahead and growl, see if I care."

"That was supposed to be impressive," he said, digging into the bag of food.

"And I'm sure it was." She tore a bite from the en-

ergy bar and wrestled with its cold chewiness, bending
over the open map. "Remind me to make some sort of
suitable reaction later. Right now I want to find us the
fastest way out of here."

The spoon hesitated on the way to his mouth. "It's
not that easy." He cleared the rest of the ragged feeling
from his throat and took that bite, swallowing—eating
faster now. "They found us, Ana. They *followed* us."

Her tenuous cheer evaporated. "I don't see how."

"The same way they always do. One of us is marked
somehow." He offered her the food, and she shook her
head—knowing well enough that the accelerated healing took a toll on him. It was Core Education 101.

He tipped the rest of the stroganoff into his mouth for
a high-calorie chew-and-swallow and set the bag aside,
pushing the jacket off his shoulders to check his pockets and coming up with nothing but lint.

Ana quickly did the same, going so far as to check
the rolled cuffs of her pants. "Nothing," she told him—
and then muffled a startled cry when he reached for
her, patting her down as thoroughly as anyone could,
hands impersonal as they traced the seams of everything from her shirt and pants down to her bra. Her face
flared with a new and unwelcome warmth. "I suppose
I deserved that."

He cast her a startled glance. "*Deserve* has nothing
to do with it. Right now I think it's safe to say that I
know more about how the Core works its enemies than
you do."

"Enemies," she said, musing on it with a prick of
hurt. She'd never done anything but try to be what they
wanted...without losing herself in the process.

"Don't get tangled in it," he said. "Isn't that what we decided?" He rubbed his temple with a weary gesture.

On impulse, she reached for his hand. They sat together for a long moment of silence during which she was ridiculously aware of the way his fingers overlapped hers, the faintly rough nature of his palm and warmth of it. His fingers twitched slightly, and she found a wince at the corner of his eye and reached to soothe it.

Gratifying that he closed his eyes to rest briefly against her touch. Once he straightened, he said, "They tracked us somehow. We need to know how."

"Can't we just make a run for it?" Ana asked, thinking herself sensible. "Surely once we return to the retreat—"

"Don't count on my people for help," Ian said, more sharply than she expected. "Not if Lerche told the truth about seeding that place with silents—and triggering them."

"I thought...if your brevis is already on alert...won't they send more help?"

"On wings," Ian said. "If they're not here already. But they'll be in crisis mode. And who knows if they'll be able to shield from the damned silents, no matter how careful they are. Although if they can get Maks on the scene with his uber-shields..." He trailed off, stopping himself. "Never mind. The point is that they're vulnerable. There's no way I'm leading the Core straight back at them."

"Then you should rest." The contents of one backpack sat on the ground before her, and Ana spread them out with one hand. A change of socks, a compass, a first aid kit, energy bars—and most importantly, in the middle of it all, a thick stack of chemical warmers, bundled together with a rubber band. "We've got what we need for now, if we're careful."

His grim smile disabused her of that notion. He said, "We bought some space, but not much. Lerche absolutely can't afford for me to live—once he doesn't hear from those men, he'll act quickly. He has too much understanding of what I can do, even if he has no idea I solved the silent amulet."

Ana reclaimed her hand, threading her fingers into her hair, head bent to look at the ground before her—the scattering of supplies from the pack, the coat that overlapped her crossed knees and then some. The evidence that they'd killed and fled and killed again. "I just can't even believe this," she said. "In what world does *any* of this make sense?"

"No particular world," Ian admitted, and recaptured her hand. "Look, Ana. You had the right of it. We can't stop to make things make sense. We just have to trust. And to follow."

"Follow you, you mean," she said bitterly. "Just like I followed Lerche for so long."

He sat silent for a long moment. Far *too* long. When she dared to glance at him, she found the weariness she expected, and the strain on his face. But she also found a less expected grief.

He gave her hand one last squeeze and released it. "Not if you don't want to." He rubbed a hand over the back of his neck, rotating his shoulders within the drape of the jacket. "But give me a chance to work out this tracking thing before you make up your mind."

Ana froze on understanding. He didn't intend to *make* her do anything. He didn't even intend to insist. He was hurt and tired and doing his best, and yet he was willing to let her walk away.

She didn't know whether the realization pierced her heart, or freed it.

Ian wouldn't force her. Not after what she'd been through, and especially not because of what she believed him—the Sentinel- -to be.

In the end, he didn't even know if he'd be willing to let her go her own way. But if he couldn't stop her, then he'd damned well make sure she wasn't carrying a tracker. Sure, he could have done with a little more time. He didn't have it. So be it.

He'd tasted the posse concussion amulets in spite of his illness and injury—he'd been able to perceive them from afar and been able to trigger them. So he trusted that he'd have similarly felt any tracker planted on Ana.

Not that they hadn't searched her—and him— thoroughly enough.

It meant that if they were being tracked by amulet, it was a silent one. Silent and so well hidden that there was no point in continuing a physical search.

He was about to put his new system to the test.

*Not ready.*

Not physically, when he still burned from the inside out, his thoughts slippery and his bones sore. Not skill-wise, either. No finesse, no established parameters— only a blind fling of energy. "Just give me a moment," he told her as grimly as before. Not that she'd leaped to her feet. She was, he thought, still processing the fact that her choices from here were entirely her own.

Not a situation in which she had practice.

Besides, he still held her hand. In fact, he drew

strength from it—knowing, if not understanding, why it made all the difference in the world. Enough so he was able to close his eyes and find one small, quiet, still place inside himself. From that he drew the purest note of energy he could find—a fine-tuned thing of highest clarity.

He sent it out in a single smooth pulse.

Chaos instantly pushed in on him, and he held it off—listening from that same quiet place, the only place from which he had the faintest chance of hearing—

*That.*

The response bounced back at him so quickly he almost missed it—and then again, three quick pings tumbling over one another at not quite the same strength.

He lost hold on the quiet, shuddering faintly as the chaos slammed in around him again.

"Ian," she said, bending close to him, the scent of her hair a soothing spice and her breath warm against his neck.

He opened his eyes to find her there. That close, with the daylight reflecting into the deeper honey glow of her eyes and the faint freckles completely revealed, concern written all over her face.

She had no idea.

And they didn't have time to soften the news.

"It's you," he said. "And them, for what it matters. But mostly it's you."

She understood immediately.

*Almost.*

Her hands flew to her blouse, leaving him to fight the impinging chaos alone. "I'll change," she said, glancing down the hill where three men lay still clothed. "If we can't find the thing, I'll just leave it all behind."

He put his hands over hers, stilling them—getting

a frown of response. Cold still blushed her cheeks and nose, but behind it her complexion had pinked up to a healthier warmth. No point in getting her cold all over again. Especially not when he was pretty sure it wouldn't do any good.

"I mean," he said, "it's *you*."

She looked at him with a distinct horror. "What do you mean, it's *me*?"

"*In* you," he said. "I'd bet on it. Just as Fabron Gausto did to Jet."

"I don't—" Her confusion said it all. Ian knew more about the activities of the deceased regional *drozhar* than she did. Knew more about the Core altogether—if not about how those such as Ana lived within it. Or about how the Core managed them.

Although he was getting a pretty damned good idea.

"*Ian,*" she said, pulling her hands away and tucking herself inside the absurdly oversize jacket. "My very own people are using me—they're trying to *kill* me. And now my very best ally, my *lover*, is the enemy I've always known couldn't be trusted at all." She worked herself up to a glare. "I've had *enough*. So you just come right out and *tell me what you're talking about*."

He blinked at her. Felt amusement welling up and didn't try to hide it. "When you put it that way, babe, it does seem only fair." He rotated his shoulders again, taking the stretch through to his torso—testing his ribs. Wincing at the scrape of pain but nonetheless lifting his arm to brace against the tree trunk. Testing himself. Limbering himself.

Because now it was about to get ugly in a way he hadn't anticipated.

And she was waiting.

"Short version," he said. "From scratch. Gausto was developing a working to force a shapeshift on non-Sentinels. He wasn't getting anywhere, so he worked it from the other direction—forcing the change on animal subjects."

Unexpected understanding crossed her face, a startled distaste. "Jet," she said. "The woman I met yesterday."

"She's here?" Ian felt a surge of hope. "Excellent. Lerche's workings aren't likely to affect her the way they'll affect the others."

Ana took that in with a nod, but not without vexation. "What's that got do with me?"

Ian released a gust of impatience. "God, my head is a mess. The point is that once he had Jet, he used her—but she was and is a wild thing. So he found a way to keep track of her that she couldn't thwart. He implanted an amulet." The amulet had been a multitasker, full of less benign workings, but Ian left that part alone.

Ana froze, looking down at herself with renewed horror. "*In* me," she said, suddenly understanding. "Oh, my God, he can track us just because I exist!"

"Unless," Ian said gently, "we can do something about it."

"I don't—*how*—" But she froze, understanding. "Take it out. You want to take it out. You want to *cut me open and*—"

She jumped to her feet, clumsy in the cold and the jacket, and Ian made no move to stop her. He could hardly blame her. Even if he wasn't Sentinel, even if she wasn't wrestling with her whole world flipped inside out. She turned her back on him and took the three stumbling steps to the edge of their little scoop of shelter, and he didn't try to stop that, either.

He said, "I'll be back in a few moments."

She made a muffled sound he didn't even try to interpret as he stood and slipped his arms into the jacket sleeves—slowly, carefully, unwinding muscles stiff from the night and protesting all the abuse they'd taken along the way.

He was just as glad Ruger wasn't here to tell him what he'd done to himself with that explosive release of amulets. Or to tell him what he was doing to himself by interfering with his body's attempt to heal.

He ducked out beneath the massive tree trunk and made his way downhill to where the two posse members lay—sans their jackets, their bodies already taking on that peculiar stillness of death. The concussive amulets, released from such close proximity, had left them splayed as if trying to escape themselves, resulting in an instant rigor that must have resisted the removal of their jackets and now made searching them even more of a challenge.

But before he searched, he circled them—alert for the stench of amulets that might have gone untriggered when he'd targeted the concussive workings. Perceiving nothing, he steeled himself, slipping around the edges of the necessary focus to ping them for silent amulets.

*Come* on. *Get it together!*

But he didn't and couldn't. Not until he extended his awareness back up the hill to where he'd meant to leave Ana her privacy—not intruding so much as reminding himself of the peace she'd always given him. From that first moment in the retreat yard, in the kitchen…even in those moments when she'd been planting that first lethal amulet.

She was right. There'd be no untangling this mess

between them. There'd only be allowing what they felt and seeing where it took them.

Where it took him now was into the quiet zone. A brief respite, and just enough to ping for silents, sending that faint pulse out and away.

From the men, he got three faint, damaged pulses.

And from Ana, he received the same quiet response he'd felt before.

Just frigging awesome.

Ian made short work of his remaining tasks—searching and finding the men's more conventional weapons. Two handguns, about which he knew little other than the fact they were semiautomatics. A Leatherman multitool and two combat knives of modest length. Their phones, which might come in handy if he and Ana ever found a signal.

He stuffed the bounty into the various pockets of his newly acquired jacket and let his mind drift as he circled a little farther out, found a moment of privacy behind a cluster of little junipers, and slowly made his way back up to Ana.

She greeted him with eyes reddened but dry, delicate features pinched with both the cold and resolution. "Okay. Then how do we find it?"

"The amulet?" He barely waited for her nod. "We can try to triangulate. Don't know if I'm up for that, honestly. It's a kind of fine work I've had no practice in, and my ability to concentrate at that level is fractured at best." He gave her what felt like a lame grin and no doubt was. "On the other hand, even with healing workings, it should have left a mark. We can just look. Starting with here." He touched her neck, slid his hand down beneath the jacket to stop at the grace of toned muscle where her neck met her shoulder. "This is where they put Jet's."

Her eyes widened; her hand raised to cover his. "There's a spot there..." she said. "It always itches. Since right before we came here..."

"Don't tell me. Right about then you had some sort of twenty-four hour bug."

She gave him a skeptical look. "You couldn't know that."

Ian laughed without humor. "I know how the Core works, babe. I know they made you sick so you wouldn't notice the clues that they'd done this thing. Probably just a day or so, but pretty miserably so."

"I had an awful headache—it lasted two days." She closed her eyes, struggling with the reality of it. "I'm not prone to them. I should have—"

*"No."* He said it with such vehemence that it shocked her into looking at him—unguarded, eyes wide. "You can't blame yourself. They were very careful to make sure you never had reason to suspect what they could and would do to control you." He stepped closer. "What they were doing *all along*. Don't ever forget that, Ana."

She held his gaze for a long moment, then sighed. *Acceptance.* "Fine," she said. "So now...?"

Ian couldn't help his grim look. "Now," he told her, "we get it out."

Easier said than done...but done as quickly as Ian possibly could.

He raided their acquired first aid kit, not surprised to find disposable scalpel and hemostats. And with Ana's jacket and blouse open and pulled aside far enough to expose her bra strap and the swell of her breast, he found the faintest hint of a scar. The stroke and prod of his fingers located the tiny lump of an implanted amulet.

She drew back in alarm when he produced one of the combat knives, but settled back even before he reassured her, curling her fingers into the exposed roots at the base of their shelter.

"Silly," he told her with much affection, and bounced the knife pommel against the old scar fast enough to set up a vibration and long enough so she frowned at him again.

"What—?"

*"Now,"* he told her, and made the quickest of incisions, feeling the faint bite of metal against the blade and swapping the scalpel for the hemostats. Ana squeaked with surprise and jerked, biting her lip hard, and by then Ian had the thing.

He swabbed her shoulder and made swift work of the butterfly bandages, placing a gel skin bandage over that and leaving Ana with a stunned expression on a pale face.

"You're done?" She ran her fingers over the thin and flexible covering.

"Aim to please," Ian told her. "It might need stitches when we get past all this, but no big deal."

"I'm not even sure I felt that." She laughed, if not quite convincingly. "You and your bouncing knife."

He held the nubbin of an amulet up for her inspection, and then flicked it down the hill toward the dead men. "Just in case they have any trouble finding their own."

"Goodbye, Lerche." Ana's words should have held finality, but Ian heard a sadness there, too.

Not that he could blame her. Goodbye to a way of life,

to a way of thinking. To a big part of what she'd always been and always believed.

He tucked away the first aid kit and the trash he'd generated, grabbing the meal wrappers while he was at it—leaving Ana to her silence while he distributed the contents of the third pack between the first two, and then helped her to her feet and adjusted the pack to fit—as best it could, sized as it was for the man who had worn it.

Ana glanced down the hill. "We just leave them?"

He understood her reluctance. "We do. Someone from the Core will track them down. They had their own trackers—damaged with concussion release, but yours is there, too." For above all, the Core knew better than to leave the evidence of its behavior lying around for the mundane world to stumble over. "They would have found us, too, if we hadn't made it."

She tucked newly gloved hands around the pack straps. "I know. It's just…none of this seems right. I just can't help but wonder if this isn't so much about the Core as it is about Lerche, and if I head on in…report what's happened…"

Something in Ian hardened. "Lerche," he said, jamming an arm through his own pack strap. "Eduard Forrakes. Fabron Gausto. And all the men who ever thought it was okay to belittle you and demean you and keep you so beaten down. Who think it's just fine to hurt Sentinels whenever it suits them. What happened here isn't about any single person, Ana, and it's not even about you or me. It's about a culture that sees bullying and *taking* as their right."

Ana sent him a strange look. "Funny," she said. "That's what Lerche would say about you."

Ian settled the pack into place. "Then you've got some decisions to make, don't you?"

"I don't—"

"Stay," he said, "and your Core will find you. Probably not Lerche's people by then. Or go on your own way, and find the Core. Or come with me. I'm heading to the Sentinels, and I'll take down as many posse members as necessary to get there."

"That's hard," she said, the faintest tremble at her mouth—and anger lighting her eyes. "That's damned hard."

He knew she wasn't talking about the choice. She was talking about *him*. And he couldn't disagree. "I want you with me, Ana. But I'll do what needs doing, and I'm not going to debate it at every turn. So, by God—" he shook his head, the words stuck in his throat for that instant "—I hope you'll come with me. Just be sure you know the choice you're making. And that you can live with it, one way or the other."

"No," she said, and her voice wasn't strong—nor that steady. "I won't let you define my terms. I can come with you now...and walk away later."

He reminded himself of how she'd grown up. Of what she'd been told. Of what she'd been plunged into the middle of. He reminded himself that he would probably never know how much strength it had taken her to say those words.

"Yeah," he agreed, and didn't do what he wanted so badly to do—snatch her off her feet like some caveman, keeping her safe. Keeping her *his*. Knowing that if he strong-armed her, he'd simply lose her altogether. "You can. But not without consequences, if you're wrong about the Core. And, just so you know, probably not without ripping my beastie little heart into some ugly pieces. But it's up to you."

With that, he struck off—his thoughts already whirling off into chaos with the distance he'd just put between them, and his body one large smoldering bruise except for the parts that simply hurt worse—his side, his face.

And, yeah, his heart. Even though it should have known better all along.

# Chapter 14

They hiked with unerring purpose, making Ana glad she'd worn her minimalist cross-trainers the day before but also sorry she hadn't put on hiking boots. Ian led them from sun to shadow and back again, cresting unexpected slopes and curving around sharp points. Always one foot slightly lower than the other on slanting ground, her feet straining to find purchase among the accumulated bedding of needles and snagging in the sly tangle of underbrush.

She drank when Ian suggested; she ate the energy bar he dug out of the pack. She unzipped her jacket to let the cool air circulate beneath, finding herself plenty warm even without the rising temperatures of the day and the direct beat of the sun. Her feet turned leaden early, and she learned to place them with even more care. When she asked if they'd make it out before nightfall, he'd said only, "Maybe."

She didn't press. She heard the strain in his voice.

She knew what it had taken from him to walk away from their discussion, leaving her the space she needed—she knew how he cared. How deeply. Because she knew, now, how passionate he was about his people. What they did. What they'd suffered at Core hands.

No matter why the Core had done what they'd done. They'd caused suffering. That, Ana knew.

Because he was right. She'd experienced it all along, in her own way, even before Lerche had turned a torturous amulet on her. Or sent three men to kill them. Or before she'd known he'd hidden a tracker in her body.

She shifted the pack straps away from the tiny wound Ian had dealt her to free her of that tracker. Even in hurting her, he'd touched her with more care than she'd experienced since she'd been torn from her home.

Ian made a sound she hadn't expected, stumbling— righting himself against a tree and striking out again. Another dozen steps and he tripped again, this time landing heavily on his hands and one knee. He didn't bounce back up.

"Ian?" She ran a few hasty steps to reach him, and then wasn't quite sure what to do when she got there. She couldn't fix this any more than she could undo the moment she'd planted that amulet in the retreat kitchen.

"Awesome," he muttered, sitting back on his heel and dusting his hands off. "Big bad Sentinel."

"You're pushing too hard," she said as if she had the right to tell him of his own needs.

Ian glanced up at the sky; without thinking, she followed his gaze.

The sun was well on its way back down toward sunset, low enough to shine in her eyes if she'd been looking up instead of at her feet.

She'd had no idea they'd lost so much time tucked away in their little shelter. She'd been judging by the warmth of the day, unable to factor in the chilling effect of the altitude or the way the rugged folds of the mountain kept them in shade.

And given the healing heat that still radiated from Ian, given the strain on his features and the obvious way his body still chewed through resources, she knew without hesitation that he pushed on her account—trying to get her off the range before night fell.

"I'll be fine," she told him. Sharper in tone than she'd meant to.

Not to mention a statement utterly without merit. She had no idea how she'd get through another night out here.

She sighed in capitulation. "I don't understand." This time her voice held the weariness of their situation. "We escaped Lerche in the evening, and made it to that little hidey-hole sometime in the middle of the night. Why would it take us so much longer to get out?"

Ian let his head drop back, his hands resting flat against his thighs; he released a weary gust of breath. "Because then, we weren't navigating. We were just *running*. Because the *running* took so much out of us. Because we've got to take a different route to get out of here or we'll end up right back in Lerche's territory—and that route has to be one that takes us into trailhead area and not over a cliff." He opened his eyes just enough to send her a meaningful look. "That explain it for you?"

"Yes," she said, numb at the hard edge beneath those words. Not the Ian of compassion.

Just, she thought, Ian when pushed past what he could actually do.

She slipped the backpack strap from one shoulder, then the other. Ian had taken his stumble on a south-facing curve, and the sun hit them full on, illuminating not just the fatigue over handsome features gone a little too sharp, but painting the hill in strong light and shadow.

Easy enough to find the gentle places on the terrain—the little hollow above them where rock and tree retreated, leaving an area of matted needle and leaf.

She struck out for it.

"What," Ian asked without opening his eyes, "are you doing?"

She tossed her backpack; it landed at the edge of the hollow. She tossed the jacket after it, glad enough to shed it during this time of warmth and in the wake of their unceasing activity. "Here's a spot," she said as if they'd come to some mutual decision.

"I told you I wouldn't argue. I meant it. This is my way, or no way."

"Fine," she said. "Leave me here, then. Maybe you can send someone to look when you get out."

He made a decidedly unfriendly sound. A growl. Something so deep and primal she thought he hadn't consciously decided to do it at all.

"Look," she said. "We're not going to make it before dark, are we?"

"We'll get closer. Close enough. I can see in the dark—well enough to get us the rest of the way. Didn't your Core ever teach you that?"

As if the Core would fail to disclose any small detail of the Sentinels' advantages over normal humankind when fear of the Sentinels lived at the heart of Core culture. *Fear of them. The need to stop them.*

*Stop them from what?* Ana suddenly wondered.

Because the Sentinels could no more allow their people to reveal their nature than the Core allowed their own to employ workings in any visible way. If any Sentinel misbehaved...

*That's what Lyn does.*

Sentinel tracker. A woman who tracked her own, bringing them to Sentinel justice.

*This is so messed up.*

"Ian," she said gently, "we won't make it out of here at all if we don't do it smarter than this."

For a long moment, he didn't move. Then he rolled his shoulders, one after the other, and pushed himself to his feet. She stood at the edge of her chosen spot and held out her hand, and when he made it up to her, she slipped around to tug the backpack off his shoulders, setting it beside hers.

"It's a bad idea," he said under his breath, dropping his coat beside hers as well, and then dropping down onto it sitting cross-legged.

"No doubt. But it's the best one we've got." She settled down beside him. "Close your eyes for a moment. I'll pull out one of the MREs and get it ready."

He rubbed a hand over his eyes. "Ana, if I close my eyes, they're going to stay closed for a while. We could end up spending the night right here."

"We'll be okay."

He shook his head, dropping his hand to look at her, and she stilled, not expecting his tortured look or the way his jaw worked. "Ian, what—?"

"*We're* not the only ones in trouble," he said. "You met Fernie. You *liked* her. And Lyn, and Ruger, and Shea? I'm the only one who can save them." His voice dropped. "If it's not too late."

"I'm sorry," she said. "Whatever the truth is about the Core or about the Sentinels… Lerche is a monster. I can't believe I didn't see it before now. I just can't—" She bit her lip, hunting words. Overwhelmed by a surge of guilt.

"Don't," he said harshly. "We've been through this.

He made very sure you didn't see it. And, Ana, I want to make this easier for you. I want to make it all *fucking go away*. But I don't have the energy for it, so, please... can we just not go there right now?"

To her surprise, Ana found these stark words more comforting than she could have imagined. Just matter-of-fact truth. Ian couldn't make this better.

In fact, *no one* could make the shreds of her life into some magically okay thing. Lerche had systematically created what she was and what she'd experienced, and now all she could do was break free of it to make her own decisions.

She shifted to her knees, bringing herself closer to him—close enough to touch his face and let her fingers linger there. He closed his eyes, and she wasn't sure if he couldn't quite bear her touch or if he simply needed it just that badly.

"Ian," she whispered. "You mean so much to me. In these few short days...you've changed my life into something I never could have imagined."

He swallowed hard, muscles working in his throat and jaw, eyes closed so hard she could all but feel his pain herself. She stroked across his cheek—the strong angle, the clean lines. She let her fingertips dust across dark lashes, ridiculously long lashes with the smudge of the big cat around the edges of his lids. She drew a whisper down the straight, strong line of his nose and touched his mouth—clearly defined, with a full lower lip that felt so very good against hers.

And was so very good at carrying off the faintest wry little smile he now offered her. "Colder than you could have imagined? More stupidly tired? More profoundly lost?"

Ana laughed, and it came out a throaty sound. *"Alive,"* she corrected him, and didn't bother to move her fingers before bringing her mouth down on his.

"Mmph," he said in surprise—but seemed to understand her need not to be kissed, but to do the kissing. His hands lay quiescent on his thighs as she explored his lips beneath hers, a sensation becoming familiar—just as was the sound of his quickening breath, the firmness of his response and the way he knew just how to woo her—one moment gentle, the next leaning into her kiss with a demanding clash that warmed her blood so much faster than any sunshine ever could.

Her hand found the hem of his shirt, slipping beneath it to touch smooth skin and inspire the responsive flutter of hard muscle. His groan sounded of frustration, and his hands lay quiet no more, instead reaching to her waist. Lifting her to straddle his lap just seemed to *happen*, and he left his hands there, thumbs curled around her hip bones and fingers splayed out just above the curve of her bottom. She shuddered at that sudden jolt of pleasure and he gasped against her mouth, his hold tightening in reflex.

In an instant he'd rolled her onto her jacket, his legs straightening to pin hers and his hands sliding up her sides to her arms, finding her fingers to interlace his own. "This," he growled, "is the stupidest damned time to—"

"Shut up," she gasped. "It's the perfect time, and you know it. Don't you dare start *thinking* about it—"

*"You* shut up," he said, and covered her mouth to make it so.

Or almost so, because she spoke right around their kiss. *"Fine,"* she said. "Take *this*." And with no hesitation at all, slipped her hand right down the front of his pants to find his erection.

Ian froze. "Cold," he said, his voice sounding strangled. "Cold, cold—"

But when she stroked him he stiffened into her, and she did it again, scratching lightly at velvet skin. "Not so cold?"

"Just—" he shuddered, his eyes squeezing shut "—just...*perfect*."

She rose up just enough to whisper in his ear. "Too many clothes, Ian."

He must have agreed. She quite abruptly found herself without a shirt, her pants unbuttoned and yanked off all but one ankle, his pants unbuttoned and out of the way. She reached for him again, owning him—fingertips and gentle pressure making way for a few firm strokes while she had him.

*"Gah,"* he said on a gasp. "Wait... Ana... I don't have—"

Right. Condoms had been the last thing on anyone's mind as they fled Lerche's mansion.

"I'm safe," he said, on his elbows over her and trembling with the effort of control as her hand stilled but lingered. "Sentinels...we can...we learn to..."

Didn't matter. He'd be healthy—Sentinels were. "I'm protected, too," she managed. Because the Core required it, demanding the use of an implant, demanding regular health tests. Controlling even that.

"Your choice," he said, holding himself there by pure evident dint of will.

"I already made that choice," she told him. "Remember? In all ways, Ian."

"Ana," he breathed, and it sounded like something

else. Something more important. *"Ana."* Whiskers brushed her skin as he buried his face against her neck, burying himself inside her. She arched up into him with a cry of welcome and a hot flare of pleasure, clutching as he retreated and thrust again—more deeply and then stilling there to absorb the feel of it. His teeth scraped her neck with a faint pinch that sent a delightful shock zinging along her skin; one hand roamed her body to find her breast beneath shirt and bra and gently roll her nipple.

She arched up into that, too, stunned by the fast-gathering heat of a climax and preternaturally aware of every inch of his touch. His breath on her neck, his lips and tongue soothing the spot he'd only just nipped, his fingers rough and perfect over her breast, the amazing sensation of her own body throbbing around his and his body throbbing within hers.

And though he somehow held himself still within her, trembling against the anticipation, she could do so no more. She twisted, writhing up against him, insisting… Her hands found the tight muscle of his beautifully rounded bottom, and she grabbed it, hard—pulling him in while she took him just a little bit deeper, reaching for that miraculous gathering of bright liquid imminence.

He cried out as he had before, a startled thing—a wild thing, set suddenly free and thrusting hard. A man, shouting in beautiful, vulnerable surrender. And again, and again, each shout bringing her nearer and closer and *oh. Please. Yes—!*

Ana spilled over into the hot shards of orgasm, her fingers digging into his backside, aware of nothing but the sensation he wrung from her, his final gasping thrusts and the guttural groan of his own release—not just a momentary pulse but a sensation that rocketed between them, building into something that was bigger than either of them and, in the end, leaving Ana with a sob stuck in her throat.

Ian slowly relaxed above her, his touch more languid as he stroked her beneath her shirt—gently on her tender breast, lingering on each rib, his thumb dipping into her belly button. His lashes brushed her chin as he raised his head, kissing that chin and then each corner of her mouth. "Ana! Are you crying?"

She nodded, a quick little surprised motion. "Yes," she said. "It's just so... It was..."

"Beautiful," he whispered, and kissed her again— briefly, before he laid his head on her chest, letting the weight of it settle slowly. She lifted her own head just enough to kiss the disarray of his silvered hair, and found his hand to interlace her fingers again. He briefly returned the touch with a squeeze of his own, and just that gently, relaxed into sleep. Still covering her, still keeping her warm.

Ana found his discarded jacket with her free hand, tossing it over his back with an awkward flick of her wrist and tugging it into place. Covering them both, and smiling into leftover tears as she let his presence lull her away into sleep beneath him.

Ian woke with a start, rolling away from Ana to land in a crouch—face lifted to the breeze, the night a sharp wash of blue-tinted detail around him and his hands flexing against the ground, phantom claws deployed.

*The leopard awake.*

Slowly, he relaxed—understanding that there was no danger, no enemy on approach. It was only that the leopard, so repressed, so sickened, had come back to him in such a tidal surge of awareness.

Ana stirred within the gentle hollow of ground where they'd sheltered, still buried beneath his recently acquired jacket. They'd made love, they'd slept, they'd woken to disarray and satiated kisses, and they'd eaten… and then he'd acknowledged the inevitable.

It wouldn't have done his friends any good if he'd made it off the mountain in record time only to falter upon reaching the retreat. Especially if the Core was already there.

*Waiting.*

Not just for him. For Ana.

And he was far, far too close to that point of exhaustion.

So they'd slept again, one jacket beneath them and one above, Ana's gently heavy breathing lulling him back to sleep.

It had almost sounded like purring.

"Ian?" Her voice came sleepy from the hollow; material rustled as she pushed the jacket away from her face. "Ian—?"

"I'm here," he said, keeping his voice low only out of respect for the night. "Go back to sleep."

She made a disgruntled sound, and the rustling subsided. Ian stood, uncoiling to his full height. Aware of the leopard as he couldn't ever remember being.

*Ana.* She'd done what she did best, quieting him. Giving him the room to heal—and now, to feel the depth of what he'd always been. An Ian Scott that he'd never truly known, with his world too full of thought and motion and intent.

A quiet breeze slipped over his arms; he felt the chill of it for the first time since...

Since he'd first been affected by the kitchen amulet.

He stood a moment, still in the way only the leopard could be—in a way he'd never truly allowed of himself. Absorbing the understanding of how deeply—and how quickly—those amulets had affected him. Absorbing, too, the perfidy of such a subtle attack. He was the primary AmTech of this region, and if he hadn't felt the insidious nature of the damage being done, how would anyone?

*Ana was right.* Right to insist that they stop here, right to insist that they rest, that he heal. Because more important than the need to save those people he loved so fiercely was the need to convey the secret of the silent amulets as quickly and widely as possible. If he stupidly sacrificed himself along the way, that would never happen. No one would even know he'd solved the riddle—or that it was even possible.

Another breeze slipped over his arms, riffling his hair and evoking a shiver. The leopard pushed at him, whiskers bristling, the skin over his shoulders twitching. Ian glanced back at the small quiescent lump that was Ana under the jackets and then back out into the clarity of the night, stepping out into the silence of it—*bounding* out into the silence of it—and reaching for the leopard as he moved.

*Coiled power, the graceful snap of a long tail, broad paws quiet against the earth, breeze a mere ruffle of fur, hunger growling in the emptiness of a body chewing through resources to heal.*

Ian went hunting.

* * *

Lerche cursed the sling that bit into his neck, and he cursed the raking claws of the working still crawling through his system—one of those from the case Ian Scott had triggered *en masse.*

Lerche hadn't known him to be capable of any such thing. Hadn't known *any* of them to be capable of such a thing. And even if he'd known...

It wouldn't have occurred to him that any sane man would do it. Not when too many of the powerful workings were constructed to target the nearest Sentinel—unlike the workings that Scott had very clearly managed to direct away from himself and away from Ana. Across the household and onto Lerche and his men, so many of whom had been badly injured or died outright.

He hadn't had so many to waste. And now he hadn't heard back from the three posse members he'd sent into the mountain, readily following the silent amulet he'd had embedded in Ana before this operation.

She'd gone to bed without it. She'd woken with it. And she'd never known the difference.

Too bad the tiny silent blanks were so precious. Lerche could foresee a day when all his people carried such trackers, instead of just those who most needed to run silent.

But not until—*unless*—he got things under control before the regional *drozhar* ran out of patience. The entire Southwest had undoubtedly felt the ripple from the mass amulet release—including the Tucson Sentinels. Brevis reinforcements would already be on the way.

They'd be too late for those at the retreat. He was confident of the deadly web he'd woven there—silent amulets, triggered in unison to enclose the retreat and trap the occupants within its effects. If they weren't dead, they were dying. Brevis couldn't get here in time—because there was no *in time*. Until the working faded or the amulets were destroyed, any and all who entered that retreat would die, leaving the Sentinels only the need to clean up after them, bereft of evidence and hushing events to protect their own clandestine nature.

Just as Lerche now cleaned up after his own, whipping up the few men left to him. By the time the *drozhar* arrived, there'd be no one to contradict his story.

And it was a good story.

*Ian Scott gone mad in the wake of Ana's assignment gone awry, Ana gone rogue and misusing amulets in an attempt to succeed in her own small assignment.*

Of course Ian Scott had then come after Ana, tearing through the mansion with no regard to Core lives... and he had triggered the final amulet attack before fleeing into the hills, dragging Ana with him. There they'd both no doubt expired.

Things were well in hand. Lerche could be reasonably certain that Scott hadn't completed his work with the silent amulets, or he would have detected them on Ana long before Lerche ever had a chance to take him prisoner. Those results alone would justify his initial operation—the one he'd put on the record with the *drozhar*—and the Sentinels and Ana would take the blame for the rest.

Lerche resisted the urge to scratch his healing arm, and instead reached for his new phone—sliding it open and scrolling down the contacts to the men who ought to have returned from the mountain by now. They should certainly be within an area of reception.

"Answer, damn you," he muttered, glaring at the phone.

No one did.

# *Chapter 15*

Ana saw Ian leave.

She saw him *change*.

And she froze with fear beneath the bundle of jackets, understanding for the very first time—truly understanding—what Ian *was*.

He was gorgeous. He was power and danger and primal energy.

He was *beast*.

Just as Lerche had always said. Just as she'd always believed, but as she'd not truly been able to comprehend.

Who *could*?

She'd made love with this man. She'd declared herself to him. She'd opened her heart to him.

And he was more dangerous than she ever could have imagined.

"I'm done now," she whispered into the night. "No more hard stuff, universe. It's somebody else's turn."

Intense gut-level fear, it seemed, was every bit as strong as any trust.

She pushed herself up from the ground, rising slowly to pull the jacket on and zip it up; the temperatures had fallen to their usual remarkable degree, and she had no intention of getting cold all over again.

After she found herself a bush, she hunted up hat and

scarf from one of the backpacks, covering her ears and neck and then stuffing her hands in a pair of scavenged gloves. They flopped off her hands like clown fingers, and she laughed darkly into the night as she put both hands in one glove, salvaging warmth.

Waiting. Unable to sleep, knowing that he was out there. That the *leopard* was out there.

Snow leopard. A glimmer of pale spotted white as he prowled away, an amazing length of tail, small ears tucked tight to a beautiful feline head. Not the biggest of the cats, which suited him. He wasn't a brawny man, after all. He was all lean frame and muscle, broad shoulders and coiled movement.

Ana pulled the arms of the bottom coat up into her lap, making it into as much of a robe as she could, and huddled into the results.

Waiting. Watching for that glimmer of pale movement. Listening for the rustle of a big padded foot against the ground.

And therefore nearly missing him when he did return, walking upright and quite humanly in the darkness. His nearness startled her all over again and she sprang to her feet, tripping over the bottom coat and recovering herself.

"Thought you were asleep," he said, his voice low and conversational.

"I had to use a bush," she told him. "I…saw you leaving."

"Ah." His voice held understanding. She couldn't read his face.

She suspected he could very easily read hers. Sentinel night vision was a well-known thing—a combination of human and nocturnal physiology, with their earth powers thrown in. Clear, bright and detailed.

He didn't try to come any closer. "You gave me back the leopard, you know."

She didn't know. In fact, she didn't understand at all.

"I haven't been able to find myself since that first amulet started working on the retreat." He shook his head, a motion she could see in the rising moonlight. "To be fair, it's been a very long time since I could cut through the overlapping thoughts in my head to let the whole of the leopard through."

Ana struggled to absorb the meaning behind his words—hearing in his voice a reverence, a *relief*, that she found distinctly hard to comprehend. "It's that important to you?"

Ian laughed outright. "Is breathing important? Is *living*?"

She didn't quite know how to answer.

"Yes," he said, more quietly now—beginning to realize that her hesitation came not just from a failure to understand, but from her own reaction to the leopard. "It's that important. I'm sorry if I frightened you. I'll never hurt you, Ana. *Never*."

She discovered she'd wrapped her arms around her stomach, holding herself tight. "When I first saw you on that trail with the cougar…"

He'd been beautiful. He'd been charging into a fight with a creature significantly larger than he was, and even in her fear of the power he held, she still remembered most vividly the bittersweet desire to have someone who cared enough for her to do the same.

But now he waited, and she made herself ask. "I wondered then…how much of yourself do you retain when you're leopard? How much of your humanity?"

His silence let her know the question came as something of a blow. His lingering distance told her the same. "What has the Core told you, Ana? That we're all beasts? That when we take the change we become the worst of both worlds? All the ugliness of humanity, all the ferocity of the animal? Killing machines?"

It took all her strength to stick to her truths. She wanted to say *no, never mind, I'm just being silly*. She wanted to find some appeasing response that would take the tension from his posture and make everything feel all right, even if it meant burying her fear.

She had learned well how to stay safe in her world.

But Ian had always been truthful with her. And he was teaching her that the only true way to be safe was to be honest with him—and with herself. So she said, "Yes. That's exactly what I learned."

Not from her family, in those early years when she'd learned what it did feel like to be loved. But after.

Ian's bitter, self-aware tone took her by surprise. "God, they suck."

And then he startled her again. "You need to figure it out, Ana. What you see against what you've been told. What you've experienced with me against the words of a culture that showed you how to live in disrespect and fear."

"I…" She started talking because it seemed necessary, and trailed away because she wasn't even sure what to say. Finally she managed, "I know. I just don't know *how*."

He took a step closer. A challenge of sorts—knowing he'd frightened her and now daring her to get past it as he finally answered her earlier question. "When I take the leopard, it makes me more than either of us. Everything that's me, free to glory in everything that's leopard. But the leopard doesn't control me. The leopard *is* me."

Ana took a step back. Not from fear—for this was Ian, the man who had held her and loved her and risked his life for her. Just because she needed…

*Space.*

Because at some point, that *one more thing* had simply become too much to process, in too little time.

He didn't pursue her. But he didn't back down, either. "We use who we are to keep this world safe from those who would harm it. We patrol wilderness areas, we find toxic dump sites, we work in zoos and parks. If we're not supposed to embrace who we are while we're at it?" He snorted. "Pardon me, but fuck that."

*Embrace who we are.*

It's what Lerche had tried to take from her, too. Pushing and squeezing and molding her to the understanding that what she was could never be enough. That she needed, somehow, to be somebody else.

"Whatever," Ian said as if it hadn't mattered at all. But it had, and she knew it. It mattered very much. And still she was all jumbled inside. Unable to offer him the responses he needed—not and be honest.

Ian cut her silence short by stepping up to pull the packs together. "Time to move out," he said, rummaging and discarding. "I think we can get this stuff into one pack, if we use the jacket pockets." He held out a handful of energy bars, and she belatedly stepped forward to take them, stuffing them into all the nooks and crannies of the jacket. He flattened the trash from the MREs and layered it into the bottom of the pack, offering her the final dinner along the way. "Here. You need it."

"So do you," she protested, finding herself with words again.

He gave her a glance that she couldn't read in the darkness, moonlight or no. "I've eaten."

The *leopard* had eaten, he meant. She swallowed hard and refused to think about it—and took the dinner, tearing it open to initiate the heating process and meanwhile tucking its little side packets into her pockets with the energy bars.

He zipped and buckled and hefted the pack. "It's good," he said. "We'll tie the jacket to it. I'm afraid you'll have to carry the second pack, too, but it's light."

"Why—" she started and stopped, looking for better words than *why do you have to be the leopard?*

"You can stay here if you want," he told her, reminding her of their earlier conversation. "Or go your own way."

"That's not what I meant." She drew on that new courage and stood her ground. "I can carry the packs, and I will. I'm only trying to understand."

He handed her the full pack. "Because the leopard can see better, hear better and move better. And if we run into trouble, I'm in a better position to do something about it."

"Okay," she said.

He gave her a sharp look that she felt even through the darkness. "And because I've missed it. I *want* it." He took a step closer, close enough so she could see his features and see the gleam in his eyes, and the yearning. "Because I *need* it. I'm not ashamed of that. Pretty much the opposite, in fact."

With that he turned her around to help her with the pack, and tied the jacket on it, and stepped away. Not just one step, but half a dozen—where he hesitated only long enough to say, "I won't let you get lost," before he spun into a silent blue-white explosion of energy and strobing light, and emerged from it as leopard.

Beautiful, graceful, *deadly* leopard.

Ian quartered the terrain before Ana, clearing it not only of a prowling bobcat but confirming the absence of human presence now that they neared the trail he'd been targeting. Never out of her sight long enough so that she felt alone, never so close as to frighten her.

When a small gathering of coyotes lowered their heads and trotted away with a collective sneer, he knew two things—that dawn was close, and the trail was closer. Coyotes packed up near the base of the range, skimming that intersection between humanity and the wild where rabbits, squirrels and small house pets kept them fed and entertained.

Ana greeted his return with less apprehension and more relief. He sat before her, long pluming tail wrapped around his feet, wishing he could explain how magnificent it was to prowl inside this other skin, soaking up scents and sounds that the human never noticed. How exhilarating to give way to the instinctive impulses of the leopard—from the leap that clapped broad paws over a mouse only to sit and twitch whiskers as it scurried away to the sudden dash across open ground, tail flipping along behind in the glory of muscles in play, bunch and leap and pounce and then *oh, did I do that?*

How *alive* it made him.

How important it was that this deep connection with his leopard had been restored.

*By Ana.*

But she wasn't ready to hear any of that, and he wasn't ready to be the human without letting the leopard shine through. He turned and padded away, leading her in such a deliberate manner that she understood they were close.

Just as well. Faint dawn and Sentinel sight painted deep shadows of fatigue beneath her eyes and hollows beneath her cheeks. He knew he'd look no better when he returned to the human—visibly gaunt in the wake of the extensive healing, worn by the pain and circumstances.

Not that he was complaining. Not even to himself. He didn't want to think too deeply on the state he'd been in, or what he'd have done without Ana's help.

The trail at this point was a narrow thing of marginal footing, but when they reached it, Ana released a huge sigh of relief. Ian turned to give her a cat grin, his rump perched ridiculously high on the slope and his paws braced below, jaw dropped just the slightest bit. But it only made her hesitate, one hand on a bracing tree.

When he moved out she waited for a decent distance between them before she followed.

As soon as he judged it light enough for her human sight to follow the emerging trail on her own, he slipped off to parallel it. The track widened; another trail merged into it and drew them around in a flattening loop toward the parking area. Ian drifted to shortcut the loop, stealing a few more moments with the leopard as the trees thinned and the bunch grass rose up, studded with juniper and hiding the oddball prickly pear.

Ana's unexpected voice drifted to him on a level parallel to his, out on the far part of the loop. Ian hesitated, ears swiveling, the rest of him frozen so as not to generate his own noise.

He couldn't hear the words…he didn't like the tone. Not just a greeting to an unlikely dawn hiker. Not a conversation with herself.

The rumble of a male voice cinched it. Demanding. Rude.

Ian swerved in that direction, trotting with purpose and long, loose strides. Not sprinting yet—the snow leopard didn't have a lot of sprint, and he'd save it. But pushing hard, with several hundred yards between them.

Until Ana cried out. *"Ian!"*

Then he ran, legs pumping, claws digging into earth—bounding over brush and dodging trees, ears flattened and tail counterbalancing even the most improbable leap.

He felt nothing of *Core*. Nothing of lurking amulets or the stinging taste of a working in progress. A crude, ping of wild energy returned no hint of a silent amulet.

Ana cried out again, this time in anger—in obvious struggle. She was brave enough, his Ana, and had struggled her way through an emotional and physical ordeal that would have left others a weeping mess. They'd *made* her strong, always holding victories and successes just out of her reach, creating a world for her in which *just keep trying* was the only option.

But she wasn't big enough, or strong enough, or trained enough, to overcome Core posse.

Ian bounded in without a hint of stealth, getting his first glimpse of them—Ana hampered by the oversize jacket and pack, not one but two men grabbing at her. Not yet trying to hurt her, not being the least gentle…

They must have waited here, taking a chance on the

location. This was the closest egress from the mountain, barring one that would return them to the mansion. It was familiar, the one from which they'd taken Ian the first time.

Where they'd gotten the men, Ian didn't know. But he'd screwed up. He'd thought them safe. He'd thought to steal a few more moments as the leopard.

*He'd left Ana alone.*

Now there was no stealth—not with Ana's struggles fueling his fury. If the men had no amulets, then they had conventional weapons, and Ian could only bear down on them hard and fast, kicking it up into that burst of a killing sprint. Taking them by surprise, simply because they'd never trained against such an opponent before.

They weren't as unprepared as all that. One of them shouted alarm; the other flung Ana away and snatched at his side—not quite fast enough with a gun as Ian leaped with claws extended, slapping the man in a quick series of swiping blows.

The gun went off, plucking a trail of fire along Ian's upper arm—and with it came an equally fiery rain of whipping blows across his back. He turned a snarl on the second man and his tactical baton, snagging the thing in one paw even as he came to rest on the man screaming beneath him.

The fallen man flailed, and Ian turned on him with the fiercest of snarls, all his teeth in the man's face—freezing him in gut-level terror.

Ana's scream came not in fear but in warning—no time to form words, just her own human cry to beware. Ian looked up to find that the second man had a gun, too, and now he had a shot, with his partner flat on the ground and out of the way.

Ana launched herself at him, arm raised, a blade glinting briefly in the barely risen sun. The man thought to shove her carelessly away and then jerked in surprise as she struck, whirling around to bat her down with a cruel blow.

By the time he turned back to Ian, he found himself face-to-face with an enraged snow leopard—one already inside the line of his gun, ears flat to his skull and teeth bared in the clearest of threats.

The man froze, instantly opening both hands so the gun sat only loosely in his palm, his finger off the trigger.

Ana scrambled back up to hands and knees, lurching beneath the pack and making her way to the other man—wrenching his gun away and backing off to the sweet spot where she was out of his reach but still close enough to call point-blank.

Under Ian's glare, his captive eased his own gun to the ground and stepped away. Ian batted the thing toward Ana.

She gathered it, too, breathless and wild-eyed, a smear of blood trickling from her nose and the split of her puffing lip. "This one looks pretty bad, Ian."

Ian didn't look away from his own captive. *Pretty bad* was likely an understatement. Sharp claws, soft neck. The man hadn't understood his fate before Ian had snarled him into compliance, but Ian thought he'd figure it out very soon.

This other man, though...

Ian gave him a hard eye, took a step in his direction. A stalking, deliberate step, head lowering.

"Hey," the man said. *"Hey."*

"Try sitting down," Ana suggested, a little starch

coming back into her voice. Grim starch, as she, too, realized the likely fate of the man before her, but starch nonetheless. "In fact, try cuffing yourself with whatever you were going to use on me."

Irate nastiness bubbled out. "You watch yourself, bitch. When Lerche gets his hands on—"

Ian snarled. All teeth, all narrowed eyes, lowering over his shoulders. Taking another step.

"Okay, okay! Whatever!" The man sat as if his legs had gone out from beneath him, which might well have been the case. "Godammit, she stabbed me!"

Oh? Ian cast a glance over at Ana, a twitch of whisker. *Good for you.*

Her expression in return didn't give him any warm fuzzies. A grim thing, her mouth flat and her eyes looking trapped rather than relieved.

Ian stalked an unhappy, grumbling path around the surviving Core posse member, flicking his tail in the man's face as a reminder. The man cursed again, digging into his pockets—freezing just for a moment as he started to withdraw his hand and discovered himself under intense feline scrutiny. *"Handcuffs,"* he said, snarling the word. "Just like you said."

Ian sat. Watching. The man snapped the cuffs into place and held them up for inspection. "Okay? You happy now? You just going to let Levv die, or are you going to let me call someone?"

Ana's voice sounded remote. "Unless you're hiding an amulet with a miracle working on it, it's too late for your friend." She sat back on her bottom, legs loosely crossed and the gun in her hand as if she couldn't quite remember how to hold it.

Because, Ian knew, she'd been through *just.*
*Too. Much.*

And he wasn't helping.

He moved to the edge of the trail, making sure the
gunshot hadn't attracted the attention of an early morning hiker. The surviving man glared and Ana cast him
a distracted glance, but they were alone in their little
tableau, and Ian stepped into the human—straightening
and reaching for that place within himself. The one that
stood tall and sharp-eyed and still full of the leopard.

Full of concern for the woman who would never
be anything but beloved, no matter what she could or
couldn't cope with in the end. "Ana?"

"I'm okay," she said, and then laughed, a short sound
with dark notes to it. "I mean, relatively speaking, right?"

Ian cursed—silently, sharply—and got to work. Gathering the gun, finding the knife that Ana had dropped,
stuffing them into the backpack she'd also dropped. He
checked the man's cuffs, ratcheting them down tight
without concern for the man's sneer or the implied threat
behind it.

It meant only that he and his buddy weren't the only
ones looking for Ian and Ana, and it was information
that Ian was glad to have. He stood and stepped away.
"Who drove?"

The man's sneer only grew stronger, turning an ill-
defined face into something ugly.

"Whatever," Ian said. "If I cut your jacket off to
empty the pockets, you're going to get cold fast. If your
pants come off, you'll be hanging in that breeze. Maybe
you'll have a phone to call for help, maybe not."

The sneer shifted to narrowed eyes and a mean resentment, but the man's eyes cut to his partner.

Ian moved around to the other side of the dead man where he could keep an eye on the living, and patted the man's front pockets. "This is how it starts," he told Ana, keeping his eyes on their captive. "He goes back to the Core and talks up the way I overpowered him with my animal nature. How his gun was of no use. How I slaughtered his partner." He risked a glance at her, catching her gaze only for an instant—big and brown and shattered. "I mean, my God! I stopped him from killing me! What is this world coming to?"

*"Us,"* she said, no strength behind her voice. "You stopped him from killing *us*." But she scooted back slightly, leaving the gun behind. "But…look at his throat, Ian. Look at his *throat*."

Ian didn't need to. He hadn't used his teeth—hadn't bitten through spine or taken a suffocating hold on the man's throat. He simply hadn't put the man's safety above his own, risking himself to make sure he pulled those blows.

"I know what happened to his neck," he said, grunting as he rolled the man up to one hip for a better angle into his pocket. The keys came to hand fairly quickly, and he retrieved and reseated them firmly in his grip. "Was it less civilized to use claws in defense than it was for him to shoot me in the first place?"

That got her sharp attention. "Did he— Oh, Ian! Your arm!"

Just a flesh wound. Bleeding freely, hurting badly, through the bulk of his biceps and out again. "Yeah," he said. "But never mind. I'll heal, right? That's what makes it okay to hurt us and hurt us and *hurt* us, isn't it? Ask Lerche what he thinks about it, why don't you?"

She sucked in a breath and stared at him as if she'd never seen him before.

Maybe she hadn't. Maybe he'd protected her from the impact of Lerche's actions. From the impact of the Core on the Sentinels.

Maybe he wouldn't do it any longer.

He grabbed the back of the man's jacket and dragged him off the trail and into the trees—damned if that didn't hurt, too, or if a wash of light-headed sweat didn't flush across his brow and prickle down his back while he was at it. Too much accumulated insult at that, even if this one had made the leopard nothing but mad. Without the amulet working at him, without the clutter of extra chaos in his thoughts, that clear connection to his most basic self remained strong.

Damned strong.

Damned fine.

And nothing to apologize for.

He returned to find Ana standing off to the side, their captive still sitting sullenly in the middle of the trail. He wasn't into explanations; he hooked a hand under the man's arm and hauled upward, adding enough of a pinch in that tender spot to inspire compliance. From there he led the man to his partner and pushed him down into a sprawling sit. "Phone?"

The man gave him a wary look but only a momentary hesitation. Lessons learned. "Inside jacket pocket."

Ian tugged the jacket forward, unzipped and searched first one side and then the other—impersonal and efficient and finding the thing. But when the man grabbed for it, Ian held it just out of reach, just as efficiently thumbing the battery free. The man's protest died on his lips when Ian tossed the battery at his feet and then hurled the phone into the trees. "Have at it," he said, and left the man there.

Ana greeted him with a baffled stare. "What did you—?"

"He'll be a while finding the pieces of his phone," Ian said shortly. "It'll buy us some time." She stared into the trees, frowning, and he sighed. "No, Ana, I didn't kill him, though I have no idea how badly you might have hurt him with that not inconsiderable knife blade. But we need to get moving. I'm tired of bleeding, and I'd like to try to save my friends now."

She startled just a little, looking down at her own hands and the blood there. "I did stab him," she said, her voice low. "I don't think it went very deep."

"Doesn't matter if it did," Ian said. "Unless you want to buy into the Core mind games and call yourself the monster because you didn't want to die."

Her head snapped up. "That's not fair."

"Yeah," he told her. "It is. Come or stay, Ana. Your choice."

He really hoped she would come as he headed for the parking lot, scooping up the fallen pack on the way. He didn't think getting behind the wheel of a car was his best choice just now. Especially not as the stench of the car and its considerable amulet presence made its impact on his senses.

No wonder they'd been so clean. They'd divested themselves of workings before setting out. Smarter than the last two, or maybe they'd just learned their lesson.

Or just maybe they knew more of what they were about. It made him wish he'd lingered to question the survivor. If Lerche had called in reinforcements...if those reinforcements were of a better caliber posse...

Just what they needed, if the regional *drozhar* had gotten involved.

He reached the car, a ubiquitous pale SUV, and unlocked it with a click of the key fob. He yanked a back door open without much care and tossed the pack inside, only then hesitating to take stock of Ana.

"I'm coming," she said, from only a few steps away. "I'm seeing this through."

It held no promises, and it gave him little comfort. But it was something.

# Chapter 16

"What do you mean," Lerche said, annunciating each word with precision, *"they got away?"*

Budian's voice didn't hold the respect it should have. "Not from me," he said. "I'm still keeping an eye on the retreat—not for long, though. Someone's got to go clean up after Stephan's mess in the mountain, and there aren't many of us left. In case you hadn't noticed."

Lerche stood too quickly from his massive desk, bumping the backs of his knees against the sturdy chair as light-headedness struck. But only briefly, and he was already on his way to the balcony, throwing the door open to scowl over the rolling foothills that fell away into the city. "If this posse had performed adequately, none of this would have happened!"

"Sure," Budian said without the convincing note he should have injected. "But things are looking good here. Not a peep from inside the retreat, and no sign that the amulet field has so much as a glitch. Plus, I hear that Tucson's on the way, so I figured you'd want to focus on wrapping things up here."

"Tucson?" Lerche said the word with a sharp alarm he hadn't meant to display. Not to Budian—not to anyone. "The *drozhar* himself?"

"Grapevine," Budian said as if it was completely acceptable for the man to have received such news before Lerche. "But about Stephan. He's cuffed out by the trail, and Levv is dead. Scott took their car, and you can bet he's on his way to the retreat. Not only that, Scott and Dikau must have taken down the first team—they wore our jackets and had our packs. Hell, Dikau stabbed Stephan with one of our issued weapons."

"Ana *stabbed* him?" No. *No.* Ana was *his.* His to command, his to use, his to *own.* Pathetic little bitch, her Sentinel contamination too light to be of any experimental use and too heavy to make her of use within the posse.

Ian Scott couldn't have her. The Sentinels couldn't have her. She was Lerche's to spare or to use or to put out of her misery. *His* misery. His fist clenched within the sling, his other hand tightening around the cell phone.

"You want me to deal with Stephan and Levv?" Budian said, left too long in silence. "I mean, I can stay here, but I figure you want that scene sterilized before anyone from Tucson—"

"Go," Lerche said, hearing his own voice as if from a distance—a veil of disbelief, and a veil of growing fury. Ana had betrayed him. She'd thought she could break free from him, and she should have already paid the price for that. Instead she dared to work against him—wounding his man, siding with the Sentinel Am-Tech. Who even knew how many secrets she would betray along the way?

Not that she'd ever known anything of import to begin with. But even one word was too much. Her very *presence* was too much, and would confirm things the Sentinels might only suspect.

"Go," he repeated, more harshly this time. "Take care of Stephan, and clean the area. I'll deal with Ian Scott."

*And Ana Dikau will be mine again.*

\* \* \*

As if Ana intended to allow Ian to drive when he was bleeding again. Didn't matter the confusion that lay between them, or the confusion that lurked so deeply within her.

*Love the man. Trust the man.*

Fear the leopard.

Fear everything about a man who could *become* leopard.

Even then, she knew better. He didn't become. He *was*.

And the rest of her world was upside down around him.

Still, she knew how to drive. So she plucked the keys from his hand and did just that, taking Ian into the city where his friends were at such risk.

Ian jerked, wincing, one hand going to his temple. "Annorah!" It sounded like both imprecation and relief, and Ana slowed, looking for and not finding a place to pull over as they wound through the foothills community and toward busier streets. Ian glanced at her. "It's all right. It's just…okay, a little hard to explain. A voice in my head." He turned his gaze inward—and Ana was certain he spoke out loud for her benefit. "Turn it down a little, huh?"

A voice in his head. Something Sentinel. Someone who could help?

Ian snorted. "She says it's always hard to break through to me and it always takes this volume, wants to know what changed."

*Me*, Ana thought. *I did that for him. Somehow. Just by loving him.*

She did love him. She just couldn't pretend she didn't also fear him.

Ian said, "It's a long story, Annorah. And yes, I'm talking out loud, and I'm relaying. I'm with Ana Dikau. That's another long story."

A pause, and he shifted, closing a hand over his arm—not the injury itself, but below it, as if he could rub the pain away from there. "She says she tried to reach me last night and couldn't. No surprise there. Southwest Brevis felt the amulet bomb I set off. They're sending help." She wasn't surprised when his jaw tightened on the last, and then he forgot to relay at all. "Nick's coming? Warn him off, Annorah—warn him off *right now*. The retreat is under a working—I don't *know*—just warn him off!"

In the silence to follow, Ana asked, "Is she…gone?"

Ian waited while she navigated a four-way stop. Closing in on the retreat, where Ana wasn't at all sure she wanted to be.

She'd liked those people. And she would never make assumptions about Lerche again—how far he would go. How many lines he would cross.

She already knew.

Ian rubbed his arm, his face pinched. "Yes. She'll warn him." He glanced at her. "Nick is our brevis consul."

"The Southwest commander," Ana said. "Right. I've heard of him. Nick Carter. He's a wolf."

"He belongs to the woman you met. Jet." He took on a wry expression. "I use the word *belongs* with some purpose. Point is, he knows she's in that house."

"She's the wolf," Ana said. "If Lerche used a Sentinel-specific working, maybe she's all right." She found herself hoping so. Jet had been frightening...but compassionate, and her eyes held an honesty that Ana had trusted.

Ian cursed short and hard, and this time Ana did pull over, making use of a generous shoulder. "Is she back? Is there a problem?" She glanced in the rear and side-view mirrors, looking for any sign of the Core.

"I didn't tell her how to find the silents," he said, self-recrimination written so clearly on his face that she couldn't help but reach out to him, her hand over his and holding tight.

"Call her back?" she suggested with no idea how it actually worked.

*"Can't,"* he said, hitting the word short and hard. "Some people can. I'm not one of them. *Damn!*" He hit the door armrest with explosive force, startling her—but he hadn't moved his hand out from beneath hers, and she ran a thumb over his knuckles, the only comfort she could offer. "God, if only I'd gotten my head out of my butt earlier and gone *active* on the silents..."

*"Hey,"* she said, a single sharp word that got his attention. "It's only been what...a little over a year since that night?" The night they'd all learned about the silent amulets, when Fabron Gausto had launched an attack of such perfidy that even within the Core, it was spoken of in hushed tones.

At least, among those who had worked at Ana's level—those who had worried about the ramifications, perfectly aware of how deeply vulnerable Gausto's attack had made the rest of them.

"Something like that," Ian said. "We lost so many... and then I got messed up when I went to help Maks." He stopped, as if realizing she'd known nothing of it. "We got distracted by Eduard's work…and then the situation in the Sacramentos."

"Wait," she said, still catching up. "I don't know about those things, but…*wait*. You were *hurt*? And then someone else from the Core went after you?"

He gave her a look of such patience that he caught her attention completely. "Ana," he said, "they've never *stopped*. Not since Gausto kicked things into gear. Meanwhile there's someone else joining the party — someone who figured out we both exist and wants us both dead. And we're too busy with stuff like this to figure *them* out."

It was her turn for patience—but she had none. "My point is, you were hurt! And busy! And now you're all pissed at yourself because in the middle of all that you didn't turn your thinking inside out when it comes to these silents?"

He opened his mouth. Closed it. Muttered, "Pinging the things seems obvious enough *now*."

"It's only obvious after you think of it." She crossed her arms, bumping the steering wheel. "Not when you're building on an entire history of never having to do it before."

"But I should have—"

"Ah!" She made it a scolding sound, freeing one hand to hold up a finger of punctuation. "Stop it. Get your head out of your butt *now*."

His eyes looked startled, bright blue and clear in the morning sun. His mouth didn't quite close on his unspoken words.

"I get it," she said. "It would have been better if you'd been able to detect the silents earlier, and it would have made things easier right now if you'd had the chance to give that information to Annorah, but honestly—do you think anyone but you can do anything with that information in the next fifteen minutes? In the next day?"

He frowned, but instead of irritation she saw uncertainty. Possibly no one had ever called him on his overblown expectations of his own genius before. Probably they'd never *scolded* him for it.

Eventually he said, "No. Probably not." He caught her hand, reaching across his body to do it with the arm that wasn't injured. The other still bled—they'd made no effort to bind it—but she saw the flow of it had much reduced, and couldn't help but wince at the memory of his bitter words. *I'll heal, right?*

He'd been right to think she'd been so indoctrinated in what the Sentinels could do that she no longer considered the extent of his pain, or what it took out of him. Out of any of them.

Ian stroked her hand, turning it over to trace the lines of her palm. Still, she thought, taking something from that contact between them. He said, "The thing is, Ana, I'm going to save my friends now—or to damned well try. Whatever that means. Lerche could be there. The amulet field could be more than I can handle. I don't have my gear, I barely have my brains, and my people are probably dying."

He hesitated on the next words, but she knew. Her response came out as a cry of dismay. "You're not counting on getting through it!"

He said with grim but careful words, "I'm not making assumptions."

Because Lerche would kill him if he got the chance. Ana didn't doubt it—not any longer. Not in her heart or her mind.

And Ian was tired. She saw that clearly enough.

Still, she found herself unaccountably annoyed. *"Fine,"* she said, and reached past him to flip the glove box open. "Write a note and leave it in the car. Or put it in your pocket."

"You can tell them," Ian said.

She froze. "What?"

"You," he said distinctly. "Can tell them."

She sat back. "You're assuming that I won't run like a rabbit. I don't want anything to do with your Sentinels, Ian. I don't want anything to do with the Core." She realized the truth of the words even as she spoke them. "I want my freedom, and I want to find out who I really am, and what I really want."

He went as still as a hunting cat. "And if I'm around when this is over? What then?"

"I'm getting the impression that *'this'* is never over," she told him darkly. "But I'll tell you what. You stick around, and you'll have a chance to find out."

"Hard bargain." The corner of his mouth twitched.

"I learn fast." She put the car in gear, checking the rear and side view. "Faster than Lerche will give me credit for."

"Idiot," Ian said of Lerche, muttering it. He rotated the wrist of his injured arm, flexing the hand. Keeping it moving, such as he could. "Let's go for it, then."

She pulled away from the curb and they drove in silence—into the city, into the little greenway area and the surprisingly undeveloped land that ran alongside it. Driving with swift assertion and no idea what they'd do when they got there.

"Pull over," he said, abruptly enough so they skidded slightly in the dirt and gravel road in front of the retreat.

They came to a stop beside the low adobe wall where she'd first met him, when she'd still believed this to be both nothing but a routine surveillance assignment and her big chance to advance in the Core.

On the other side of the wall, a large man lay where he'd fallen, awkward and unmoving at the base of the porch stairs. Ana didn't recognize him—and from the faint frown on Ian's face, neither did he.

But it was evidence enough that Lerche hadn't been bluffing about amulet workings. Or that they were just as effective as he'd claimed—possibly against them all. Humans included.

"Is he breathing?" she asked, unable to see it from the driver's seat.

"Can't tell." Ian flipped the door handle and hesitated with one foot out the door. "You should probably wait here. But it's up to you."

She undid her seat belt, her hand already at the door. "Wait here because it's safer, or because there's not much way I can help even if I want to?"

"A little of both." He disembarked into the narrow space between the SUV and the wall, and stuck his head back inside. "A *lot* of both."

"Then I'll wait," she said. For now.

But it didn't last long.

Three of them came at Ian as he moved toward the gate—not men she recognized, and to judge by his wariness, not men he knew, either. He stopped short, putting his back to the wall, his wounded arm held close. Ana slipped out of the vehicle without thinking about it, but hung behind the open door.

They didn't seem like Core—they wore jeans and cargo pants, T-shirts and button-ups under light jackets. Nothing black. Nothing silver. And their complexions varied from pale to dark brown, their eyes likewise.

But their expressions, to a man, weren't the least bit friendly.

"Don't know who you are," Ian said, standing with deceptive quiescence, "but you'll want to back off now."

"Don't know who *you* are," said the largest of them, big and burly—the darkest of them, and there was nothing of quiescence about him. "But you stink. Your car stinks. And the woman stinks."

"Then put some distance between us," Ian said, and something sparked in his eyes. A man reaching his limit.

Ana saw it, and she had no doubt the three men saw it, as well—and in their way, heeded it. Standing out of reach and on the balls of their feet, never mind that they all three outweighed him, standing taller and broader. She searched them for what she saw so easily in Ian—the sense of coiled strength, the hint of *other* in his movement and carriage.

Maybe it was there. But she didn't see it. So maybe these were Sentinels and maybe not—because according to Ian, a third faction had developed, an interloper group trying to dispatch both Core and Sentinel. Fully human and unfettered by the need to hide their most basic natures.

What they could get away with, they no doubt would.

She slid back into the car and rummaged for the nearest pack—and then rummaged within it, her hand closing around the crosshatched surface of a cool metal grip. But after she withdrew the pistol, she rested it beside her, one foot on the ground and the other on the running board, propped against the seat and waiting.

If anyone noticed, they gave no sign of it.

Ian was done waiting. He turned back to the yard without completely turning from the men, holding his hands out just a little, one higher than the other but the blood no longer dripping at all. *Searching.* As if he'd extended all his senses, and not just the invisible awareness that Ana had never quite fathomed. The uniquely Sentinel perception of the world.

"Hey," said the palest man, apparently also no stranger. "*Hey.* He's gonna—"

They moved as one—but only a single step. Ana straightened, both feet on the ground...a perfect line between her position and the three men, right through the triangle of space separating the curve of the metal door and the car body, the gun at her side.

They still failed to notice her. They stopped because Ian turned back on them, teeth slightly bared. Not in a way that looked dramatic or faked, but an entirely natural, completely effective threat.

If they had guns, they didn't reach for them.

*The Core would have guns out already.* The Sentinels, she thought, would respond as Ian had—and would respond *to* him.

That meant these men were from the third party. The unknown, inviting themselves into this conflict.

"People are dying in there," Ian said, his eyes dilated to darkness and revealing the *wild.* "You must know that. *Your friend* is dying." Not quite complete thoughts, distracted by the amulets as he was. "I can help them."

"You've done enough." The big man stood with fists clenched, muscles bunching, his restraint writ large across his body. "If it weren't for your kind—"

"Really?" Ian snapped. "You want to go there? Because I know who you are. And if it wasn't for your interference in the Sacramentos, this might not have happened at all!"

*Yes. The third party.* Ian believed it, too.

The big man laughed. "Nice," he said. "We wouldn't even exist if it wasn't for you and your counterparts."

"That's what our *counterparts* said two thousand years ago, and look where it's taken them."

Ana pressed a hand over her mouth at the truth of his remark. It smelled of gun oil and powder, sharp scents that only reminded her how the weapon had already been used this day.

By her own people.

The ones who'd begun just as Ian said, but who now seemed able to justify far more than monitoring the Sentinels and stopping their bad behavior. Who now simply persecuted them.

As these men would inflict themselves on her. On Ian, as he strove to save lives.

Ian bit off a curse. "I don't have time for this. Either come and get me or leave me alone." He turned back to the yard. Searching, as she'd known he would, for the working that threatened his friends. Or that had already killed them all.

Of course, the interlopers didn't leave him alone.

But they didn't attack all at once, either, and even Ana knew that to be a mistake. The middle man, the one with Middle East coloring and second largest in size, broke first.

She jerked the gun up, realizing then how little use it was. She could never bring herself to shoot a man in cold blood, and she wasn't good enough to hit them without hitting Ian. Not cold enough to do it, even knowing Ian would most likely survive.

He'd been hurt enough at the hands of her own.

But Ian didn't need her help. He was ready—he was waiting. And injured or not, he was so fast that Ana barely followed what happened as he moved—ducking under the man's attack, rolling in behind to box his ears, kicking his knee away and landing on his chest, just barely pulling a mortal blow to the neck.

As leopard, that blow had torn out the side of a man's throat. As human, even pulled, it left the man gasping for air, a bruise rising around critical blood flow.

Ian crouched beside the man, ruffled but with a stillness that Ana had come to understand presaged a preternatural alertness. *Ready to move.*

"Ana," he said, not looking at her, "tuck the gun away and see if there are extra cuffs in that car. And an ice pack in the first aid kit. These men will wait quietly for the moment, if they want their friend seen to."

Ana straightened, startled; the men seemed to see her only for the first time.

Ian had known about the gun all along, for all that he hadn't even seemed to notice. And he'd made sure the men knew about the gun, too, now that he'd asked her to come out in the open.

She tucked the weapon into her back waistband and did as he asked, quickly scaring up a set of restraint cables and the vehicle's first aid kit. She gave the two men a wary glance on the way by, going all the way around the SUV so she could approach Ian from along the wall.

"Ice his neck," Ian said, moving away once she got there, taking the restraints with him. "And sit on him."

Ana did just that, taking Ian literally as she was meant to. He whipped the restraints into place, threading them through the man's belt to keep his hands pinned there, and stood aside, looking at the men from beneath his lowered brow—a gaze that only underscored what Ian was. What he could do.

What he *would* do.

He shifted his shoulder, the single evidence of discomfort from his arm, and spoke to them in inexorable tones. "Now leave me alone, so I can try to save some lives. Or else come at me now and get it over with. Because if I have to come at you, I'm going to do it as fast as I can, and at least one of you is never getting up again."

Ana believed him. She thought the men believed him, too. They exchanged a look, took a step back...

A single step.

Early morning along a scarce-used road, and they stood in a standoff. One man dying in the yard, the Sentinels within and Ian at the end of his patience. No longer willing to coddle them along, or spare them from what he intended.

Ana drew a sharp breath as his gaze went inward, recognizing the nascent flicker of energy and light that came with that focus. She glanced along the road in alarm, but quickly realized that of course Ian had already checked and knew the area was clear.

For the moment.

By then the energy had blossomed into full light, crackling strobes that lashed and tangled, snapping out to touch Ana. She flinched and cried out—but only for that first instant.

For that touch had been soft. It had been a mere whisper of light and presence, and it left her arm tingling with an unexpected pleasure as Ian emerged.

*Leopard.*

The men bit off curses and stepped back—not so much flight as strategic retreat, repositioning to support each other and reaching for the weapons they'd not yet employed.

Ana lifted her gun, sure enough of her aim at this range so she didn't need to fake her confidence. "You'll want to drop those," she said, and of all the choices she'd made recently, of all the confusion she'd faced with them, this one left her no qualms. Protecting Ian from those who would do him harm simply because they felt entitled to interfere.

Not so different from the way Lerche had behaved. Or from the other things the Core at large had done, things they never revealed to those such as Ana.

The men hesitated on dropping their guns, of course. Enough so that Ian lowered his head, crouching slightly.

One leap and he'd be on them.

"Over here, by the wall," Ana told them. "And then you sit down." When they still hesitated, she felt her patience snap. "Quit being such babies. You came, you stuck your noses in and it isn't working out. Deal with it! We don't care if you walk away in the end—we only want to be left alone."

Not so different from the sentiments Ian had expressed about the Core.

A car turned onto the lane, moving without haste, its tires crunching slowly over the scattered gravel.

"Ian," Ana said. But of course he'd noticed it. A swift blur of movement and he crouched low to the ground near the gate, his tail still, his body flattened behind the clump of towering hollyhocks.

The men moved, too, angling themselves off the bumper of the SUV and using their considerable size to block any casual view of Ana and the man she sat on. *Of course*, she realized. They didn't want outside interference any more than the Core or Sentinels did. They wanted to enact their vigilante excesses without the inconvenience of legal oversight.

The car curved slowly out of sight, obscured by the high wall of the adjoining property.

The men darted forward at Ana, moving before Ian did.

Or thinking they had.

He was a streak of pale beauty and flowing tail, knocking Ana aside and bounding to intervene. His paws flashed and Ana cried out, having seen more violence in this single day than she'd seen in her entire life. One man went down beneath the thrusting impact of his attack, grunting hard and fighting back—as if there was anything to fight. Ian had already doubled back on himself to leap at the man who hesitated on the trigger of his gun, unable to fire without hitting his buddy.

Down they went, and this time the victim fought back, slamming his gun against the side of Ian's head. *Hurting him.*

"Stop it!" Ana screamed, not knowing if she spoke to Ian or to the men he'd attacked. *"Stop it!"*

She hadn't meant for the gun to go off. She screamed when it did—startled at the sound and the recoil, horrified that she could have pulled the trigger without meaning to…relieved as dirt chipped up in response. *Only the road…*

The men froze. Ian froze, too—but just for the merest instant before he bounded away, suddenly back beside the wall with his whiskers lifted in a silent snarl and no weakness to be seen.

Ana leaped up to stomp on the fallen gunman's hand with both feet, stumbling back when he shouted in pain and then dashing forward just long enough to wrench the weapon away from fingers that no longer quite held it.

The man was too busy realizing himself still alive to fight over the piece. And Ana was too staggered to search for the other gun. For Ian had pounced, and he'd taken them down, but he'd left no blood in his wake. She could still feel the terror where his fur had brushed her on the way past, but...

No blood. No *claws*.

More civilized than they were. Than *all* of them. Maybe even more civilized than Ana herself—having the power, wielding it and walking away.

Ana had pulled the trigger.

A strained new voice broke their silence. "Ian!"

For all the effort behind that voice, it barely carried out of the yard—but it still got everyone's instant attention.

Shea sat on his knees in the doorway of the retreat, slumped against the door frame, scowling hard. "For fuck's sake," he said. "Get away from the fucking yard. There's a silent—"

Ana ran up to the wall—but didn't touch it. Didn't get nearly close enough for that. "Are you all right? What about the others?"

Shea laughed, a harsh sound. "Fuck, no, we're not all right. Never saw it coming. Lyn's down hard... Jet, I dunno... Ruger's trying. Got shields up then, but... too late. Can't hold them much longer. No idea about this poor fuck." He gestured at the prone figure in the yard. Then he tipped his head and looked directly at

Ana across the distance, his gaze a shock of accusation. "Did you do this?"

Ana recoiled. "No!"

Shea slumped a little farther, straightening with obvious effort. "Just stay away," he said, sounding weary. "We never saw it coming. Fucking silents...can't be found. Maybe Lyn, but she's..." He glanced over his shoulder and didn't finish the thought. Didn't have to.

Not nearly far enough away, the snow leopard growled.

No, not growled. Just a sound in his throat. Inquiring.

Ana stood suddenly straighter. "We can find them!" she said. "Ian can do it! He's got them figured out!"

Shea lifted the head that had started to droop. "Has he, now? Irony, that. Because all his isolation gear is in the house, isn't it?"

Ana had no idea what that meant, in particular. But she knew that Ian had had hope and intent, and she clung to that. "We'll find them," she told Shea. "You just hang on. All of you!"

Shea didn't respond, slumped where he was, and Ana realized he'd passed out. She bit her lip, looking back over her shoulder to the two men just now climbing to their feet. They looked stunned, their faces red from the blows they'd taken, a few scratches trickling blood.

She readjusted her grip on the gun she'd never dropped. "Just leave us alone," she said. "We're trying to save them. To save your friend, too, if we can."

The one man cradled his hand. The other had relocated the loose gun, but held it low...and then he raised both hands slightly in capitulation. He slowly returned the gun to the flat holster inside his waistband, nodding at her clenched grip on her own weapon. "Nothing as dangerous as a gun in the hands of someone with a trigger finger like yours."

That, she thought, was likely true.

"But watch yourself," the other man said. "Because we're sure as hell going to be keeping track."

But Ian had already moved on, pacing to the corner of the yard with a stalking grace even as the wounded leg gave way slightly beneath him. He crouched to let another car pass by and lingered there, his ears canted back in focus.

After a moment he just barely turned the corner, hesitating there, and then returned to his original spot, reaching a large paw to the adobe wall and extruding claws to leave the most deliberate of marks.

*Triangulation.* Just as he would have done with the amulet in her shoulder, if they hadn't found it through dead reckoning.

Then he paced on down the wall, paralleling the extended driveway. It split to enter the retreat property while the other branch continued to the undeveloped property beyond; he stayed with the retreat fence line, finishing the section of latilla fencing and moving onward to the idiosyncratic corner of tall adobe. Ana followed at a distance, pausing when he did and moving on as he did, and altogether too painfully aware that the interlopers trailed her once they'd dragged their stunned friend behind the SUV where he wouldn't draw attention. Their low conversation revealed that the man was coming back to himself—that they felt he would be back in the game soon enough.

Also not reassuring.

But then, here she was following in the wake of a man no longer human, a beast the likes of which she'd always been warned against. She'd defied her direct superior, she'd contributed to the death of her fellow Core members, and Nick Carter was on his way. So she was about to find herself a captive of either the Southwest Brevis Consul himself, or the unknown organization that wanted to do away with them all. Unless she escaped, in which case the Core would no doubt hunt her down.

*Reassuring* wasn't even an option.

# *Chapter 17*

Ian padded unevenly along the fence line. He had the taste of this particular working, now—knew it to be destructive and indiscriminate, a powerful thing that would simply suck the life out of anything within its bounds. He narrowed his focus, searching swiftly—sending energy out, waiting for the response, moving onward to triangulate.

He'd found two amulets so far, both at the eastern corners of the enclosed property. He very much expected to find two more at the western corners, once he'd circumvented the adjoining property along that side. And though his heart beat hard and fast with fear for the Sentinels trapped inside, he felt the thrill of the moment, too. At the potential unfolding before him.

Because anyone skilled at sending and receiving subtle energies could be trained to perform this kind of search. It wouldn't take Ian's skill; it wouldn't take Lyn's talent. It wouldn't even take an AmTech team.

*Got you*, he thought at the Core. *Got you good and hard.* The silent amulet code was broken; the amulets themselves would no longer be the ever-looming threat they'd become.

It was a short-lived thrill. Finding today's amulets

didn't come close to disabling them. The greater work was yet to be done.

And it was a thrill diminished by Ana's expression as he'd charged past to defend her on the road—her unthinking terror at the brush of his fur.

Not to mention a thrill diminished by the presence of the two men still following behind along with Ana, making no attempt to interfere. *Yet.* Ian wasn't sure if they'd been convinced, scared or simply bided their time.

He skirted the back of the enclosed area, moving swiftly now in spite of his limp—the third amulet already targeted and pinging back its sly stench at his ongoing outreach. To the south, behind the house, lay a patch of undeveloped land, grown up in junipers and tall high prairie grasses—here, the two men waited, keeping their distance and still keeping their eyes on Ian. One of them snapped a phone closed and slipped it away; Ian could only hope that if it was a call for reinforcements, they'd be some time in getting here.

Two outbuildings snugged up against the high section of adobe wall at the corner, and then the wall fell away to nothing more than a token rail fence. At the juncture of the adobe and rail, dark metal gleamed.

*The third corner.* Ian knew where he'd find the final amulet—off in the clumpy weeds in the other back corner of the property, just inside this same rail fence.

It told him everything he needed to know.

He might not be able to disengage the working, and he might not have his isolation equipment, but with a boundary-enclosed working like this one, the fastest solution was simply to bring all the amulets together and let them run down together.

*Simple.* He growled softly to himself. Not so simple

at all, when there was no safe way to touch the things or to move them. Without nullifying tools, the amulet would conduct through any buffer—metal faster than wood, wood faster than rubber.

He crouched outside the fence, tail flicking. A shovel from the shed might do it, if he moved quickly. Start at the far corner, scoop up the diminutive amulet, run counterclockwise from around the corners and dump all the amulets with the one in the front west corner, leaving them until they could be dealt with. They might even run out quickly. The Core couldn't afford to leave an undiscriminating working of this magnitude lying around.

Ana moved up beside him, looking over the fence with him—surprising him with her nearness. Ian slid a paw under the lowest rail, pointing it at the amulet. It took all his control to resist cat impulse—the slap of a stunning paw, the flick of small prey into the weeds—

*A car on gravel. Someone comes.* His tidy ears snapped forward—and then flat. A car on the lane was nothing; a car coming up the long drive was very much something. *Nick, I told you to hang back.*

But it wasn't Nick.

It was a gleaming high-end SUV, a thing with more luxury than utility. And black, here where the strong sun made such things a constant folly. Not a Sentinel vehicle at all.

Ana made an uneasy sound. "Ian..."

The SUV came on with an inconsiderate speed, spitting gravel against the latilla fence and slewing slightly around the bend. Even through the darkened windows, Ian recognized the occupants—Budian behind the wheel and Lerche in the passenger seat.

No time to become the human and grab a shovel; no

time to gather amulets. Ian faced the vehicle with his ears slanted back and his tail flicking into cold anger, crouching just enough to make his intentions plain—he could and would take them down at the first sign of threat.

No matter that the Core would simply use such an incident to decry his lack of humanity.

Lerche disembarked with stiff discomfort, his arm in a snug sling. He had no amulets, silent or otherwise. A quick check revealed that he—and Budian and the car—were entirely clean.

Lerche had learned that much, it seemed.

It meant only they'd have other weapons to hand. Budian hadn't yet done more than open his door, and it was to him that Ian looked for trouble.

Lerche held out his good hand to Ana. "Come, my dear. Time for you to return home."

Ana didn't move. "You didn't come here for me. I don't matter that much."

"It's true, I'm also here to clean up this mess before the *drozhar* arrives." Lerche let his hand drop. "But you're also wrong again, I'm afraid. It matters very much to me what happens to you. And how."

Ana's voice came stronger. "Only because if someone's going to hurt me—to *kill* me—you think it should be you."

Lerche smiled. The smug cruelty behind it made Ian want to slap the expression right off his face, claws extended and sharp. He quivered with the effort of holding his place, whiskers bristling and a growl growing in his throat.

Lerche said, "You are exactly correct, my dear—you personally matter to me not at all. But no one else has the

right to touch what's mine. You should have considered
that before you allowed yourself to care for this Sentinel. You sealed his fate with your actions."

Ana made a noise that might have been taken from
Ian's leopard. "I don't *care* for him," she said, moving
closer than Ian had ever expected of her.

Not while he was leopard. *Beast.*

Ana rested a startling hand behind one leopard ear,
her fingers sinking into deep, plush fur. "I don't care for
him," she repeated. "I *love* him."

The peace of her touch flowed through him, open in a
way he hadn't yet felt. More than just calming, but full of
*Ana.* Full of everything that Ian needed in that moment.

He moved, putting himself between Lerche and
Ana—perfectly aware of her trembling, and even more
aware of the fact that she leaned into him instead of
away from him.

Lerche's face darkened. "Maybe you think you do,"
he said. With his restless motion came the scent of gun
oil. "Had we more time, I would show you the error of
those ways. But the *drozhar* is coming, and I expect the
Tucson Sentinels are, too."

Budian said something from inside the car, too muffled for even Ian's keen ears to catch. Lerche looked
sharply over his shoulder. "Ah," he said. "Already here,
I see. Well, we should get on with it, then. Before the
beasts work up their nerve."

"They're not Sentinel." Ana's voice had an angry edge
pushing behind its tremulous note. "Did you and the
others think you could keep pushing and attacking and
hurting people without drawing attention? Because if
you did, you were wrong. You were wrong about everything, and you were really, *really* wrong about me! I'm

not yours, I'm *mine*. And if I want to give everything of myself to Ian, I'll do it."

"By all means," Lerche said, straightening the edge of his sling, hand lingering there—and then reaching within. "Just as I do what you've forced me to do."

Such a perfect place to secure a gun, that sling.

Ian gave Lerche only enough time to dip his hand into the sling before he leaped—a single reaching bound, a hard impact—

Ian jerked as the gun discharged inside the sling. Ian sprang away, crouching with lashing tail and flattened ears, while Budian scuffled with someone on the other side of the vehicle.

Lerche looked down at himself, the gun in his hand now. The sling obscured his torso, but the tang of blood in the air and the stunned look on Lerche's face said enough. He'd been hit, and hit badly. And he knew it.

When he raised his eyes, he pinned his gaze on Ana. "That's a shame," he said, his voice strained. "But you're still mine."

Ana stood straight and tall—not very tall at that, and not very large, but with a fresh certainty in her voice. "No," she said. "I'm not."

A new car turned into the driveway, large tires on the gravel—and another, not making quite as much noise. Budian, now caught up between the two lingering interlopers, nonetheless had line of sight along the curve of the drive. "The *drozhar*," he said, his voice pitched low to carry. "And more of *their* people."

*Nick, dammit! I told you to stay away—*

Not that he'd truly expected it to happen.

But he hadn't expected the mad look that crossed

Lerche's face, the sudden hard gleam in his eye as a
surge of blood soaked through his suit.

He hadn't expected the man to charge forward—at
*Ana*.

Ian leaped for him, too late—catching the back of
his shoe, tearing out the back leg of Lerche's trousers.
And Lerche bowled into Ana, knocking her against the
rail fence, flipping her over it to land hard on the dried
grass of packed ground.

*Inside the amulet perimeter.*

"No one moves!" bellowed one of the interlopers, a
man who no doubt now had Budian's gun. Nick's voice
responded with calm authority, words unintelligible past
the roar in Ian's head, the sudden chaos of fear and understanding and complete and utter absence of *Ana* in
his senses. His awareness narrowed down to that one
single view—her attempts to scramble out from beneath
Lerche, her cry of fear as Lerche's body weighed her
down and the amulet working sank into her, weaken-
ing her just that fast.

"Ian!" she cried, hardly more than a hoarse, whispering shout, "I can't—"

*The amulet.* It gleamed newly exposed beneath the
tangle of the fence.

*No shovel, no tech gear, no options.*

Ian pounced, scooping the thing up with a flick of his
paw—feeling the instant drain of direct contact, his paw
burning with a cold fire that ran along all the small bones
to his wrist, hooks already setting into his forearm. The
amulet settled between his toe pads and his heel pad and
he closed his paw around it, tail lashing terribly as his
whiskers drew back in a silent, terrible snarl.

He meant to carry it to the other corner and instantly

knew he couldn't. He flipped his paw, clumsy now, and the amulet tumbled through sunlight toward the other back corner—redrawing the boundary and freeing Ana as it disappeared into the dry grass.

*Not too late. Please, not too late!*

But the house still lay within the field, there where Shea had worked so hard to shield his friends and Ruger had done his best to fortify them. *Not too late! Please, not too late!*

Ian pounced on the amulet, defying the heaviness of his legs and giving the thing an expert flick into the far corner—redrawing the amulet boundary once more, this time to cut diagonally through the house. *No way to tell where they are in that house...*

He fell to a brief crouch, panting heavily and drawing on every bit of what he was. Drawing on what Ana had taught him about quieting his thoughts to send out the finest, purest pulse of energy.

It bounced back at him from right beside the first one—and once he'd found that again, he quickly saw its gleam, an uneven chunk of slightly darker metal.

Leaden legs took him there, his pounce still quicksilver fast but taking the last of such speed from him. He scooped up both amulets in one swipe—tumbling back into the human as he rolled into the rough adobe of the far wall. Only then did he hear Nick's astonished commands to *stop the hell what you're doing!* and Ana's weaker cry of dismay— *"Ian, no! Ian!"*

And yet behind those protests lay the anguish of what Ian already knew.

Without this, his friends would die.

If they hadn't already.

He staggered upright and along the wall, his gaze focused on the spot where the interior courtyard met the wall—as far as he could go, and far enough so the amulet field would cut only across the very front corner of the house. The man in the front yard might yet lay within that brutally damaging field, but Shea would be free of it.

The ground met Ian's face with bruising force; he couldn't remember falling. Back to his feet, his vision tunneled to include only the courtyard's wrought-iron fence…falling…back to his feet again with one unfeeling foot clomping down in front of the other, his arm turned to stone and a shaft of volcanic cold making its way down the long bones of his arm to his shoulder.

*"Ian."* Nick's voice came just behind him—full of understanding and full of inexorable command. "It's far enough. *Enough*, Ian."

Another step and he'd fall against the wrought-iron bars, wavering so uncertainly before him. Ian held out his hand and stared stupidly at it, willing it to open.

*Dead dull flesh, nothing of his own.*

Nick moved in beside him, reaching for the hand— Ian turned on him, snarling him off. Impotent threat if Nick chose to ignore it.

"Ian!" Nick snapped. "You know better. *I can stop it!*"

Because Nick could. Nick, among them all, had the knack of focusing down on an amulet to burn it out in a flash. But it was a knack the Core knew nothing of and could never know of.

Supposing the working didn't leave Nick instantly incapable of any such thing.

Ian had no words. He had only the snarl, the lift of his free hand in warning, fingers lifted to reflect the dagger-tipped spread of the paw beneath.

"Then *get rid of it*!" Alpha fury underlined the snarl in Nick's own voice.

*Volcanic cold, creeping through his shoulder, along his collarbone and tracing his ribs, reaching for his spine...*

Ian turned his threatening fingers on his own hand, prying at deadened, clutching flesh. Something snapped and he didn't feel it, though Nick made a grinding sound of horrified dismay. Another snap and Ian clumsily turned his hand, the first spark of pain radiating down his spine as he shook his wrist to dislodge the amulets from his grasp.

A single dull pebble hit the ground, bouncing into the mowed scruff.

Ana's voice cut through the roar of amulet-dulled senses—weak but coming closer, full of horror. *"Ian!"*

"No!" Nick grunted with impact, and then snapped a curse over the ensuing sounds of struggle. "Dammit, don't—!"

But Ana's hand landed on his back—ever so briefly, a stunning infusion of light and emotion and love before Nick wrenched her away.

Ian sucked in a mighty breath and somehow managed to drop the last amulet from the crease of his palm. But a final lingering shard of fire lanced along his spine, arching him back and twisting him from agony down into darkness, leaving him only the final echo of Ana's scream.

Ana blinked her eyes open to bright New Mexico sky. The sun tingled against her face and stubby dead grass poking through the back of her shirt, and she rolled over just enough to push up on one arm.

"Ana, I presume." The man crouching before gestured impatiently to those outside her view, commanding them to come on.

He wore such an intensity about himself, such obvious *other*, that Ana gasped and flinched away from him—from his pale green eyes and black hair rimmed with hoarfrosted silver and from the very palpable effort to restrain all of it to human expectations.

He didn't seem to notice her recoil. "You fainted. Be still. There's a lot going on, and if I have to manage *you*, someone else is likely to die. Maybe even Ian."

Ana could only gape at him—and realize instantly that his hard, no-nonsense words were ones she could trust. *Nick Carter. Brevis consul.*

And no wonder.

"Mariska, the house!" Nick said, a command snapped across the yard to those who had come with him. "Report! Maks, get this place shielded—and no more of our visitors leave!"

Meaning someone had already gone. Ana lifted her head to discern who remained, but there were too many figures in motion, and she wasn't nearly steady enough to sort it all out.

She looked for Ian instead.

Nick's attention snapped back to her. "I told you—"

"I'm not going anywhere!" But she was tired of taking orders from those who hadn't earned the right to give them, and she was tired of being afraid. And Ian...

Sprawled beside her, his body limp but still reflecting that final wrenching cry before he'd collapsed. It hurt so much to look at his mangled hand, a thing of gray flesh and unnatural angles. Ana slung a defiant look in Nick Carter's direction and crawled the few feet to reach Ian, her own limbs dull and heavy in the wake of even brief exposure to the amulets.

Ian had *held* them. *Carried* them.

She rested a hand on his shoulder, finding it cold. Rested her forehead beside his hand, trembling there. Reaching out to him in the way she'd learned and finding no sense of a presence in return, no impression that he heard her. "Ian," she said, shaking him ever so slightly, and then more insistently. "Come out of there and follow me!"

A woman's voice called from the house. "Alive! Nick, they're alive—all of them! But they're weak as hell— Joe, get your ass in here!"

Nick jabbed a short gesture at the house. "Do it," he said, voice raised for the distance. "Stabilize them and get back out here."

"Healer?" Ana said, watching in dismay as a big man in a flannel shirt and jeans broke away from the cars and ran to the house, hopping over the fence to reach the gate the woman Mariska had unlocked. "But Ian—"

"Not our healer," Nick said shortly. "Someone who can give them back some of the energies they lost." He lifted his chin to indicate the approach of someone from behind, and Ana twisted to find a slender woman with large eyes and an uncertain demeanor, a gear bag slung over one shoulder. "Katie, see what you can do for Ian until Joe gets back out here."

As Katie went to work, Mariska jogged up to them— short and sturdy and athletic, her deep complexion full of brown tones and her eyes rimmed with darker coloration, her hair darkest black and pulled back into a short French braid. "Jet's as good as any of them," she said, her mouth thin with strain. As she looked back to the house, her silhouette showed the slight rounding of early pregnancy. "Ruger is pretty rugged, and so is Shea. They tried so hard to protect everyone. Fernie... I really don't know. She and the others had been through a lot before the Core set off this particular bomb."

"Fernie!" Ana said in dismay.

Mariska looked at her with a ferocity that sent Ana flinching away. Another field Sentinel, this one, and furious to boot. "Yes," the woman snapped. "*Imagine.* We're people, just like you. Ruger is mine, and if anything happens to him, I will never stop coming for you. *Never.*"

"Mariska," Nick said, but his tight voice spoke volumes, and he caught Ana's gaze with those pale green eyes. "We'll figure out Ana's story before we condemn her."

"And if Jet—"

"She won't!" Nick snapped. "Lyn is in there, too—Joe will find a way to give back what they've lost until Katie can figure out—"

But Katie interrupted him in turn, her voice grimmest grim. "I'm nowhere near Ruger's league with this stuff," she said. "I don't know if I can reverse whatever this working did. I don't even know *what* it did."

Words fell from Ana's mouth. "Then let me help."

Nick regarded her with narrowed eyes. "How?"

Ana lifted her gaze to the clump of figures milling by the cars. If Budian had been correct, one of those men was the region's most recent *drozhar*. Budian would know what the working was...and the *drozhar* could command him to talk.

"I know how they think," she said. "I know how to talk to them. I can learn what we need. Just don't—"

she faltered, looking down on Ian; it seemed to her that even in these last moments, his color had worsened, her sense of him diminishing. "Please. Don't let him die."

Katie had unzipped the gear bag, digging efficiently into pockets to pull out vials and shake them vigorously; already she unscrewed the top of one to withdraw its full eyedropper. "It's not my intent," she said. "But I need a clue, and I need it fast."

"Mariska," Nick said. "Go with her. Don't let them intimidate her." As if he somehow already understood that they would.

Mariska bared her teeth. "No fears."

But the Ana who could be manipulated by the need to belong to these people no longer existed. She'd already lost everything she'd hoped to have with them... and she'd already gained so, so much more in return. She would get the information they needed, and she'd get it fast.

She gave Ian's shoulder a final squeeze and climbed unsteadily to her feet, grateful for Mariska's helping hand. "Oh," she said, remembering her promise. "Ian... he told me to make sure you knew. He figured out how to find the silents. I know how he does it. If it comes to that... I can explain."

Nick stood to look down on her. "If they find out you just told me that—"

"Oh, yes," Ana said. "They'll kill me. But then... what's new? I'll get what we need to know—I can do it." The *drozhar* would have to learn about Lerche—his activities, how he'd compromised them, how the Core could position themselves to blame the man and minimize his damage. Budian could tell him nothing without damning himself—but Ana could. She had exactly what she needed to get what the Sentinels required. "And then you help Ian. Help the others."

"You get it, and I will," Katie promised fiercely—but she, too, glanced over her shoulder at the detained *drozhar* and his evident temper.

"They can't hurt me anymore," Ana said—and then laughed a little with the true understanding of it—of her freedom to hand. "And they can't have me anymore. Besides, I choose my own people." She looked down at Ian, crouching to cup his face one last time before facing all her fears at once. *Defeating them.* Ian Scott, dark lashes shadowing his cheek, silvered hair in charming disarray, lean strength captured by injury but the *other*...

The *other* still lingered there, making him everything that he was. *Snow leopard. Human. Lover.*

*Hers.*

# *Epilogue*

Ian beat a quick drum tattoo against the standing height worktable in his home lab—one of a series of such tables, with a single token chair tucked away beneath stacked gear. Steinman rolled out over the speakers, all drama and operatic rock, as Ian bounced between scowling at an amulet case design and his ongoing text chat, where two of his AmTechs struggled with a streamlined approach to teach the new silents detection method across the whole of Southwest Brevis.

Or at least, to those who had even the faintest ability to manage it.

Start with bouncing off something loud, he typed.

Although in actuality, the message read Strt w smthng looud, because even fingers raised on a keyboard couldn't type well when encased with plaster. Or whatever they'd used in this particular cast.

It turned out that bones broken in the thrall of that particular deadly working didn't heal any faster than anyone else's. Slower, in fact.

But he was alive.

Ana was alive.

Fernie was alive, and Ian's friends were alive, if all just now recovered these weeks later. Katie had been filling in for Ruger until recently, augmented by Joe

Ryan. The man's deft skill with undefined earth energies allowed him to replace—slowly, carefully—what the working had stolen.

Joe had had plenty of incentive. Along with Ruger, Joe's partner Lyn had been nearly consumed by the working.

But now Lyn was back at work, Ruger was splitting his hours between brevis and preparing for fatherhood, Shea was out shielding the unwary, and Jet was off visiting her former pack. Only the very human interloper who'd stumbled into the working was just as dead as everyone had thought him to be.

His three partners had left quite smartly during the immediate aftermath of the convergence of the three factions. It had been Nick's decision, Ian gathered, to let them go. There'd been enough to deal with already, between the injured, their shortage of manpower...and the Core's regional prince, the *drozhar*, to manage.

The text pinged back at him. Start with something loud, what?

Gahhh. Ian typed, intro thm to prss dammt procss w big honkn loud aml dammt am.;/ fck!

Let them chew on that for a while. He was done typing. Such as it had been. He returned his attention to the work case design, and most importantly, to the swatches of buffering material on one workbench. Experiments to do, oh, yes. He turned up the music.

A draft of moving air signaled invasion of his Am-Tech turf.

*Ana*. She stood in the door, still dressed for what passed as winter in Tucson, her arms crossed and a wincing amusement on her face.

Ian scooped up the sound system remote and hit the mute button. "Hey," he said. "Soundproofing!"

"The house still vibrates after a certain point," she said drily, tugging off her gloves and unzipping her jacket.

Hmm. Maybe so.

"Anyway, I wanted you to know I was home." She only entered the workroom by a few feet, always respectful of this space.

Not that she didn't have good reason. The activity here was, on some days, the equivalent of defusing bombs in the basement.

The text screen bleated a plaintive request for clarity. Ian dropped out of the chat with a click of the mouse and put his back to the worktable, propping his casted hand on the forearm of the other. It was as close as he could get to crossing his own arms. "How'd it go?"

She waved a dismissive hand. "The Core is…the Core. They're trying to pretend they're not appalled that Southwest's new liaison is a woman."

"One with tainted blood at that," Ian said, his expression a dramatic nonverbal of *Oh! The horror!* "So basically, still stalling."

"It's okay," Ana said. "They're also still talking."

"Nick knew what he had with you," Ian told her. "He's like that."

A new liaison. A new *perspective.*

That perspective was the reason Nick hadn't hesitated to move Ian to this home workspace once Ana had walked into his brevis lab and said, "No wonder!" And she'd turned on Nick and said, "How can you expect him to think in this space? It's full of everything and everyone! He's already got enough going on in that head of his."

Nick had sent a stunned look to Ian—still in a wheelchair at that point, still under close care at brevis where doctors combined conventional skills with Sentinel needs and healing—and Ian had only shrugged. He'd learned to trust Ana's eyes. Especially when it came to the things to which he'd long inured himself. He was a snow leopard with an overactive mind and never enough quiet, and it hadn't truly occurred to him that things could work any other way.

"You people have time to secure and equip that gaping workroom in his basement before he gets out of your private little hospital," she'd said, hands on hips. "Why don't you?"

So they had, and she'd moved in to make sure it was done right—and Ian's echoing bachelor pad slowly showed increasing signs of actual inhabitation. A few more pieces of furniture, a small collection of cooking utensils, actual throw pillows on the couch...

She'd made herself at home. She'd made it into *their* home, and more so every day. Not with any great declaration, because they'd already done that, each in their own way. But because she belonged there.

"That's an interesting smile," she told him. Daylight LED lighting revealed every bit of her in blossoming health—a little more curve to her hips, less strain in her face. And no bruises at all.

"Just thinking," he said, though he knew he wouldn't get away without explaining, and there—she'd already cocked a brow at him. "About changes."

He hadn't meant for that alarm to cross her face. "You're feeling okay?"

"Fine," he said. "Totally fine." And then, because they both knew better, he added, "Okay, still taking naps. But it's getting better. And there's nothing wrong with a good nap."

"Why, no," she said, straightening. She slipped off the jacket, tucking it over her arm, and went straight for her top blouse button. Ian found himself coming to all kinds of attention.

One button. Two. "Nothing wrong with a good nap at all," Ana said, glancing at him with an innocence that Ian didn't trust. Not for one moment. "In fact, I think I might just take one."

"Ana," he said, giving it a bit of the leopard.

Ana looked at him over her shoulder as she turned away, heading for the stairs that bypassed the main house and led directly to the second-story bedroom. "I thought you might want to follow along, see where it goes."

Ian turned off the collection of monitors with a flip of a switch and the light banks with the flip of another, putting him not very far behind Ana as she ascended the stairs. "Ohhh, yes," he murmured. "Entirely my choice."

And Ana laughed softly, and led him into the rest of their lives.

\* \* \* \* \*

**Denise Lynn** is an award-winning author who lives in the USA with her husband, son and numerous four-legged "kids." Between the pages of romance novels she has traveled to lands and times filled with brave knights, courageous ladies and never-ending love. Now she can share with others her dream of telling tales of adventure and romance. You can write to her at PO Box 17, Monclova, OH 43542, USA, or visit her website, denise-lynn.com.

### Books by Denise Lynn

### Harlequin Nocturne

*Dragon's Lair*
*Dragon's Curse*
*Dragon's Promise*

### Harlequin Historical

*Falcon's Desire*
*Falcon's Honor*
*Falcon's Love*
*Falcon's Heart*
*Commanded to His Bed*
*Bedded by Her Lord*
*Hallowe'en Husbands*
*Bedded by the Warrior*
*Pregnant by the Warrior*
*The Warrior's Winter Bride*

Visit the Author Profile page
at Harlequin.com for more titles.

# DRAGON'S PROMISE

## Denise Lynn

Braeden was for Brenda, Cameron for Cheryl…

And for my sister Sandy,
I grant you Sean, along with all his passion
and his magick. With much love, always.

# Prologue

*Ancient castle ruins on the east coast of Ireland—*
*October 3. Two years ago*

Candlelight flickered in the drafty cell, casting eerily
dancing shadows on the wall behind the altar. Pacing
before the altar, Nathan the Learned paused to stare into
the undulating flames, before gazing down into a crystal
bowl. The water filling the bowl had been blessed by the
light of a full moon to lend more power to his scrying.

He scried not for hints of what the future held, because he knew that once his deeds this night were completed, his future would be secure. Instead, he wanted
to see the past. Not just a hazy memory of days gone by,
but a clear reckoning of what had brought him to this
long-sought-after moment of greatness.

With one hand on the head of the naked, bound
woman kneeling at his feet, he waved the other over
the bowl. The water rippled outward from the center,
as if disturbed by a falling pebble.

A wavering image of a medieval castle appeared. *Mirabilus*. The medieval stronghold where it all began so
very long ago. The water stilled, permitting the reflection to become clearer. A cold breeze, not unlike the one

he'd felt that fateful night, brushed across his cheek. The shape of an amethyst dragon formed over the image of the castle. It wavered as if trying to take flight and then it cracked, splintering into a million pieces, just as it had that fateful night. He then saw himself as a child hiding within the darkness of a curtained alcove as the High Druid, his uncle Aelthed, killed his own brother—Nathan's father. The terror of the child flowed into the man he'd become, settling cold in his belly. He had vowed revenge that night and would soon taste the victory he'd craved for so long.

The image of childhood faded, permitting a new one to appear. Again Nathan saw himself, this time a man full grown, leaning over the High Druid Aelthed as he lay gasping his last breaths upon his bed. He cared not that the wizard suffered in his final moments. The man deserved whatever pain and agony plagued him—not just for killing Nathan's father, but for also seeing to it that he had been laid to rest in an unhallowed grave, unable to ever attain life after death. Worse, when the time had come for Nathan to be named Dragon Lord of Mirabilus, the honor had gone to another, along with the ancient family grimoire and the two remaining dragon pendants.

Nathan shook with unforgotten rage. Oh, yes, the wizard had paid dearly for those mistakes. As Aelthed's soul had sought escape from his withered body, Nathan had trapped it in a wooden puzzle box that locked with such an intricate, complicated set of moves no one would ever be able to free his soul. For nearly nine centuries, Aelthed's soul had remained imprisoned. And for most of those years, Nathan had kept the puzzle box close at hand, guarding it like a prized possession.

Until he'd dropped it while trying to escape death at the talons of a Drake's magical dragon when he'd tried to destroy the eldest Drake and his wife.

Now all the items he needed—the puzzle box, the pendants and the grimoire—were together under the protection of the current Dragon Lord. From what he could discern, the Drakes had been unable to break the spell holding the wizard's soul captive. So, just as he'd planned, Aelthed's spirit was still confined, waiting for Nathan to set him free.

Once again the image faded. This time it was replaced by the reflection of his son, pale and cold in death. Nathan screamed in agony and waved the recent, too painful image away.

Tapping the handle of the braided leather whip he held against his thigh, he seethed. A few years ago he'd nearly lost his own life to the current Dragon Lord. Sorely wounded, he'd nurtured his hatred and desire for power, using that dark energy to survive. Which was more than what could be said for his son. The Dragon Lord's twin had taken his sole remaining son—once again preventing him from reaching his goal.

He cursed the Dragon Lord and his family. They were the only obstacle in his way—the only thing that kept him from attaining supreme power.

For all these centuries, the Drakes had stood between him and his place as Hierophant, supreme ruler over all.

But no more.

This time he would gain possession of the Drake family grimoire, those accursed pendants and the ancient puzzle box—along with its spellbound occupant. Once all of the items were in his hands, he could finish the spell he'd worked on for centuries, and then the position of Hierophant would be his. And when he alone held supreme power, nothing and no one would ever again be able to repudiate his will.

Nathan laughed. And this time he wouldn't have to lift a finger to defeat the Drakes.

They thought themselves unreachable, hiding behind a specialized security system that made breaking in to Dragon's Lair undetected, impossible for anyone possessing more than human capabilities. And they were far too cautious, their sixth sense too well developed for him to be able to attack them away from their stronghold.

But he had another option at hand. He glanced at the woman kneeling on the stone floor before his altar. A necessary link. With her help, this time he would use a Drake to beat them.

Now that the full moon had finally risen, he was anxious to set his perfect plan into motion. He screamed at her, "Say the words!"

When she refused, he snarled and then raised his arm asking, "Do you enjoy the bite of pain?"

At her silence he flicked the whip in his hand, making it hiss and whistle as it snaked toward its victim. The crack echoed in the nearly empty chamber. The tips of the braided leather scored her naked back, adding yet another row of bloody lines to the pale flesh.

Her shoulders flinched, but she gave no other sign of giving in to the agony—yet.

Nathan narrowed his eyes and trembled with a surge of unbridled lust. This gypsy mage could give him many weeks of untold pleasure. Even after his rather ardent lovemaking last night, she was still lovely. The lingering traces of his touch on her luscious breasts and full hips only made her more desirable. He saw the bruises as his marks of ownership, and he ached to once again possess her.

*Not just yet. Soon.* His mind whispered for him to be patient, and Nathan drew in a long, shuddering breath.

First he needed the ancient curse against his enemies to be spoken. He had repeatedly tried activating the simple yet powerful curse himself and found only failure. He'd studied the curse's history over and over until discovering that it was not Druid. It was of Romani origin, and he was certain this beautiful gypsy mage possessed the magic to give the curse life. He'd cloaked himself in the allure of youth then seduced her with the promise of riches and whispered of nights filled with tender, fulfilling lovemaking.

But when she'd seen his true self, discovered his lies and the reason for the curse, she'd sworn to never say the words. Her reaction made him more certain she could bring the curse alive and one way or another, he would force her to do so.

Nathan dropped the whip at his feet and grabbed a handful of her thick, raven-hued hair. Tugging on it until the hairpins he'd used to secure the luxurious tresses atop her head and away from her back slipped free.

He slid his other hand along her neck, closing his fingers one by one tightly over her windpipe. "Do you seek death out of some misguided notion that it will save those I wish to harm?" He leaned down and whispered against her ear. "It will not work. If you refuse me again, I know another mage…another *gypsy* mage…one much younger than you who will be more than grateful to escape your fate."

The woman tensed beneath his touch, obviously realizing that he spoke of her younger sister.

"Perhaps we will try one more time." He relaxed his hold around her neck slightly.

She swallowed hard and then nodded.

He released her and stepped back to retrieve the whip and send it sailing to snap loud on the floor beside her. "Say the words."

When she bowed her head and began to whisper, Nathan lashed his weapon once again across her back, shouting, "Louder, so I can hear you!"

"Not a dragon born—" she paused, gasping as if the words burned her throat more than the lashes across her flesh "—yet a dragon you shall be."

Nathan tossed a pinch of dark reddish powder into the flickering candle atop the altar. When the flames danced around the dragon blood, he nudged the woman, ordering, "Finish it."

"Once this beast has taken form, it will answer only to thee."

Nathan dropped clippings of his own hair into the candle. As the stench of burning hair filled the air, and the flames of the candle sparked, he proclaimed, "I am thee."

He stared down at the woman. Now that the curse had been given voice, his lust vanished. While there was no way to know how long it would take for the curse to work, her task had been completed. The time had come to end their partnership. "I fear I have no further use for you, my dear."

He let the whip fly again and again, chuckling as it cracked loudly across her shoulder. Disappointed that she didn't beg for mercy, or so much as raise a hand in her own defense, he worked the deadly weapon until her ragged breaths were nothing more than a few mewling gasps.

Drenched in sweat and gasping for breath himself, Nathan let the whip fall from his hand and leaned over the dying woman now curled in a ball on the floor. She opened one swollen eye and whispered, "St. George will set you free."

He growled at her and then shrieked, "You bitch!" before drawing what little life force she had left from her body.

With her last choked breath, she once again whispered, "St. George will set you free."

# Chapter 1

*Outskirts of Detroit—One year ago*

"Man, now that is one fine-looking piece."

"Yeah, how'd you like to have a taste of that?"

Inwardly seething, Sean Drake's only physical display of disgust was a slight tightening of his grip around the beer bottle in his hand at the juvenile comments the thugs in the booth behind him were making about the woman who'd just taken a seat at the bar. Their antics and crude behavior were starting to chafe at his last nerve.

These men were petty thieves and thugs. One was a large, hard-drinking bully, and the other his smaller, junkie buddy. Both low-life slugs.

He'd run into them a few weeks ago when they were casing the neighborhood around his current apartment. They'd been looking for their next target, and he'd made certain to accidentally bump into them that night to thwart their plans.

He should have killed them instead.

Had he followed his gut instinct, they wouldn't be here tonight, intent on harassing someone weaker and smaller than themselves. He wasn't about to let that happen. He didn't care what trouble they brought on themselves, but they wouldn't be permitted to hurt anyone else.

Sean tossed back the bottle of beer he'd been nursing and realized with a start that it was time to go home. Not to his sparsely furnished, one-bedroom apartment at the edge of the city, but home to the forested mountains and Dragon's Lair. He choked back a laugh at that thought. Barely eight months had passed since he'd left the Lair, but it felt like years. Actually, he hadn't simply left. Confused, half-dead and afraid for his life, he'd run away in the middle of the night.

It had taken him most of this time alone to come to the conclusion that he'd deserved the beating the Dragon Lord had given him. After all, his unwillingness to control his new, and unwanted, powers had put not just himself at risk, but he'd also become a danger to his brothers and their families. As the Dragon Lord, Braeden had been forced to choose between knocking some sense into the new changeling, or killing him.

Thankfully, even though it would have been within his rights as the lord, his brother hadn't chosen to take his life. Sean knew he should have been grateful, but at the time, the boulder-sized chip on his shoulder hadn't allowed him to see reason. Instead, he'd convinced his sorry self that everyone hated him, that nobody understood him—basically, he'd reacted like a spoiled, self-centered child.

But he hadn't been a child. He'd been a relatively normal twenty-six-year-old adult with a college degree, and more wealth and opportunities than most people would see in a lifetime. He had a good position in the family business and a family who'd cared about him.

Until just over a year ago, when he had been torn from a dark dream by the sounds of a striking whip and an evil cackle, followed by what sounded like a raggedly chanted curse. He hadn't been able to make sense of the breathless words, just snippets of a woman's pain-filled voice. A demonic urge to change into a dragon had filled him. With it came an unrelenting need to seek Drake blood. Since he wasn't a changeling, he had chalked it up to being nothing more than remnants of a nightmare.

His shape-shifting into a dragon would have been fine as far as Braeden or Cameron were concerned. Since both of his older brothers were changeling wizards and possessed dragon blood from birth, they would have welcomed his newfound ability. But it wasn't fine with him. He had always been the normal one, the human brother without any power to read minds, transfer thoughts, slide into dreams, shift into a dragon or materialize someplace on a whim.

For many long weeks after the nightmare, he'd been edgy, moody, confused and unreasonable. As the next month passed, instead of fading away, the troubling urges from that dark dream grew. At the time, he'd thought he was losing his mind. But then, when the dream turned real and he had shifted to dragon form, he'd felt invincible and driven with only one purpose in mind—to kill his brothers. Aunt Danielle had been convinced that he'd been cursed—and since he had heard bits of a chanted curse in his nightmare, he agreed with her assessment, but could do nothing to break whatever spell had been cast over him, except wonder who had cast the spell and why.

Cameron had spent the next two months trying to teach him how to use this new unearthly power and how to control his urges, but Sean had been reluctant to accept his brother's training. One night, in a moment of what he could now only consider pure insanity, he'd shifted into dragon form and attacked Braeden.

While he'd known that as the Dragon Lord his brother was a powerful wizard, he hadn't truly known just how powerful until Braeden's beast gave him a beat down he'd survived only by some miracle.

Sean rubbed the side of his neck. Just remembering that night made his scars burn like fire. How would his brothers—and their beasts—react when he showed up at Dragon's Lair? Would they let him come home? If so, what would it cost him to gain entry back into the family fold?

A sudden flash of sensual heat flowed through him, interrupting his musings and drawing his attention to his surroundings. The brilliant green eyes of his slumbering dragon flickered open. The black, elongated pupils narrowed and widened, dilating with curiosity and interest.

Sean tensed, focusing on the unexpected awakening of his inner beast. He controlled the urge to shift and then studied the other occupants of the bar. Who—or what—had roused the dragon from its slumber?

His gaze settled on the exceptionally attractive woman at the bar—the one the thugs were still drooling over as they kept up their running commentary of what they'd like to do to her.

Their shallow imaginations leaned more toward control and force than pleasure. The urge to show them exactly how control and force felt grew stronger by the minute.

Yeah, it was definitely time to go home before he did something that would terrify the humans of this world.

Curious about the woman, and his dragon's rapt fascination with her, he rose from his seat at the booth and grabbed his empty beer bottle from the table. Seemed the perfect time to get another one.

Crossing the uneven floor of the seedy neighborhood bar, Sean knew he was ready to pay whatever price his brother demanded. In an effort not to draw unwanted attention from his family, he'd avoided touching his bank account. Now, he was tired of drifting, tired of picking up one meaningless job after another just to eat and beyond tired of trying to act normal among humans who would never understand or accept what he'd become.

Sean leaned over the empty stool next to the woman, put the bottle on the worn bar top and nodded when the bartender reached to pull a fresh longneck from the cooler.

Intentionally turning to face the woman, Sean breathed in deeply. He couldn't quite put his finger on it, but instead of some floral or botanical perfume, her scent was enticing—like exotic spices and promises. Lusty promises that curled around him, twisting, swirling, drawing him ever closer.

He leaned in until his lips were mere inches from her cheek. When she turned her head to look at him, her scent grew stronger, filling his mind and his blood with the need to possess her. He wanted to taste her deep red, full lips, run his fingers through those auburn- and coppery-colored waves curling halfway down her back and get lost in the warmth of her brandy-hued eyes.

When she didn't lean away from him, he motioned for the bartender to refill her drink then tossed the money for the beer and her drink on the bar.

"Thank you."

Her low, throaty whisper raced warm and enticing across his face, leaving him almost trembling with lust. The dragon's rumble of desire deepened to a guttural roar, demanding he claim this woman as his own.

Surprised by both his and the beast's intense responses, he was certain this was no mortal woman. He freed his senses and brushed his mind briefly across hers.

Instead of discovering nothing of interest, a rush of familiarity, of like meeting like, confirmed his assumption—she was another preternatural. His knowledge about others of his kind was limited, gained from the few details his family had provided and from stories told by a vampire he'd run across a couple of months ago. It didn't require an abundance of knowledge to know from the instant, sensual heat of her returned touch and the seductive half smile playing across her mouth, that she was a succubus looking for much more than just another drink.

Her sense of desperation swept over him. She wasn't seeking just a quick night of pleasure. Sharp, painful pangs of hunger gnawed at his gut—she needed to feed from someone strong enough to withstand the draining she would unleash on them.

More than able to satisfy her craving, Sean smiled back at her. She could feed on his life force for days without draining him.

Before he could understand exactly what was happening, or offer protest, Sean's beast gently blew an invisible puff of fire and smoke in her direction, marking the woman as his.

Didn't the dragon understand that the two of them were one being? The beast couldn't claim a mate without committing Sean to the same person. He resisted the urge to gasp at the implication. Of course the beast knew exactly what it had done.

Sometimes Sean wished he'd have paid more attention to what his brother had tried to teach him. Even though he didn't possess the ability to materialize elsewhere or slide into another person's dreams like his brothers did, he was able to shift and to communicate telepathically. While it made him more like them, more of a Drake perhaps, he still didn't understand his beast the way his brothers did theirs.

Why had his beast chosen this moment to mark a woman when it had never considered doing so before? Was it because he'd recently been thinking about returning to Dragon's Lair and his family?

And why this woman? Sean held back a chuckle. The answer to this question was obvious. He wanted this beguiling temptress with every fiber of his being.

She said nothing, but the slightest widening of her eyes let him know she'd felt the mental brand.

He pushed the drink he'd bought closer to her then grabbed the beer, deepened his smile and nodded before returning to the booth without saying a word.

Caitlin watched him leave. A less-perceptive woman might have been deflated by his nonverbal response, interpreting it as a dismissal. However, she knew better. He may not have spoken words, but his brief touch across her thoughts had felt like a warm, possessive caress against her cheek. His inner beast had marked her, meaning this was no mere mortal man. Whatever nonhuman traits he possessed were apparently from the animal kingdom. But his mental touch hadn't permitted her entry into his mind to tell her which one.

However it didn't require any degree of perception to notice that he hadn't simply *walked* away—he'd sauntered, swaggered—as if confident of her interest and daring her to follow him.

Caitlin curled her fingers around the glass he'd pushed toward her. The imprint left by his touch was still warm under hers. Beneath the warmth churned a hunger as deep as her own. She shivered with anticipation, knowing her bed wouldn't be cold or lonely tonight.

Of more importance had been the feeling that his interest in her was purely physical—an interest that she welcomed with relief. Because of a vow to her mother, she hadn't fed in over a month, and now blood flowed through her veins like a thick, slow-moving sludge. The lethargy weighing her down was nearly unbearable; she needed something—someone—to refill her life force.

The fastest, easiest way to gain the life-giving power she needed to survive was to simply suck the force from another being. However, that required her to know when to stop before completely draining the *donor*, and right now her hunger would make that nearly impossible.

But the most pleasurable way to obtain what she needed, the fairest way for the other participant and the longest-lasting method was through hot, intense sex. Finding a willing partner wasn't a problem, since as a succubus, men and women were always drawn to her whether she summoned the attraction or not. Unfortunately, most humans didn't possess enough life force, or the driving need—a near-insatiable hunger—to survive mating with her.

Hence the reason for promising her mother that she'd refrain from feeding on them—again. Since this man wasn't human, he stood a better chance of living through the event.

The old cliché "killing two birds with one stone" came to mind. She would still be honoring her parents' request by not seeking out a human, and by morning she might gain enough life force to last weeks.

She raised the glass to her lips and then paused before putting the drink back on the bar without taking a sip. Already weak and slow, Caitlin knew the booze would only make her feel worse. She'd come in here as a last resort, looking for a *donor*, not to get drunk.

Now that she'd found what she wanted—what she so desperately needed—it was time to go. Not for one second did she worry about him finding her. She'd strategically leave enough of her scent lingering in the air that he'd find the way to her home with ease.

"Aren't you a hot little thing?"

*Hot?* Always. *Little?* Caitlin resisted rolling her eyes at that description. She hadn't been a *little thing* since she'd hit just under six foot tall at age twelve.

A yellowish glare from the streetlight at the end of the alley danced in the droplets of sleet rolling down the thug's drawn blade. She forgot about his comment and took another step back from the two men stalking her, luring them farther into the dark alley.

They'd been in the booth behind the changeling at the bar. She'd heard their crude comments when she'd entered, felt them watching her when she'd left the bar, and she'd seen their reflections in the smoked-glass window as they followed her out. She'd expected *him* to follow her, but these two were another story.

With a quick touch of her mind to the humans, she

discovered that while their goal also included sex, it wasn't the passionate kind they wanted. She quirked an eyebrow at their stupidity and kept walking backward.

They had corralled her into the alley a block away from the bar where no one would see them—mistakenly thinking she was an easy target. She might be drained, but her tired muscles and slow reactions would still be more than enough to handle these two.

One man swung a knife at her, laughing as she jumped back from what he thought was a lethal blade.

"Yeah. Come on, cut her, cut her." The smaller of the two men squealed like a child. From the glassiness of his eyes, the lack of meat on his bones and the jerkiness of his movements, he was obviously juiced on something more than beer.

The changeling with a body even she would die for approached frowning, but said nothing to stop the other two men. He hung back. A quizzical expression drew his brows together as if he was waiting for something.

*"Do you want my help?"* She jerked slightly at the intrusion of his silent query.

*"No."* Caitlin scoffed at his offer, adding, *"You know damn well that help with these two isn't what I want from you."*

Once again he gave her a smile full of promises and passion.

She drew her full attention to the thug with the blade, and because the question was usually expected in these situations, she asked, "What do you want?"

Knife man smiled. "Why, darlin', we want you."

*Of course he did. Everyone wanted her whether the desire was mutual or not.* Caitlin shrugged out of her unzipped jacket, letting the buttery-soft black leather hit the wet pavement. "Oh, big boy, all you had to do was ask."

Her unexpected, brazen comment stopped them in their tracks. Only the twitching drughead seemed upset by the sudden turn of events. But his most dangerous response was to twitch faster.

Needing just a drop of energy before taking on these two humans, she reached out with her mind and touched the junkie, recoiling instantly from the contamination and disease he carried deep in his soul. No way in hell would she place a finger on him and risk poisoning herself needlessly.

She focused on the knife wielder. He possessed a vile darkness that wouldn't kill her, but it would eventually make her physically ill. From their encounter in the bar, she knew the changeling would give her the opportunity to heal herself long before she became sick.

The blade sliced through her silky tank top and across her rib cage as the thug closed his hand boldly around her left breast. "Teasing will get you killed."

Caitlin didn't flinch at the knife tip's burn. The lost blood would soon be replenished, and the cut would heal momentarily. And while his hold on her body irritated her, it didn't hurt.

But he'd ruined her favorite top. That was completely unacceptable.

She tilted her head and smiled before placing the palm of her hand against his cheek. "Teasing?"

The knife fell from his hand, his pupils dilated and he moaned raggedly with a sudden, unexpected flare of lust. Humans were just so damn easy. She threaded her fingers through his dark, greasy hair. Resisting the urge to shiver with disgust, she cupped the back of his head and drew him closer, whispering, "I would never tease about anything as important as a new top."

When their lips nearly met, she exhaled softly, filling him with mindless desire and near-excruciating need.

His eyelids fluttered closed—he was hers to do with as she willed. Caitlin tightened her hold and inhaled almost every last ounce of his life-giving force until he whimpered like a little girl.

"Enough."

The preternatural's one-word command shocked her into releasing her grip on the human. She let him drop to the pavement like a rock. Nobody outside her parents, or the royal circle of elders, gave her orders. Who did he think he was?

The junkie stared down at his buddy in open-mouthed shock. Jerking his head and shoulders, he screamed, "What? What the hell did you do?"

Mr. To Die For popped the little guy on the jaw and dropped him with one hit.

Caitlin staggered, gasping in confusion and worry at her sudden inability to function, or focus. She'd known she would be ill from sucking the life out of the thug. But not this quickly, never this fast. This wasn't normal. Something was wrong. Her heart thudded fast and hard inside her chest. What was happening to her? What was so different this time around?

She stumbled and then bounced off the garbage Dumpster. Just great. Her parents would be so pissed off if she went and got herself killed now.

"Come here." The male she'd wanted pulled her against him right before she collapsed into a puddle. Cupping her chin, he tipped her head up and brought his lips close to hers. "Eat. Drink. Whatever it is you do."

She weakly slung an arm around his neck. "How romantic."

"Yeah, that's me, Mr. Romance at your service. Shut up and feed."

"Not a vampire." Her words sounded disjointed to her ears.

"No shit."

Caitlin's stomach cramped; her legs shook. Had he not been holding her so securely, she wouldn't have remained on her feet for much longer.

When her arm slipped from around his neck to dangle uselessly, she knew there'd be no way she'd be able to exhale anything from him. Hoping his intent was truly to help her, she whispered, "Kiss me."

The first touch of his lips against hers sent a lightning-charged zing of energy clear to her toes. She sighed with the most exquisite longing, forgetting even to draw in his energy as she reveled in the utter completeness of the moment for a split second before darkness overtook her.

Caitlin's first awareness was the feel of cool, satiny-smooth sheets against her flesh. Her second was that she felt more alive than she had in months. She opened her eyes and gazed into the grassy-green depths of the eyes staring back at her.

"Morning, Red."

Normally, that clichéd endearment would send her ire skyrocketing, but his voice was so deep, his overused, outdated greeting so easy and familiar that for the first time in her life, she felt her face flush with embarrassment. His one-sided smile—a seductive, knowing smirk—only lent more heat to her cheeks.

Confused by her odd reaction, she asked, "Where am I?"

"According to your directions, you're home. If not, then we've invaded someone else's privacy for the past three days."

*Three days!*

She sat up quickly, glancing around to make certain she truly was home. The deep forest green of the walls were adorned not with any feminine ornamentation, but with only the tools of her trade—a centuries-old broad sword and a pair of even more ancient crossed daggers— mounted near the door let her know they were indeed in her bedroom. No other woman would have decorated their bedroom in such a manner. Satisfied with her location, she held the sheet tightly to her neck. "Three days? What have I been doing?"

"If you don't know, then I haven't given it my all." He sighed then chuckled softly and drew a fingertip down her spine. "Feeding."

For three days? And she couldn't remember any of it? She was in bed with a man who possessed the chiseled body and face of a Greek god and she couldn't remember the feel of his body on, or in, hers? Either she'd lost her mind, or he was some type of preternatural she'd never met before.

She closed her eyes tightly, trying desperately to remember. Then slowly, bit by bit, the fog started to clear, permitting snippets of their time together to trickle into her mind.

They'd met in a bar and had been attracted to each other from the beginning.

His inner animal—the part that made him preternatural—had marked her. She wasn't certain why it had done so, only that for some reason it had chosen her. More importantly, she hadn't turned him away.

Images of the thugs in the alley floated through her mind. When she'd become sick immediately after draining the one attacker, this man, the one now in her bed, had been there to catch her before she fell to the wet pavement. He'd given her energy—his own life force, without question.

A shiver of lust raced down her spine as more, broken bits of memories poured forth. Not quite visual memories, but more like remembered feelings. The warmth of his mind-robbing kiss as his tongue had swept across hers. And the certainty of his touch when he'd stroked and caressed her to a fevered pitch that left her gasping for air and wanting so much more.

All of this was so foreign to her, so strange. She'd never let a man into her bedroom. She'd never been so swept away by a kiss that she'd lost the ability to think. She'd never met a man who could willingly fill her life force and live.

Never before had she desired, longed for, lusted after a man who possessed an inner strength that was on a level she couldn't quite understand, and while it excited her, it also frightened her.

Though she could remember the feel of his touch, the taste of his kiss, she couldn't pull his name from her memories. It was an odd time to ask, but she wanted to know.

Caitlin took a breath, looked at him and asked, "Who are you?"

He tugged on the sheet, dragging it down to her waist, and sat up far enough to slide his tongue along the curve of her breast. "Ladies first."

She shivered. How many times had he done that the last few days? Caitlin swallowed her moan. Had she enjoyed it as much as she did now? "Caitlin St. George."

The man froze, his eyes widening for a split second before he moved away from her. His smile faded into a deep, menacing laugh, wiping away her desire to lean in to his caress.

Fear slid in behind her lingering passion, pushing it away, flowing over the warmth to bury it with a cold, foreboding chill. Maybe she should have asked *what* he was, instead of *who*.

Before she could part her lips to voice her question, he shifted into the form of a smoky dragon and was gone.

# Chapter 2

*Dragon's Lair, Drakes' Resort*
*in East Tennessee—today*

"Sean, we have a problem."

Without taking his attention away from the lines of coding on his monitor, Sean reached out to absently hit the button on the intercom. "What now?"

"The security alerts are going insane. Again."

"Be right there." He saved the program he'd been debugging, shrugged into his suit jacket and headed out of the private office in his suite.

Sean reminded himself to be patient. Harold was doing the best he could. The security tech had called in sick this morning, and he didn't have time to sit and watch the monitors himself.

The rest of the family had left for the family's medieval stronghold on Mirabilus Isle a few days ago, and he wasn't about to call either of his brothers, or his aunt, home for something this minor. Not when this was the first time since his return they'd left him in complete charge of the Lair.

So when Harold, the family's right-hand man, sometimes chauffeur, mechanic and occasional handyman, had volunteered to watch the cameras, Sean had accepted his help.

Of course, today was the day when everything that could go wrong, did. Now, for the third time this morning, Sean's new tweaks to the system were having fits.

Walking into the basement security room, Sean glanced at the half-round bank of monitors. "Which one now?"

"The lobby." Harold rose and moved out of the inner circle.

Well, at least it wasn't in the kitchen again. Sean sat down and swiveled the task chair back around to glance at the screen to the lobby.

The temperature bar at the bottom of the monitor was blinking red—something very hot, or on fire, was in the lobby. He knew if he turned the sound on, that the alarm would be barking in time with the blinks.

"I didn't see anything out of the ordinary." Harold leaned over his shoulder, pointing at the check-in counter. "But it went off when she entered."

A woman stood at the counter. Either the modified alarm system was a total bust, or it was finally doing its job correctly.

Sean tapped in another view of the counter and cursed softly.

The system was working just as it should—monitoring the temperature of the guests' bodies and alerting the security staff to the presence of a nonhuman.

She hadn't changed much since he'd last seen her. A little paler, with lines of distress marring her forehead, making her appear drained and weak. Shadows of worry framed her amber eyes. If anything, her apparent vulnerability made her more enticing now than before. Caitlin

St. George—the magic dragon slayer—was checking in to Dragon's Lair.

When she'd first told him her name, he had gotten the impression that she didn't realize what her name even meant. But then, since he'd refused her entry into his thoughts, she hadn't known who, or what, he was, so there'd been no reason for her to put two and two together.

Actually, other than her name—which could be nothing more than a strange coincidence—he'd had no reason to vanish the way he had. Granted, she was a St. George and he a Drake—the dragon slayer and the dragon—but as far as he knew, the days of killing dragons had ended centuries ago.

Yet at hearing her name, something sharp and menacing had poked at his dragon, enraging it beyond reason. So he'd done the only thing he could upon discovering he'd been sleeping with what his beast seemed to distrust—laughed at the complete irony of the situation and then vanished from her life.

What was she doing here at the Lair? Something was obviously wrong. But why would she come to him? After the way he'd deserted her so abruptly, it made no sense for her to be here.

Sean cleared the event from the system and reset the lobby's alarm. "There you go, Harold. It's all reset now."

The man frowned at him and asked, "Who is she?"

He brushed by Harold, answering on his way to the elevator, "An old friend."

"How old?"

Sean knew what Harold was asking in his roundabout way. He wanted to know if this was someone he'd met during those long, endless months his family all referred to as "Sean's dark time."

Knowing Harold wouldn't like the answer and that the man wouldn't be able to keep the information to himself, Sean hit the close button on the elevator's panel and said, "I met her at a bar in town." It wasn't exactly a lie—he *had* met her at a bar, in a town, just not a bar in this town.

Checking his reflection in the smoke-tinted mirrored wall, he straightened his tie and raked his fingers through his hair. Why his appearance mattered was beyond him. It wasn't as if his beast was going to let either of them remain dressed for long.

Stepping out of the elevator when it stopped a floor above, he crossed the resort's lobby, almost missing a step as a nearly forgotten bolt of raw lust surged through him, awakening the slumbering dragon within.

He could feel the beast turn its head to stare intently at the woman. He heard the ragged chuff as it picked up her scent and recognized the mate it had hungered for, yet oddly wanted to avoid.

He rolled his neck, fighting the urge to give in to the heated desires washing through him and leaned over the counter next to Caitlin to tell the clerk, "I've got this one, Brandy. Give me a suite key on thirteen." He glanced at the floor, then asked, "Do you have any bags?"

St. George was cool, collected—unlike her response at their last encounter. She didn't flinch, didn't even bat an eyelash. However, she stared at him, her eyes shimmering, and swallowed hard, apparently as affected by his presence as he was by hers. "My luggage is in the car. I don't need a room, but we do need to talk."

Sean placed the keycard back on the counter and

nodded toward the row of elevator doors. "If you'll follow me?"

She seemed hesitant, not moving until he placed a hand on her shoulder. "Come on, Red, I'd really hate to embarrass both of us right here in the lobby."

That, too, was a lie. At this minute he didn't care where they were, or who was around. He wanted nothing more than to shred the clothes from her body with his talons and taste every delectable inch of her naked flesh.

Beneath his touch he felt her flare of lust roar to life, only to cool just as quickly. Sean wasn't fooled by her controlled disinterest—it was a method of self-preservation that she'd obviously learned, and perfected, during this last year.

Damn shame, actually.

She let him guide her to the elevator. Once the door slid closed behind them, he moved in, stalking her, backing her into a corner. "Welcome to Dragon's Lair."

She pushed against his chest. "I said we need to talk."

Talking was the furthest thing from his mind. Sean leaned against her, his chest pressing into the softness of her breasts. He narrowed his eyes as the heat of her body drifted into his. "Talk about what?"

"You do remember what I am, don't you?"

With a soft throaty growl, Sean nodded. "Yeah, mine."

"Really? Your abrupt departure said the exact opposite. Trust me, I am *not* yours."

Sean settled his thighs more firmly against hers and feathered his lips against her neck. "You'll soon forget that I ever left so hastily."

Caitlin closed her eyes at the reminder of their last encounter. It had taken days, but eventually all of her memories had flooded back and she'd remembered every second of the time they'd spent in her bed.

She hadn't been as uninvolved as she'd first hoped. In fact, if her memories were accurate, she'd urged him on a time or three and had begged—*begged*!—him to stop teasing her, to end his achingly hot torment of her body more than once.

Never before had any man satisfied her so completely—and lived.

Her body seemed to hum as it, too, remembered and hungered for a command performance. She placed her hands flat on his chest, biting back a sigh at the feel of his muscles beneath her palms. "Please."

He clasped both of her hands with one of his own and dragged them down the length of his chest and past his waist. "You don't need to beg—at least not right now. We can save that for later."

When he bent his head to once again feed her shivers with his lips, she turned slightly and sank her fangs into his neck.

He pulled free from her bite, still smiling. "New trick?"

"A gift from my father. You should be grateful that unlike him, I don't suck blood."

"Oh, sweetheart, there isn't anything you could do to me that I wouldn't like."

"Sean, please." She shoved him farther away and paced along the back of the elevator. "I'm not here on a pleasure run. I need your help."

Her worry settled cold in his blood, effectively cooling the wayward desire. He watched her carefully. Her stride as she paced was brisk and determined. Yet she repeatedly curled and uncurled her fingers while shooting him brief darting glances. Nervousness was mixed in with her worry.

Sean silently swore. How did he so instinctively know that without delving into her mind? What was this *thing* between them? Why the instant attraction before and again now, and why did he so easily pick up on her moods? And why was his beast so conflicted between desiring her and wanting to tear her to shreds?

The only thing he understood about any of it was that he didn't like it—at all. It was an interruption in his life that he didn't need right now. This was something he couldn't control. And the safety of his family and his own life depended on his ability to control the vile urges demanding their deaths that still haunted him at times.

Without looking, he reached over and hit the stop button. When the elevator bounced gently to a halt, he asked, "I haven't heard from you in nearly a year, what sort of help do you think I'd be willing to offer?"

She paused to look at him with narrowed eyes. "I gave up trying to contact you after about four months."

"I never received a call or any other contact from you."

"If by *other contact* you mean telepathy, I can't do that unless I can see you. So summoning you with my mind was out of the question. Since you'd shifted into a dragon, it wasn't that hard to guess your identity. There aren't that many dragon clans left, and the way you reacted to hearing my name made it fairly obvious you were a Drake. After that, finding the phone number to Dragon's Lair was easy." She resumed pacing, her arms crossed against her body. "Unfortunately, I kept getting the wrong Drake. I spoke to your aunt. The last time I called she told me that you were recently engaged and to leave you alone." The look she turned on him was frigid. "So I did."

He felt her rising anger. However, it was nothing compared to his own. *Engaged?* That was the best Aunt Dani could devise? "When was this?"

Caitlin shook her head and sighed as if bored with this conversation. "The first time was about a month after you disappeared from my bedroom."

She'd called while he was still debating whether to come home or not. Which explains why he had never received word that she'd called. However, he'd returned to the Lair shortly after that, so why hadn't his aunt mentioned the calls?

That was something he'd take up with Danielle later.

"I'm sorry. I wasn't living here then."

"Ah."

He was taken aback by the shortness of her answer. "I am not engaged."

She rolled her eyes and shrugged. "That doesn't matter."

"What did you—"

She turned to face him, throwing up her hands to stop him from talking. She screamed in frustration and then nearly shouted, "Our son has been kidnapped!"

The beast reared back and growled with enough force to send him stumbling backward. The growl turned menacing as it vibrated inside his chest. Between that unexplained bout of temper and the sudden roaring in his ears, he wasn't certain he'd heard her correctly. After taking a deep breath and shaking his head, he asked, "Our what?"

"Son. Our son."

"That isn't possible."

"Yes," she shot back. "It is possible." She covered her face with a shaking hand for a second before adding, "I don't have the time, nor the inclination, for this."

He repeated, "It's not possible." He would have known. The beast should have known. This woman had been marked as its mate, why hadn't the beast known, or at least sensed this had happened?

"Damn it!" she yelled. "Do you think I sleep with so many men that I don't know who the father of my child is?"

"No." His mind swirled with an effort to make sense of this. First, however, he needed to defuse her anger before she managed to give the beast a reason to be uncontrollably enraged. "That isn't what I meant. Calm down. Give me a minute to—"

"Would you like a calculator?" She jerked her purse from her shoulder, rummaged inside and slapped her smartphone against his chest. "Here. We were together a little over a year ago. He's three months old. You do the math."

Sean cursed and pushed the phone aside. "I assumed you were on the pill."

Not only was it lame, it was the flimsiest excuse he'd ever used. Especially since he knew what her response would be.

"Oh, of course you did. And I suppose you also assumed that human birth control pills would somehow be effective?"

He closed his eyes at the expected reply. He'd never had to worry about any type of danger inherent with spur-of-the-moment sex, since his beast had the uncanny ability to sense when something wasn't quite right and would steer him away from the encounter. As for birth control—his brothers had assured him that it was a non-issue since he could only impregnate his...*mate*.

Sean wanted to kick himself. Once they'd walked into her bedroom he'd been so wrapped up in lust, need, desire and her that he'd never given a second thought to the fact his dragon had marked this female at the bar. How had he let himself get so out of touch with reality? It wasn't as if he could blame the alcohol—he'd only had two beers. Regardless, intoxication wasn't an acceptable excuse for anything. Especially not for this.

Caitlin dropped the phone back inside her purse, and then she grasped the lapels of his suit jacket. "I don't care if you believe me or not. I know he's your son, and he's in danger."

Sean looked down at her as he willed the snarling dragon to calm down enough for him to think. "I never said I didn't believe you."

"He's just a baby." Tears welled in her eyes. Her chin quivered. "Please, help me."

He could hear the beast's roar in his ears, saw it thrash back and forth in his mind. The dragon was feeling trapped and angry, but the woman in front of him was afraid and worried. His beast would soon get over its hissy fit. However, Caitlin couldn't be expected to do the same. He stroked her cheek and brushed away a falling tear. "Yes. Of course I will."

She fell against his chest with a cry. "Thank you."

Ignoring a sudden bout of heartburn caused by the dragon's displeasure with this entire situation, Sean restarted the elevator and then, against his better judgment, he wrapped his arms around her. "It'll be fine. We'll get him back safely. Have the kidnappers asked for a ransom?"

She nodded against his chest.

"That's good. Money isn't an obstacle."

"The ransom isn't money."

The kidnapper didn't want money? Then what was the demand? "So you've talked to the kidnapper?"

The elevator doors whooshed open, and Caitlin stepped out of his embrace. She shrugged one shoulder and then said, "In a manner of speaking, yes."

Sean frowned at her elusive answer. "My suite is right around the corner. We can talk there."

He escorted her down the hallway in silence. Once inside his apartment suite, Sean crossed the living room to open the sliding door to the balcony. A blast of cool, late-autumn air flowed into the suite. He breathed in deeply, hoping the crispness of the air would help to quell the uneasiness in his chest.

Stepping away from the door, he motioned Caitlin toward the sofa. "Would you like something to drink?"

She shook her head as she settled into a corner of the couch.

Instead of taking a seat himself, he perched on the arm of the chair across the room from her. "Why don't you start at the beginning."

"The day before yesterday, something broke into my room while I was napping."

"Something?"

"Yeah—*something*." She shrugged. "At first I thought it might be you, until the icy evilness of it washed over me, taking away my breath."

As far as he knew, that type of evilness could belong to only one being. A sickening feeling in the pit of Sean's stomach formed, growing with each passing word of her explanation.

"It was as if it knew I'd realized the thing's vile intent, because it conjured a spell that threw me against a wall and pinned me there until it exited with our son in tow."

"Can you describe it?"

"At first it was wispy with no real identifiable form."

That explained why she'd thought it might be him. His dragon form was little more than smoke unless he—or the Dragon Lord—willed it into something more solid.

"And when it started to take shape, it was like a beast from a nightmare." Her lip quivered, but she quickly turned her head away as she continued, "A monster has our son."

Sean's beast growled with rage. Not with a vague undirected anger like it had upon first seeing Caitlin, but with murderous intent toward the wizard who had taken its offspring.

"You'd said it spoke to you and demanded ransom?"

She nodded, but didn't answer.

Sean rose and crossed the room to kneel before her. He stroked her cheek, coaxing her to look at him. "What, Caitlin? Tell me, what does it want?"

"The book, the box, the emerald and sapphire pendants." She stared at him. "And for you to complete your task."

Sean jerked back as if he'd been burned. While the items demanded as ransom told him that his suspicion had been correct—Nathan the Learned had his son— it gave him no clue as to what task he was supposed to complete.

Caitlin edged around him and stood up. With her hands pressing into her stomach, she moved across the room—away from him. Staring out the open balcony

doors, she asked, "How are you involved with this...
this thing?"

"I'm not." Even though as far as he knew he wasn't
working with any malevolent being—at least not of his
own free will—his answer felt...off...not quite right
somehow. It felt as if his subconscious was vaguely
aware of something that hadn't yet fully registered in
his brain yet.

"Then why did it place so much importance on this
task of yours?" She leaned against the doorjamb. "It
laughed when it repeated itself more than once."

"*It* has a name—Nathan—"

"No!" She spun around with a cry before he could
complete his sentence. "Not Nathan the Learned?"

Tightening his grasp on the arm of the sofa, he
frowned. What did a succubus know about a Druid wizard? He straightened and turned to face her. "How do
you know about Nathan?"

"My father is a vampire."

He rubbed his neck. "I already gathered that much."

"He's been around long enough to have run into the
Learned a time or two. Besides, my father has a seat
on the High Council of our kind, so there isn't much
he doesn't know, or hasn't heard." She shrugged again.
"And what he doesn't know, my mother can usually find
out."

He almost didn't want to ask. "And your mother is
a...what?"

"Dead."

Sean resisted the urge to vanish. A few years ago he
would have walked out of the apartment at such a sense-
less answer. But he'd seen and learned so many things

the last two years that he was fairly certain this wouldn't be anything new. "Dead as in a zombie?"

Her eyes widened. "Gross. No. Dead as in physically deceased."

"Ah." Feeling foolish, he offered condolences. "I am sorry for your loss."

"No need. She's still here."

Maybe he hadn't learned everything just yet. "What?"

Caitlin rolled her eyes. "She refuses to move on without my father, so her spirit is still here."

"That raises more questions than I want to get into right now. But I don't suppose your mother can find out where…" He paused, realizing that he didn't know the child's name.

"Sean."

"What?"

"Sean. His given name is Sean Alexander Drake II."

*Just. Simply. Wonderful.* Since there was no way for her to know that what she'd done in naming the boy went against centuries of Drake tradition.

"Is there a reason you made it so easy for him to be found by any dragon slayer out there?"

She shrugged. "Since I'm the slayer, it actually didn't cross my mind. Besides, his name had nothing to do with you or what you are."

"Right." He didn't buy that for a minute. "Then why make it so obvious he's my son?"

"Because it was the easiest way to piss off my parents."

"And I'm sure you succeeded."

"Completely."

Why she'd want to enrage her family in such a manner was a question left for another time. "I don't suppose your mother can find out where Junior is being held?"

She cringed visibly at his use of *Junior*. "Sean—his name is Sean."

"Can she find out where Sean is being held?"

"She already has. He's in a castle ruins on the east coast of Ireland."

Sean found it interesting that the wizard had holed up about as close to Mirabilus Isle as he could without being easily detected. His family had taken the larger jet, but Braeden's personal one was still in the hangar at the airport. He pulled out his cell phone and directed Harold to have the jet fueled and ready to go as quickly as possible then tapped it off without explaining why. He and Caitlin needed to get to Mirabilus, and she had no means of otherworldly transportation.

Turning his attention back to Caitlin, he asked, "Does your mother know if he's harmed the baby?"

"Our son is fine—for now."

That was a relief. Although there was no telling how long that might last. A flash of heat coursing down the back of his head, then down his spine, distracted him.

"He'll be safe for a week."

Sean frowned at the way she'd answered his question before he'd asked, and then he realized her intrusion had caused the flash of heat. "Stay out of my head, Caitlin."

"I'm sorry. Since we're physically so close, it's just easier."

"Easier isn't always right." Before, at the bar, she hadn't complained about him delving into her mind, but he wondered how she would react to the same type of trespass now and reached out to brush her thoughts.

His touch seemed to crack the mental dam she'd been

using to rein in her needs. At first a trickle of weak, nervous energy flowed free. Then, as if the dam burst, the hunger she'd been holding back rushed out, nearly overwhelming him. Her raw, aching need was stronger now than it had been the night they'd first met. She was literally starving to death.

He studied her closely. While her copper-streaked auburn hair still fell in waves down her back, the shimmering luster had dulled, as had that twinkling spark in her amber gaze. Her attempt to hide the circles beneath her eyes might have worked from a distance, but now, standing before her, he could see the darker areas where the makeup had worn away. Her face seemed thinner, and her cheeks gaunt.

He lowered his focus, briefly noticing the line of padding in the shoulders of her jacket, before seeing the stark definition of her collarbone.

Sean cursed silently. This hadn't happened in the hours since their child had been taken. Without thinking, he backed her against a wall, pinning her forcibly with his body. "What have you done, Caitlin?"

"What are you talking about?" She pushed at his shoulders. "Nothing. I've done nothing. Let me go."

He ignored her feeble attempt to free herself. Instead, he opened himself to the emotions battling for escape— an avalanche of need, hunger, anger and fear cascaded against him—a tide of emotions he could easily calm, if she'd let him.

Her hunger and craving tore at him, creating a sudden urge to care for her. He didn't question the urge; she was the mother of his child and his dragon's mate. She was his responsibility, and he would do whatever he must to ensure her well-being.

Seemingly over his early bout of anger, his beast chuffed in agreement and then sniffed the air around her. Sean wanted to groan at the lack of life force surrounding her. How many weeks, or months, had she gone without feeding? How many more would pass before she perished?

"You've done nothing?" He slipped a hand beneath her jacket and felt her ribs. "Nothing?" The dragon raged with an unfamiliar worry. Fighting to control his own concern at what she'd done to herself and the beast's anxiety, Sean said, "You will be of no use if you are dead. You need to feed."

She sighed raggedly and leaned against him. With her lips against the hollow of his neck, Caitlin agreed. "I know."

Letting one claw form, Sean hooked the dragon talon into the neck of her silky blouse, warning, "If this is a favorite top, consider it gone."

"Don't," she whispered, but offered no resistance.

"You are spent." He trailed a line of kisses along her cheek. "Let me help."

At her soft sigh, he shredded the fabric and then slowly traced the smooth curve of his talon across her stomach, drawing a moan from her lips.

She shrugged out of her jacket and torn blouse, letting the clothing fall to the floor, and placed her hands against his chest. "What are you going to do to help?"

Her touch was like ice, cold and lifeless against his skin. He again sensed her fear and hunger. He knew the fear would only be calmed once her child was back safely in her arms. But her hunger twisted in his gut with an unspoken desperation that only increased his desire to feed her.

"First you are going to gain some strength." He retracted the claw and covered her hands with one of his own. "Then we're going to Mirabilus to get our son back and kill that bastard wizard once and for all."

When she only nodded, he dipped his head to ask in a whisper, "What use will you be to the child if you've starved yourself?"

She tried to free her hands, but he held them securely against his chest. "I'm fine."

Sean laughed softly at her lie. "You are far from fine." He pulled her into his embrace asking, "When did you last feed?"

"I don't remember."

He cursed at the shakiness of her answer, released her from the circle of his embrace, swung her up into his arms and headed down the hall toward his bedroom.

She stared at him in shock. "What are you doing?"

"I would think that was obvious." He kicked open the door, crossed the room and dropped her onto the bed.

When she scrambled, almost backstroking toward the far edge of the bed, he easily grasped her legs and pulled her back to him. Kneeling on the bed, he leaned over her and held her head between his cupped hands. "Why didn't you come to me?"

Caitlin swallowed a cry of frustration at the concern she heard in his voice. She could claim that she had tried everything to contact him, but they'd both know that was a lie. Even though she'd been unable to reach him via the phone, she could have searched for him, driven here to Dragon's Lair. While tracking him down might have angered him, he would have come to understand the need.

Or she could say she hadn't wanted to tell him about the baby, but she would know the strength of that lie.

She had wanted to tell him, wanted him by her side during the pregnancy and delivery, but her parents and the High Council had insisted vehemently that she hold on to that secret, going so far as to imprison her—a near death sentence for her—when they discovered that she had reached out to him by calling Dragon's Lair.

Still, at this moment, she'd be safer back in her cell. This was the last place she wanted to be—and the only place she longed to be. Beneath his unwavering stare, she finally answered, "Because I don't want to need you."

His easy smile was her undoing. That smug, knowing, self-satisfied, all-male half smile was enough to make the walls she'd painstakingly erected around her emotions crash to her feet as nothing more than tiny shards of broken glass.

His gentle touch stroking her cheek, brushing the hair from her face, tracing her lips, coaxed a strangled cry from her.

Blinking back unwanted tears of shame and disgust at the ease of her surrender, she slipped her arms around him and whispered, "Damn you to hell, Drake."

"At least I won't be lonely with you by my side."

Between his feathery kisses, she exclaimed, "I hate you."

Again with that smile, he answered, "I know."

"I'd rather we didn't—"

He covered her mouth with his, effectively cutting off her words.

When his tongue swept across hers and he exhaled, his breath filled her. It warmed her and fed life into her starving soul. He had every reason to be angry with her, but still he freely shared his life force. How could she not set aside her misgivings?

It didn't matter that she was a St. George, a slayer of dragons, or that he was a Drake and supposedly her mortal enemy. Nor did it matter what her family or the High Council thought best. She needed this—she needed *him*.

She had craved his touch for so many months now that she no longer cared what her parents or the council had said. They were wrong—all of them were wrong. They'd insisted that her obvious path was to kill the dragon and had expressed disappointment that she hadn't done so when she'd had the chance. But she knew with a certainty she couldn't explain, that her only path in life was to not *kill* the dragon. Without the beast, and the man, she feared she might be the one who died.

Without releasing her, his cell phone hit the nightstand right before she heard their clothes rustle to the floor and felt the cool breeze rush across her flesh. She greatly appreciated some of his more than handy skills.

He rolled onto his back, pulling her atop him, and broke their kiss. "Now, if you're done complaining and protesting, let me help you. Take what you need, Caitlin."

She sat up to straddle him, her hands flat on his chest. His expression was serious, no hint of teasing quirked his lips. His heart beat strong and steady beneath her palms, no uneven thumps to give evidence of a lie.

She wanted to accept his offer, but knew full well that she was so starved for his touch that things might get out of control this time. If she drained him, killed him, she'd never see her son again, and she'd spend the rest of her life running from his family. Worry for his well-being prompted her to admit, "I don't know if I can stop myself."

"Darlin'," he drawled in his best tough-man voice, "I think we both know full well that you can't hurt me."

When she still hesitated, Sean reached up to thread his fingers through her hair. He cupped the back of her head, and she shivered at the tingles running across her scalp.

His bright green gaze held hers, and she swore she could see the dragon within coaxing her closer as the man pulled her down. Memories of their last time together filled her mind, heated her blood and gave her the oddest sense of belonging. Coming here had been the right thing to do.

When their lips barely touched, he challenged, "I dare you to try draining me."

How could she possibly resist such an offer?

# *Chapter 3*

Sean knew Caitlin would be unable to resist his challenge. He relaxed beneath her as she hungrily kissed him, inhaling as much of his energy as she could.

Knowing that a kiss, a drawing in of his breath, would never be enough for her to gain full strength, he slid his hands down the smoothness of her back, chasing the rising goose bumps with his fingertips, and grasped her hips to lift her.

He wanted her healthy and whole—needed her to be at her very best for what was to come. It would take both of them to defeat Nathan and rescue the child. And she would need all the strength she could summon for what would come afterward.

He shifted beneath her and eased her slowly down the length of his erection. Her moan echoed his as she curled her fingers into his shoulders, her nails pressing hard into his flesh.

Sean closed his eyes, savoring what was more than just a physical union of their bodies. This intimate act was more than just a way to replenish Caitlin's energy, or to satisfy the hunger between them.

It was a way to feed their beasts—to soothe the anger emanating from their souls. The growing heat of their bodies, the touch of their lips, transformed the hurt into a power that could very possibly keep them both alive.

Through a thick fog of desire he heard the security alarm scream from his office down the hall. His cell phone vibrated off the nightstand.

Before he could respond to either, Caitlin rolled off him with a harshly gasped curse. Her wide-eyed gaze flew to the bedroom doorway. "Mother! What are you doing here?"

Sean quickly spelled their clothing back on, swallowed hard and then rose from the bed. He stared at the uninvited, semisolid, still-forming woman walking into his bedroom. "Mrs. St. George?"

His beast twitched, backing away in the same manner it did when confronted by an angry Aunt Danielle. Sean rolled his eyes at the adolescent behavior of his dragon.

Mrs. St. George ignored him. Instead, once fully visible, she pinned Caitlin with a hard glare. "I thought we discussed you having anything to do with this... this vile animal."

Animal? The dead wife of a vampire thought *him* an animal? Sean was amazed at the woman's audacity.

"Like it or not, Mother, he is my son's sire."

Narrowing his eyes, Sean frowned at the term *sire*. He was the child's *father*, not his overlord. But that was a detail he'd take up with Caitlin later. For now he chose to silently watch the byplay between the two women. He hoped it would give him a chance to catch his breath and regain some composure.

"This is how you defy the council? They gave you orders to keep your mouth shut and to stay away from this beast. Instead, you lied to us about where you were going and like some cheap whore, come running to the enemy's bed?"

"He is not *my* enemy."

Mrs. St. George flung her arm out and pointed a shaking finger at Sean. "That is a filthy beast. Your father would run him through with a sword and roast him on a spit like the pig he is, if he knew what you were doing."

The dragon within shook off its initial apprehension at Mrs. St. George's appearance. He focused his growing rage, intent on self-preservation, on the older woman. Never before had the desire to kill been so strong and overpowering—not even when he'd felt driven to murder his brothers. Who did this…ghost…think she was to threaten him in such a manner? *Roast him on a spit?* Sean clenched his fists tighter at his sides as he fought the unrelenting urge to shift into dragon form, rear up and do a little roasting of his own.

"What the hell is going on here?" Braeden materialized in the doorway, breaking the beast's murderous focus by his unexpected appearance. Had Sean been thinking, he would have realized that Harold would eventually contact Braeden, who would then spell himself directly into the middle of the action.

While he was grateful for his brother's timely interruption, Sean groaned at the speed Harold had obviously used in contacting his brother, instead of ordering the jet. "I've got this. Go back to your wife."

His brother cocked an eyebrow at him before studying Caitlin, who was still on the bed, flushed and looking as rumpled as the sheets beneath her, and then at her mother, who had turned to face him. A smirk lifted the corner of his mouth. "Why, Mrs. St. George, how's the hubby doing these days? Does his leg still bother him?"

Sean frowned in confusion. His brother drifted into his mind to fill in the missing piece. *At the last meeting of the heads of the preternatural families, St. George and I had a minor...tiff. He lost.*

Caitlin's mother stiffened at Braeden's question and raised her chin a notch. "That's Baron St. George to you, Drake."

Braeden leaned casually against the doorway and inspected his fingernails as if bored. "*Lord* Drake."

Sean knew his brother's nonchalant stance was nothing but an act. The deep steadiness of his voice had been a dead giveaway. He waited to see how Mrs. St. George would react to the Dragon Lord's reminder of who held the higher rank. Regardless of the families involved, St. George was just a baron in his circle, and while titled, he still answered to others. Braeden was the High Lord in his, answering to no one.

Finally, with a look that could kill a mortal, Mrs. St. George dipped her head slightly in deference. "The baron is well, my lord."

Braeden straightened and walked into the bedroom. "So, anyone care to explain what's going on here? Why has Lady St. George come to the Lair?" He paused by the bed to stare down at Caitlin. "And why is the dragon slayer's child in a dragon's bed?"

Caitlin corrected him. "My father's daughter is no longer a child, nor is he the dragon slayer. I am."

Braeden arched his eyebrows at her statement. Before the situation could get completely out of control, Sean insisted once again, "I can handle this."

Caitlin's mother visibly shook before exclaiming, "My daughter bore that vile beast's spawn!"

Sean cringed when he saw Braeden stiffen. This wasn't how he had wanted his family to find out.

Without asking permission, Braeden stroked Caitlin's cheek. His touch lingered far too long for Sean's comfort. He might not have been born a preternatural, but he knew enough about his brother to realize Braeden was mining information whether Caitlin wanted him to or not.

Finally, after what felt like hours, but was in fact mere seconds, Braeden lowered his arm and turned to glare at Sean. It was obvious from the darkness of his eyes and the tick in his cheek that he knew everything. "Could you have been any more foolish?"

"I…" Sean trailed off at the elongating of Braeden's pupils. Now was not the time to poke a stick at the one being that could kill him and his child's mother in the blink of an eye.

"You do understand what this means?"

"Yes." Of course he did.

Now.

He was mated…

For life.

Not only was the child his responsibility, so was the mother. Getting Caitlin to understand that would be the questionable part.

"Good. Have you thought about getting into Nathan's stronghold?"

"Haven't had time yet. I was seeing to another…problem first."

Braeden shot a hard gaze from him to Caitlin and back. "And you thought relinquishing a portion of your own strength would help the situation?"

His dragon bristled at the insinuation of weakness,

but Sean wasn't going to argue this with his brother at this very tense moment. So he simply nodded.

Thankfully, Braeden didn't press the issue. Instead, he said, "This explains your need for a jet. Mine will be ready within the hour. In the meantime, figure this—" he paused to wave a hand between the two of them then continued "—*problem* out. I'll head back to Mirabilus and nose around Nathan's stronghold. Either I, or Cam, will be in touch." Braeden nodded toward the older woman. "For future reference, whatever you do, don't let her, or her husband, get anywhere near my nephew."

Sean opened his mouth to ask why, but before he could utter a single syllable, Braeden was gone.

Still refusing to meet his gaze, Caitlin's mother stepped closer to the bed. Addressing her daughter, she said, "I will not have some beast telling me what I can or cannot do."

Beast? She called the Dragon Lord a beast in his own home? Sean had reached the limit of his patience. "Get out." When she didn't move, he let his dragon give the order. "Get. Out."

The raspy, deep command got her attention, although not in the manner he'd intended. She turned to look at him with all the concern of someone being pestered by a gnat. "I beg your pardon?"

Her shoulders sagging, Caitlin implored the older woman, "Mother, please, just go."

"Not without you, I won't. Your father has secured Baron Derek's signature on the prenuptial agreement. It seems that after careful consideration, and a substantial increase in the dowry, the baron is willing to ignore your childish escapades this last year. Besides, the elders have located a suitable family for the bastard you bore, and they'll be at the manor the day after tomorrow to collect him."

She turned to address Sean directly. "Now, if you'll just hand over the items we need for the ransom, we'll be on our way."

The woman couldn't be serious. He glanced at Caitlin, but she kept her head lowered, refusing to meet his gaze. They were going to give the baby to strangers? Just like that? Without even consulting him first?

It wasn't as if the two of them were too young or immature to care for a child. And it most certainly wasn't as if either one of them couldn't afford to care for the baby. There was no logical reason to give the child away to strangers. And to talk about it so callously, as if they were doing nothing more than giving away a lamp, was more than he could tolerate.

Rage burned in his chest. But he didn't know who he was angrier with—Lady St. George for her unforgivable rudeness, or Caitlin for acting as if this was all fine with her. He could deal with Caitlin later. Right now, however, he wanted her mother gone.

Sean didn't bother trying to hold his temper. The woman didn't deserve any type of restrained behavior from him. She could count herself lucky that he didn't unleash the dragon spitting and snarling inside him.

He strode across the room until he stood between Caitlin and her mother. Staring down at her, he once again ordered, "Get out of my apartment. Get out of the Lair. Now!"

She sighed and then motioned Caitlin to join her. "Come, it is time to leave."

"No!" Sean yelled at her while reaching back to hold

on to Caitlin's shoulder, keeping her pinned in place on the bed. "*You*, get out of here. She stays."

Lady St. George's eyes widened, and she grew more opaque with each passing second. Right before she completely disappeared, Sean said, "And don't come back."

"That wasn't necessary."

Sean spun around to look down at Caitlin. "I didn't ask for your opinion, did I?"

When she rose from the bed, he asked, "Where do you think you're going?"

"They aren't going to let me stay. I need to go home."

"*Let* you stay?" He didn't even try to hide the sarcasm in his voice. "What are you, ten years old?" Sean pointed at the bed. "Sit down. You aren't going anywhere."

"But—"

"But nothing." He interrupted her. "Oh, that's right, *Baron Derek* is waiting for you." The physical act of simply saying those words aloud sent the beast into a raging fit.

She shrugged her shoulders and said nothing.

"What makes you think I'm going to let the mother of my child marry another man?"

"What do you care? It's not as if I was ever going to marry you."

Sean laughed at her. "Oh, darlin', I don't remember asking you to marry me."

"Then what the hell are you talking about?"

He hadn't planned on giving her the news in this manner, but now was as good a time as any. "Didn't your daddy tell you? Must have been an oversight on his part. Why do you think he's so anxious to get you wed to someone else?"

She sighed and looked away. "Because he's tired of

hearing others talk about his daughter in such a degrading manner."

"Yeah, right, Caitlin. You know better than that. Do you really think St. George cares what anyone else says or thinks?"

"When it comes to me, yes, he does. He hates the dishonor I've brought to his door."

"You brought a baby to his door—my baby. Since when is there dishonor in creating life?"

"When that life is conceived out of wedlock and isn't of royal blood, there is plenty of dishonor."

And here he'd always thought Braeden had cornered the market on acting like a medieval lord. Apparently, he'd been wrong. Sean made a show of looking around the room. "In what century do you people live?"

She raised her hands, only to lower them back onto her lap. "You don't understand."

"Oh, hey, I get it. Wealth and power don't replace titled nobility in your little world." He moved closer to her. "Actually, it's you who doesn't understand. The reason your father is marrying you off as quickly as he can is because he knows that dragons mate for life."

"Mate?" She jumped up from the bed and glanced toward the door. "You talk like an animal."

"Of course I do." If she thought she was going to make a break for it and get out of this room, she was sadly mistaken. He stepped close enough that he could feel her confusion. "Do you forget *what* I am?"

Before she could answer, the wispy form of his dragon rose up from him, surrounding him. He stood in the center of the smoky creature and stared at her as his beast leaned forward to capture her gaze.

Spellbound by the glittering stare holding her captive, Caitlin shivered at the display of control and power before her.

Sean crossed his arms against his chest and asked, "Are you afraid, Caitlin?"

The beast lowered its head, sniffing her, chuffing her scent, and then rose up, its mouth open, fangs bared, growling in obvious displeasure.

"You should be afraid. Far more afraid of me than you are of your parents."

Caitlin respected her parents, didn't want to disappoint them any more than she already had and yes, to a certain extent, she did fear their wrath. However, her fear of him had the added element of possible death—hers. Summoning as much bravado as she could, Caitlin stared at him, asking, "You plan on terrifying me to prove that point?"

"No. But you need to understand there are no options for you."

"There are always options." There had to be.

"No." He circled her slowly, his beast moving with him. "Any option was lost when you carried the child to term. Had we not been mated, it's doubtful you would have been pregnant in the first place and even if by some chance you had, you would have lost the baby long before it was born. It's the nature of the beast—a way to prevent unwanted changelings."

A tiny part of her mind wondered if that was the reason her parents had essentially locked her away during her pregnancy. Since she had been ravenous the entire time, they'd said it was to protect the human population. Had they lied? Had it been done in hope that the baby would perish? *No.* She swatted down the thought. Even though they had withheld this mating information, she was certain they would never stoop so low. "Even if that's true, and we are...mated...it doesn't mean we have to have anything to do with each other once Sean is rescued."

"True. You're right." He agreed with her but then added, "However, there are two problems with having no contact. No matter what happens, you will never marry another man. Ever." The smooth curve of a talon traced her spine, making her shiver with fear and unexpected longing. "Do you understand me?"

"No. I don't. That doesn't make any sense. We aren't in love. We have no intentions of marrying each other."

"Perhaps not. But dragons mate for life."

He'd already said that. "And?"

"I can never take another mate while you live."

She closed her eyes. This was too much. She heard his words, but they made little sense. Pinning her gaze back on his, she asked, "So, if I don't stay with you, you'll spend the rest of your life alone?"

"Since I have no intention of raising a son without a mother, no, I would not live alone."

That meant— Her mind screamed. *Wait a minute!* No. He couldn't be serious. Could he? She felt as if she were choking on her own breath. "You would kill me?"

He lifted one eyebrow. "How dark is that cave where your mind goes?" He shook his head. "No, I have no intention of killing you. But you are my mate. You are *my* child's mother. And that's where the second problem comes into play. If you want to see the child grow up, you'll need to live here and trust me, you aren't doing so with a husband in tow."

Her stomach knotted at the implication. "Are you planning to take him away from me?"

"Absolutely. He is mine." A low, menacing growl raced hot against her ear. "What do you care? You were going to give him to strangers."

She trembled with dread. Her heart ached at the idea of losing her son forever. "That wasn't my idea."

"I didn't hear you argue with your mother about it."

Argue with her mother? That would have been a fine waste of time, since the woman would have simply ignored her. Never, for one second, had she worried about giving her son away—she'd had every intention of escaping with him and disappearing for good. "You don't understand."

"What don't I understand? That you were going to give my child to another family in the St. George clan?" His voice was tight with what she recognized as anger. "What were they going to do with him?" He grasped her arms and threw her mother's words in her face. "Run a sword through him and roast him on a spit like a pig?"

"No!" She tried to jerk free. "It's not like that."

"Then tell me what it is like." His hold on her arms tightened. "Tell me how much love and affection the child would have received from a clan who so obviously despises what he might become."

"Stop it. You don't know what you're talking about."

"It does make me wonder, though. Would you have attended the child's funeral wearing black? Would you have mourned his death? Or would you have avoided the event altogether?"

Her heart beat hard and fast, making breathing difficult. The smooth huskiness of his voice, more beast now than man, frightened her more than she ever thought possible. She kicked at him, twisted her arms to claw at him.

He threw her onto the bed, landing on top of her. She swung her fists. When he did nothing more than laugh, she bared her fangs and hissed.

Sean nearly laughed in her face. "You want fangs?" He turned her head with the palm of his hand, shoving her cheek into the pillow, holding her still, and sank the tip of his fangs into the tender curve where her neck met her shoulder.

His bite laced anger through Caitlin's growing horror. She struggled to shove him away, but he tightened his hold, sending a wave of pain shooting across her shoulder.

"Let me go."

His beast only growled, making her wonder who was in control—the man or the dragon.

Immortality had been her birthright from her father. She'd always taken comfort knowing that outside of having her heart, or head, ripped from her body, or starving to death, nothing would end her life.

However, with Sean's deadly fangs lodged so close to her neck, her immortality was in grave danger. The sticky warmth of her own blood soaking into her clothes only served to confirm the danger.

*Submit.*

The deep raspy voice of the beast flowed into her mind. But submitting to him wasn't an option. While the Drakes and St. Georges may have become slightly more civilized these last few centuries, after today that would change.

Her resistance gained her another deeper level of pain as his jaw tightened and he shook her.

*Submit.*

How? Caitlin sobbed at the futility of trying to fight this beast.

*Caitlin, for the sake of our child, submit.*

This deep voice, while still raspy and hoarse, did not contain the undertone of a beast. It was human, and its plea touched not just her mind, but something deeper, too.

With a sob, she fell lax beneath him.

After one final halfhearted shake, he gentled, releasing her, then soothing her injured flesh with his tongue, wiping away the blood and the pain as he tended the wound. His touch knitted muscle and flesh until it was once again whole.

Satisfied the injury had been healed, Sean lifted his head to look down at her and warn, "Don't ever fight me again."

"You have to be kidding. I'm supposed to bow to your every whim out of fear for my life?"

He heard the angry bravado in her trembling voice. Relieved that her terror had begun to subside, he lightened his tone. "See how easily you understand?"

"You are not some commanding deity that I need to mindlessly obey."

"Damn pity. However, it doesn't change the fact that I am responsible for your well-being and safety. It's instinctual. Things will go easier for you if you just do as you're told."

When she didn't respond to his flippancy, or statement of fact, he rose from the bed. "I need a minute alone, and I'm sure you could use some time to yourself, too. But we obviously have a plane to catch, so be quick." He glanced around the bedroom. "You said your luggage was in your car?"

She nodded and Sean headed toward the door. "I'll have it sent to the plane and your car parked in the garage. Join me out front when you're ready."

Caitlin waited a few minutes after he'd left the room before she rolled over and buried her face in the comforter on the bed. Why had she come here? What made her think that Sean would help her get their son back without any conditions of his own? She'd known he was a dragon changeling. She also knew what that meant—demanding, possessive and oh, so arrogant in his assumption that he alone was right. Yet she'd never had so much as a second thought about coming to him.

Her breath hitched, and she swallowed the urge to cry. Was her son warm? Was he dry? Had he been fed? Did they hold him when he cried?

They wouldn't know that he didn't like to be rocked; he'd rather be bounced. So if they rocked him, it would only make him more upset, more agitated. What if his anxiety was more than they could handle and prompted them to do something horribly reckless?

Dozing in the corner of the ancient puzzle box, Aelthed opened his eyes and tilted his head to one side with a frown. Something was…different. There was a certain *something* in the air swirling about his eternal jail.

It felt like… He leaned forward, his arms wrapped around his bent legs, studying the chemistry in the air. It felt like animal lust.

Need.

Desire.

He shook his head. From where had this emotion come? Who was the object of such primordial passion?

Even after more than eight long centuries of captivity, he understood and recognized the intense longing that charged the air swirling about him like lightning in a thunderstorm.

The dragon twins were already mated, so neither of them were the target. And he knew that it was not Danielle Drake. Her passion was for him, and it felt warm, comforting, enticing and nothing at all like this brewing storm.

"No." Aelthed rose and paced, hoping the movement would clear his mind of what was impossible. "It can't be."

The newest changeling wasn't a dragon born. It couldn't be him. His beast and power came from a curse alone, not from family blood. So why would that dragon's emotions flow all the way from Dragon's Lair to Mirabilus, into his cell and mind? Unless… Aelthed frowned. Was there more to this curse than he'd first feared?

Sending his thoughts out into the air, he whispered, "Danielle, come, talk to me."

Just saying her name eased the tension from his body and the frown from his face. Danielle Drake possessed far more than just guardianship of his prison—she possessed his heart. Since he'd forced himself into her hands a couple years ago, he'd come to care for her deeply and he was well aware she shared the same feelings for him.

After Nathan the Learned had dropped the box that kept Aelthed imprisoned at the feet of the Dragon Lord's wife, Alexia, they had put him in the basement with their weapons and forgotten about him. Which suited him fine, because it gave him the chance to listen and learn.

When it became necessary to gain assistance, he'd sought out Danielle Drake. Aelthed laughed softly remembering the first time he'd spoken to her. At that moment he'd been grateful for two things—that Danielle was telepathic and that his nephew Nathan had kept him updated on the current languages through the decades. Otherwise he never would have been able to converse with the woman.

He might have only been a spirit imprisoned in a puzzle box, but that didn't stop him from noticing how beautiful she was with her womanly curves and long raven tresses. He'd been drawn to her from the first moment she'd touched his box and made him gasp at the warmth that had flooded through him.

She was so easy to talk to, quick of wit and old enough to know her own mind. Which she had to be, considering she'd raised her three nephews alone after their parents had been killed at Nathan's hand. It was a shame she'd never married, never had the opportunity to share a life and experiences with someone her own age. But she'd insisted more than once that her life had been full and she was content with her lot—especially now that she had Aelthed to share her joys and troubles with.

He'd once lamented the huge difference in their ages and she'd laughed at him. While it was true that he was over nine hundred years of age and she only sixty-two, he'd only lived as a man for eighty of those years. As far as she was concerned, he wasn't all that much older.

He didn't argue with her logic, because it made no difference while he was locked in a wooden cube.

Within moments, he felt her warm touch on the box as she lifted it from her nightstand. "What is it, Aelthed? What do you need?"

He shivered at the low, seductive timbre of her voice. Oh, to be alive again, to be a man capable of gathering her into his arms for an embrace, a kiss, a prelude to making love. A wry smile briefly crossed his lips. Dreams and wishes were all he had and of late, they weren't nearly enough.

Opening his mind to his surroundings, he brought her into view. He nodded with approval at the way she'd been wearing her hair down lately, instead of twisted up into a tight bun. She looked younger, more alive with the raven tresses streaming along her back. Forcing his attention back to the subject at hand, he asked, "Your nephew, the youngest one, is he still back at Dragon's Lair?"

He felt the woman's hesitation before she answered, "Yes, he is."

"And tell me, Danielle, what troubles him?"

She sat on the edge of her bed and sighed. "I'm not sure of all the facts since Braeden just returned from the Lair. But it seems Sean got a vampire's daughter pregnant. She had a son, and he's been kidnapped."

A vampire? The changeling lusted after a vampire? "Good heavens, not St. George?"

"Of course. Would one of the Drake boys choose anyone…normal?"

Aelthed chuckled at her long-suffering tone. Even though she'd done a fine job, she never should have had to raise three Drake males on her own. "No. It would make your life all too boring if they did."

Danielle nodded in agreement. "I suppose so." She placed the puzzle cube on a pillow and stretched out on the bed. "So, what can you tell me about St. George?"

"Well, it's your great-great-great-grandsire's fault that he's a vampire. If I recall the rumors correctly, the two of them got into a fight—the dragon and the dragon slayer—and when the dragon managed to knock the slayer out, he left the man tied to a tree in the forest assuming someone would come along and free him."

"I can guess the rest." Danielle snorted. "He was found by a vampire, not another human."

"Yes. Which explains the deep-seated hatred between the two families."

"Not that they ever would have been the best of friends in the first place."

"Perhaps not, but we can do nothing about the past. Only the future. How did the cursed changeling get a vampire pregnant?"

"She's not exactly a vampire. Braeden says she's a succubus."

Aelthed considered that possibility then shook his head. "Doubtful. I think the Dragon Lord may be mistaken on this one. Although I am willing to guess that if she's not a full blood-sucking vampire, that she may be a psychic soul-sucking one. Does she have fangs?"

"I don't know. I haven't met her."

"This babe she bore, is it human—or otherworldly?"

"I'm not sure." Danielle shook her head and sighed. "But since its mother isn't human, doesn't it stand to reason that the babe might not be, either?"

More to himself than anyone else, Aelthed mused, "I wasn't thinking of the mother."

Danielle's frown deepened. "Surely you don't think this curse on my nephew carried over to his child?"

"Considering the oddities of late, it's something we need to consider." Even though Aelthed could already guess her answer, he had to ask, "I don't suppose you know if the babe has shown any habits that might be considered…purely Drake?"

"I can't answer that, either. I know nothing more than

you." Danielle picked up the cube and held it out before her. "Right now all I know for certain—" she drew the cube closer and then dropped her voice to little more than a whisper "—is that your nephew, Nathan the Learned, has the child and is using him as leverage to get his hands on the grimoire...and you."

# Chapter 4

Caitlin awoke with a start, uncertain where she was at first until a warm hand brushed down her arm. Then it all came rushing back—her arrival at Dragon's Lair, her mother's intrusion and boarding the plane.

When they'd boarded, she hadn't paid much attention. It'd been easy enough to fall asleep when they'd left Tennessee, but not so much now. Even though she was still exhausted, she looked around the dimly lit cabin. The only description she could think of off the top of her head was air yacht. The Drakes' private jet wasn't a short-hop plane. From the size of it, the baby could easily do transcontinental flights with ease.

The interior looked nothing like any plane she'd ever flown on before. She stretched her legs out before her, pressing her back into the baby-soft leather of the seat. No wonder she'd fallen asleep so quickly; this was easily the most comfortable recliner she'd ever sat in before.

From behind black-padded doors toward the rear of the plane, Sean's voice drifted across her ears. Apparently, he was on the phone again, meaning she was free to go snooping.

Caitlin felt the side of the chair for a button to lower the leg rest. Instead, the one she pressed extended the chair out into a bed. Comfortable? Yes, but not what she wanted. She pressed another button and this time righted the piece of furniture to a chair and then swiveled away from the window. She rose and stepped around the chair next to hers—there were four of them, one on each side of the aisle and the chairs could swivel to face each other if the people seated wanted to hold a conversation.

Behind this setup was another, but while still recliners, the chairs were more like airplane seats in that they didn't swivel around. Between the two sets of chairs was a table that folded down against the wall.

She turned around and walked past the swivel recliners into a small kitchen—or galley, she supposed—and pulled open the fridge to take a bottle of water. The closed doors beyond the galley probably led into the cockpit. She had no desire to see what was there, so turned around and walked into Sean's chest.

"Looking for something?"

"No. Just being nosy."

He laughed. "It's a winged travel home. Braeden does nothing in half measures." Pointing down the aisle, he added, "On the other side of the first set of doors is the head...bathroom. Double sink, shower, toilet. Beyond that is another set of doors that leads to another cabin with more private seating for four. Beyond that a sound-proof door concealing the bedroom, where there's two sofas that fold out to beds."

Then he slid open a small panel on the wall next to the galley door and pressed a button. A huge screen slid down in the center of the cabin. "And if you want to watch a movie, you can do that in any of the cabins. Including the head, except that screen's a little smaller."

Caitlin widened her eyes. "Impressive."

"No half measures whatsoever."

"I can't imagine his travel trailer."

Sean laughed. "Where did you get the idea that Braeden goes camping?"

"No?"

He escorted her to the double chairs. "Hardly."

They no sooner sat down than his phone rang again. "Excuse me." He rose and walked down the aisle.

She turned her attention out the window to see only the blackness of the night. They were headed to the Drake family's medieval stronghold on Mirabilus—an island somewhere in the Irish Sea.

It was said that the glamour spell cast over the isle, more than a thousand years ago, still held, and that any mortal who looked upon it saw nothing but mist and fog obscuring their vision.

She couldn't begin to imagine a magic that strong. What sort of power did it take to cast such a permanent spell? This island had been in his family's possession since the beginning of time. What sort of powers did he and his brothers hold?

Caitlin glanced toward Sean before looking back out at the expanse of darkness. He was still on the phone. Had one of his brothers discovered something about her son? She folded and unfolded her hands, fighting the impatience gnawing at her. It had only been a few hours, but her worry for her son made her anxious and left her wondering why this seemingly top-of-the-line plane was taking so long to get to Mirabilus.

"Soon." Sean sat back down and covered her fidgeting hands with one of his own. Obviously, his call had ended. "We'll be there soon."

When she only yawned then nodded in response,

he slipped his arm across her shoulders and pulled her against him, asking, "Tired?"

"Very." But the knowledge that they were getting closer to her son now had her nerves on edge. Besides, his fingers circling her shoulder, and the warmth of his side against hers, had her wishing for something more than sleep.

Even though she didn't feel his presence in her mind, his deep chuckle let her know that he was tuned in to her thoughts and she tried to pull away, but he simply swept her into his arms and across his lap as if she were nothing more than a rag doll.

"Where were we before your mother appeared?"

The warmth of his breath whispering against her ear sent shivers down her spine. Caitlin sighed and pushed against his shoulder. "Not in public." She had no intention of joining any mile-high club.

"There's no one here." He made a show of looking around the empty cabin. "It's not as if we're aboard a commercial airliner."

"Was that your brother on the phone?" She tried to change the direction of their conversation before it got out of control.

"Of course." While he followed her lead with the conversation, he didn't stop caressing her shoulder. In fact, the free hand he'd placed on her stomach was now inching higher.

"Anything I should know? Did he discover something about little Sean?"

"No. We were discussing our living arrangements at Mirabilus."

"What do you mean by *our* living arrangements?" She

sucked back a soft gasp as he brushed his hand along the underside of her breast.

"As in where we'll be sleeping."

He'd easily, and all too conveniently, ignored the intended emphasis she'd placed on the word *our.* Caitlin wished she could just as easily ignore the warmth of his hand that had trailed away from her shoulder to steadily stroke the sensitive spot beneath her ear. With all of the calmness she could muster, she asked, "Any reason we can't have separate rooms?"

"A few." He leaned his head down to rest his lips behind her ear. "For one thing, while it may be a castle, it doesn't have near unlimited supply of empty rooms."

"Uh-huh." She closed her eyes, savoring the rush of sexually charged pleasure rippling to life. She really should stop him.

And she would…soon.

"For another thing—" he paused to graze her earlobe with his teeth then continued "—why wouldn't we share a room?"

His lips joined in the play along with his teeth. She wasn't certain which would make her lose focus first— the light nips from his teeth or the gentle suckling of his lips. She'd had no idea earlobes could be that sensitive. Caitlin leaned away, but he just followed along.

"We aren't a couple." For some reason her tone didn't sound too sure of that fact even to her own ears.

"No?"

He brushed his thumb across her breast. Her nipples strained through the layers of clothing to get closer to his touch. She gritted her teeth to keep from crying out with longing, swallowed hard and finally said, "No. We aren't."

He caressed her thigh, making her jump in surprise. When had he moved his hand from her breast? While she was still sorting through that quandary, he asked, "So, we don't have a child together?"

"Yes, we do." She grabbed his hand, stopping him from sliding it between her thighs.

"So at some point in time we were most definitely a couple."

She couldn't argue that point. However, she responded, "We were only together a few nights."

"And days."

He relaxed the hand on her leg. Caitlin followed suit, easing up on the confining grip she had on his hand. Sean entwined his fingers through hers and lifted their joined hands to his lips.

Wondering what he was up to now, she looked at him. The shimmer of his eyes warned her that she wasn't going to agree with whatever plot he was devising.

He kissed the back of her hand before moving his lips to hers.

She closed her eyes, not fighting the kiss or the empowering breath flowing into her, feeding her sorely depleted stores. Her mind seemed to spin in a whirlwind of colors that beckoned her to lose herself in the brilliant maelstrom.

Then a touch, the stroke of palm against flesh, unfettered by clothing, brushed slowly down the length of her body.

Caitlin froze. He'd slipped into her mind with his kiss and she'd been too weak, too tired to sense his presence until he was inside. But that didn't mean she had to quietly accept his intrusion.

She pulled away from his kiss, but he held her close

and whispered, "Accept my offer, Caitlin. I have enough energy for both of us, and I freely give you whatever you need."

When she hesitated, he rested his forehead against hers and said, "I swear to you, we can argue and fight about it later. There'll be plenty of time. For now, if you won't feed for yourself, do it for our son. He needs you."

Unable to withstand the lull of his voice and the heat of his mental touch, she relaxed in his embrace, accepting the return of his kiss and the strength he offered.

Sean knew this wouldn't last for long. The Caitlin he remembered from their brief tryst would never have rested so pliantly in his arms, permitting him to have his way. Nor would she have surrendered so easily to his physical, or mental, touch. Doing so attested to her near starvation.

She wouldn't have done this to herself. The thought that anyone would have starved her in this manner sent his blood boiling. And the thought that they'd probably done so because of the child added his beast's rage to his own. They would pay—with their lives if the dragon had any say in the matter.

Her throaty moan tore him from the darkness of his thoughts. He frowned, realizing that this mental play, this stroking and touching, no matter how focused, wasn't going to be enough to satisfy the hunger tearing at her.

Sean knew he couldn't do this without his beast's help. After all, that had to be where the magic originated, so he hoped the brute would behave himself. He gave control of this mind play to the dragon, trusting the beast wouldn't harm his own mate.

While they physically stayed in the seat they shared,

in his mind the dragon came to life. A mass of foggy mist swirled into the form of the beast before dissipating, only to return in the shape of a man. He glanced over his shoulder and for a split second, Sean saw the elongated emerald gaze of his dragon.

The power and lust in that brief glimpse sent a shiver down his spine. But the tremor evaporated, replaced with a heat so intense Sean wondered if they'd burn alive.

A woman appeared out of the lingering mist. Not any woman, but Caitlin. A timid smile crossed her lips, but her amber-hued eyes held a wariness that couldn't be denied. She didn't trust the beast—didn't trust him to hold control.

He'd have to prove her fears baseless.

He reached for her and the plane lost altitude as if it would fall from the sky. It took a moment for Sean to realize the motion of the jet was real—it wasn't some imagined feeling of bottomlessness.

The Fasten Seat Belt light blinked on. At the same time, the pilot's voice filled the cabin. "Sorry about that. We've hit a pocket of turbulence. Should be out of it soon."

It was all Sean could do not to growl in frustration. This was one of the many reasons he didn't like flying in planes—the utter lack of control.

Caitlin scrambled back into her seat and fastened her seat belt. She was flush, shaking, and it didn't take a genius to know it wasn't from the plane's sudden movement.

He leaned over and captured her lips beneath his. Their kiss was brief since that wasn't his intent. When she parted her lips, he exhaled as much of his energy and power as he could, willing her to absorb what little he could offer in this manner.

She stroked the side of his face, rested her hand against his cheek and slowly inhaled. Her fingers against his skin trembled. When she started to pull away, he cupped the back of her head and held her steady. Regardless of what she thought, or feared, she couldn't drain him. His beast would never permit such a thing to happen.

Once her heartbeat slowed, and her fingers stilled, he released her. "Will that hold for now?"

"Yes. Thank you." She turned away to stare out the window.

The plane hit another patch of turbulence and she grasped his forearm. "Sean!"

He patted her hand. "It'll be fine."

"No. Look!"

He followed the line of her finger to the outside of the plane. The turbulence hadn't been caused by any weather formation. The dark shape of a demon beast near the tip of the wing was the reason the plane's flight pattern had been so erratic.

"What is that?"

Sean had the distinct impression that he somehow knew this demon, but how? "I think the question is *who* is that, not what."

"Fine, then, who is it?"

"I would guess our son's kidnapper."

Caitlin gasped. "Do something."

While reaching for his cell phone, Sean looked at her to ask, "What exactly do you want me to do?" He wasn't about to slip into the demon's mind to try forcing him away, and he wasn't able to materialize on the outside of the plane. If that thing was Nathan the Learned, as he feared, he would be literally risking not just his own life, but those of Caitlin and their child, as well.

He hit speed dial on his phone. "Cam, we have a problem here."

Not bothering to wait for an explanation, his brother rushed into his mind and pulled out just as quickly, leaving Sean reeling from the rush.

Within seconds, two dragons appeared behind the demon.

"Your brothers?" Caitlin asked.

He studied them briefly then shook his head. "No. Cam and his wife, Ariel."

Surprised, she asked, "She's a dragon changeling, too?"

"Only when she's pregnant." At her questioning look, he explained, "She takes on the abilities of the baby she carries." Which obviously meant another Drake was on the way soon.

"How did they get here so quickly?"

Sean explained, "Just like Braeden, Cam is also able to materialize where he's needed in an instant. Since he was most likely with Ariel, it's a fair bet she demanded to come along."

"But how did he know what was happening? Are they watching us?"

"In a manner of speaking, yes. This jet is Braeden's pride and joy. He was probably keeping his awareness on it and knew when trouble threatened."

The dragons double-teamed the demon with a div-ing-bombing aerial assault. They worked in perfect uni-son, and Sean could only imagine the exhilaration they felt at their spiraling maneuvers. The demon beast was no match for the two larger and faster dragons, and it quickly disappeared into the night sky.

Cam hung back long enough to peer in the window at Caitlin. She leaned away. "What does he want?"

"Thank you. Now go home." Sean tapped a finger on the glass. "He's just being nosy. He'd never admit it, but it's a common ailment for him. Especially in beast form."

"Sort of like a dog?"

The dragon reared back as if it had heard her comment, which he probably had, and spun away.

Sean snorted in amusement, but said in a more serious tone, "I'm not too sure that's the way to talk to something who just rescued you."

"I wasn't thinking." Caitlin sighed. "I'll apologize later."

The seat belt light blinked off.

His phone rang. Sean absently looked at the caller ID before responding to Caitlin. "You do that, but right now get some sleep. We'll be at Mirabilus soon."

She shook her head. "I can't sleep."

There were things he couldn't do like his brothers could, but this wasn't one of them. He placed his palm over her eyes and whispered, "Sleep, Caitlin, just go to sleep."

Once certain she was resting comfortably, he rose and disappeared into the rear cabin to return Braeden's call.

Someone touched her arm, startling her from her odd dreams of demons, dragons and wizards.

"Caitlin. We're here."

She blinked the sleep from her eyes and frowned before turning an accusing glare toward Sean. She'd been unable to fall asleep until he'd placed his hand over her eyes and ordered her to go to sleep. How many other powers did he have that would also prove unwelcome? "You knocked me out."

He ignored her and moved away to the already open exit door. "Coming?"

She followed him down the steps onto the runway and into a waiting limo. "You have everything at your fingertips, don't you?" She winced at the snippiness of her tone.

"And you don't?" Sean shook his head at her comment. "If it all disappeared tomorrow, I'd still know how to survive. Would you?"

Caitlin looked down at her lap. He'd basically been decent to her during the entire trip. He could have grilled her about what had happened in his bedroom with her mother, but instead he'd seemed to have declared an unspoken truce—at least for now. What was wrong with her? Why on earth was she picking the stupidest fight possible? "No, probably not."

He reached over to cover her folded hands. "Is this really an argument you want to pursue?"

"No." She slid her hands from beneath his. "I don't know what's wrong with me."

He chuckled softly and raised a hand to count off items on his fingers. "One, you were locked in a cell and nearly starved. Two, our son was taken from you by force. Three, you're here with me when you seem to have a fiancée to deal with. Four, again, you're here with me, your family's enemy, at my family's stronghold. Five, I don't think you've taken in enough energy to have the strength to think rationally about much of anything. Need me to go on?"

"No." He might have been right on all counts, but he didn't have to sound so smug.

The limo drove beneath a huge set of gates, at which point Sean said, "Besides, there'll be enough to fight about in a few minutes."

His comment as they pulled up to the castle sounded more like a warning than anything else, and it confused her already drowning senses. "If you're so certain we'll end up arguing with our next breath, why were you so kind on the plane?"

"I don't like to fly. Why would I willingly step into a tin can with wings, give up control to someone else, when I can move quicker and safer by myself?" He paused to shrug. "It seemed it might be easier to not spend the time aboard the craft fighting."

"I could have flown alone."

"Right. And who would you have called when trouble showed up at the wing?"

"Again, thank you."

"Don't thank me." He waved toward the gathering near the doors. "Thank Cam and Ariel."

The car came to a smooth stop, and Sean opened the door to exit. He stopped and then turned half around to face her. "By the way, Aunt Danielle is already planning our wedding."

"Our what?"

Her expected shout would have been laughable had he not been so serious. Sean stepped out of the car and offered her his hand. She looked at the appendage as if she contemplated removing it from his arm.

"I warned you that we'd be arguing soon."

She took his hand and slid across the backseat. "Arguing?" Caitlin swung her legs around. "There's no sense arguing about something that will never happen."

He pulled her from the car and against his chest to whisper into her ear. "We're in agreement there, but arguing with Danielle Drake will only ensure it happens."

"So we just agree with her instead?"

Sean sidestepped and rested his palm on the small of her back to escort her to the castle doors. "Don't agree to anything. Hedge."

He paused in front of Braeden. "You two have met." His brother nodded.

Caitlin's soft intake of breath let him know she'd noticed Cam. How could she not? Other than the color of their eyes, he and Braeden were identical.

Quickly filling her in on who was who, Sean slipped into her mind. *"You obviously realize the twins are Braeden and Cameron. Braeden's eyes are amethyst, Cam's are sapphire. You might notice that Braeden has just a touch more silver streaks at the temples, but don't mention it, he'll only argue. The older woman with the long black hair is my aunt Danielle Drake—she's not a changeling. The woman with the dark brown hair is Ariel, Cam's wife, and she can only take dragon form when she's pregnant. Braeden's wife, Alexia, is probably upstairs with the children. You'll recognize her by her red hair, and she's not a changeling, either."*

Caitlin sighed, then responded in the same manner, asking, *"And I'm supposed to remember all of that?"*

"Sorry to intrude." Ariel stepped forward. "You'll figure us all out soon enough." She extended her hand to Caitlin in welcome. "You should try to tell the twins apart when they're wearing colored contacts."

"I think I'll pass on that." Caitlin asked, "Were you one of our rescuers?"

Ariel waved off the question as if it was nothing more than a common, everyday occurrence. "Glad to help."

"I do thank you." Caitlin glanced to Cam. "And you, too."

As talkative as his twin, Cam simply nodded.

And then to Sean's complete surprise, his brother barked like a dog. Just once, but it was enough to make Caitlin flush with embarrassment. She managed to choke out, "I apologize," before looking as if she wished she had the ability to disappear on whim.

Aunt Danielle's eyebrows rose a fraction of an inch before she chastised Cam with a piercing look.

Braeden cleared his throat and motioned to the door. "Let's move this inside."

Once the heavy doors thudded closed behind them, Ariel and Cam wandered off arm in arm with nothing more than a wave over their shoulders. Aunt Danielle hung around until Braeden stared her down and she made her own exit up the curved staircase.

The moment Caitlin parted her lips, Braeden raised a hand. "I have nothing in the way of news. You'd already told us that Nathan holds the child in his castle ruins, but a quick flyby came up empty. I spoke with Baron St. George, and he had nothing new to impart. I have men searching the area but until they return in the morning, there's not much else I can tell you."

Sean felt her pain; it twisted in her gut like the sharp blade of a knife and slammed into her chest with the force of an unseen battering ram. He pulled her to his side, wishing there was a way to spare her the agony she suffered, asking Braeden, "Is my suite ready?"

"Yes." His brother paused a split second then added, "And her bags were just delivered."

"Let's go upstairs." Sean coaxed Caitlin to come with him, fully prepared to carry her if need be.

To his relief, she shook off the utter doom surrounding her long enough to bid Braeden good-night. Then she followed him to the rear of the Great Hall, where an elevator was concealed behind a large tapestry.

They'd made a great many updates to modernize the medieval keep over the last few years. Nearly all of them welcome improvements as far as Sean was concerned.

Caitlin's eyes widened briefly as the elevator door slid open, prompting Sean to offer, "We could use the stairs if you like."

"This is fine." She entered the cab. "Have many improvements been done?"

He hit the button to close the doors. "You mean like running water and electricity? Yes." Leaning against the wall he leveled his gaze on her. "But if you're looking for a dungeon, it's been turned into a gym."

She grimaced, making him wonder why the mention of a dungeon would bother her.

Caitlin asked, "I take it the truce is officially over?"

"Apparently." She had to have known they'd be back to this conversation eventually. There were still too many unanswered questions. Such as what exactly did she think she was going to do with their son—his son—when they got him back? And who was this Baron Derek?

When the elevator bounced to a stop, he led her through the open doors and down the hall to his suite, where he placed his index finger to a touch pad outside the door. After the barely perceptible sound of the lock tumbling into place reached his ears, he pushed the door open. Not having to carry keys, or keep track of a keycard, was just another modernization that made life easier.

He ushered her inside a suite that looked fairly identical to his apartment at Dragon's Lair. Sean checked the bedroom to ensure her luggage had indeed arrived then came back out to the living room.

"Your luggage is in the bedroom. Are you hungry?"

"No. But I'd like to take a shower and change my clothes."

"Feel free." He waved toward the bedroom. "Take your time."

He watched her walk down the hallway and wished for a moment their truce was still in effect. Perhaps then she wouldn't be taking a shower alone.

His wandering thoughts were cut short by the sound of items thumping and clattering onto the kitchen counter.

Sean stared at the items that had suddenly materialized on the kitchen counter. The jewel-encrusted, worn, leather-bound book was the family grimoire. Since it'd been locked away in Braeden's office safe, obviously his brother had sent it to him.

Two dragon pendants, one emerald, the other one sapphire, appeared next to the book. Sean rolled his eyes. Those could only have come from his sisters-in-law, which meant Braeden hadn't wasted a moment getting the rest of the family on board.

He flipped open the grimoire to glance at the first few pages. Sean knew, from his brothers' experiences, that he'd likely see nothing that could help him without Caitlin being present, so he closed the book and then opened the fridge, looking for something to wash the dryness from his mouth. Not finding anything that looked remotely interesting, he closed the door, only to open it again, pull out a pitcher of orange juice and then pour a glass.

He glanced at the clock. Nearly an hour had gone by since they'd entered the suite. What was keeping Caitlin? He'd told her to take her time, but hadn't expected her to avoid him this long.

She couldn't have disappeared. He hadn't detected that ability in her, and he was certain that if she could, she would have when the demon showed up outside the plane. No, she was still in the bedroom, intentionally avoiding him in all likelihood.

Sean placed the glass in the sink and then left the kitchen to stand before the open sliding doors that led out to the balcony. The ever-darkening forest beyond Mirabilus seemed oddly comforting. Lengthening shadows creeping slowly closer to the castle, along with the creaking and moaning of the pines as they swayed against the brisk sea breeze, served to calm his dragon.

Over the passing months Sean had discovered that his beast took comfort from things others considered dark or eerie. Instead of causing tension or putting him on edge, he found himself relaxing, easing peacefully into the crash of thunder, streaks of lightning and the approaching darkness of night.

Howls and growls of beasts in the distance, generally unheard by human ears, set him at ease. Just knowing that nature was performing as it should was enough to lull him into deep, blissful slumber.

At one time the low chuff or growl of a bear would

have caused him concern, as would the mournful howl of a wolf. But now, as much beast as he was human, the territorial protests of the forest animals caused him nothing more than a second's notice—a mere heartbeat of recognition before it was swept along with all the other *nonevent* moments of life.

Sean glanced toward the hallway. A *nonevent* kind of moment was what Caitlin should have been. She should have remained an extremely gorgeous woman he walked by on his way out of the bar. Instead, he'd had to meet her, had to mark her, had to spend three days and nights in her bed.

And because of all those *had tos* he was now a father and mated. And his child was stolen, a bargaining chip in a game as old as time.

Being a father wasn't a bad thing. It actually made him feel as if he'd accomplished the miraculous feat alone. And being mated also wasn't exactly a bad thing. Although Sean wished he'd had more say in the matter, more time to decide if this was truly his mate before the beast had up and taken the decision out of his hands. While it was too late now, it would have been nice if the dragon could have chosen someone who actually wanted to be mated to him.

Some type of shared wanting would come in handy for this wedding his aunt was planning. The woman was going to be sadly disappointed when it came to her youngest nephew since he wasn't at all interested in getting married.

But right now he had other, more important things to concern him. Like the little fact that he was essentially lying—withholding the full truth—to Caitlin about something that really wasn't quite so little, after all.

How was he going to tell her that everything she thought she knew about him was a lie, or at least not the whole truth? He wasn't a dragon born. His beast existed because of a curse, and he had no way of knowing what would happen once that curse was broken.

Hell, he didn't know if it could be broken. And even if he discovered a way to rid himself of this curse, did he want to surrender that part of him?

# Chapter 5

Sean turned away from the panoramic view and headed down the hall to see what was keeping Caitlin, meeting her as she opened the door, rubbing a towel over her head. "I was coming to get you."

She peeked at him from beneath the bath towel. "You told me to take some time, so I did." She snatched the towel from her head. "I assumed we weren't going out anywhere, but I didn't really bring anything comfy-casual to wear, so I borrowed some things from your dresser. I hope you don't mind."

Sean lowered his gaze from her wet hair. He couldn't remember his T-shirt or sweatpants ever looking quite so beguiling before. Of course she had to choose one of his old, small, thin, white T-shirts that suddenly seemed nearly transparent where it hugged her body. Even though she'd lost far too much weight since he'd last seen her, there was still enough padding beneath her smooth flesh to provide curves worth exploring.

Caitlin shoved the wadded-up, damp towel against his chest. "They're called breasts, and you've seen them before."

Unable to speak through the dryness making his tongue stick to the roof of his mouth, he stood there in silence and watched her sashay down the hallway toward the kitchen. The gray sweatpants—also threadbare and too small even for her—accentuated each and every dip and curve.

Oh, yeah, she'd chosen clothes from the bottom of the these-are-too-small drawer of his dresser on purpose. If she thought to distract him, the tightening of his groin and heavy thudding of his heart proved her effort successful.

Where his instinct was to protect and command, hers was to tease and tempt. And when she wasn't outright exhausted, she did a damn fine job at both. He tossed the towel behind him, not caring if it made it to his bedroom floor or not, and took a deep breath before following the bewitching temptress into the kitchen.

"Are these what I think they are?" Caitlin touched a fingertip to the grimoire before picking up the emerald and sapphire dragon pendants. "What about the box?"

"That's in Danielle's possession. I don't expect to see it tonight."

She frowned and then slid her gaze from the sparkling gems to him. "You're going to let me give the book and pendants to Nathan?"

Sean shook his head. "Hardly."

"Not even in exchange for our son?"

Only if it became absolutely necessary and he had a surefire way to ensure the items stayed safely in Drake possession. But he wasn't going to tell her that. "We'll get our son back."

"Not if we stand here chatting."

It was only natural for her to be upset over the kidnapping, so he wasn't surprised by the coldness in her voice. But her words chipped at his patience. "You didn't think I was coming here just to rush pell-mell into the Learned's stronghold without a plan in place first, did you?"

When she didn't respond, he stared at the flush coloring her cheeks and realized that was exactly what she'd thought. "Just how stupid do you think I am?"

"I never thought you were stupid. Just..."

"Gullible? Easily beguiled? Quickly seduced?" He leaned on the counter next to her. "You thought what? That you'd walk back into my life, surround me with an aura of lust and I'd hand the ransom over to you without question?" Sean dipped his head closer to hers. "What made you think I would do that?"

"He's our son."

"I know that. But the Learned has used every trick conceivable to gain possession of these items. Since the only thing he craves is power, it's apparent that somehow having these items would make him too powerful for anyone to stop. You yourself said that you felt his evilness. That is not someone who should be permitted to live, let alone rule the world."

"So, you will risk our son's life to stop Nathan?"

He would risk his own life to stop the Learned, but not the child's. "We will get the boy back."

"How?" She slapped a hand flat on the countertop. "How are we going to get him back?" Her voice rose with each word until she paused, gasping, then breathlessly asked again, "Will you risk his life to stop Nathan?"

The shakiness of her voice let him know that the minuscule amount of strength he had given her earlier aboard the plane was fading. Sean moved behind her.

She stiffened, but then her body softened, welcoming his warmth, and he pressed against her.

"Caitlin, I know you are frustrated and that everything seems to be taking forever, but I promise you, the child will come to no harm. Nathan may be twisted and brutal, but he is far from stupid. He knows the child's value. He knows full well that if he harms the boy, he'll get nothing. And I assure you, Nathan isn't going to risk coming up empty-handed." He grasped her shoulders and squeezed lightly. "We have a small leeway of time to plan his rescue. So try to unwind a little. We will figure this out."

Once she relaxed slightly, he reached around and opened the grimoire. "This is the history of the Drake family from the Middle Ages until now." He turned the pages slowly, letting her look at each one.

"What do I care about your family's history?"

"This book contains spells that only a dragon and his mate can see. It might have some answers for us."

"Why do you have it, then? You didn't know you had a mate until recently."

"While I waited for you to join me, it just appeared on the counter."

"Simply appeared?"

"Yeah, I'm told it does that on occasion."

"Wonderful."

By her tone of voice, he didn't think she thought it was *wonderful* at all. To ease her concern, and uncertain if it was true or not, he said, "Braeden spelled it here."

He flipped the first two pages and then paused. "That wasn't here before."

"What do you mean, it wasn't there?"

"I just looked at these first few pages while you were

in the bedroom, and this one wasn't here. Apparently the history of this book is true."

"In what way?"

Sean turned back a page, then flipped back to the new image. "It seems that part of the book's magic is that it'll paint scenes meant only for us."

"Do you think it will tell us how to get Sean back?"

"We'll have to go through it to find out."

Both of them looked at a picture of two young women kneeling on the floor with a wooden chest between them. He studied the image. It looked as though the women were using two of the dragon pendants as keys to unlock the chest. One pendant was sapphire and now belonged to Cameron's wife, Ariel. The emerald one, which currently belonged to Alexia, wasn't in the picture. He'd never seen or heard anything about the amethyst one the other woman was using on the chest.

He shook his head. This was something he'd have to ask his brothers, or Aunt Dani about, because if the picture was right, there was still one pendant missing. And the wooden box was nothing like the cube Aunt Dani kept close at hand at all times. The one in the grimoire was shaped more like a small chest.

Sean turned to the next page. This picture was still in the Middle Ages and was of an old, white-haired man on a bed, with a crazed-looking younger man leaning over him holding a puzzle box.

This one he understood. He tapped the image of the younger man. "This is Nathan the Learned. Unfortunately, he is a distant relative."

"Is that the box he wants?"

"I'm sure it is. It contains the soul of his uncle Aelthed." He pointed toward the older man. "That must be Aelthed."

At Caitlin's frown, he explained, "In the twelfth century, Nathan conjured a spell to capture his uncle's soul the moment it left his body, and it's been there ever since. He did so because Aelthed killed his own brother, Nathan's father, for committing what amounted to treason against the family and then buried him in an unhallowed grave. At the time, Aelthed was the Druid High Lord and when his death was at hand, he refused to pass the power on to Nathan."

Caitlin brushed a fingertip across the image of the puzzle box. "So even if Nathan wasn't evil from the beginning, he was pushed into it?"

"I don't know for certain. I can only guess that he was evil from the day he was born and Aelthed's actions were the tipping point." Sean turned the pages, letting each flip past in vivid illuminations. Every page propelled them through the decades.

"Stop!" Caitlin grabbed Sean's wrist to stop him from turning over that page. "That's my father." She stared at the picture of a man tied to a tree while a half man, half dragon loomed over him.

She pointed at the sword near the man's side. "That's Ascalon."

He'd seen the dragon slayer's sword somewhere before. An image of it hanging against a dark, forest green wall flitted in and out of his mind. A shiver trickled down Sean's spine. "Isn't that one of the weapons mounted in your bedroom?"

Caitlin nodded. "It's been handed down through the centuries and was passed to me on my twenty-first birthday." She pumped back an elbow into his gut. "It was supposed to keep me safe from dragons."

Sean was fairly certain that had she been in full control of her body and mind, she would have realized who she'd led to her home that night and would have used Ascalon. He tensed against another shiver. Just the name of the weapon made him break out in a sweat. There was no defense against the sword. It was pure magic. One small cut from the blade would leave any dragon changeling defenseless. He had no way of knowing if it would work on a cursed dragon or not and had no desire to find out.

So far his beast's magic had kept him safe through its ability to heal almost instantly. However, if he wasn't immune to the weapon's power and his skin or scales were so much as nicked with Ascalon, the magic would drain from the beast, leaving it and him without the ability to heal. As a man, he would be rendered motionless. In beast form he would be reduced to nothing more than an oversize lizard. In either case, a death blow would then become—fatal.

"Are you afraid, Sean?"

He snapped his attention back to Caitlin. She hadn't moved, and her voice was so soft, so steely, that he wasn't certain she'd actually spoken.

"Are you?" She repeated her question.

He cocked an eyebrow. If nothing else, she bounced back quickly. While he still sensed her anger, the fear had been replaced by a cold, ice-forged steel. "Why would I be afraid?"

"You should be."

The weapon had been hanging on her bedroom wall. Sean frowned then directed his attention to her luggage in his bedroom. One was long enough to carry a broad-sword. He tilted his head and extended an arm.

Caitlin jumped at the sound of her heavy bag thudding onto the kitchen floor behind them.

"Did you bring your sword with you?"

She laughed softly. "Would you go into the lion's den unarmed?"

He spun away from her, grabbed the bag before she could react and tugged down the zipper. A length of forest green velvet had been wrapped around the weapon. Carefully reaching inside, Sean lifted the sword out and placed it on the countertop.

"That's mine." Caitlin tried to force by him and reach for the weapon.

Sean easily pushed her out of the way. "Touch it and I swear, Caitlin, you'll regret it."

He jerked on the free end of the fabric, unrolling it until the sword clattered onto the counter. A leather-wrapped, wooden scabbard protected the blade. He traced the cross-bindings, wondering if they were as old as the weapon before sliding the blade free.

His beast screamed in wild-eyed rage and abject fear. Shocked by the depth of the reaction, Sean silently crooned to the agitated dragon until it quieted. At the beast's questioning glare, he promised, *We have the blade. I'll put it someplace safe where it can't harm us.*

Sean was surprised by the lack of ornamentation on the weapon. The hilt was bare save the worn, well-oiled leather wrap, the pommel nothing but a metal ball. He lifted the sword, holding it out to test the swing, and was impressed with the balance. Even though it was impossible, it was as if the blade had been made specifically for him.

Caitlin leaned against the counter. "That's part of its magic. The fulcrum changes with each person who wields the weapon. It will always feel perfectly balanced in the hand of a preternatural."

"You would think that wouldn't be the case if a dragon held it."

She shrugged. "Yeah, well, it was assumed that the St. Georges would rid the world of the beasts, so maybe that wasn't a consideration."

He ignored her to look closer at the etching on the flat shoulder. A rough picture depicting a dragon slayer standing over a dead dragon had been etched from the crossguard and down the spined blade.

"Check this out." Caitlin reached toward the weapon.

Sean jerked back; his beast snarled.

She stopped and extended her index finger. "Just let me touch the blade. I won't try to take it away."

He took a breath and nodded, but stayed on alert for any sudden movement on her part.

When Caitlin placed her fingertip on the tip of the blade, the spine glowed a deep amethyst color. She slowly trailed her touch up the ridged spine. The glowing light pulsed, expanding and contracting, as it followed along behind her finger.

She drew her hand away and the light disappeared. "I think that's the magic."

"Does it do that when you use it?"

"I've never run into a dragon before." She grinned. "We could find out."

Sean slid the blade back into the scabbard, rolled the velvet around the wooden case and then held the bundle up with one hand. "This is going somewhere safe. I'll return it to you…later."

He released the bundle and willed it into the safe in his office. Not only was the strongbox made with a twelve-inch-thick casing and locked with a combination lock, it also had a fingerprint sensor. The digitized print was synced to the ring finger on his left hand. A joke his brothers teased him about all the time—insisting he was married to his safe.

To make the safe even more impenetrable, Sean kept it constantly secured with magic. There would be no way for Caitlin to retrieve her deadly weapon until he was ready to give it back to her.

Once he heard the faint click of the safe's door closing, he willed the dial on the lock to spin and then lowered his arm. "There, now everyone is safe."

He glanced at Caitlin and frowned at her smirk. For some reason she didn't seem too concerned about being separated from her sword. When she arched her eyebrows, he asked, "What?"

She didn't reply. Instead, she extended her right arm and crooked her index finger.

To Sean's shock, Ascalon, minus the scabbard and velvet wrap, flew directly to her hand. She closed her fingers around the hilt and twirled the blade. Only then did she return his stare to ask, "Tell me, Sean, *now* are you afraid?"

His heart pounded at her repetition of the exact same question he'd asked her in his bedroom back at the Lair. The hairs on the nape of his neck rose, a cold sweat beaded on his forehead and his snarling dragon's gaze was riveted on the glowing blade. Fear didn't begin to describe the tumult of emotions making him nauseous.

"You should be." She threw his own warning in his face.

Sean took a step back, wondering if Braeden would be outraged to learn that *yes*, he could be more foolish. Not only had he welcomed the dragon slayer into their lair without giving it a second thought, he now found himself at the pointed end of the one weapon in existence that could easily end his life along with the lives of his brothers and their families.

Caitlin tossed the weapon in the air, sending it spinning end over end before her. She easily caught the sword, rested the blade across her forearm and extended the hilt toward him. "You can return this to your *safe* hiding place."

She didn't need to add the obvious—no matter what he did with the sword it would always answer her summons.

"Who else has that power?"

"As long as I breathe, only me."

The fact that she'd freely given him that information somewhat eased his concern. Sean grasped the sword and willed it back into the safe. Even though it wouldn't protect him from Caitlin, at least it would keep the sword out of anyone else's hands and sight. He didn't know what his brothers would do if they discovered such a dangerous weapon on Mirabilus.

Then, as if nothing had just transpired, Caitlin moved back to the counter and turned to the next page in the grimoire.

The dragon shook off the lingering dread and stared intently at the woman with a new, albeit disconcerting to Sean, gleam in his gaze.

Too many thoughts crowded his mind, making it impossible for Sean to decipher what his beast was thinking.

"Who are they?"

Caitlin's question drew him from his uncertainty. He once again took his place behind her and looked over her shoulder. A picture of two people in a burning car going over the edge of a mountain had caught her attention. "My parents."

He pointed to the dragon hovering just behind the car. "And that is Nathan."

She turned the page. "And these are?"

"Me, Braeden and Cameron, when we were much younger, with our Aunt Danielle."

Caitlin leaned over to get a closer look at the grimoire. The softness of her hips pressing into his groin instantly changed the direction of his focus.

"So, you were raised by your aunt?" She shifted from one foot to the other.

The perspiration running the length of his spine was far from cold and had nothing to do with fear. Sean clamped his hands on either side of her hips to keep her from swaying side to side. "Uh, yes."

Caitlin paused then smiled to herself. So he wasn't as put off by her actions as she'd thought he would be. After she'd brazenly called Ascalon to her hand, she'd thought for certain that Sean wouldn't want anything else to do with her. She was honestly surprised that he hadn't ordered her from the island.

Apparently, his need to be responsible for her welfare was stronger than she'd realized. Regardless of this whole dragon mate connection idea, once her son was rescued from Nathan's clutches, she would prove to Sean how little she needed, or wanted, his protection.

Although, right now, she did want something from him and from the hardness pressing against her, she was fairly certain the only connection he was concerned with at the moment involved naked bodies and moans of pleasure.

From what she remembered, the sex they'd shared had been indescribably mind-blowing. And she knew from the make-out session on the plane that his touch and kiss still had the power to make her heart race and her toes curl. More than that, she still wanted him with a desperation she couldn't explain.

Her natural instinct was to simply take what she wanted. However, they'd never had the opportunity to fully replenish her energy, and the power she'd used to draw her weapon to her hand had just about drained what little life force she had in reserves.

She longed to turn around and tell him exactly what she wanted, what she needed. But Caitlin feared she had already flogged his ego with Ascalon. She desperately needed his help to rescue her son, and while this was so out of the ordinary for her, it would probably be wiser to let him take the initiative—for now.

However, since it wasn't in her nature to let anyone else take the initiative, she found herself unintentionally sighing softly, exhaling just the tiniest hint of lust, before she shifted back to her other foot. At his barely perceptible gasp, she bit her lower lip, determined to remain in control of her desires and let him do all the teasing and leading of this sensual dance. Pointing at the two older boys in the picture, she asked, "The identical twins are Braeden and Cameron, right?"

"Yes." He buried his face against the side of her neck. "Except for their eyes."

She didn't even try resisting the urge to moan at the feel of his hot breath and lips moving against her flesh.

Tilting her head to give him easier access, she asked, "Anything different besides their eyes?"

"Not really." He paused beneath her ear. "Do you really care?"

The frustration evident in the tightness of his voice made her quickly swallow a burst of laughter before saying, "No. But you're the one who wanted me to go through this book before we devise a plan to rescue our son. The least you can do to speed this along is answer my questions."

Sean groaned before resting his chin on her shoulder. "You're right. Continue."

She nodded, then turned the page to see an iridescent dragon peering up at her. "That's gorgeous." She reached toward the picture, wanting to see if it felt as detailed as it looked.

"I wouldn't do that."

The dragon's head seemed to morph into three-dimensional life as it rose up from the page and hissed at her.

Caitlin blinked, uncertain that what she'd just witnessed wasn't a figment of her imagination—or something placed there by Sean. To make sure, she tentatively touched the tail.

Before she could withdraw her hand, the tiny beast sunk its teeth into her finger.

"Damn!" She jerked her arm back. Shaking her hand, she asked, "What the hell was that?"

"I warned you." Sean flicked a finger at the blood-thirsty creature, sending it scurrying back down into a one-dimensional painting. He turned her around and grasped her wrist to bring her hand to his mouth, then ran his tongue slowly across her wounded finger.

The temperature in the room increased by at least a hundred degrees. Caitlin struggled to draw in breath. Her stomach turned and tumbled when he once again drew his tongue along her finger. She tried to pull free, but he simply glanced at her and shook his head.

From the gleam in his eyes, he was enjoying her discomfort far too much.

"Sean, that's enough. It's healed." Caitlin closed her eyes. *Could her voice possibly tremble any harder?*

His soft chuckle answered her unspoken question.

Everything about him was a role reversal for her. Even though it had been her intention, she wasn't used to someone else doing the teasing. It was unfamiliar, uncomfortable and she wasn't at all certain she liked not being the one controlling the levels of lust and desire.

Once again she tried to pull free. "Sean, please, don't."

He released her hand then cocked an eyebrow and looked at her. "So, I misread your signals?"

His heated gaze trailed down her body and back up until he pinned her with a hard stare. "The tight-fitting clothes, come-hither pheromones and that shifting from one foot to the other had nothing to do with teasing?"

Caitlin wondered if flames would spark to life from the heat burning her cheeks. Most men wouldn't have called her out. For one thing, other men would have been too far under the spell of her pheromones to be able to form a complete sentence. And for another, they wouldn't have had the guts to question her.

"No, you didn't misread anything. I was leading you on, but I changed my mind." She knew from the more pronounced arch of his brow that he didn't believe her.

"Fine." He reached around her to pick up the grimoire

and pendants. "I'm going to finish looking through this in my office. If you want to join me, feel free."

He turned and took a step before stopping to look over his shoulder at her. "I'm not into guessing games. You want something from me, ask for it."

*Ask for it?* Speechless, she watched him walk away. *Ask?*

# *Chapter 6*

The woman would drive him out of his mind, Sean realized. A succubus who turned down an overture after she'd been the one to start the sensual dance? It wasn't in her nature to blow hot and cold like this.

He realized she was worried about their son and knew that played a huge part in her indecision. Still, something wasn't quite right. Hard as he tried, it seemed as if the answer was just out of his reach, and he couldn't quite grasp it.

Her mother's untimely interruption had been unwelcome, as had his brother's and the demon's, but none of those instances were responsible for this oddness between them. Something else was causing this strain. *What?*

Sean dumped the grimoire on his desk, cringing when the ancient tome landed near the edge, slid halfway off and then teetered. Cursing at himself, he lunged for the book. But his fingertips barely touched the binding as it rushed beyond his reach to hit the floor with a heavy thud.

The pendants he'd closed inside the book skittered out from between the pages to shoot in different directions across the floor. The emerald dragon pendant slid under his desk, while the sapphire one sailed to the other side of the office and smacked into the base of a bookcase before ricocheting back across the room.

A flash of amethyst split between the other two, skipping across the gleaming dark walnut floor like a flat stone flicked across the smooth surface of a pond, coming to a dead stop in the open doorway at Caitlin's feet.

"What is this?" She bent down and picked up the gem.

"I don't know. I've never seen it before." Sean retrieved the grimoire, quickly checked to be sure it was still in one piece and placed it on the center of his desk before scooping up the emerald and sapphire pendants and sliding them into a pocket of his jeans.

He reached for the gem. "Let me see it."

Instead of handing it to him, she just held out her hand. The dragon-shaped amethyst glowed on her palm as if it had a heartbeat.

Sean stared at it.

"Where did it come from?" Caitlin held it closer to her body and stroked a finger down the dragon's back.

Sean shivered as he felt the gentle touch against his own back. Had his brothers not told him about this effect, he might have been caught completely off guard. They'd gone into great detail about their wives teasing them at the most inopportune moments. While his beast and Caitlin seemed to be mated, he wasn't about to give her that kind of power over him. As if nothing was amiss, he waved toward the grimoire. "It came out of the book when it fell."

"That explains the noise I heard." She walked into the office. "But how could it have fallen out of the book if it wasn't there to begin with?"

He resisted the urge to shrug. "How did the dragon

picture come to life and bite you? I can't tell you how anything with this grimoire works, except to say by magic."

"That makes sense." She sat in an armchair before the desk.

"I'm glad it does to you." Sean dropped into his chair and rested his arms on the desktop. "Can I see it?"

Caitlin leaned forward slowly as if reluctant to part with the piece of jewelry, then handed it to him.

The instant he touched the pendant, the glowing stopped, leaving it dark and lifeless. He frowned. "Interesting." He held it out to her. "Here, take it back for a minute."

The glowing heartbeat resumed when she held the dragon in her hand. "Do you think it's alive?"

"Yeah, and obviously it likes you better."

She frowned at him then placed it on the desk. "No need to sound so snappish about it."

"I'm sorry." He hadn't intended to sound irritated, only stated the facts as he saw them. "I've never seen it before, so how would I know if it's alive or not?" He picked up the now-dark pendant and held it between his index finger and thumb. "Besides, it is apparent the thing does somehow respond to you."

Caitlin leaned forward, reaching toward the gem. "Well, I can fix that easy enough." She flicked the tiny dragon on the end of its nose as if it was a misbehaving puppy.

An unseen fist slammed into Sean's nose hard enough to bring tears to his eyes. The pendant clattered to the desk as he slapped a hand over his nose. "Damn!"

Staring at him, Caitlin's eyes grew large. "Your nose is bleeding."

He wiped at the warm, sticky blood and fought not to respond to her statement of the obvious. While his brothers had told him about the pendant's ability to transmit sexual desires and wishes, they'd said nothing about this.

She narrowed her eyes, and the beginning of a purely evil smile teased the corners of her mouth. "Did what I think happened, just happen?"

Sean cast a wary gaze between her and the pendant. He never should have given it back to her in the first place. With what he hoped was a fierce frown, he said, "Don't get any ideas."

They both reached for the gem at the same time. He groaned when she nabbed it from beneath his fingers.

Leaning back in the chair, with the pendant securely in her grasp, Caitlin batted her eyelashes. "Why, Sean, I think this little piece of jewelry is charmed especially for you. Just like a little voodoo doll."

He didn't like the lilt in her voice, nor the glint in her eyes. It was one thing for him to know the power contained in the piece of jewelry, but to have her figure it out would be like playing with fire. He needed to get that pendant back in his hands where it, and he, would be safe from mischief.

Sean held out his hand. "Give it to me." As soon as the words were out of his mouth, he knew he'd made a mistake. What was he thinking? It was doubtful she'd interpret that as an order, or command—no, Caitlin would take it as a challenge.

Her slow smile only confirmed his fears. She raised the pendant to her lips, making him shiver with anticipation. Sean took a deep, steadying breath. While she might think she held all the control, she'd soon discover her error. He'd make sure of that after she made the first move.

She paused, her lips barely brushing the spine of the carved gemstone. "Aren't you worried in the slightest?"

He ignored the warmth of her breath against his back and shook his head. "No. You aren't going to hurt me until after our son has been rescued."

"Who said anything about hurting you?" She slowly drew the tip of her tongue along the back of the pendant.

Savoring the heat racing along his spine, he channeled it into the now-wakening beast within then returned her smile. "I hope you receive as well as you give."

She paused, frowning.

Before she could make sense of his warning, he coaxed his beast into daydreaming about Caitlin. It was a simple enough task. Unfortunately, there was no way for him to avoid the desire and lust rippling through the dragon.

Sean relaxed in his chair and watched the play of emotions and desire rush across her features. His dragon chuffed, and her eyes widened momentarily in surprise. When he imagined stroking his fingers along the length of her neck, she tilted her head to give him better access. He sensed her desire, felt it in the echo of his own drumming pulse.

Caitlin sighed. And once again, he sensed that something wasn't quite right. He focused more closely on her response, and while the aura of lust clung in the air around her, he didn't sense any wanting...or any longing for him on her part. She wasn't beckoning him closer.

That lack made him pause. Whether they had sex or not wasn't an issue. This teasing on his part had been nothing more than a warning to let her know that she wasn't the only one who could manipulate desire, just a continuation of the experiment he'd started on the plane to see how far he could go using nothing more than his dragon's lust and his own thoughts.

He reined in his thoughts, ignoring his beast's disgruntled groan, and leaned forward to rest his forearms on the desktop. "What's wrong?"

Caitlin closed her eyes for a moment at his question. Everything was wrong. She shouldn't have come to him for help. Now she was essentially trapped on an island with a man who had the power to manipulate her desires with nothing more than his thoughts. That was her forte, and she'd never expected him, or any man, to have the same sort of power over her. Simply knowing he could set her heart racing and send her desire soaring with nothing more than his thoughts was unsettling, to say the least. Yet a part of her couldn't help but wonder just how far they could go in such a manner.

They would test those limits…someday. But now wasn't the time.

She took a deep breath and then looked at him. To her relief, he didn't appear angry. His frown conveyed more concern than anything else. "I won't deny that I find this experiment rather…enjoyable." After placing the pendant on the desk, she continued, "But maybe this is something we can explore…later."

"After we get our son back."

To her surprise, he'd finished her sentence so easily. But after all, that was her only reason for being here at Mirabilus.

She nodded and placed a hand over one of his. "I'm sorry, but I can't focus on much else right now."

He laced his fingers between hers and stroked his

thumb along the side of her hand. The warmth of his touch, the gentleness of his action, made her heart flutter. "Then let's figure out a way to get him back."

That suggestion sounded good to her, but how? "And what do you propose?"

He released her hand, reached behind him to grab a chair and pulled it beside his. "Join me."

Caitlin narrowed her eyes. Across the desk wouldn't work just as well? "Seriously?"

"Totally." He pulled the grimoire toward him and flipped it open. "We need to be together to finish going through this tome. And with the size of this desk—" he waved a hand at the expanse of mahogany "—it would be easier if we werc on the same side while doing so."

With the two of them within touching distance, she could only imagine how this would end. But he had a point. It would be easier than sliding the grimoire back and forth across the desktop. Before she could overthink the idea, she moved to his side of the desk and purposely scooted her chair a few inches away from his then sat down.

"Comfy?"

Since she'd now have to lean over to see the pages clearly, not really. But she wasn't going to admit that. "Yes."

His soft chuckle should have been a warning. But before it completely registered as such, he hooked a foot around the leg of her chair and dragged it against his own. When she leaned away, he slung an arm over her shoulder and drew her close. She was effectively pinned by the arm of her chair on one side, his warm hard body on the other and the desk in front of them.

"Now, isn't that better?"

Strangely enough, she didn't actually feel trapped or imprisoned. With the warmth of his body and arm surrounding her, she felt…safe. And oddly calm and comfortable—something she hadn't enjoyed in what seemed like a lifetime. With her parents, Derek and the council, these last few months had been a living hell. Caitlin stiffened, knowing that this was something she could all too easily come to enjoy.

Craving this comfort, she would be fine with his calming touch, if she had any intention of staying with him. But she didn't. She couldn't. Except for their son, they shared nothing in common. Nothing that would keep them together for what could be a very long time, given neither of them was burdened with a human's short life span.

Besides, they were different species—even enemies as far as her parents and the council were concerned. It wouldn't be fair to him, her or little Sean to even consider sharing a life together. Someone would only end up getting hurt, and she feared that someone would be her, or worse, their son.

Caitlin peered down at the grimoire. The image quickly filling the page took her breath away. She gasped.

Sean drew lazy circles on her shoulder. "What do you see?"

It was like watching an old black-and-white photo being developed. The unadorned concrete floor, ringed by cement block walls, steadily grew clearer. Then light from a single bulb hanging from the ceiling glowed eerily off the empty opening where steel bars had served as a door.

Couldn't he see what the invisible hand drew so accurately? She hesitantly touched the corner of the page. "That's Sean's nursery."

"Looks like a dungeon to me."

Obviously, he did see the pictures on the page.

He leaned closer to her, his breath rushed warm against her ear. "Where is the rocker, the stuffed animals and the night-light? I thought those things were unspoken requirements for a nursery."

Caitlin shrugged. "It actually used to be a dungeon a few centuries ago." Even though it had been updated for her use, it still was a dungeon—a prison cell that had effectively done its job.

He traced the tip of his thumb along her neck. "And what exactly was our son doing there?"

"It's where I lived, so why wouldn't he be there, too?"

The brief tightening of his arm still resting across her shoulders was the only clue to his opinion of her questioning reply.

"St. George's home is so small that there were no other rooms to use as your living quarters or a nursery?"

She didn't know how to answer him. If he didn't like knowing that the nursery was in the dungeon, what would he think if he knew she and their son had been imprisoned there?

More details were etched into the picture. She closed her eyes, suddenly aware that she wouldn't have to tell him anything.

"What is this, Caitlin?" He leaned forward, pulling her toward the desk along with him. He tapped a finger on the page before leaning back, giving her room to breathe. "Are those bars?"

"Yes." Her voice was so soft, she wasn't certain he'd heard her response.

"Beg pardon? I didn't hear you."

She cleared her throat then repeated a little louder, "Yes."

"I've seen you in action. While you can suck the life from a human with little effort, I doubt you pose the same danger to your family or the rest of their kind. So why would you need to be confined behind bars?"

"Because I *can* suck the life from a human."

"Are you telling me that you have no control over yourself whatsoever?"

"Of course I can control myself—under normal circumstances. But there's nothing normal about being pregnant."

He was so close his snort of disbelief ruffled her hair. "You make it sound as if you had some kind of disease."

"We didn't know how I would react, so my parents thought it safer this way."

"You might convince someone else of that, but I'm not buying it."

She tried to pull away. "Let me go."

"No." He curled his fingers into her shoulder, holding her in place. "Look at me."

Caitlin swallowed her groan. If she did as he requested, he would be able to see the doubt in her eyes.

He grasped her chin and turned her head toward his. "Caitlin, tell me again why they locked you up."

She paused, blinking, hoping to give herself time to be certain of her answer. "So I couldn't kill anyone."

One eyebrow winged over his eye. "Whose brilliant idea was that?"

She hesitated before answering, "My parents'."

"You had to think about it?" Sean brushed his thumb along her jawline. "Want to try again?"

He saw through her half truth too easily. Her answer hadn't exactly been a lie. When the High Council convened to determine her fate upon learning of her pregnancy, her parents hadn't come to her defense.

She'd been appalled and hurt by their lack of support, but they'd insisted that since the consequence of her actions with Sean would affect the safety of the entire clan, it was imperative that the matter be decided by a higher authority. Before she could formulate a feasible argument to their unwarranted fear, she'd found herself before the council.

She sighed. "The High Council."

"And how did they expect you to feed? Did they provide any life force for you—other than the baby you carried?"

His suggestion, that she would stoop so low as to harm her own child, made her ill. She jerked away from his touch and stared at him in disbelief that he'd even think such a thing. "What are you insinuating?"

"After seeing this—" he once again tapped the picture "—I'm trying to figure out how much danger your family and their council pose. How can you be certain they aren't working with Nathan?"

Caitlin shoved her chair back, breaking free of his hold to escape his nearness, and rose. Pacing back and forth along the far wall, she said, "That's ridiculous."

Thankfully, he didn't move from his chair, but his gaze seemed to bore into her, making her spine tingle with building worry.

"Really? Is it? They want nothing to do with the baby, nor do they want you to have anything to do with him."

"That's quite a leap, don't you think?" She tried to find a way to get him off this track.

"How so?"

"They were ashamed of what I'd done." That much was true. "They confined me so I wouldn't harm anyone." She'd believed that—at first, but after they'd let Derek visit her, she'd begun to wonder and now she wasn't sure at all. "To jump from that to accusing them of seeking to intentionally harm my baby is one hell of a jump." She could only hope that was true.

What sounded to her like a low-pitched, threatening hiss echoed in the office. She stopped pacing and turned her attention to Sean. The look of disbelief deepened to anger, turning his face into a frightening mask of rage. His narrowed eyes met hers, and when he curled his lips she swore venom dripped from his exposed fangs.

He rose, slowly, and she backed away until her escape was stopped by the wall. His hand trembled as he pointed to the grimoire. "What is this?" Laced somewhere between man and beast, his voice was rough, raspy and filled with hatred.

Caitlin knew what scene had filled the page without having to look at it. That cursed book was showing him Derek's *visit*. A visit that nearly ended her life. She glanced at the safe that secured Ascalon from all but her. Just knowing the weapon was close at hand gave her enough courage to hold her ground.

She said nothing, simply waited for him to figure it out on his own. And it didn't take long.

"I will kill him."

"And I won't stop you." She blinked. From where had that response come? It was heartfelt and honest, but she'd not meant to say it aloud. As far as anyone knew, she was still going to go through with her marriage to Derek. What they didn't know was that she'd see him dead before she'd exchange any vows with him. There were other uses for the honed sharpness of Ascalon's blade besides slaying dragons.

"This…this is your Baron Derek?"

She nodded, unwilling to give him more than what he'd asked for.

He rubbed a hand across his neck where she'd bit him earlier. "What are you?"

"I was born with fangs. Useless fangs that can tear and rip, but I'm not a vampire. Our son wouldn't permit Derek to change me."

"What do you mean?"

Caitlin swallowed hard; remembering that night wasn't something she wanted to do. Every time she did let that memory invade her thoughts, her stomach twisted at the way she'd been tossed about the cell, before he'd pinned her to the bed. She recalled the abject look of hatred in his eyes the second before he tried to latch his fangs into her neck. "Derek tried to turn me."

"Why?"

Looking at him, she shrugged. "I don't know. To make me a better fit as his wife, I suppose." Because the truth lurking at the back of her mind was still too hard to face, she lied.

"You are mine."

"No. I am not." He really needed to get that idea out of his head. "Had I been yours as you insist, you wouldn't have left the way you did. But I wasn't going to be his, either." She spread her arms, hands out, begging him to understand. "I fought him as best I could. He's a vampire, Sean. He's stronger than I'll ever be, and I couldn't risk letting the baby be harmed."

"He raped you."

"Not physically, but yes, essentially you could say that's what he tried to do. He did force himself on me against my will. But your son wasn't going to permit anything to happen."

Sean looked back down at the grimoire. "You were still pregnant, what could he do?"

A small smile flitted at the corner of her mouth. "Make my blood so vile that the second it touched Derek's lips he turned violently ill."

"And your parents still want you to marry this bastard?"

"The whole thing was probably their idea to begin with. All I know is they were angry afterward. At me. Not him."

She closed her eyes against the memory of the bitter fight she'd had with them after Derek had stormed away. A shiver tracked nearly down to her toes.

With a soft, nervous laugh, she looked at him and admitted, "I was overjoyed that the baby had stepped in, so to speak. It's hard enough being a psychic vampire who requires living energy to survive. I don't ever want to need blood, too."

"And yet you stayed with them."

"What choice did I have? I can't disappear at whim as you can. Those bars held me captive as easily as they would a human. I was never let out of that cell until after Sean was taken."

"And you came straight to me." He leaned on the desk. "I wonder, was it because you wanted to, or because they sent you?"

She debated. Should she tell him the truth or add more lies to the ones she'd already told? With a sigh, she lifted her chin and held his stare. "In a way, both, actually." At his questioning look, she explained, "It was my idea to come to you. If things hadn't played out as they had, I'd have come to you long before the baby's birth."

"And?"

"And yes, it was also my parents' idea. They told me to do what I must to get the items the Learned demanded to save our son."

"Considering they're so willing to give him away, that doesn't sound logical at all. Since he's such a stain on their pristine reputation, I would think the child's death would serve them better." He frowned. "I have to wonder if the baby was anything more to them than bait."

She'd had the feeling that her parents had given in to her plea to come to Sean far too easily, but hadn't yet had time to sort out why. "Bait for what?"

"Me. My brothers. Nathan's goal in life is to see us dead."

"Why would my parents help him?"

He looked at her as if she'd completely lost her mind, before asking, "Why would the dragon slayers want to see the dragons die?"

She couldn't help rolling her eyes at the absurdity of his question. "Sure, maybe a few hundred years ago, but aren't we all a little more civilized now?"

Sean snorted. "If we were human, perhaps. But we aren't. It's ingrained in our DNA to hate each other."

"So you've hated me and my family since the moment you were conceived?"

"Not exactly." His gaze darted away before it returned to her. "But we weren't talking about me, were we?"

So, she wasn't the only one in this office keeping secrets. Did he really think she wasn't going to ask? "What do you mean—*not exactly*?"

"We were talking about you."

She'd expected that answer. "Yes, we were." She slowly walked toward the desk, noting the frown had left his face. Now he looked more...not quite worried. She doubted if he really worried about much; maybe a better description would be...concerned. *Why?* "But since Sean is your son, if there's something I need to know, perhaps now might be a good time to share."

He glanced down and shook his head. Pushing the grimoire toward her, he said, "Looks like I won't need to tell you anything."

She studied the still-forming picture of a dark-haired woman curled into a ball on a planked floor. Bloody stripes crisscrossed her back and trailed across her arms. Nathan stood over the naked woman with a whip in his hand.

Caitlin gasped as the woman's pain surged into her blood, hot and agonizing. The rage beneath the pain was palpable, nearly alive with its intensity. She grasped the edge of the desk to keep from being overwhelmed by the emotions flooding her senses.

Sean touched her shoulder, startling her, to ask, "Are you all right?"

She brushed away his disquiet to study the words forming above the image. Reading aloud, Caitlin recited, "Not a dragon born, yet a dragon you shall be. Once this beast has taken form, it will answer only to thee."

She waited for the grimoire to fill in more words, but it seemed to have come to a stop. Sean reached down and turned the page. There, a lone figure, Nathan, had taken shape. A wicked, satanic smile curled his lips into a grimace. Pure evilness shimmered in his eyes. She read the words above his picture. "I am thee."

She shivered as a cold hand of dread seemed to close around her heart. Was this curse meant for Sean? Had his dragon been conjured into being by the Learned?

"Sean…?" Uncertain how to ask him if he was Nathan's minion, she let the question trail off and shifted her attention to the man standing across from her. If his ashen complexion was any indication, she wasn't all too certain he'd known very much about this curse before now.

"Look," Sean whispered, his focus drawn to the facing page.

Once again the woman appeared. But this time she lay facedown on the floor, her body shredded by the whip. Her dying gaze transfixed not on Nathan, but on whoever might be seeing this depiction of her last breath.

*"St. George will set you free."* The words, a mere breathless whisper, hung on the air surrounding them.

Caitlin glanced quickly around the room. Neither she nor Sean had said anything, and those words were just now coming into sight on the page. So who had spoken?

Then, once again, this time a little louder, the strange voice said, *"St. George will set you free."*

# Chapter 7

Strong waves, dark and foreboding, pounded against the rocky cliffs below the castle. The thundering crashes echoed relentlessly through the stone fortress, bringing peace to none within.

High above the roiling waves, Nathan the Learned stared out an open window in the east tower. His attention focused across the wild sea toward Mirabilus.

Very few beings—human or preternatural—have ever seen Mirabilus. The glamour spell the ancients had cast upon it centuries ago held as strongly now as it had that day.

The residents' daily lives had been disrupted only by the actions of Aelthed. He alone had brought humans to the druid island. First it had been the medieval Comte of Gervaise, who had promptly won the heart and undying love of Mirabilus's queen. She had given birth to the first half-bred twins. The idea of a halfling female ascending to the throne of Mirabilus had been so reviling that his own father had tried unsuccessfully to kill both of them.

Between the ineffectiveness of the hawthorn sickle used as a sword of judgment and the utter lack of planning, his father's men had failed in their quest to rid the world of the halfling heirs. Those followers had died at the hand of the second human Aelthed saw fit to guide to Mirabilus—a medieval knight by the name of Faucon.

At least the knight had taken one of the half-bred daughters off the island as his wife. But the other one had remained to become queen. And her husband—Nathan swallowed the bile that churned from his stomach to his throat—her husband had ascended to Dragon Lord of Mirabilus.

A position of power that should have been his.

The door to his chamber creaked open. "My lord?"

Nathan swung away from the window, his heart thudding fast and angry with a long-lived hatred, fueling his eternal thirst for vengeance.

One of the nursemaids trembled in the doorway. The wail of the baby she held broke through the haze of rage and the roar of the crashing waves. Nathan's lips curved up into a sneering smile at her unexpected stroke of luck. Had the babe not been in her arms, he'd have spent his anger on her.

"What do you want?"

"The...baron—"

"Get out of my way." Her words were cut short as a flurry of black pushed by her and stopped in the center of the room. The man swung toward the nursemaid and pointed at the door, his dark cape hanging from his arm like a wing. "Leave us and take that squalling abomination with you."

Nathan nodded toward the woman, giving his permission for her to withdraw, before turning his attention on the baron. "To what do I owe this pleasure?" If the uninvited guest in his castle couldn't read the annoyance beneath his words, the man was denser than what he'd first thought.

"Why is that…thing…still alive?"

It was all Nathan could do not to laugh at the man's obvious distaste. "It is good to see you, too, Baron Hoffel." He shrugged at the baron's lack of response and then moved away from the window. "Had you fulfilled your end of our deal, Derek, all of this would be over, and the child would no longer be here."

"And you know I tried."

A little too hard as far as Nathan was concerned. The idea had not been for Hoffel to kill the child or the mother. That pleasure belonged solely to him. No, the dimwit was supposed to have freed the woman from her cell and brought her here.

"I don't know what else you wanted me to do."

Hoffel's whine threatened to crack the tenuous hold Nathan had forced on his temper. As much as he wanted to relieve the man's head from his body, he might come in handy for a time.

"How was I supposed to know she could poison her own blood?"

Another point of disagreement. Nathan didn't think for one minute that St. George's daughter possessed that type of magic. It was more likely that the unborn dragonette had instinctively protected his own life by turning his mother's blood vile in response to the vampire's attack.

"Besides, what difference does it make? You still have the child."

Yes, but he'd wanted the mother and the child—before the birth.

It had all seemed so simple. Yet every action in his quest to gain supreme power had gone so wrong of late.

The gypsy mage's forced assistance with the curse had worked—the youngest Drake had fully transformed into a dragon, the birth of his offspring was proof of that. However, the beast had failed to follow his master's orders. Nathan had repeatedly ordered him to kill his family, but somehow the Drake had found the strength of will to fight those commands.

When the beast had run away from Dragon's Lair, Nathan had been tempted to kill him for his disobedience. But he'd stopped himself, knowing that the young one's death would serve no purpose. He'd guessed that eventually Drake would return to his family, and he had.

Unfortunately, he'd returned with stronger control over his urges. Nathan knew he'd have to excise more power over the beast to get him to do as ordered, but the strengthening ritual required him to have the beast chained to his altar. The chaining would be the easy part. Getting the man to his castle would be tricky.

He was still trying to devise a plan when he'd learned from his spy on the vampires' *sacred* High Council that Baron St. George was looking for a family to adopt his daughter's bastard half-breed child. Nathan knew he'd found a way to draw the Drake he'd cursed to his castle.

His plan had been to simply kidnap St. George's daughter and bring her here as bait. However, the High Council in all their wisdom—or lack thereof as far as he was concerned—had ordered the baron to lock his daughter away in a cell. He still wondered at that decision. Were they hoping to starve her to death for her betrayal in mating with a dragon?

Nathan gritted his teeth. Violence was one thing and

it was oft times required, and while he had no qualms about torture, starvation was the action of someone weak and depraved.

When he achieved supreme power as the Hierophant, the first thing he would do was dissolve the vampires' council. The idea that a sitting group of old vampires should act as an all-powerful judge and jury over their kind was outdated and would be useless under his reign.

That was when he'd decided to use Hoffel. He glanced in the man's direction and bit back a curse at the ineffectiveness of that idea. Nathan had thought that since the Hoffels and St. Georges were working on a betrothal between their two heirs, it would be easy enough for the man to whisk the woman out of her spell-proof cell.

Obviously, while both sets of parents agreed the betrothal was a good thing, the participants didn't. It seemed to Nathan that they hated each other more than anything else.

When that plan fell through, Nathan took matters into his own hands and waited until the baby was born. He didn't need the woman, not when the child would be enough to draw the beast to its aid. No dragon, pure born or curse created, would be able to ignore the need to protect its offspring.

It had taken him a while to come up with a solid plan. He'd had to discover the guards' timetable and then wait for the baron and his wife to be gone from the residence. Finally, once he'd learned the council had called a meeting of the families, Nathan had slipped into the vampire's mansion.

His research had paid off. True to form, the guard waited until the baby and its mother fell asleep for an afternoon nap and then left his post to spend a good twenty minutes in the restroom. Everything had fallen into place exactly as planned. Knocking the fool out and swiping the key to the cell was child's play.

Quietly, Nathan had unlocked the cell and took great pains to give the appearance of Drake's misty dragon when he'd entered. The woman was easy to deal with since he'd caught her off guard, and when she thought to protect her son, he'd slammed her across the room, scooped up the child and issued his demands before he'd left.

Since the baby was in his possession, the only thing he needed to do for now was wait. He knew Drake wouldn't permit St. George to bring the grimoire, pendants and puzzle box. The items were too important to entrust to a nonfamily member. No, he would bring them in person.

Which was the whole idea. Once Drake was here, in Nathan's fortress, he would be powerless to stop what would happen.

And when Nathan finished strengthening his curse over the dragon, he would add one, compelling the beast to kill himself after his family was dead. The only thing Nathan would need to do was sit back and watch as the youngest Drake killed the others. He shivered with excitement at the thought of such a spectacle.

After that nothing would stand in his way of attaining the power he sought.

"What—"

Not willing to listen to the man's whine any longer, Nathan waved a hand toward Hoffel, cutting off the vampire's words and sending him into the cells in St. George's dungeon. He might have some use for him later, but for now, Nathan had more important matters to attend. For now that the Drake was near, ensconced at Mirabilus, he had an altar to prepare.

Something cold like an ice-chilled finger stroked along Aelthed's neck, startling him from his dreams. He shook off the lingering traces of his slumber and frowned. What had awakened him?

The fine hairs on the back of his neck rose. His breath quickened with the feeling of being watched. Why did it seem that he was no longer alone in his solitary cell?

He inspected his cube, with his eyes and his mind, to ensure that he was indeed still the only soul in residence. Certain that his odd sensation of not being alone was nothing more than his imagination, he closed his eyes and brought the grimoire into view.

A strangled gasp tore from his throat. *No. It wasn't possible.* He and he alone had the power to bring pictures to life in the ancient tome. It mattered not if he was awake or sleeping, a part of his mind was always focused on the grimoire.

Creating the pictures was easy; he had only to get the book into the hands of a dragon and his mate, then he would harvest their thoughts, their fears, their memories, along with his own, to draw scenes that would help them understand what they needed to do, or what they must discover.

But this—he shook his head and once again stared at the picture of a gypsy mage in the throes of her final breath—he hadn't drawn this. How could he? It wasn't a memory from either the youngest dragon or his reluctant mate. And it certainly wasn't any memory of his own making.

So who possessed this type of power?

He raised his arms, spread his fingers and pulled the memory to him, drawing it in, making it a part of himself.

Aelthed trembled at the woman's pain. He wept for the loss she suffered, the days she would never know, the years she would never see. Yet he steeled himself against the pain, hardened his heart to the near unbearable loss and breathed deeply, drawing in more and more of the memory until it was as clear as it had been on the day the event took place.

He opened his eyes and watched the scene unfold before him.

His nephew's rage washed over him, cold and heartless, as he lashed the woman, tormented and threatened her until she spoke the words of the Romani curse that turned the youngest Drake into a changeling.

Even as mortal death closed upon her, she tried to give the changeling a way to save himself. Into the universe she'd whispered his salvation.

Aelthed waved the memory back to the mist from which it'd formed, and he wondered if it had been the gypsy's soul, or the whispered words, that had had the power to add these scenes to the grimoire. Either way, her magic was strong. She'd spoken the words and created a changeling. Perhaps her final words could save the cursed beast.

Unable to stand the heavy silence that had fallen over Sean's office, Caitlin asked, "What does that mean, *St. George will set you free?*"

He dropped down onto his chair. "I know as much as you do. Nothing more."

She hated to ask, she really did; he looked terrible.

Ashen would be a good description for the current color of his face. His eyes held a sadness in their depths that turned her cold with worry. But her son's life was at stake, and she needed to know if she'd made a huge mistake in coming to him. Sitting on the edge of his desk facing him, she took a deep breath then in a rush asked, "Do you work for Nathan?"

The harsh stare he focused on her made her slide along the edge of the desk, out of his reach. "What you're really asking is if I'm involved in this kidnapping. So instead of dancing around the subject, just ask."

"Are you?" Why did that two-word question make her feel as if she was betraying him? She didn't know him, not really. Outside of a three-night fling, a lingering thirst for each other and their son, they shared nothing.

"You saw the same thing I did."

"That doesn't answer my question."

"No. I had nothing to do with the kidnapping. Hell, since you didn't see fit to tell me about him, I didn't even know the child existed."

She flinched at his accusation, but said nothing.

"As for working with the Learned, what do you want me to say?" He leaned forward and spread his arms, palms up. "I don't know." He pushed out of the chair, shoving it back so hard that it bounced against the wall. Heading for the door, he added, "If I am, it's not by choice."

She blinked. Seriously? He'd disappeared on her after learning who she was. He'd walked out of the bedroom after the scene with her mother and his brother. Then he'd walked out of the kitchen when she'd changed her mind. So now he was walking away again? Was this his usual method of coping? "You're just going to walk away again? Is that how you deal with everything?"

He froze in the doorway without turning around. She saw the bunching of muscles in his shoulders and arms and wondered if she'd made a mistake. Now seemed a prudent time to put his oversize desk to use, so she stood up and moved to the other side of it. As an inanimate object, it offered no protection, but at least it made her feel as if there was a solid barrier between them.

"Yes." Slowly, he turned to face her. "That's exactly what I'm going to do." He clenched and unclenched his hands at his sides. "Otherwise, I might do something we'll both regret."

Caitlin shot a quick glance toward the wall safe. "As we both know, I am more than capable of protecting myself from you."

Before she could blink more than once, he was before her. He'd cleared the distance from the door, and around the desk she'd considered a barrier, in a blur of effortless ease. Wrapping his fingers around her arm, he dipped his head to nearly growl against her ear, "If you're so intent on using that damn sword, do it."

His voice was rough, gravelly, and so filled with unexpected anguish that it caught her off guard more than the speed with which he'd moved. Confusion and concern kept any anger or fear at bay.

Caitlin stared up at him and gasped. This was far more than just worry or rage. Without stepping into his mind, she had only her senses to go by and heightening them was easy enough to do. The coldness of his glare, the hard line of his mouth, tenseness of his body and the rapid beating of his heart screamed fear in her mind. *Fear of what? Or who?*

She lifted her hand and placed it against his cheek. "Talk to me, tell me what's wrong."

Instead of jerking away from her touch as she'd expected, he pulled her roughly against his chest. "Talking is the last thing I want to do."

She hadn't intended to send out any seduction pheromones, but apparently controlling the level was completely out of her ability when it came to him. There was no denying that, yes, she wanted him as much as he seemed to want her right this second. But not like this, not when anger and unexplained fear permeated the air around them.

Caitlin knew that fighting him would only serve to intensify the dark emotions battling for release, so against all common sense, she relaxed in his hold to hesitantly ask, "Sean, does anything seem out of place or wrong to you?"

He wrapped a hand into the hair at the nape of her neck and pulled her head back. One eyebrow winged up as he answered, "Yes, you're still talking."

Caitlin forced herself not to hiss in frustration at his response. She slipped her hands between them and pushed as hard as possible against his chest. "Stop."

A human would have been sent stumbling backward. But not only did her shove fail to set her free, it earned her a low, guttural growl, too. She looked up at him, and from the elongating pupils knew the sound had come more from the beast than the man it possessed.

Regardless of what she wanted, it was obvious she wasn't going to get the chance to talk reason to the man—not with the beast in control.

After taking a deep breath, Caitlin reached up to stroke the side of his neck. She held his gaze, marveling at the sudden need flowing into her. How had he so easily flamed her desire for him against all of her better judgment?

A throaty rumble answered her unspoken question. The sound took her breath away with its deep intensity. The arm he held around her tightened, pulling her feet from the floor, and swung her onto the desk. He released her long enough to jerk the T-shirt over her head before pushing her down on the cold polished wood.

She gasped as his surging need enveloped her, setting her on fire. She wondered again what caused this unnatural heightened level of desire. But her wandering mind snapped back to focus when he wedged his body between her legs and leaned down to suck the cool tip of one breast into his hot, moist mouth.

Lost in the haze of lust, she grasped at his shoulders, wanting more. Sean caught her wrists and pinned her arms above her head, holding them there with one hand while tugging at the sweatpants she wore with the other.

Caitlin lifted her hips to make his task a little easier. "Let me—"

Her offer of help was met with teeth scraping against her nipple before he lifted his head enough to stare at her. "Stop."

Her breath caught in her throat at his gruff tone, then kicked into short gasps of air as a thin rim of gold shimmered to life around the deep green of his eyes. A part of her mind warned that she should fear the beast. It was stronger than she was and could tear her to shreds with one sharp talon.

But another part, the side that was seriously in need of mental help, coaxed her to let him have his way.

Caitlin closed her eyes, unable to make sense of anything beyond the growing need to be possessed, to have him carry her over the edge of desire into satisfaction.

He came over her, whispering, "You are safe. Trust me." A rush of warm breath against her neck, the tip of his tongue trailing her earlobe and his deep, rumbling voice in her ear promising her safety, made up her mind.

With a soft moan, she surrendered, more than willing to let him take control, to use sex to banish whatever devil seemed to be haunting him, certain she would come out of this encounter physically satiated and whole.

He turned her arms, placing her palms flat against the desk, and curled her fingers over the edge. Not interested in any slow, leisurely lovemaking, Caitlin sighed with relief when he didn't waste time peeling off her sweatpants or his jeans. The instant their clothing vanished, she wrapped her legs around his hips, pulling him closer.

He eased the hard length of his cock into her with agonizing slowness. She wanted to scream at his teasing, torturous motion. He released her hands and grasped her hips, holding her in place, preventing her from pushing up against him.

"Sean." Uncurling her fingers from the edge of the desk, intent on reaching up to pull him closer, Caitlin gasped. Invisible bonds held her arms pinned to the slick smoothness of the desk.

She stared up at him. The gold rim around his emerald eyes shimmered. Yet the heartrending half smile on his lips was all human—and filled with pure male arrogance in his certainty of what he was doing to her.

Caitlin swallowed the whine threatening to escape. She didn't understand what was happening to her. She'd been swept away with lust when they'd first met, but this—this near-unbearable need was unfamiliar, and far from normal in its intensity.

She didn't want to need him like this, didn't want him to have this much power over her. When her son was safely back in her arms, she'd never see this man again, and the last thing she wanted was to miss his touch, ache for his kiss as desperately as she had this last year.

He deepened his thrust, filling her, completing her in a way no one else could. A white light flickered in her mind, shimmering as it grew brighter, feeding her sorely depleted life force.

The ease in which he fed her, the flow of his strength rushing into her, chased away any concerns about the future. The only thing that mattered was right now, this very moment. One way or another, tomorrow would take care of itself.

# Chapter 8

Like a pesky gnat, something small and irritating kept teasing at her ear. Caitlin batted a hand toward the irritation.

Her unsuccessful attempt to rid herself of the pest drew a groan from her as she became fully awake. Anxious to escape, she pulled the blankets up and rolled away, intent on falling back into her dreams before the lingering thread beckoning her to return disappeared.

It had been such a long time since she'd found her dreams welcoming. This last year or so they'd been more of the nightmare variety. She didn't appreciate being torn from a pleasant one of her, Sean and their son enjoying a family outing. Since something like that would only ever happen in a dream, having the idyllic situation disturbed was even worse.

The tickling against her ear returned, and she batted at it once again. But this time she made contact with something definitely more solid and much larger than a gnat—it felt more like a face. From the stubble beneath her fingertips, it was a face in dire need of a shave.

She patted the cheek, muttering, "Go away, Sean."

He ignored her suggestion and instead slid beneath the covers to rest against the warmth of her back. "That isn't going to happen. But as much as I would love to spend the rest of the day in this bed with you, we have to get up. My brothers will be waiting for us in Braeden's office soon, if they aren't already."

Caitlin's stomach tightened, and her mind whirled her fully awake. She desperately wanted her son back safely in her arms, yet her gut instinct told her that involving the Drake family would somehow be dangerous.

She frowned at the thought—it was illogical, considering that deed had already been committed the moment she'd come to Sean. Besides, how could it possibly be dangerous when more help in this matter—help from beings far more powerful than she and Sean—would be beneficial, not dangerous?

Regardless of what the Drakes may or may not think about her family, they would combine forces to rescue one of their own. It was natural, instinctual at a basic level for any form of beast to protect their own kind—more so when the being in question was a baby.

A vision formed in her mind, clouding over her rationalizations. A vision so strong that it forced her eyes shut. Dragons—not one, but three—lay bleeding in the agony of their death throes on the stone floor of a ruined castle.

Standing over them laughing, with Ascalon in his hand, was Nathan. Neatly trapped in his free arm, her son wailed.

Caitlin gasped. No. She couldn't—she wouldn't let them help. Not if it meant leading them to their death. Especially when in the end, her son still wouldn't be free from the demonic wizard holding him.

The warmth of Sean's lips against her neck startled her out of her dire musings. How was she going to do this on her own? As much as she longed to explain, or to discuss this with him, she knew that telling Sean would be a mistake. For one thing, he would never back off. In fact, it would most likely prompt him to act on his own without any assistance from his brothers.

"What's wrong?"

"Nothing." She took a deep breath to calm her riotous emotions before rolling over onto her back to look up at him as he leaned over her.

His eyebrows shot up at her lie. "Are you upset about last night?"

It would be so convenient to use that as an easy excuse to explain away her obvious discomfort. After all, his initial love play had been rather...forceful.

A tremor of desire rippled down her spine. Oh, yes, forceful and very focused on her satisfaction. By the time they'd made it to the bed, she'd been more than just satisfied; her life force had been filled to the brim and then some.

But she didn't want to cover up a lie with another lie. Doing so would only become confusing. Instead, she ignored his question to ask, "Any food in your kitchen?"

"Hungry?"

"Famished." On cue, her stomach growled.

Sean traced a fingertip down the length of her nose then sat up. "It would be rude to let you starve." He patted her leg. "I'll go find us something to eat while you get dressed."

She watched him leave the bedroom without another word. He'd acquiesced too easily. The tone of his voice had changed from playful to...noncommittal—flat. He knew something was up other than her simply being hungry.

Caitlin threw off the covers with a sigh. It didn't matter. He could think, wonder and suspect all he wanted, but until she told him of her plan, he wouldn't know for certain. And since she had no intention of telling him anything, he'd simply have to keep wondering.

She hadn't figured out how she was going to rescue her son without help from the Drakes, so it would be a bit difficult to discuss it with him. Besides, it would be better this way. Not only would she be sparing his and his brothers' lives, she could then prevent Sean from trying to take her son away from her, as well.

That wasn't going to ever happen regardless of what he thought. She'd never had any intention of letting her parents or the High Council give her son away, so she wasn't about to let Sean take him from her, either.

It wasn't going to be easy. But what she needed to figure out right now was how to get possession of the items Nathan demanded without Sean or his family finding out. That wasn't going to be easy, but she knew where the grimoire and pendants were located.

Sean poured a cup of coffee and sat on a stool at the kitchen bar. She was up to something; he sensed it in the change of the air surrounding her. It had flashed warm when he'd awakened her, then cold as he'd reminded her of the meeting with Braeden and Cameron, and then hot.

Since she hadn't seemed angry, at least she'd claimed not to be, and they hadn't been engaged in any sexual act, he could only surmise that the heat came from racing thoughts.

He should have reached inside her mind to investigate, but he'd decided he was going to gain her trust. After all, she was the mother of his child and his beast's

mate. So if they were to have any semblance of a relationship they had to share something more than sex.

He wasn't looking for love, or any declaration of her
heart. But they would be partners in raising their son,
so some type of shared bond, a friendship maybe, would
prove useful. Perhaps learning to trust each other would
lead them in that direction.

The only thing he could do now was to see if it was
possible to get her to talk to him. His dragon grunted
and rolled his eyes. Sean ignored the beast's obvious
doubts. One way or another he would see this through.

"Did you find us something to eat?"

At her question, he rose to get her some coffee. "More
or less. I normally eat down in the dining room."

She accepted the cup and after a swallow, took a bagel
from the plate of pastries he'd offered. "Right now anything is fine, thank you."

He took a seat and pulled out the stool next to him.
"Join me."

She did so, asking, "Have either of your brothers
called with any news yet?"

"No. But that doesn't mean they don't have any to
share. They could just be waiting for us to arrive below."

"How do you think they'll be able to help?" Picking
at the bagel, she continued, "I mean, what can they do
that we can't?"

Sean leaned closer, his shoulder resting against hers.
"What are you thinking, Caitlin?"

"I don't like this waiting. If we just took the items
we have to Nathan, maybe it'd be enough. Then this
would be over."

"You know, I get it. I can't blame you for being impatient. But if we went to Nathan with less than what he demanded, our son would be left without parents."

She leaned away. "Yes, but if we keep dragging this out, I could be left without my son."

His beast rumbled as her voice rose. Sean took the opportunity of swallowing more coffee to gain control of his dragon and temper his response. Certain both were in check, he set his cup down and took one of her hands between his. "Look, first of all it's our son. *Ours.* You aren't in this alone. Besides, I thought we discussed this yesterday. It's safer to confront Nathan with strength."

"You mean magic."

"It doesn't matter what you call it. The force and power of three beasts will succeed far better than you and I ever could."

She paled at his statement and closed her eyes. Sean slung an arm across her shoulder and pulled her close. "Tell me what's wrong."

Caitlin shook her head, but he could feel her cold fear as it seeped into him, chilling him to the bone. "What are you so afraid of? Tell me, let me help."

She jerked away and moved to the glass doors. Staring out at the mist-shrouded forest, she said, "You can't help."

He remained where he was, ignoring the urge to enfold her in his embrace and protect her from whatever had her so worried. "And why would you say that?"

Not saying a word and not moving away from the door, she shook her head.

This wasn't like her. This odd, discomforting nervousness. At least it wasn't like what he knew of her. Trying to talk to her, to reason with her, was getting him nowhere, and he wanted to know what had frightened her so between last night and this morning.

Uncertain which tactic to use, he fell back on what was familiar to him. He rose and headed toward his office saying, "Don't tell me, then. But it changes nothing. Cameron, Braeden and I will get our son back with or without your input."

Caitlin spun away from the door with a gasp. "No!" When he didn't pause, she followed. "You'll just die in the attempt."

Die? What was she talking about? Why would she suddenly be so certain of that happening?

A shimmer from his desk caught his eye. Sean frowned then stopped in the doorway and turned to face Caitlin. She bumped to a stop against his chest.

He grasped her shoulders and asked, "What did you see?"

She looked away for a heartbeat then turned her attention back to him. Fear etched her features, leaving her looking more pale and drawn than she had upon her arrival at the Lair. "The three of you dead. And Nathan laughing over you as he held Sean."

"He can't kill all of us."

She glanced toward the safe. "With Ascalon he could."

He swallowed a curse before asking, "When had you planned on telling me this?"

"Never."

A kick in the gut wouldn't have taken his breath away as fast. Releasing her, he stepped into his office. "So you were content to let me go on a mission you were convinced would end in my death?"

So much for building any trust with her.

"No. I had planned on going alone."

Now his beast gasped for breath. "Alone? You're convinced that three beasts will fail, yet you believe you would succeed?"

She was either far more brazen that he'd ever assumed, or she'd lost the ability to reason. It had to be one or the other, because nobody in their right mind would think like that.

"What made you believe for one second that I would ever let you do that alone?"

She shrugged. "You couldn't stop me if you didn't know."

"Right. Because I'm completely clueless and wouldn't notice you weren't here."

"I hadn't thought that far ahead yet."

"Obviously." It was impossible to keep the biting tone from his voice.

Was she always this impetuous?

If so, they were going to be in for a rockier road together than he'd ever imagined.

As it was, his beast was already gnashing his teeth at the mere thought of her traipsing off to Nathan's stronghold by herself.

Sean sat down before his desk and waved her to the chair on the other side. "Show me where you saw this warning."

She glanced at the grimoire. "It wasn't in the book. It was more of a mental flash."

For some reason, that just made it worse. She'd planned on risking her own life because of some fleeting thought? "You sure it's not just an overactive imagination?"

"No." Frowning, she shook her head. "It's stronger than that."

His attention was once again captured by the pulsing glow of light coming from the grimoire.

"Apparently, there's something we need to see." He flipped open the ancient tome to the last picture they'd observed then turned the page.

Caitlin sucked in a loud breath and shoved her chair back from the desk. "There." Her hand shook as she pointed at the forming picture. "It isn't just in my mind."

Sure enough, taking form on the page was the scene she'd described.

He and his brothers were on a stone floor, broken and bleeding, the vaporous mist of their life forces flowing into Nathan as he stood over them laughing. In one hand he held Ascalon—blood dripped from the blade. In his free arm he held a crying baby.

Then, as Sean stared at the image, a thick chain began to form. One end was shackled to his ankle, and link by link it stretched across the floor to an altar where that end had been secured.

From the items on the altar—the burning candles, the crystal cauldron, jewel-encrusted chalice, dragon statues of emerald and sapphire, along with a wooden, curved-blade athame—it was obvious that Nathan had been casting spells. Ones that apparently included him.

His dragon screamed. The rage made his hands tremble. Sean curled his fingers, tightening his fists in an attempt to stop the anger threatening to overtake him. He needed to focus on the rest of the still-forming image.

On the floor before the altar was the body of a dead woman with long black hair. Thin, bloody stripes, as if caused by a whip, marked her naked body.

As if sensing his attention, the woman turned her head and stared at him.

*"Yet a dragon you shall be."*

The words of the curse echoed in his office. Caitlin's eyes grew large, shimmering against the paleness of her face.

His beast ceased to breathe as his own heart raced, pounding hard inside his chest.

Sean pushed away from the desk, unwilling to witness any more that might be shown to them. He didn't need further evidence of why he'd been cursed into a changeling. The task he was to complete for Nathan was obvious to him. He'd been so concerned about his urge to kill his family that he hadn't taken any other scenario into consideration.

He didn't need to kill them; all he had to do was to lure his brothers to Nathan's castle. Unwittingly he would do so under the guise of helping him rescue his son.

Caitlin had been partly right—while he would go to rescue their son, Braeden and Cameron couldn't be permitted to help. He would not be responsible for killing the Dragon Lord and his twin.

"Sean, look!"

He followed Caitlin's wide-eyed gaze back to the page with trepidation. On the facing page, a dual picture formed.

One half of the page was a desolate image of the world with Nathan in supreme control. The other an idyllic setting with him, Caitlin and their son surrounded by his aunt, brothers and their families.

*"St. George will set you free."*

Once again, the confusing promise filled the air.

He moved back to the desk and turned the page, hoping another picture would form, explaining how he could defeat Nathan.

Caitlin moved behind him. Placing a hand on his shoulder she asked, "You don't think it'll be that easy, do you?"

Sean reached up and covered her hand with his own, wondering if he should be uncomfortable with the way she'd so easily read his mind. "No. But sometimes it doesn't hurt to hope."

His cell phone vibrated, and he glanced at the screen. "Your brothers?"

He nodded in reply to her question and hit the intercom button on the desk phone, opening a line to the office. When it beeped, he said, "On our way."

Sean rose, scooping the dragon pendants from his desk drawer, and slipped them into a front pocket then grabbed the grimoire. He extended an arm toward the door. "Ready?"

Caitlin paused at the huge metal-studded door that Sean held open for her. She felt as if she were being ushered into a medieval lord's chamber for an audience that would decide her fate. She supposed that in a way, it would. Together would they all be able to come up with a plan to save her son? Or would they spend their time devising a plan that would only get them killed?

Did she want to be a part of that? She glanced at Sean, who raised a questioning eyebrow at her hesitation. Whether she wanted to be a part of this or not wasn't an option. She took a breath and entered the room.

Her feet sank into the plush, dark midnight blue carpet. A thin ray of sunlight filtered into the room through an opening between the drapes. The light shimmered off the jeweled hilt of a sword, one of many weapons mounted on the walls, and bounced off the face of a sapphire dragon perched on a marble pedestal. The flicker of light against the dragon's eyes made it appear as if the gemstone beast was looking at her, watching her, waiting for just the right moment to pounce.

She turned her attention to the two men standing before the desk. Their exchanged greetings were brief since she'd met the men.

Her thoughts drifted to the three pendants—amethyst, sapphire and emerald. She sat in one of the chairs in front of the desk with a glance to each man, once again noting the color of their eyes.

A dragon for each brother—was that by coincidence or design?

The grimoire had shown sisters with eyes the same color as the pendants they'd used. Perhaps these brilliant hues were common in the Drake family. If so, was it possible that the brothers had the wrong pendants?

"Sean?" She thought it worth mentioning. "Do you remember—"

Braeden's rousing curse cut off her question. He rose to glance out one of the many tall, narrow windows of his office. "What is Baron Hoffel doing here?"

Caitlin groaned and sank as far back into her chair as possible, wishing it would just swallow her. "I didn't invite him."

Sean sat down in the chair next to her. "I didn't think you had."

Cameron leaned against the desk and asked, "Someone care to clue me in?"

Before she could explain, Braeden said, "Hoffel is Ms. St. George's betrothed."

"How cozy." Sarcasm dripped from Cameron's voice. "Can anyone explain how he found his way here?" He stared at her as he asked.

"I don't know." Caitlin shook her head. "It's not like I could, or even would, give him directions."

Without another word Cameron left the office. She presumed it was to escort their *guest* to the meeting.

The silence in the room as Braeden and Sean stared at her while waiting for Cam to return with Derek, was thick and heavy with unasked questions. It was all Caitlin could do to draw in breath. She sank her nails into the arms of her chair, hoping the act would lessen her worry.

While hell would freeze over before she married Hoffel, she didn't relish the idea of having to explain his death to the High Council, or her parents—or his own parents for that matter.

Sean placed a hand over hers and leaned closer. "If you don't kill him, he'll leave here whole."

She'd been so caught off guard by Derek's arrival and so worried about how the Drakes would react, that she hadn't even noticed Sean's mental intrusion.

But at the moment that was the least of her concerns. There'd never been any intention of marrying the baron, regardless of what her parents or the council thought. However, her plan had been to string everyone along until her son was safely back in her care. Then she and little Sean would leave—before the marriage and well before anyone else could take him away from her.

But her success with getting away from her parents, Derek and the High Council with all of their antiquated rules and stifling expectations depended on her ability to not become the target of their suspicion.

After Derek's attack in the cell and the subsequent blame laid at her feet for his atrocious behavior, it had been all she could do to retain the appearance of civility. In reality she wanted nothing more than to slide her sword through his neck.

*"Bloodthirsty, aren't you?"*

The voice racing through her head didn't belong to Sean. Nor did it feel anything like him. She shot a glare toward Braeden. He raised his eyebrows then silently added, *"Don't worry, I won't say a word."*

Sean's fingers tightened slightly over her hand. She drew her attention to him. Apparently, by the way he glanced from her to his brother, he knew something was up. And when he tried to force his way into her thoughts, Caitlin closed her eyes and dropped a solid wall between both of the men and her mind.

The last thing she needed right now was for Sean to discover what she planned after they rescued her son. He'd demand she stay at his side, where he could protect her and little Sean. She didn't need nor want his protection, and she wasn't about to run away from her controlling family only to go straight into his arms. For reasons she couldn't quite pinpoint yet, that idea felt as if she'd simply be trading one set of chains for another.

A knock at the office door made her heart race. Hoffel was here. Why he'd come to Mirabilus was beyond comprehension. It was one thing for her to walk into the beasts' lair—she had a very good reason for doing so— but for him to follow her defied logic.

Sean briefly tightened his hold over her hand before

releasing it and then leaned closer to whisper, "He can't hurt you."

"I know." She was well aware that Sean's dragon wouldn't permit Derek to lay one finger on her. But she wondered what his beast would think, or do, when he saw her greet another man as if she welcomed his presence.

# Chapter 9

Sean couldn't help but stare at the man who'd entered Braeden's office. It was impossible not to, considering he appeared to be dressed up for Halloween—entirely in black. From the theatrically swirled cape as he strode through the door, to the tailored suit—tie, clip and cuff links included—down to the wing tips, not one speck of color broke the darkness.

He'd seen funeral directors who dressed less somberly than this.

It wasn't just his attire. The man couldn't be more than five and a half feet tall. Which would be fine if he had either the build or the attitude to go along with his stature. But he didn't. His flamboyant entrance made him appear to be more of a low-budget character actor than anything else. And his beady-eyed glare would be more appropriate for a teenager of about sixteen.

His bearing and appearance would make him look like a child standing next to Caitlin. Sean wondered how old Hoffel had been when he'd been turned. Perhaps he hadn't yet been an adult at the time. If so, it would explain quite a bit.

Braeden stepped forward to shake the baron's hand in welcome. "Baron Hoffel, what brings you to Mirabilus?"

"Caitlin shouldn't be alone at a time like this. I came to see that she had the support of her husband-to-be."

His claim on Caitlin, while stated in a thin, reedy voice, couldn't have been made any plainer.

Sean watched silently, curious to see Caitlin's reaction as she rose and went to the baron's side. "Thank you. I'm certain my son's father and his uncles appreciate your added assistance as much as I do. After all, this could turn out to be a bloodbath, and every hand could prove useful."

Obviously, Hoffel wasn't the only one who saw fit to stake their claim. Caitlin had just done a pretty good job of it herself by making it plain that these men were her son's family, not Hoffel. But that wasn't what surprised him the most. It was the baron's reaction that had caught his interest.

Granted, Hoffel was a vampire, and his complexion was on the pale side to begin with, but Sean was positive the man had turned a rather ugly shade of white at Caitlin's words. If ever there was a time when he was torn between outright laughter and pure blood rage, this was it.

For all of Hoffel's theatrics, for his great bravery in abusing a woman, there was nothing alpha about him. In the end, the man was nothing more than a coward and a bully.

Sean had little use for either.

Braeden returned to his desk and waved the others toward the chairs.

With as much restraint as he could muster, Sean let the baron claim the chair closest to Caitlin. It wasn't as if the man could hurt her—if he so much as thought to lift one finger to cause her pain or harm, Sean would basically rip his head from his body and serve it for brunch.

Caitlin looked at him and gasped softly. Sean felt her warm touch brush across his mind. He frowned. How had she done that since he'd been intent on not letting Hoffel in and had put a secure lock on his mind?

Her hand, inside the pocket of the jacket she wore, moved slightly. A slow touch trailed up his spine to linger at the base of his neck.

*How in the hell had she gotten a hold of that pendant?*

No sooner had he asked himself the question when he'd come up with the answer—before they'd left his suite he'd given her a hug for encouragement. The snitch had obviously pilfered it from his pocket without him even realizing it.

He quickly checked his pocket. Sure enough, only two of the pendants were inside. This meeting could turn out to be more interesting than he'd ever imagined.

Obviously tired of waiting for Braeden to ask, Cam barreled ahead. "Care to tell us how you got here?"

Hoffel shrugged. "Luck, I suppose." He smiled sheepishly, adding, "I became lost and followed a small fishing boat into shore."

Surprised his brother left the brazen lie alone, Sean asked, "And what do you plan to do to help in my son's rescue?"

The baron quickly covered his sneer with a cough before offering, "I've had the occasion to meet the Learned once or twice. I could be in a position to mediate the boy's release." He reached over and clasped Caitlin's hand in both of his own. "After all, Cait and I need to make sure he arrives at his parents' house safe and sound."

Braeden's eyebrows rose. Cam's eyes widened in

shock. Sean leaned forward in his chair. "I can assure you that isn't ever going to happen."

Hoffel placed a light kiss on the back of Caitlin's hand and held Sean's stare. "That isn't up to you, is it?"

Sean resisted the urge to rise and tower over the man. Instead, he forced himself to remain seated, but warned, "If you want to turn this into a pissing match, feel free. But you aren't going to win. That is my son and he will be raised here, by me."

Danielle Drake chose that moment to waltz unannounced into the room. "Gentlemen, let's keep this civil, shall we?"

She breezed past the baron to reach out and take Caitlin's hand. "You and I need to get acquainted. Why don't we let the men have their little discussion and we'll rejoin them soon?"

Without another word, she led Caitlin from the office, but not before issuing a silent order to Sean and he was sure his brothers. *Get rid of him. I don't care if you toss him in the ocean or kill him. But he's up to no good.*

Caitlin didn't release her breath until they were outside the castle. She hadn't been aware of holding it until she gasped for air.

"Thank you." She studied the other woman then said, "If I remember correctly, you're Sean's aunt Danielle."

"Yes." She laughed. "Guilty as charged." And then she led Caitlin to a stone bench. "Please, take a seat. We really do need to talk."

Once Caitlin was seated, Danielle pulled a wooden cube from the pocket of her brightly colored dress. "And this—" she lifted the cube before her "—is Aelthed."

"The druid from the grimoire?" Caitlin marveled at the concept. "He's real?"

"Yes, and you're the second person to meet him other than me. He met Ariel, Cam's wife, a while back out of necessity."

"What about your nephews?"

"There's been no reason for them to be introduced."

Amazed, Caitlin asked, "Why me?"

Danielle set the cube on the bench between them. "I'll let him answer."

Before Caitlin could question the woman, a voice floated up from the wooden box. *"Because, my dear, you are going to free me and my nephew from our prisons."*

Caitlin stared at the seemingly inanimate object a moment then asked, "How am I going to do that?"

*"I'm not quite certain yet, but we'll find a way while you're rescuing the dragonette."*

Danielle placed a hand on her leg. "You really aren't going to marry Hoffel, are you?"

Seeing no reason to lie, Caitlin said, "Not in a million years."

"Good." The older woman frowned. "And you aren't giving the child away, either, are you?"

Caitlin smiled and shook her head. "No. It would be easier to tear my heart out with my bare hands."

"Excellent. Then it's settled."

A sinking feeling in the pit of her stomach urged her to hesitantly ask, "What is settled?"

"All of you will figure out a way to rescue the baby and kill Nathan. Then you and Sean will wed—"

"No. No. No." Caitlin raised her hand. "Hold up. I have no intention of marrying your nephew."

"Yes, dear."

Oh, no! She'd forgotten Sean's warning about not arguing with the woman. She was supposed to have hedged. Sean would have to deal with this on his own. Right now her only concern was her son. "If none of you will give me the items the Learned demanded, how am I going to ever get my baby back?"

"What items would those be?"

Was it possible that nobody had told her yet?

Caitlin lightly tapped the cube. "He wants this cube and the grimoire, along with the emerald and sapphire pendants."

Visibly flustered, Danielle Drake waved her hands before her. "No. He can't have those things. It would mean the end of everything. Literally, just everything."

Sean had said something along the same lines, in a less frantic manner, making Caitlin wonder exactly how much magic these items held.

Danielle picked up the cube and held it tightly to her chest. "No. He is not getting Aelthed." Tears shimmered in the woman's eyes.

Had she known the older woman would get this upset she never would have said anything. Caitlin patted the woman's shoulder. "Shhhh. It's okay. I'm sure it won't come to that. Please don't worry."

Now the woman was rocking side to side on the bench. Caitlin's heart fell. What had she done? She glanced over her shoulder toward the castle. "Please, let's go back inside."

"No." Danielle pulled away from her touch. "They'll take him away."

"I won't let them. I promise."

"You can't stop them!" Danielle flapped a hand at her. "Go away. Just leave me be."

Caitlin rose and looked again toward the castle then back at Sean's aunt. "I don't want to leave you alone like this. Come in with me."

"No!"

Seeing as how urging her only made the woman more agitated, Caitlin turned away and headed back to the castle. She'd let Sean and his brothers know what she did as soon as she got back in the office.

*"Danielle, beloved, really. Was all that necessary?"* Aelthed chided.

Danielle sneaked a peek over her shoulder to ensure Caitlin had indeed gone back inside before she sat up, straightened the skirt of her dress and then put the cube back down on the bench beside her. "I got what we wanted, didn't I?"

*"While traumatizing the poor girl."*

"She'll get over it. It's not like she's not hiding things, too."

*"Did you notice her hesitation when she mentioned the pendants?"*

"Yes, I did. Do you think she found another one?"

*"No. That would be impossible. Lady Rhian's amethyst one was shattered into a million pieces. By now it would be nothing more than dust and memories."*

Danielle sighed. "True. But wouldn't it be wonderful if we could somehow re-create that needed key and set you free once and for all?"

*"Perhaps."*

"Yes, well, right now I'm relieved to know the woman isn't working with her family, Hoffel or the Learned. At least I don't have to worry she's only here to hand the boys over to Nathan."

* * *

"Sean!" Caitlin burst into the office without pausing to see if she was interrupting anything or not.

He immediately came to his feet and met her halfway across the room. "What's wrong?"

"I did something stupid."

He led her over to the chair she'd vacated earlier—the one right next to Hoffel, who to her dismay was still present. "Sit down and tell us what you did."

Catching her breath, she explained in a rush, "I said something to upset your aunt, and no matter what I did she only became more and more flustered. I think she's having some sort of panic attack or something."

All three Drakes stared at her a moment before exchanging an odd look with each other. Finally, Braeden rose and addressed Hoffel as he headed for the door with Sean and Cam on his heels, "We'll have to continue this discussion later. I'll have one of the men show you to a room you can use."

He paused at the door. "Caitlin, come with us, please."

His voice was so stern and commanding that she didn't question him. She simply followed the three men from the room.

Once they walked outside, the three of them ducked around the side of the castle, pulling her along.

Cameron broke into laughter first. Then Sean. While Braeden's only show of amusement was a half smile and shake of his head. At her frown, he explained, "Our aunt has a bad habit of engaging in dramatics. She apparently wanted some information from you, got it and then chased you away."

"You have got to be kidding me!" She would strangle the woman for wasting her time in such a frivolous manner.

"Oh, no, that's Danielle Drake. What did you tell her that *upset* her so?"

"I told her about what was demanded in exchange for my son."

Braeden sighed. "She apparently hadn't believed me when I relayed that information and wanted to hear it directly from the source."

The other two started laughing again.

Caitlin glared at Sean. "I'm glad you're so amused. Perhaps you'll find this just as funny. Our marriage *has* been planned and, oops, I forgot to hedge."

With that, she turned and stormed away.

"What a bunch of jerks." Their amusement grated. Especially Sean's. There was nothing funny about any of this. Her son's life was in danger, and they were guffawing over some prank their aunt played?

Fine. They could laugh and waste all the time they wanted. She, on the other hand, wasn't going to sit here doing nothing any longer.

Tonight, after all of them were in bed sleeping, she was going to make her way over to the Learned's stronghold with that damn grimoire and the pendants. It was doubtful she'd be able to get her hands on the cube, but she could tell him where it was—in Danielle Drake's possession.

She stomped into the elevator and punched the button for the third floor. In the meantime she needed to make sure she could pick the lock to Sean's desk, so she could more easily get the items. And then she would have to find a way across the water—even if she had to steal a boat to do so.

* * *

Terror ripped her from the nightmares chasing her. Caitlin reached across the bed, finding only empty air where she'd instinctively thought to find Sean and the comfort just a touch would provide. She gasped at the chilling stab of loss and sat up, hugging her arms about herself in an attempt to dispel the shivers racking her sweat-soaked body.

They'd argued after he had returned to the apartment about his finding so much humor in his aunt's trick. He didn't appear to be taking any of this seriously enough for her satisfaction. His easy manner and mirth had been the last straw of her temper and patience. The rest of the day and evening had been spent in fuming silence on his part, and focused planning on hers. Finally, when she couldn't stand to be in the same room with him any longer, she'd gone to bed. She'd been so certain that sleep would elude her, but it hadn't. She'd quickly fallen into nightmare-laden rest.

Visions of Sean's death circled in her mind with the rotating wildness of a tornado. The same gruesome scene played over and over as she watched helplessly. Her body was frozen in place, unable to go to his aid.

He was naked, chained to Nathan's altar. She heard nothing as if suddenly deaf, but she could see the anger in his furrowed brow and blazing eyes. His lips parted in a soundless shout—a yell of rage that was met with Nathan's vile laugh. The evil, humorless laughter ended as the wizard thrust the tip of Ascalon through Sean's chest.

In distorted, slow-motion frames, Sean fell to the stone floor. His life blood flowing from him along with his soul. A curling fog streamed from his body, and Nathan gleefully pulled the departing energy into himself.

"No." Caitlin threw off the covers. She couldn't let that happen. What she was about to do would enrage Sean, but she'd much rather endure his anger than lose him forever.

Regardless of what he would think, or say later, she knew this was the right thing to do. Hadn't they both witnessed the grimoire drawing the same horrible image of his death? This wasn't the first time she'd had this dream—it had haunted her before his family's book had put her nightmare into pictures.

She had to trust her instinct on this. These images were more than just pictures or vague warnings, and far more than simple worry on her part. They were portents of the future—omens that she could no longer ignore.

Caitlin quickly tossed on the first clothes she grabbed and tied her hair back with a stretchy band. Knowing she would need something to carry everything in, she rooted around in the closet, snagged her long duffel bag and then left the bedroom. As quietly as possible, in case Sean had returned from wherever he'd headed after she'd gone to bed, she stayed against the wall while she crept down the hall and peered around the corner.

Her soft *whoosh* of the breath she'd been holding rushed into the darkness of the empty living room. She approached the door to his office with her fingers crossed. Hopefully, it wouldn't be locked. He'd be angry enough without her breaking into his office.

To her relief, the door opened at her touch. She flipped on the desk lamp and held out a hand, calling Ascalon to her grip. After sliding the weapon into the bag, Caitlin swept the grimoire on top of the sword.

Since she'd already practiced earlier, picking the lock to his desk was easy enough to accomplish after a couple tries. Once she had possession of the two dragon pendants that Nathan had demanded, she dropped them into the bag, too.

She felt the front pocket of her jeans to ensure the amethyst pendant was still there. Nathan hadn't asked for it, nor did she have any intention of giving it to him, but as far as she was concerned, since it responded to her—it belonged to her.

Now she just needed to get out of this apartment and to the dock where Hoffel waited for her as planned. Earlier in the afternoon, she'd realized that he actually had had a good point about mediating. He *had* met the Learned, and he might prove as useful as he thought he could be, so she'd approached him. Her selling point had mirrored his—rescuing the baby so they could get on with their lives.

And the man had bought it.

Right now she didn't care. She'd willingly use whomever she had to use to get her child back where he belonged.

Once Caitlin exited the apartment, she rushed down the hallway to the stairs where she thought she'd have less of a chance of being caught.

To her relief she encountered no one on the stairs and saw no one when she peered down and out into the Great Hall. After taking a deep breath, she raced across the hall, wincing as her footsteps seemed to echo off the stone of the walls.

But thankfully, her moves had all been well planned so far because she made it outside into the night air without mishap.

She hugged the castle wall as she skirted around to the side, avoiding the lights before darting out into the open expanse of ground between the castle and the beach area.

Halfway across the open ground she felt rather than heard or saw someone fall into step alongside her.

"Going somewhere?"

The sound of Sean's voice made her heart stutter and stomach turn.

He took the bag from her hand, flung it into the air where it disappeared, then grasped her upper arm and steered her back toward the castle. "I'm afraid your lover's already been detained."

Between gritted teeth she said, "He is *not* my lover."

"Really? You might want to fill him in on that."

She ignored his dig to ask, "What did you do with my bag?"

"Put everything back where it belongs."

"You really didn't expect me to just sit around and do nothing like the rest of you have been, did you?"

When he didn't respond, she continued, "He is my son. My son! I can't just leave him to die at Nathan's hands. Why can't you understand that?"

Again, he kept walking without saying a word.

"Damn you, Drake! What is wrong with you? How can you not care about your own son?"

He came to an abrupt stop, swung her around before him and slapped his hand over her mouth. Standing nose to nose with her, he shouted, "Shut up. Just. Stop. Talking."

Caitlin flinched at the gravelly tone of his voice— more growl than anything. She leaned away from the brilliant emerald shimmer emanating from around his elongated pupils.

Yes, she feared the beast evident in every fiber of Sean's being. But she refused to back down.

She tore her face away from his hand. "No! I will not shut up." She poked a finger into his chest. "Why don't you act like the beast you claim to be and save our son!"

Before she fully knew what was happening, he shifted, quickly—almost instantaneously from man, to misty dragon, to strong, solid beast. An angry, muscular beast, who grasped her by the nape of the neck as if she were nothing more than a piece of paper before taking to the sky.

Caitlin's scream followed them into the nighttime clouds.

# *Chapter 10*

Sean's beast flew low over the choppy waters, letting the icy cold spray cool him and hopefully the woman still clutched securely in his talons. Her screams hadn't lessened, but they were borne of anger, of rage, having nothing to do with fear. She was mad because her plans had been thwarted.

Too bad.

Didn't she realize that her plans would have gotten her killed? He longed to shake some sense into her. But the human part of his mind knew that if he started, he'd be unable to stop, and harming her would serve no purpose.

So for now they would soar until her ire abated enough to hear reason and his anger eased over the fact that in the end, she'd chosen to go to Hoffel. That stung.

It wasn't as if he and Caitlin had a relationship; they didn't. Outside of the child she bore, they shared nothing other than over-the-top sex.

He understood his dragon's rage—the beast was jealous, plain and simple. Somehow he'd have to get over it and learn to live with the fact that he and his mate were never going to share a life.

His own anger confused him—oh, sure, the mere thought of being passed over for that weaselly, snot-nosed bully Hoffel was a huge slap in the face as far as his ego was concerned, and there'd be no getting over that.

But why did it feel like more than just a bruised ego?

He hadn't been sitting around all day doing nothing like she'd suggested. He'd spent most of the day with his brothers and some of Mirabilus's men, devising a way to rescue the child and kill the Learned without the loss of too many lives.

He and Cam had flown at least half a dozen missions, scouting every speck of the Learned's stronghold. They'd charted each and every weakness, while noting in detail the strengths that would prove difficult to overcome.

He'd even seen their son.

The boy was fine. He'd been screaming his lungs out, but he hadn't appeared harmed, just throwing a fine temper—like his mother. The nurse had fretted over him as if she'd actually cared about his distress and was doing everything within her power to ease it.

At one point Sean swore the child looked directly at him. But that must have been wishful thinking because his beast had been nothing more than a sliver of fog weaving in and out of the mist.

It had been all he could do not to slip in through the narrow window opening and take the child from the castle ruins. But how? In solid form he wouldn't have fit through the opening—he was unable to control his size in solid form; he would always be a big, lumbering hulk. And in smoke form, he had no way to physically carry the boy.

He would have told Caitlin all of this. For that matter, she could have helped with the plotting and planning, but she'd been in a snit because she thought they'd laughed at her over Danielle. Had she let him explain, she'd have known that they'd been laughing at Danielle's antics, not Caitlin's gullibility. But she'd stomped off.

And when he'd gone to the suite to talk to her, she'd stormed into the bedroom and slammed the door closed. He could have forced his way in and made her listen, but instead, he'd done his own storming off.

Sean rolled his eyes. Anyone watching them would think they were a couple of hormonal teenagers instead of adults at times.

When he'd gone back up for dinner, the chill in the suite had been too cold to bear for long. So again, he'd left her alone, thinking that was the easiest option.

Finally, when he'd realized that the ignoring routine was getting them nowhere, he'd gone up to talk to her, only to find her, the grimoire, the pendants and Ascalon gone.

While searching for her, Cam had called to inform him that Hoffel was on the beach with a boat, waiting for Caitlin. Sean tracked down Caitlin, leaving his brothers to deal with Hoffel. At least they wouldn't kill the fool.

"Sean, are you in there?"

He shook himself out of his woolgathering and noticed she wasn't screaming anymore. He dipped his head to peer down at her. She was seated on the pad of his... foot with her back resting against one of his curled talons.

"Ah, you do hear me."

Of course he heard her. But his first instinct was to keep ignoring her, even though he knew that would get them nowhere. The problem was that he was in beast form, and he wouldn't be able to keep the dragon's feelings out of any conversation he had with her. And the human side of him feared that in this short amount of time the beast had become far more attached to the woman than was good for either of them.

She stroked her hand down a smooth talon and then leaned over to rest her forehead against it. "I just needed to do something to get our son back. Surely you can understand that, can't you?"

Wonderful. She was going to appeal directly to the dragon. He couldn't allow that. Sean focused his energy on her. He might not be able to speak out loud, but he could still get his thoughts across.

"Leave him alone, Caitlin."

"I'm just explaining myself."

"There's no need. We aren't confused in the least. You chose Hoffel."

The dragon huffed and soared higher.

She wrapped her arms around the talon she'd been leaning against. "Only because you and I weren't speaking."

"Bull."

"You can't seriously believe I'd ever choose the baron for anything, can you? You met him. He's a vicious coward."

Maybe it was time she was confronted with the truth Braeden had discovered about her fiancé and perhaps her family. "He's the Learned's henchman. How do you think he found his way here? It was no accident. So, tell me again how neither you, nor your family, are involved with Nathan."

"What? No."

"Don't play dumb, Caitlin. I know better. Isn't that why you came to me in the first place? So that I'd get myself and my brothers killed trying to save our son?"

"Sean, I swear, I would never do that. I don't believe my family would do such a thing."

He wanted to believe her, but he'd be risking far too much to do so. And he wasn't willing to risk everything for her. "Really? You don't believe your kind, loving, blood-sucking family would ever do anything to harm another person?"

"It's not like they're out there slaughtering the villagers."

"No. They're just out there roasting dragons on a spit."

She sighed. "This is getting us nowhere."

"No kidding. Why don't you just tell me the truth and be done with it?"

"I have told you the truth."

"Your truth has too many holes in it."

He strengthened his focus, determined to discover the truth on his own and reached out to touch her mind. To his surprise, she let him in with little resistance. Sean shivered against the pain he met. This time it wasn't her hunger that threatened to tear him apart—it was the cold, twisting ache of what could only be a mother's loss.

Since her immediate, basic needs had been met— she'd been fed and was no longer starving—her nurturing and maternal needs had rushed in to fill the void. There existed an ache inside her that could only be soothed by the return of her child.

Yes, he was angry that the Learned had his offspring. He was horrified that the St. Georges had done their best to kill the child before it came into the world. When he'd seen his son, he had been filled with overwhelming awe and a warmth inside like nothing he'd ever felt before.

And if the child died, he would be angry, sad, beside himself with grief.

But it would be nothing compared to Caitlin's pain. Hers would be unbearable.

Through no choice of his own, he'd not yet had the chance to imprint with his son. He would mourn the loss of something he never got the chance to know.

Caitlin would mourn the loss of a part of herself.

Sean's beast crooned, soft and low, seeking a way to provide Caitlin with temporary solace. He would never be able to convince the dragon that its efforts were a waste of time. Nothing it did would help. But the animal acted on instinct, and right now its mate was in pain, and it would seek a way to somehow ease that agony.

Sean let him be and pushed deeper, past the pain, reaching for memories that would give him the answers he sought.

He hadn't doubted her claims that her parents had locked her away, leaving her to starve—he'd seen the proof of that—he just hadn't given any thought to the hurt and anguish such a spiteful, unkind act had caused her. She might be an adult, but they were still her parents and they'd sought her death, or at the very least the death of their own grandchild.

Nor had he doubted that Hoffel had attacked her; the grimoire had clearly shown him that.

But neither of those were the memories or thoughts he was looking to find. So he poked around a little more.

And there, the memory he sought came into focus. Yes, just as he'd thought, her parents had directed her to come to him. That whole scene with her mother back in his bedroom at the Lair had been nothing more than one of her mother's orchestrated shows meant to manipulate him so he'd believe that she had come to him on her own.

When in truth they'd ordered her to bring Ascalon with her so that if Nathan didn't succeed in killing him and his brothers, she could.

However, she'd come to him with the firm intention of ignoring their orders. She was set on getting her child back and then leaving—everyone. Caitlin wasn't going back to the St. George family home. She'd lied to her parents, Hoffel and the High Council. She wasn't going to marry Hoffel.

But she wasn't staying with Sean, either, and she wasn't leaving her child behind.

His anger that she would blithely disregard everything he'd told her about being mated and raising the child sparked to life.

Before that spark could flare to a full-blown inferno, he stopped. Could he blame her? After everything she'd been through, could he really fault her for wanting to run away, to disappear? Hadn't he run away for less?

That was most likely why she'd gone to Hoffel tonight. She'd mistakenly believed that with his help, she would get her child back and then she would just disappear without anyone being the wiser.

Little did she know that Hoffel would have delighted in helping the Learned kill her, or at the very least watched the event with glee.

He eased out of her mind and directed the dragon back to Mirabilus.

"Sean."

"No. Just be quiet."

"But—"

"I don't want to hear your explanation. I just want you to be quiet."

The last thing he wanted was for his dragon to discover what she'd planned. It was going to be hard enough to keep the beast out of that part of his mind; he didn't want it to overhear a conversation. They could talk later if she insisted, after his beast was fast asleep and not tuned in to its human part. Until then, she just needed to keep her explanations to herself.

Sean circled the beach, landing alongside an old work shed. He set her down gently, and with the curve of a talon pushed her into the shed before shifting back to human form and then following her inside.

Aelthed shook off the regret and sadness swirling around him. The cursed changeling was upset, but being pure Drake, he wasn't about to give voice to his sense of loss or the confusion he felt because of it.

Stretching out his legs, seated in the corner of his cube, Aelthed could empathize with the changeling. It had taken him a good many months to finally understand his own sense of loss over something he'd never really had.

As a man, a human man—or as close to human as he'd ever been—he was dead. Even if he found a way out of the cube he would exist as nothing more than a disembodied soul. No matter what he did, he would never feel Danielle Drake's arms around him, never taste the sweetness of her kiss, never experience the pain or pure joy of her love.

And he'd grieved over those things for quite a while. In truth, there were still moments when despair threatened to drop him into the agonizing pits of hell.

He wished there was a way for him to help the change-ling avoid the same fate, but he knew that wasn't possi-ble. St. George's daughter wasn't ever going to give her heart to the dragon. It didn't matter whether they rescued the child or not; it wasn't in her nature.

Succubus or not, she was the spawn of a vampire. A heartless, soulless creature who cared nothing for the emotions or needs of others. That was the way she'd been raised. And that was how she would raise the dragon-ette—it's what was familiar and normal to her.

Now that was something Aelthed couldn't permit. To keep a dragon from going rogue, it needed to learn and understand the value in feelings, human feelings. Otherwise, what was to keep it from ruthlessly killing those smaller and weaker than itself?

She would never willingly surrender the child, and since she wasn't going to remain with the changeling, something had to be done; someone would have to in-tervene.

"Aelthed, love, what are you stewing about?" Dani-elle's voice broke into his thoughts. "I swear there's smoke streaming from your cube."

"Ah, you've returned." He leaned away from the wall of the cube. "What were you able to learn?"

She dropped down onto the bed and scooped the cube off her nightstand to hold it close to her chest. "Well, Hoffel is a dimwit."

Aelthed chuckled. "I doubt that. It's more likely that he's playing a dimwit to keep you from discovering any-thing."

She issued a decisive *hmmphhff* before asking, "Do you actually think the man possesses any level of in-telligence?"

"I'm not certain, but the changeling, his mate and I do agree that Hoffel is a vindictive, petty, vicious little man and worth watching."

"That's what Braeden thinks, too. Cameron isn't at all certain the baron is dangerous, but feels that it would be wiser to kill him and not have to worry about it."

"Yes, Cameron would think that."

"Well, he does like to take the direct route to solving problems."

"Are you sure that's really it? I've always thought he just enjoyed ridding the world of bad guys."

Danielle's soft laugh floated against him, leaving him awash with unrequited longing so intense he had to fight off a shiver.

"What's wrong, Aelthed? Something doesn't feel quite right."

The concern in her tone brought a sigh to his lips. She'd been far too perceptive of late. "Nothing you need worry about."

His cube moved slowly. "My love." The warmth of her breath let him know that she held his prison near her lips. "I wish more than anything in the world that I could hold you, too."

Sean waved Caitlin through the open door in the back of the work shed and into the tunnel beyond.

Someone—a worker, or one of his brothers—had lit the torches lining the wall, so at least they weren't walking blindly down the tunnel in the dark.

Caitlin trailed a fingertip along the damp wall. "What is this place?"

"It leads to Aelthed's workroom."

"Aelthed? The druid?"

"That's the only Aelthed I know."

Caitlin wasn't in the mood for answers bordering on sarcasm. She shot him a frown over her shoulder, but before she could say anything, the tunnel opened up into a circular room.

More torches lined the walls, and lit candles had been placed here and there to provide light. She walked slowly around the perimeter of the chamber. A layer of dust and grime coated countless ancient jars and containers on the shelves.

The hard-packed dirt floor was littered with broken shards of pottery, glass and other bits of objects she couldn't identify—and probably didn't want to know what they were.

In the center of the room was a wooden table—likely a casting altar from the items gathered on the worn top. She glanced down at the silver scrying bowl already filled with water.

"Sean, what are we doing here?"

He stood behind the table. "There's something I want to show you."

And he couldn't have done that elsewhere? "It has to be done in a medieval chamber?"

"No, but I like the added atmosphere."

She didn't. It reminded her too much of the High Council and the black magic they called forth on occasion.

"Couldn't we…"

He grasped her wrist and gently tugged her toward him. "Humor me."

She couldn't help roll her eyes, but she joined him, standing between him and the table.

Sean encircled her with his arms, making her feel safe. His hands stretched out over the bowl.

"You do this often?"

"Shhh." He waved his hands over the bowl.

The water started to move. Slowly at first, wavering back and forth until it settled into circular ripples coming out from the center as if a pebble had been dropped onto the surface. Then it rippled faster, before it flattened to the smooth clearness of a mirror.

"Watch."

She saw an image begin to form—faint at first, but then it grew clearer, more defined. Sean moved his hands farther apart, letting her see more of the water's surface and more of the image.

It was like she was flying. Below was the ocean—the white-capped waves rolled toward land, and high on a craggy cliff were the ruins of a castle.

She flew closer and closer until she could make out the cutaways of narrow window openings. Then she slowed and flew lower—keeping out of sight perhaps?

"Was this you?"

"Yes. Keep watching."

The fool had gone to the Learned's stronghold.

A sound rose up from the bowl. High pitched, faint, barely discernable, so she inched higher, nearer to the window. Then she heard it—

The cry of a baby.

Caitlin gripped his forearms and held her breath as she leaned forward, trying to get closer to the image on the water.

In what seemed inch-by-inch increments that took hours to cover, she rose. Finally, just when she thought she'd go mad from anticipation, she was just outside the window.

And there he was—her son.

Screaming down the castle walls. He was displaying a fine temper—one worthy of a dragon.

Caitlin reached toward the water, aching to touch even the reflection of her child, but before she could get close enough to graze his image, Sean stopped her, holding her back, preventing her from getting the tiniest bit of comfort.

She wanted to scream and rage as her child was doing, but the only sound she could make past the thickness in her throat was a ragged whine of despair.

"Just look. If you touch it, the image will dissolve."

She didn't know whether to fight against the strong arms wrapped tightly around her, holding her fast against his chest, or to melt into the safety and comfort they offered.

Her child's cries wiped the question from her mind. She didn't care about the arms around her; the only thing she could focus on was her son. She stared at him, relieved that he appeared unharmed—angry, but whole and sound.

As if he felt his mother's presence, he turned his face to her. The brilliant green, tear-filled eyes looked directly at her. His face was red from his tantrum, making the shock of light blond hair appear even lighter.

The nursemaid holding him turned away from the window, and Caitlin found herself pulling away from the view through no choice of her own.

"No!"

The harder she tried to stay near the window, the

faster she seemed to retreat, until the window, the castle, the ocean, vanished from sight.

Her chest tightened until she could no longer draw in air. Her arms ached from the emptiness she didn't think she could bear a moment longer.

The chamber spun into nothing but a cold, empty blackness.

# Chapter 11

Sean caught her before she fell to the floor. He reached out to his brother. "Braeden, a little assist, please."

The flames of the torches and candles flickered out at almost the same instant Braeden spelled him and Caitlin to his bedroom.

He laid her on the bed and checked her pulse. The strong and steady beat reassured him that she had fainted, and nothing serious was wrong. Which was what he'd assumed, but he would rather be certain.

Sean brushed her hair from her face, his fingers lingering of their own accord on the silken strands. And when she started to rouse, he spelled her back to sleep. He had things to do. He didn't want her around to argue with him, nor did he want to have to worry about what she was up to.

It would piss her off, but her mood was the least of his concerns.

He closed the door behind him when he left the bedroom and stood in the middle of the living room, looking around at his possessions. This had been his suite of rooms, his apartment—his home, on Mirabilus, since he'd turned eighteen. It would be strange not living in it.

But he wasn't going to share living quarters with

Caitlin anymore. Not even for the few remaining days she'd be here.

Once their son was back in her arms, she would look for, and find, some way to escape. He didn't want her to feel as though she had to *escape*. He'd rather she simply leave, openly—freely. Perhaps if he didn't fight her on it, didn't make her feel as if she needed to run away, she would keep him apprised of her whereabouts.

He couldn't get back the time he'd already missed, but he'd like to know his son. He wanted to be there from now on, to see him take his first step, to go off on his first day of school—he didn't want to miss any of it, not the good, nor the bad...or the hard.

And he couldn't do any of that if he didn't know where Caitlin had taken the boy.

There was nothing in the living room or kitchen that he'd need in another suite. The one he'd chosen for his temporary use came fully furnished. However, he did want some of the things from his office.

Sean flipped on the desk lamp and started putting a pile of things together on the top of his desk. He removed the grimoire and two pendants from her bag, but left Ascalon in place. The weapon wasn't his, and he doubted that she'd be using it on anyone here.

Other than his laptop and cell, the only additional item he wanted with him was the amethyst pendant. That gem was probably in one of Caitlin's pockets.

A pale, pulsing glow from the desk caught his attention. He walked over and flipped open the grimoire. The last picture they'd seen had been the one where he and his two brothers had been killed by the Learned. He turned that page over, unwilling to dwell on the implication.

The scene forming now was once again of the two women from the twelfth century. They were fitting their pendants into depressed areas on a wooden box. He leaned down to study the picture closely. It appeared that once they had the gemstones locked in place that they turned them in a specific order, and the top of the box then slid off the base.

Sean didn't know where the box was located. He'd never seen it. Was it, or did it represent, the cube Aunt Danielle kept close at hand—the one that supposedly still trapped the soul of the ancient High Druid Aelthed?

He and his brothers had never witnessed any proof that the druid's soul still did exist in the cube, but they'd had no reason not to believe their aunt.

Sean studied the page again. Apparently, he did still reside there. Why else would the grimoire have drawn the same scene more than once? More apparently, the grimoire wanted the druid freed.

He closed the grimoire and put it, along with the two pendants, into a carryall, shut off the light and left the suite.

The moment he closed and locked the outer door behind him, his beast's eyes opened. Sean sighed then warned, "Don't start."

Thankfully, the dragon's look was curious more than anything else. Even when Sean went into the suite a floor above, the creature remained calm, which actually surprised him.

Maybe the fact that they were still close to Caitlin—only the thickness of her ceiling and his floor separating them—helped keep the dragon from throwing a fit about no longer sharing a suite. Or perhaps realization hadn't fully set into the dragon's mind yet.

Not willing to bring it up, in thoughts or words, Sean dumped his bag in the office and then went into the bedroom.

The sound of light snoring let him know she was there before he turned on the light. He backed quietly out of the room.

Sliding open the glass doors, he stepped out onto the balcony. "What the hell are you doing?"

He was grateful that no one was around to see or hear what would appear to be a one-sided conversation. In his mind, he could see the dragon sit back on his haunches, cock his head and look at him in confusion.

So, he didn't know anything about Caitlin having been moved? How was that possible?

He took a breath and then spilled what was going on. "I left her. We aren't going to stay in the same suite or sleep in the same bed anymore."

The dragon glanced toward the bedroom.

"No kidding. I know she's there. She's not supposed to be. You need to move her back to her suite—our old one."

It was pretty sad when his beast looked at him as if he'd lost his wits. Great. If the dragon didn't spell her to this suite, then who did?

He knew that neither Braeden nor Cam would have done so; they wouldn't interfere like that. And Danielle, even though she wouldn't hesitate to interfere, didn't have the ability. Neither did either of his sisters-in-law.

Sean frowned. No anger, no outrage, no regret from the dragon at the news that he was leaving its mate? Nothing?

Something wasn't right. The creature may not have

moved her here, but it was a safe bet it knew who did and wasn't sharing.

"It isn't going to work. She will be leaving and you can't stop her."

The dragon narrowed its emerald eyes.

"If you try to stop her, we'll lose all contact with the boy. Do you understand that? Is that what you want?"

Other than a slight slant, the expression didn't change—it remained focused and narrowed, like it knew something Sean didn't.

*How was that possible?*

This beast, cursed as it may be, was a part of him. Hell, it was him.

Sean dragged a hand through his hair and spun back inside the apartment. This was not happening. It couldn't be happening. Because if it was, then the only logical explanation was that he'd finally lost his mind.

Grabbing his bag from the office, he left the suite and returned to his own a floor below. Without pausing to do more than toss his bag on the sofa, he strode to the bedroom door and then stopped with his hand on the doorknob. What was he going to do if she was in there?

What could he do?

Nothing other than go sleep in his office.

He cracked open the door just a hair and felt his shoulders slump as the sound of Caitlin's steady breaths brushed across his ears.

Aelthed scratched at his beard. It didn't make any sense. How was the succubus materializing from room to room? Who was responsible for the spell?

It wasn't the cursed changeling; he'd sensed no such power in him. He could move objects—a bag, a sword, or things like that, but not a person. Nor was it the other two changelings; they were each in bed with their wife. Danielle was fast asleep.

So who?

And how did the cursed dragon know?

He agreed with the changeling; that shouldn't be possible. The man and the beast were one. Aelthed rubbed his temples and revised that thought. The man and the beast were supposed to be one. In normal changeling-beast combinations they shared a mind. Each knew the thoughts of the other.

But there was nothing normal about this combination.

*"St. George will set you free."*

He spun around in the center of his cube. There was no one there, so from where had the voice come?

A glimmering image flickered in and out of view.

Aelthed stared hard at the image. It was the gypsy mage—the one who'd spoken the curse. And the one who had the power to write in his grimoire.

He fisted his hands at his sides, shouting, *"What do you want?"*

Laughter filled his cell. A tinkling, soft laugh, followed by the swish of skirts and jingle of tiny bells.

*"Trying...to help...old man."* Her words faded in and out, as did her form.

Aelthed snorted. For all the power she had, she certainly wasn't able to hold her form very well.

A silken caress, a scarf perhaps, brushed across his face, followed by another laugh. He jerked away from the touch. He'd not felt contact with another being in over eight hundred years, and he didn't welcome the intrusion.

The air swirled around him as the still-glimmering image moved closer. She extended an arm, and he leaned away.

*"I thank you to keep your hands to yourself."*

This time her laugh raced against his ear, and her fingertips stroked his beard.

*"Stop that!"*

"Aelthed, who are you fighting with in there?" Danielle's voice was filled with concern.

*"That blasted gypsy."*

"Oh!"

He closed his eyes at the shocked dismay in her exclamation. Before he could explain, he felt his cube thud down onto a hard surface and bounce once before coming to a teetering stop.

*"Dan—"*

The slamming of a door cut off his words.

Aelthed glared at the half-formed gypsy. *"So much for helping this old man."*

"Sorry."

At least she didn't laugh.

*"I don't need your help, so why don't you go actually help the abomination you created instead of just playing with him."*

To his relief, the glimmery image faded, leaving him alone to figure out how to make peace with a woman he could only talk to through wooden walls.

Sean stared at the grimoire open on the desk before him. The newly forming picture of a cube—like Aunt Dani's prized possession—appeared slowly on the page. But this time, instead of just a plain box, there was a cutaway allowing him to see into the cube. He wasn't too surprised to see that it wasn't empty. But it was odd to see an actual man trapped inside.

The cube his aunt possessed wasn't large enough to contain a person. At least not a living person.

Did the image of the man represent ashes, maybe? Were the ashes of this old man inside there?

The man in the scene shook a fist at him.

Sean leaned slightly away. Apparently, not ashes.

The dragon leaned closer and sniffed then, seemingly unconcerned, yawned and finally went back to sleep.

So...did the beast somehow know this man?

"Something new?" Caitlin asked from the office door, holding two cups of coffee.

He motioned her in. "Check this out."

She set one cup on the desk and took a seat next to him. Curling her legs up in the chair, she held her own cup close. Bending her head side to side, she said, "I feel like I must have tossed and turned all night."

Sean's eyes widened briefly, but he wasn't going to explain why she felt that way. Instead, he pulled her attention to the grimoire. "There's the cube the Learned wants."

"Is that the one your aunt has?"

"Yes. But look inside."

She leaned forward slightly, glanced at the image then calmly sat back in her chair. "I still think he looks older than he sounds."

"Older than he sounds?" Sean turned in his chair to stare at her. "Care to explain that?"

Caitlin squinted for a moment before opening her eyes. "That's right, I forgot. The three of you haven't met him."

"And you have?"

"Yes. When your aunt took me outside yesterday, she introduced us."

Sean slammed the grimoire closed. "You didn't think that worth mentioning?"

"You didn't ask. Oh, that's right, you were too busy being amused because she'd duped me."

"We're going to do this again?"

"We could gather everything up and go get our son."

"We aren't gathering anything up to give to the Learned."

"So we're going to sit here another day doing nothing?"

Sean wondered how she spoke so clearly through clenched teeth. "That's exactly what we're going to do."

Her coffee cup hit the desk so hard that coffee sloshed over the edge. "You just don't care, do you?"

"You saw him for yourself. Did he appear to be in any danger?"

"No. But you don't know when that could change."

He placed a hand on her arm, hoping to calm her and himself. "Caitlin, the Learned isn't going to do anything to harm his only guarantee. We plan on moving tomorrow."

"What's wrong with today? What difference will another day make?"

He could ask the same thing, but he knew the answer—she was anxious. "We are taking our time because we can and we must. Men are probably going to die. There's no helping it. Braeden wanted everyone to have today to see to their families and for us to go over every detail once more."

Caitlin shook her head, a confused expression on her face. "Wait a minute. You would rather have people die in a rescue attempt that may not work, instead of just giving him what he wants in exchange for a certain release?"

In an attempt to blow off some of his own agitation, Sean rose and paced. "Certain release? The only thing you can be certain of with the Learned is death. You've seen the things he's done, what he's capable of. How can you not see how much more dangerous he would be with those items in his possession?"

"I want my son!"

He walked toward her. "Caitlin, please understand."

She held up her arms, palms out, to stop his approach. "Stay away. Don't touch me."

Sean spun about and walked out of the office. She wasn't going to see reason, and he had no words to convince her that he and his brothers were doing the right thing.

He heard her crying and felt as if his own heart was going to break. There was no way he could just leave her like this, so he went back to the office and came to a rocking stop in the doorway.

She was still seated in the chair, head bowed, crying, with a glowing Ascalon held out before her.

"Do you want me to leave?"

She nodded and waved the sword at him.

Sean bypassed the elevator for the stairs, hoping the jog down them would provide some of the release he needed.

It didn't, so he kept up the pace and slammed out of the castle. He had no idea where he was going; he just knew he had to get out of there.

By the time he made it to the beach, he was moving at a dead run and saw no point in slowing. The instant his toes hit the water, he shifted to a smoky dragon and lifted into the sky.

He circled the island, flying in and out of clouds. It was too bad he couldn't just keep going higher and higher until he hit the moon, or Mars, but he knew that was a foolish wish since even dragons needed air to breathe.

What was he going to do with her? His brothers' wives were bullheaded, but Caitlin took demanding to another level. When she wanted something her way, she wanted it that way now. Not tomorrow, not when it was the right time, but now.

Had she always been this way?

His dragon snuffed at him. Yes, yes, he was being unfair. She was upset about the baby. He knew that. But he was doing everything he could within reason.

What did she expect?

Suddenly, the warmth of the sun above the clouds grew cold. The blood running through his veins chilled. Something was wrong. By the rapid beating of his heart he could tell that even his beast felt that something was off—not quite right.

He couldn't have been gone half an hour. Both Braeden and Cam were at the castle. What could have happened in so short a time? And why hadn't either of them contacted him?

When he started to direct his flight back to the castle, the dragon intervened and headed west, toward the Learned's castle. Sean's breath caught in his chest. Was something wrong with their son?

He focused his full attention on getting to the Learned's quickly, lending speed to the dragon's flight.

They didn't slow until they were right up against the

castle wall. Sean directed them up to the window where he'd seen his son and then he heard it—not the cry of a child in distress, but of a terrified woman—his woman.

# *Chapter 12*

Nathan waved a palm slowly before the highly polished mirror hanging on the wall behind his altar. The blank surface wavered and then filled with a swirling smoke before the vision he wanted came into view.

He'd been keeping an eye on the cursed beast since his arrival on Mirabilus. Waiting, plotting, tamping down his impatience because he knew that eventually, this moment would come.

A quick study of his altar assured him that all was ready.

Now he simply needed to bring the beast here.

Which wouldn't be too terribly difficult since the dragon was a juvenile and unlike his older siblings, who relied more on reason and forethought, still let emotions overrule his better judgment, especially when it came to his mate.

"Let me go!"

Nathan paid little heed to the woman chained to a pillar at the far side of the chamber. She was nothing more than a necessity—needed bait. A mortal who, in her soon to be realized death, wouldn't provide enough energy to lift his arm.

Without turning around, he snapped his fingers over his shoulder at her and smiled at the easiness of the spell.

She screamed again. "Let me— What did you do?"

Her voice changed midscream. Instead of the high-pitched, accented voice she'd used her entire life, it was now lower, the voice of a certain succubus.

He focused on the image before him. It was all he could do not to shout in triumph. No, not yet. True, the beast was now headed to what he thought would be his mate's rescue, but he wasn't yet caught fast in spells and chains.

Soon. Mere moments left.

Nathan waved his hand again, wiping away the image in the mirror and then he moved into the shadows.


Sean's throat tightened. *The Learned had Caitlin!*

No. That wasn't possible.

His heart threatened to pound out of his chest. The beast shook its head in dismay and anger. Possible or not, there was no time for planning or plotting. He wasn't leaving her in Nathan's hands one millisecond longer than necessary.

Aiming for the window, Sean entered the stronghold like a smoky arrow.

The second he cleared the window, she cried out, "Help me!"

Keeping his sense alert for Nathan, he followed the sound, through the chamber he'd entered, out into the hallway and down the curved staircase.

There, at the other side of the Great Hall, he spotted a woman chained to a pillar. Sean's beast reared back, slowing them, giving him time to shift into solid dragon form—a form that would provide him with more strength and speed than that of a human.

Once shifted, he lunged forward to get to the woman, only to slam face-first down on the cold, stone floor. He lifted his head to see a chain secured around his ankle and Nathan walking out from the shadows laughing as he threw a spell toward him and then at Caitlin.

Sean tried to shift to human form as a blazing ball of light blinded him momentarily before the heat of it washed over him. Unable to shift, the beast raged. Intent on getting to Caitlin he turned away from the wizard and reached toward her. She was no longer screaming, no longer upright. She'd fallen to the floor in a pool of blood.

Sean dragged himself as far as the chain would allow, afraid to touch her, afraid of what he would find. But he had to know. He stretched out, straining against the metal bond holding him, hooked the tip of a talon into the hem of her blouse and dragged her to him.

The dragon buried his nose in the sweat-dampened hair bunched on the back of her neck. Caitlin's scent was absent. The only things he detected were the scents of blood and death.

Unable to contain his emotions, Sean let the gut-wrenching pain of loss wash over him, sobbing as the beast's keening cry filled the chamber. He pulled Caitlin's body into his embrace then held her against his chest.

He longed to feel his fingertips against her skin, his lips—human lips—pressed to hers one more time. But he'd been denied that by the vile cretin who'd killed her.

The beast loosened his hold enough to bring her away

from his chest. Even if he couldn't kiss her, he could at least gaze on her.

He took a shuddering breath before turning his gaze down to the sight he knew would shred his heart.

As realization that the woman in his hold was not Caitlin set in, Nathan's cruel laugh rang loud in the chamber, bouncing off the unadorned stone walls.

The dragon placed the woman on the floor, drew to his full height and then growling, it turned to tear the wizard apart with his talons. As he lunged for the Learned, a puff of smoke coated his face, filled his nostrils, and he swayed on his feet as a sudden dizziness claimed him.

Sean cursed as his beast once again hit the floor and succumbed to the blackness of sleep, leaving him alert, contained within the dragon, unable to defend himself or his beast against whatever Nathan had in store.

The wizard walked behind his altar to light the candles. "Now, my beloved creation, you will learn obedience."

He picked up his curved-blade athame and approached the dragon. He drew the tip of the small weapon along the beast's chest until blood coated the blade, which he let drip into a shallow bowl back on the altar.

Sean fought against the all too familiar anger, hatred and bloodlust seeping into him. He focused his thoughts on Caitlin, their child—anything other than the dark hunger threatening to fill his soul.

Again, Nathan laughed, then chanted words Sean couldn't decipher. When the wizard finished his chants, he threw ashes over the dragon. "I wash you in death and in a hatred that only the blood of this human's kin will quell."

He walked back to the altar and then returned with a small vial. He poured the contents along the beast's spine. "Heed me in this, or your spawn and mate will die while you watch."

He then circled the altar three times, doused the candles then returned yet again. After releasing the chain on the dragon's ankle, he patted the beast's forehead and spoke to Sean, "Fear not, changeling, you won't remember a thing until it's far too late."

A darkness washed over Sean as Nathan left the Great Hall. He wanted to fight it, tried to struggle free from the descending sense of doom, but the more he fought, the stronger it became.

*"Shh, beastie, rest."*

A woman with long, flowing black hair bent over him, whispering—the gypsy mage from his dreams. She sat beside him on the floor, stroking the scales on his chest.

*"You are my boy, my big, brave boy, and I tell you true, St. George will set you free."*

Sean relaxed, no longer fighting the darkness washing over him. He gladly sank into its cold embrace.

Aelthed knew she was nearby. He could feel her in the room. Tired of this curtain of silence she'd thrown over him, he asked, *"Danielle, are you going to keep ignoring me?"*

"That depends."

When she didn't say anything further, he prompted, *"On?"*

"On whether you're alone, or with someone. I certainly wouldn't want to interrupt you if you have company."

*"Woman, have you gone daft?"* When he caught his breath, Aelthed said, *"I invited no one into my cube—it's not as if I can. The gypsy was here to explain what was going on with the grimoire and the cursed changeling's mate."*

"So, she wasn't here for you?"

*"No."*

"I'm sorry. You are perfectly within your rights to entertain anytime you so desire. I shouldn't have said anything."

Aelthed shook his head. Had she been listening to him at all? Apparently, she'd missed the part about not being able to invite anyone inside his cube. He changed tactics. *"Danielle Drake, I wish to entertain only one woman—you. I would take you as my wife if possible. I would think you knew this without being told."*

His cube bounced as she sat heavily down on the bed, sending him stumbling to the floor. Her sweet warmth invaded his space as she lifted the wooden box to her cheek.

"Oh, Aelthed, I know a great many things, my love, but that was not one of them. I'd hoped and wished that someday you could come to feel for me, but I'd not known that you had."

*"Well, I do. Now stop your nonsense."*

She sighed, then asked, "So, what is going on with the grimoire and Caitlin?"

An icy chill swept over him. He turned his head, hoping to better deduce what was happening.

"Aelthed?"

*"Shh."* He hushed her, adding more gently, *"Give me just a minute."*

He spread out his arms and waved the cold to life. It

wavered, gathered and then cleared, giving him a vision that horrified him. The cursed changeling was chained on the floor of Nathan's stronghold. Aelthed's breath caught in his throat. He moved his arm to spin the vision slightly. The sight of the Learned behind his altar casting a spell upon the beast froze his heart.

*"Danielle! Get me to the Dragon Lord, now!"*

She jumped up from the bed, clutching his cube tightly as she raced for the door to her suite. "What's going on?"

*"Just hurry. Nathan captured the youngest Drake."*

"No!" She came to a dead stop. "Is he alive?"

*"I think so. Hurry! I'll tell you what I can as we go."*

Braeden slammed the phone receiver down onto the base. "I don't know where the hell he is."

Cam tapped off his cell. "He's not answering his cell, either."

"I said eight, right?" Braeden glanced at his watch. "It's almost nine."

"Maybe we should call Dan—"

The door to Braeden's office slammed open, cutting off Cam's suggestion. Danielle half ran, half staggered into the room, dropping breathlessly onto a chair. "He's been taken!"

Cam sat down next to her and took her hand in his. "Calm down. Who's been taken?"

"Sean."

She lifted the cube. "Aelthed saw it."

Braeden didn't know whether to swear or to raise the hounds of hell. "Did Aelthed say what happened?"

She placed the cube on the desk. "Tell them."

"Hang on a second." Holding his arm outstretched,

Braeden called Caitlin to the office. She materialized—
holding what could only be Ascalon in her hand.

"Son of a—"

He dropped back down onto his chair. This was turning out to be a great start to the day.

Cam looked at the sword, then at Caitlin, then back
at the sword. "Is that…"

She nodded slowly and sank down onto a chair at
the back of the office. "I… I…" Taking a deep breath,
she placed the weapon on the floor at her feet. "I was
cleaning it."

Braeden raised an eyebrow, asking, "For anything
in particular?"

The sword disappeared. Caitlin jumped to her feet,
shouting, "Hey!"

A voice rose up from the cube on Braeden's desk.
*"I put it back in its scabbard. Can we get to the task
at hand?"*

"Is something happening I should know about?" Caitlin looked around the office. "Where is Sean?"

Danielle motioned her closer. "That's what this is
about, dear."

Caitlin took the empty chair by Danielle. "It's about
Sean?"

Braeden answered her, "Yes." He then directed his
attention to the cube. "Aelthed, if you please."

*"After their argument this morning, Sean took flight."*

Caitlin studied the ceiling, while Danielle patted her
hand. Braeden and Cam rolled their eyes.

*"It seems that he and his beast sensed something
wrong at the Learned's stronghold and went to investigate. When they got there, they heard the dragon's mate
crying for help and went in to rescue her."*

Caitlin gripped the arms of the chair, blinking. "I never left our suite. What are you saying?"

_"I'm saying that he thought he was coming to your aid and instead was captured by Nathan."_

"No!" She jumped to her feet and slapped her hands flat on the desk near the cube. "No. Not Sean, too."

Cam rubbed his temples. "What was he thinking?"

_"That his mate needed to be saved immediately."_

Caitlin stumbled back onto the chair. "This is my fault."

Braeden lowered the hand he'd been running down his face and stared at her. "How is this _your_ fault?"

"Are you working with Nathan?" Cam leaned forward to peer around Danielle at her.

"No, I don't work with Nathan. It's my fault because it was my voice he heard."

"Did you supply that voice?"

"No!"

Braeden stretched his forearms on top of the desk and folded his hands together. "Then, again, how is this your fault?"

"He was out there because we'd been arguing."

Cam leaned back into his chair. "Oh, yes, arguing with a partner is a rare thing, indeed. Especially when said partner is a dragon."

"Don't tease the girl, Cameron." Danielle chided her nephew.

Caitlin wanted to know, "What are we going to do?" Her voice was barely above a whisper. It sounded as lifeless as she looked. "We can't just leave him there."

Braeden opened his mouth, but Aelthed cut him off. _"Nothing."_

"What do you mean, *nothing*?" Her pitch rose with each word.

*"He's on his way back."*

Both Braeden and Cam checked their watches. Braeden said, "He was there about what—almost two hours?"

Aelthed answered, *"The best I can guess, yes."*

Danielle fidgeted with her hands. "What do you think was done to him?"

"If he's on his way back, he's alive."

*"It appeared as if Nathan was casting a spell on him. So he's probably dangerous,"* warned Aelthed.

Braeden spread his hands in agreement. "My thought, too."

Caitlin asked again, "So, what are we going to do?"

"I hate to kill him outright."

Caitlin stared at Braeden, her eyes wide. "I wouldn't suggest trying that."

Cam's humorless laugh broke his brother's stunned silence at being threatened by the succubus. "And why is that?"

Caitlin raised her hand and before anyone in the room could so much as blink, her sword appeared in her grasp. "I will defend my son's father. Against anyone."

"Enough!" Danielle rose to shoot a glare at each of them. She pointed at Ascalon. "Put that thing away. You won't need it."

Caitlin shook it at Braeden. "Remember, it just takes a nick."

He nodded in acknowledgment, and she lowered the weapon. Turning to Danielle, she asked, "So what do you suggest?"

"We give him a chance to explain."

Caitlin disagreed. "No. If he returns under Nathan's control, he isn't going to explain anything."

"I'm not about to let him waltz in here and threaten my family." Cam was adamant. "I won't give him that chance."

"Nor do I think you should. We need to keep an eye on him—at all times." Caitlin frowned and then added, "I'm the best one to do that. However, if anything would happen, or if I'd need help, I can't communicate with any of you if you aren't within sight."

*"Take me with you. I can call for help if need be,"* Aelthed suggested.

Caitlin and Danielle both stared at the cube. Caitlin grimaced. "Uhhh, I don't know if that's a good idea."

Aelthed laughed, then he explained, *"The temptation won't be too great since you can't run off to the Learned's with me. You can't take me anywhere I don't want to go. So there's no fear on that score."*

Braeden didn't appear too happy with the idea, but he agreed. "I can go along with this for right now. But if we discover that he's possessed…"

Caitlin leaned on the desk. "Then we unpossess him."

Cam rose and stared her down. "I'll agree on one condition. If he's possessed, you get him the hell off this island immediately and I won't kill him."

"And he doesn't return until he's completely free. Is that understood?" Braeden added.

Caitlin nodded. "I have no problem with that, except for one thing." She paused to look at each brother. "I want my son."

"Agreed." Braeden shrugged. "But we're going to have to rework our plan. I'm not going to battle Nathan with Sean at my back."

Danielle picked up Aelthed's cube and handed it to Caitlin, ordering, "Keep him safe, or you'll rue the day you set foot on Mirabilus."

Caitlin nodded then faced Braeden while she pointed up. "Could you...?"

He waved a hand, and she found herself sitting in Sean's office.

Aelthed whispered, *"Hide me somewhere. Anywhere."*

She looked around the office then headed to the hallway with the box. "Linen closet?"

*"That's fine. Just open the door and I'll bury myself up top."*

Caitlin pulled the door open and held out her hand. The box disappeared, and the door to the closet closed by itself.

She went back to the office to put Ascalon away before Sean returned. To make certain she'd be heard, she thought...*can you hear me?*

*Of course I can.* Aelthed's reply came through loud and clear in her mind.

Caitlin felt him enter the suite before she saw his misty form flow into the office. She rose, and the mist swirled around her. Desperation, fear and need seeped into her blood, making her shiver with cold dread at what Nathan had done to him.

"Sean." She raised an arm to gently run her fingers through the mist. "What's wrong?"

He enveloped her until she stood within the twirling form of the mist and smoke dragon. Yet she wasn't afraid of the beast surrounding her, towering over her, thrashing his head back and forth while crying out in a pain so great it made her ache.

What had the Learned done to him? What terrified him so?

"Shh, Sean, I'm here. Come, let me help you."

She reached into her pocket to retrieve the amethyst pendant and held it tightly against her chest, over her heart, hoping that somehow her warmth and concern would flow through the gemstone beast into the one in such torment.

A faint amethyst glow filled the air around them. It pulsed in time with her heartbeat and chased away the cold dread.

The instant the dragon calmed, Sean shifted back to human and pulled her roughly into his arms.

When she reached up to stroke his cheek, he turned his head away, but not before her fingertips felt the hot dampness of tears.

She buried her face against his shoulder and held on to him as tight as she could, trying to force her heat into his shivering body. "What happened?"

He shook his head, not answering.

If he didn't want to discuss it yet, that was fine. But she needed to find a way to warm him, to make him feel safe, and she knew of only one sure way.

Caitlin lifted her head and rested her lips against his cheek, gently exhaling enough pheromones to call to him through whatever terrors were chasing him.

He took them easily to the carpeted floor of his office and then tore the clothes from their bodies.

There was nothing gentle about his lovemaking, no foreplay, no kissing, nothing that turned having sex into making love. That wasn't what bothered her, since she could give as good as she could get. What concerned her was that he wouldn't look at her, and she didn't sense his dragon anywhere. There had to be a way to reach them both.

She took the initiative and pushed him over onto his back, rolling with him. When he reached up to pull her down in order to reverse positions, she pushed his hands away, mimicking the act of pinning his wrists to the floor. "No. Let me."

She stretched her spine, running her hands up her sides then over her head, relishing the feel of being the one in control, the one setting the pace. She shivered with pleasure and then reminded herself of the reason she was here.

It wasn't to take, it was to give.

Caitlin cupped Sean's cheek and leaned down to kiss him. Knowing she had plenty of energy to spare, she exhaled her life force and silently crooned to the beast, using what she hoped was the same tone, the same emotion he'd used on her in the work shed. She wanted to soothe him, to coax him out of hiding and to make his fears disappear.

*Oh, please hear me. Come to me. Be with me. We need you.*

Soon, to her relief, Sean's arms came around her. He reached up over her shoulder to draw her hair back, and she felt his eyelashes flutter open. She broke her kiss to rise up slightly and look down at him.

Caitlin stared down into the gold-rimmed emerald gaze of the dragon. She smiled and trailed her fingertips along his cheek. "Welcome back."

His return smile was seductive enough to curl her toes. But when she moved to rest atop his chest, he pushed her upright and held her thighs in place.

Any teasing play she'd missed before, he more than

made up for now. His touch was like liquid fire igniting not only her skin, but flowing into her blood, her heart and her soul, too. It filled her with an emotion so intense, so bright, that she feared giving it a name.

Something was happening between them that she didn't understand. Every time they came together it was as if he became more a part of her. Each time she accepted his energy, he didn't just strengthen her life force, he added his own to it.

Nothing like this had ever happened before. She couldn't explain it, didn't know if she wanted to. On one level it frightened her. Would he eventually replace her energy, her essence, with his? Or was the same thing happening to him? Were the two of them—or the three of them including the beast—becoming one?

Her ragged breath hitched with the onslaught of fulfillment. She swore the dragon took her soaring. The earth fell away beneath them as they flew above the clouds and then spiraled toward the ground at a recklessly breakneck speed that left her heart pounding.

She fell atop Sean's chest gasping for breath and laughing. "Well, that was…just…well."

They lay there until their breathing evened out. Sean wrapped his arms around her and softly said, "We need to talk."

Caitlin groaned softly. "I know. I just don't want to move yet."

His arm shifted slightly, then a warm quilt covered them. She sighed. "That's nice."

"Nathan captured me."

She cleared her mind of the conversation with his brothers, aunt and Aelthed. She wanted Sean to tell her what had happened in his own words. "How?"

"He tricked me into thinking he had somehow captured you and had you chained up in his stronghold."

That statement spun around in her mind for a moment. He cared so much about her that he'd risk his own life for hers? "And you went in to save me?"

"Of course."

She propped her chin on his chest and gazed up at him. "Why?"

"What do you mean, *why*?"

In her mind she could see the dragon looking at her as if she'd lost the ability to think. "It's not like we're married, or we've declared anything for each other. So, yeah, why?"

He lifted his head to peer down at her. "Are you hedging for a ring or something?"

"Good grief, no. I'm just curious."

"You're the mother of my child. Regardless of your thoughts on the topic, you are my beast's mate. He would have gone in of his own accord whether I wanted to or not."

He would end up getting himself killed for her. The thought of him not being here made her ill.

"I can't decide if that makes me feel safer, or more fearful for you." She drew a fingertip along his chin then asked, "What happened there?"

Sean pulled away from her touch, slid her off his chest and sat up with his back to her. With his arms wrapped around his bent knees, he said, "It's not clear. It's as if he did something to make me not remember, but bits and pieces keep coming back."

Caitlin trailed her hand down his back, running her fingers along his spine and shoulder blades. "How do you feel?"

"Like there's something I'm supposed to do."

She got the impression he didn't want to say the words, so she said them for him. "Kill your family? It's something the Learned would want, isn't it? Since you failed in that task before, it only makes sense that he do something to force your hand."

"What if I can't stop myself this time?"

"You aren't some weak-minded fool unable to control yourself or the dragon."

"He scared the crap out of the beast. When we watched you die, I thought he was going to roll over and give up." He glanced over his shoulder at her. "What will he do if that happens for real?"

Sitting up, Caitlin rested her cheek against his back and wrapped her arms around him. "I didn't die. It wasn't me. He tricked you and the beast."

"At the time it didn't feel like a trick."

His ragged voice drew a frown from her. "What do you fear the most? Losing me? Killing your brothers? Dying yourself?"

He shook his head but remained silent.

*"Get him to talk."*

Caitlin rolled her eyes at Aelthed's intrusion. As if she needed the wizard or anyone else to tell her that.

"Sean, everyone knows the Learned took you captive. You need to talk to me. You have to figure this all out before confronting the rest of your family."

"And if I can't?"

She bit her lower lip and bowed her head, resting her forehead against his back. "If I can't get you away from here, they will kill you."

# Chapter 13

Sean reached up and patted her shoulder before he rose and headed for the office door. "I'm going to take a shower. Give me a few minutes then feel free to join me if you want."

He walked past the linen closet and shook his head. Did they think he was so dense that he wouldn't eventually figure out he was being watched?

He didn't care. The moment he'd been fully aware of his surroundings, he'd pulled a secure curtain over his mind. The wizard wasn't going to know what he was thinking.

Actually, having the cube close at hand suited his purposes. Right now, however, a minute or two alone suited his purposes better. He needed to get a grip on the emotions playing havoc with his head—and heart.

After adjusting the shower spray, he turned on the hot water and stepped in. His muscles relaxed. That was what he needed, a good pelting-hot shower. Something to wash away the stench of Nathan's stronghold.

His dragon stretched under the water and sighed with relief before curling down for a well-earned nap.

He'd been confused when he'd first left the

Learned's. Confused and so terrified that his dragon had hidden away.

But he'd come straight back to Caitlin. Instinct had driven him here. A certain knowledge that she above anyone else had the ability to touch his soul. And she had.

He wasn't certain how that made him feel. At times it seemed the two of them were getting far too close.

While he wanted her to stay, because of their son— or so he told himself—he didn't ever want to need her, or anyone, as desperately as he just had.

He shook his head and wiped the water from his face. It had been a moment of weakness, brought on by the spells Nathan had cast. Surely he could set it aside.

He forced his thoughts back to the Learned's stronghold.

The gypsy mage hadn't been a dream; she was essentially his beast's mother, its maker. The Learned may have waved his hands, combined the potions and performed the motions, but she had spoken the curse that had given him life. Nor had she been wrong. St. George did have the power to set him free.

Even from Nathan.

That psychopath was in for a rude awakening.

However, his first task was deciding what to do with Caitlin. He didn't know if it was Caitlin herself who had freed his beast from the terror that had chased him into hiding, or if was her use of the amethyst pendant—or some combination of both.

It didn't matter. What did matter was that through her he was free. He had no driving need to kill his family. No fear of what Nathan might or might not do.

But he didn't want her or his family to know that.

Not until he killed the Learned and brought his son home.

He didn't want his brothers or Caitlin to go into battle with him. It wasn't their fight. It was his alone.

The Learned had killed *his* creator and had sought to control him more than once now. He had taken *his* son, captured *his* dragon and would die by his hand.

And it mattered little what happened to him. As long as his son was freed and the Learned was dead, Sean wasn't afraid of perishing in the battle.

What about Caitlin? He wanted his son raised by beings who would understand him, who could train him, teach him and see to his needs. And he wanted her safe and cared for, too.

But she had no intention of staying, and he'd already decided he wasn't going to force her. So how could he convince her that her best chance for a decent future was here with his family?

She already knew it wasn't with her family, not if she had their son in tow. He knew without a single worry that she'd never relinquish the child into their care.

Aunt Dani seemed to get along with her. At least there wasn't the strife that there had been between Danielle and Alexia or Ariel. For that he was grateful.

He hadn't yet talked to his brothers or their wives about her. They knew as little as possible, which was something he needed to change.

She needed to feel safe here, or at the Lair, and needed to feel useful and wanted. While he wasn't planning to die in this coming battle, he wanted everything seen to beforehand, just in case. Since he wasn't putting off this war with the Learned, he needed to see to those things immediately.

The door to the shower opened. "Want company?"

Sean enveloped her in a wet embrace, laughing at her squeak and pulling her beneath the water with him. "Since you're wet, you may as well stay now."

"I needed a shower, anyways." She drew circles on his chest. "Did you see our son?"

He heard the hesitation and fear in her voice. "Yes, I did, and he was fine. He was sleeping instead of screaming."

"So, what now?"

He didn't want to talk about it here. It would require more concentration than he was capable of maintaining right now. "It's something we'll discuss after our shower, okay?"

"Sure."

She slowly ran her hands up and down his side, his stomach, his thighs, before he caught her hands. "What are you doing?"

"Playing?"

"No, you aren't. You're looking for injuries."

The added flush on her cheeks wasn't from the hot water. "Are there any?"

"I think there might be a bruise on my ankle."

She eased her hands from his and started to bend over. "Caitlin."

Standing upright, she leaned against him, her cheek against his chest. "Are there any injuries?"

"No. I'm fine."

She pressed her ear over his heart. "You're sure?"

"Very."

He felt her expression change against his skin. She stood up straight and looked at him. "You *are* fine."

Sean nodded. "Yes. I said I was, and I am."

"No, I mean fine-fine."

"Ah." If he had to guess, he'd bet that somehow his dragon let her know. Should he lie? Or should he tell her the truth and then figure out how to get her to keep her mouth shut? Finally, he said, "No, I'm terribly possessed. I'm planning on killing everyone around me."

"Hmmm." She walked her fingertips up his chest and tapped his chin. "And when do you plan on holding this slaughter?"

His stomach growled, so he used the obvious answer. "After I get something to eat. I'm famished."

"Uh-huh. I would think this coming slaughter would provide you with plenty of food."

He poured a glob of shampoo on her head and started running his fingers through the building foam. "I like my food fresh, but that's a little too fresh." He turned her around.

"Am I on the list of those to be slaughtered?"

After rinsing out the shampoo, he dumped on some conditioner and started working that through her hair. "I haven't quite decided yet. If I kill you, I'm going to have to deal with our son alone. That might cramp my style with the ladies."

"The ladies?"

"Well, yeah, I'd have to go find him another mother."

She lifted her foot and stomped back on his toes.

"Or perhaps I could let you live. Then you could take care of him while I go do…my thing."

"Your thing?"

"You know, my thing."

"If I'm at home caring for little Sean, you aren't going to be out taking care of any *thing*. Besides, you're avoiding the conversation."

After pouring bodywash on his hands, he washed her arms, shoulders and back before sliding down to run his hands along her legs. Then he turned her back around to face him.

Caitlin hiked one eyebrow. "Now you're just trying to distract me."

"Is it working?"

Her other eyebrow joined the first.

He sighed. "No, I'm not possessed, but I don't want anyone to know."

At least she had the decency to look guilty when she turned her face away. "Well, I'm afraid it's too late for that."

He ran his soapy hands around her breasts. "Oh, you mean Aelthed? He can't hear us in here."

"You knew."

"That he was supposedly hiding in the linen closet? Yes, I knew. My power is a dragon, remember? He can sense an ant walking into the suite—by scent and sound. So, yes, we knew someone was here and since there was no scent, it had to be the wizard in the cube. This isn't my first go round with otherworldly babysitters. Why do you think this shower's been… Drake proofed? I needed somewhere to go where I could talk to my dragon without being overheard."

"How?"

"Tell me what I'm thinking. You're close enough."

She looked at him and tipped her head. Then she frowned and put her hands to her ears.

Sean lowered her hands. "Just stop trying to read my mind. The buzzing will go away."

She shook her head. "What was that?"

He tapped the shower wall. "It's a special white noise

system installed inside these shower walls. Whenever the water comes on, so does the sound. If you aren't trying to focus on anything, you don't notice it. But if you go silent and focus, you hear the buzz."

She finished. "And that overrides what you're trying to hear."

"That's it."

"Do the rest of them know?"

"Oh, they know there's something in here. They just don't know what."

"One day they'll figure it out."

"And the next day I'll devise something else." He rested his hands on her shoulders. "I don't like having my space invaded any more than you do. And I'd appreciate keeping this between us."

"Hadn't planned on advertising it anywhere." Caitlin shivered. "There's one small problem with this system."

He pulled her tight against him and rubbed his hands up and down her arms. "Just another bug to work out. Are you up for a little flying?"

"Flying?"

"Yeah. I'll meet you on the beach and we'll talk while we soar."

Her eyes widened. "Oh. That would work."

"Good. I'll exit from the bedroom balcony. You get dressed and meet me on the beach."

She pursed her lips then asked, "And how do I keep Aelthed or anyone else from mining for information?"

Sean laughed. "That's easy. I'll give you something to *remember* that will give them something to think about."

Caitlin groaned. "This is going to give me nightmares, isn't it?"

"It could." He ran a finger across her lower lip, before giving her a quick kiss. "But if it does, I'll be there to chase them away."

"Fine." She closed her eyes tightly. "I'm ready."

He kissed her forehead then the tip of her nose before covering her lips with his. The false memory he gave her had nothing to do with nightmares—at least not for the two of them. But it would certainly make everyone else think twice before delving back into her mind, giving her time to make her escape.

She curled her fingernails into his shoulders, clinging to him, and it was all he could do not to take her down to the shower floor and savage each other like they were in this new *memory.*

The second his dragon started to wake up and take an interest, he broke their kiss. Caitlin leaned against him trembling.

"That was…interesting." She looked up at him and batted her eyelashes. "You like my fangs that much, do you?"

He laughed. "Only as much as you like mine."

She pushed him away. "Get out of here before we accidentally test your sick fantasy."

"Just keep that on your mind and hurry up before it loses its edge." He reached to turn off the water. "Ready?"

She took a deep breath and said, "Yeah. I'll focus on fangs and blood and talk without thinking. Got it. Ready."

He turned off the water and stepped out of the shower, pausing to hook a finger around her wrist, saying softly, "Wear something warm."

She watched his long legs carry him away. He stopped

at the glass sliding doors to the balcony long enough to smirk at her over his shoulder.

No doubt she'd been busted ogling him.

Sean flexed his already tight ass muscles and then dissolved into a plume of smoke.

Caitlin laughed. Really, that was the only image she needed to focus on. He didn't have to create some gross zombie-vampire-dragon sex scene that she'd never be able to wipe from her mind.

Hopefully, he didn't actually think it would give her nightmares. It was so over-the-top that it made her want to laugh until she cried.

She dried off and pulled some sweats out of his dresser. They'd be a little big, but at least they'd be warm. She dressed quickly and left the bedroom, getting as far as the linen closet before Aelthed stopped her.

*"What did you discover?"*

"Nothing much. He isn't very talkative yet. He's obviously been through a lot and needs some air, so we're going for a walk. I'll let you know what he—"

Aelthed's gasp cut off her sentence.

She felt him poking around inside her head. He'd happened upon the memory at the forefront of her mind, and she did nothing to hide it from him.

Aelthed cleared his throat and asked in a rush, *"Are you all right?"*

She responded with a weak wave. "I will be. Don't worry, I heal quickly."

*"Uh...are you sure?"*

When he started to prod for more memories, she held her focus tightly and headed down the hallway, answering, "Yes. Very."

Caitlin managed to get out of the suite before sighing.

Sean was right; the scene of gore and sex was enough to distract them long enough for her to make a clean escape.

However, she didn't know how long she'd be able to hold this *memory* without laughing, so she hit the stairs at a faster pace.

Danielle Drake met her at the bottom of the stairs. She frowned while studying her then turned a pasty shade of white.

Caitlin shook her head, silently signaling that it was too much to talk about right now. She lightly touched Danielle's shoulder in passing and mumbled, "Please, later."

To her relief she made it out of the castle without seeing anyone else, but she could imagine the conversation that would soon be held in Braeden's office. Eventually, she was going to owe Sean's family one hell of an apology.

Once outside, she ran for the beach.

Out of seemingly nowhere, a huge claw, talons extended, reached for her, cupping her securely in its grasp and lifted her from the ground.

"You are terrible." Caitlin burst into laughter. "Your family is horrified."

"Maybe they'll think twice before intruding next time."

Caitlin's laughter faded away at the tone of his voice. She had noticed before, but never quite as acutely, that when he was in dragon shape, the deep, husky, gravelly tone bordered on harsh.

Yet it didn't frighten her. Quite the opposite, actually. It was so laced with sensual tension and emotion that it gave her shivers having nothing to do with the cold.

He flexed his foot, closing the talons more securely

around her and bringing her nearer his body. "Is that better?"

"I wasn't cold."

He didn't reply, so she let her explanation for shivering fall to the wayside; it wasn't important.

Caitlin relaxed on her perch. She was comfortable, and with his body shielding her from most of the wind, plenty warm enough. "Yes, I'm fine. The view is spectacular."

Turning her attention to the reason they were out here, she asked, "So, what do you have planned?"

"You've seen the pictures in the grimoire. I can't let Braeden and Cameron go to the Learned's."

"But you can't go alone."

"I have no intention of going alone. But I also don't intend to supply him with all three Drakes on a silver platter at once."

"You don't think showing up as a...pack would take him off guard?"

"No. The *clan* showing up at one time is what he wants."

"So if you aren't going to take a force large enough to defeat him, what will you do?"

"Give him what he wants."

"What?" Shock brought her up to her knees. She tipped her head, trying to look up at him through the separation between his talons. "You aren't serious. You can't be."

"Very."

"You were the one who told me—more than once I might add—that giving him those items was a mistake. It would give him enough power to rule everything."

"It would be a mistake for *you* to give him what he wants."

"But not you?" How exactly had the Learned damaged Sean's ability to think rationally?

"Not for me and my partner."

"Partner? *One* other person? And somehow you believe that the two of you can hand over the items he wants then walk out of there with our son and all will be well with the world?"

"Not exactly."

She sat back down and tried to read his mind. But he wouldn't let her in far enough to make sense of his plan. All she could see was a mishmash of random thoughts.

Caitlin gave up. "You need to explain this to me, because I must be missing something."

"I don't have to explain anything to you. I just wanted you to know that you will have our son back soon."

"And I'm supposed to be fine with getting little Sean back knowing you'll most likely end up dead?"

"You're going to leave as soon as he's returned, so what difference will it make?"

Caitlin narrowed her eyes. While this had been her plan all along, she didn't remember saying that to him. "I never told you that."

"You didn't need to tell me. We've exchanged enough life force the last few days that we've become bonded to each other. There isn't much I don't know. And what I don't know for certain, I can sense."

"So how does that work for you, but not for me?"

"You have the ability. You just don't access it."

What did that mean? "How are you going to walk back into the Learned's castle without killing your family first?"

Sean's laugh was far too evil for her comfort. "Simple. I'll kill them."

"What?" The longer she listened to him, the more worried she became about his mental health.

"Think, Caitlin. Mirabilus has a strong glamour spell over it. A spell that's never been broken."

"Wait." She interrupted him to ask, "What about Hoffel?"

"He doesn't count. Nathan captured one of the villagers while he was off the island doing business and forced him to bring Hoffel here."

"But Nathan was born on Mirabilus." She'd seen that in the grimoire. "So why doesn't he just come here and do his dirty deeds on his own?"

"My grandfather added a boost to the glamour spell that gets reinforced yearly. It prevents Nathan from being able to perform magic on the island. Which means he can't see what is or what isn't going on over here. He has no choice but to believe what I tell him."

"Right." She swallowed her sarcasm. "And he's not going to see through your lies?"

"By the time he figures it out, it'll be too late."

"Too late for who?" Her head was starting to ache from trying to make sense of his plans.

"For him. Once I give him the items he demands, he'll be too busy, too engrossed with them to pay much attention to anything else. I only need a minute, if that long, to put an end to his madness."

Now that did make sense. The Learned's ego would be so overinflated with the items in his possession that he would think himself immediately invincible.

However, there were other concerns. "What about Aelthed? You can't just hand him over to Nathan."

"I don't plan on it. Before leaving, I stole a potion from the Learned's stash that'll put Aelthed to sleep."

"He left you alone long enough for you to steal things?"

Sean snickered. "He thought I was so far under his spell that he left the chamber without giving it a second thought."

"Mighty full of himself, isn't he?"

"Yes. To his own detriment."

"Once you put Aelthed to sleep, how are you going to get him out of that cube?"

"The dragon figured it out. The pendants are keys. It'll just take the right combination to unlock the puzzle."

"Oh. So the picture in the grimoire of the two women opening the chest is the same way it'll work for the cube?"

"The dragon seems certain of it."

In her opinion, he was putting an awful lot of faith in the beast. "That'll make your aunt happy."

"Why?"

"Oh, please." Hadn't he figured it out? "She's in love with the old wizard."

"Well, I don't know if she'll be happy or not. I have no idea what's going to happen to Aelthed once his spirit is released. He may just disappear."

"Or be like my mother—dead, but still here."

"I suppose that's possible."

"With Aelthed's spirit removed from the box, won't the Learned know that it's empty?"

"I never said it'd be empty."

"Who or what are you going to put in there?"

"Haven't decided yet."

The certainty in his tone didn't sound undecided. It

sounded more to her as if he just wasn't going to tell her.
Did she care? Not really, as long as she wasn't stuffed
inside.

"You aren't going to try killing the Learned while
little Sean is still there, are you?" Caitlin shivered. Her
son could get fatally injured in the melee.

"No. I'm going to bring him back to Mirabilus first."

"And then go back?"

"Something like that."

Again, he was withholding information. And again,
did she care?

No.

He had a plan to rescue their son, and he seemed
confident he would succeed. While it was her place to
worry, was it her responsibility to question or point out
every flaw until he doubted himself? That would ensure
nothing but possible failure.

Even though it went against her better judgment, she
needed to trust him to do what he thought was right.
So he could keep his secrets, as long as he came back
with their son.

"When do you plan on putting this plan into action?"

"Soon. I need some time to put things into motion."

"Anything I can do to help?"

"Don't panic when you hear Braeden and Cameron
are dead. I need to spread enough rumors just in case
Nathan has someone here doing his bidding."

"I can do that." Caitlin offered, "I can even be upset
over it if that'll help."

"That's up to you. But right before I get ready to go,
I could use your help gathering together everything I'll
need."

"The pendants, grimoire and cube?"

"And Ascalon."

Certain she'd misheard, she asked, "I beg your pardon?"

"He wants Ascalon."

"For what?" It'd be a cold day in hell before she'd turn over her weapon.

"But it's fine if I turn over all my family's charms?"

She would never get used to having her thoughts read—invaded—so easily.

"Then shut me out."

"I've tried. It doesn't work anymore."

She wasn't sure if his dragon snorted or if he did. What she did know was that they were now dropping beneath the clouds. Except for a tiny speck of green below, only the sea was visible for as far as she could see.

"Where are we?"

"You'll see."

He was headed straight for the speck of green in the middle of nowhere. Once they got closer, she could see that the island wasn't as small as she'd first thought. It wasn't as large as Mirabilus, but she wouldn't feel like she was on a desolate rock in the middle of the ocean, either.

There was no shore to speak of, just rocky cliffs that dropped off to the water. Only evergreen trees and other fir-type bushes covered the ground, so they hadn't flown south. But she hadn't noticed any distinct drop in temperature, so they hadn't gone too far north.

Sean touched down in a small clearing where he released her and changed into his misty form. "There's a cabin right at the end of the path."

Caitlin followed his foggy trail. He led her along a

flagstone path that wound through a stand of trees and bushes that were probably mistletoe.

To her surprise there was a cabin in the next clearing. A very nice log cabin with a huge porch that looked as if it probably went all the way around. The swing near the front door looked inviting enough to sleep on comfortably.

The door opened, and he drifted inside. By the time she entered, he had shifted to human form, dressed, and was tucking a shirt into a pair of jeans.

She looked around, wondering if the owners were nearby. "Where are we?"

"This is mine." He walked over to the fireplace to get a fire going.

He owned an island? She shook her head. Of course he did. His brothers were into property, so why wouldn't he carry on the tradition?

"Why are we here?"

"It's time you learn how to be a Drake."

# Chapter 14

Sean didn't have to turn around to see her face to know what she thought of that statement. Her shocked disagreement threatened to burn the back of his neck. He was surprised that it took her a few seconds before she finally sputtered a reply.

"I am not a Drake. I am not going to be a Drake. So there's no reason for me to learn how to be one."

He silently finished building a fire then rose and turned around. She was still staring at him. Displeasure furrowed her brow, and her lips were drawn into a flat line.

"If you plan on raising one, you should know how to be one." It made sense to him, even if she didn't see it. While she mulled that over, he went and retrieved a tray of supplies to make coffee. It would only be instant since he didn't have any utilities here yet. But it would be warm, so it would do.

"What exactly is this going to entail?"

He glanced at her, wondering why she sounded so wary of the idea. "It's not like I'm going to teach you how to change into a dragon or anything."

After hanging the kettle of water from the tripod over

the fire, he sat down on the cedar-frame cushioned sofa and patted the space next to him. "Sit down."

She dropped down onto the chair across the coffee table from him. "I'm quite capable of raising my son. I didn't have any problem taking care of him before."

"I noticed." If he remembered correctly, *their* son was in her care when the Learned kidnapped him.

"You can't blame me for what happened."

"For the record, he's our son, not yours. And I don't blame you for what happened, but yes, actually, I can. If you had known how to defend yourself, or protect Sean against Nathan, this never would have happened, would it?"

She didn't say anything, just looked away. But he caught a glimpse of firelight shimmering off the suspicious moisture in her eyes. "Don't you dare start crying, Caitlin."

The last thing he needed or wanted was for her to get emotional, because that would only make his dragon go goofy on him. He needed everyone to remain calm and focused.

"I'm not blaming you. I never have. I simply stated a fact. You need to know how to protect yourself and our son when I'm not around."

She took a deep breath then looked back at him. "Where do we start?"

Instead of saying anything, Sean had his dragon croon to her. It was obvious she heard the beast, because she visibly relaxed. The frown softened, her lips grew less tight and the tears that had been building in her eyes disappeared.

"That's better." He suggested, "How about we start right there?"

Caitlin nodded in agreement.

"Do you have the pendant?"

She lifted the chain from around her neck. Firelight danced off the amethyst dragon. "Always."

"Good, because that's your key to Drakedom."

Although she tried, Caitlin was unable to maintain a straight face and burst out laughing.

As simple as it was, or as it should be, he liked her laugh, her smile. The way her eyes sparkled like gemstones and the dimples alongside her mouth. Those were little things that she should do often.

Focus, he was supposed to be focusing. In his mind, he asked her, *"Can you hear me?"*

*"Yes."* She answered in the same manner. *"But I'm sitting right across from you, so of course I can."*

*"That's fine. Now try to stop me from entering your thoughts. Nod when you're ready."*

"I was able to block you easily enough before."

"You've concentrated so much on hearing me lately, that it's not as easy anymore." He added, "And since we've bonded more, my getting access to your thoughts is like breathing for me."

"You do realize this is how I live, right?"

"You're a succubus, not an empath. You should choose who and what enters your mind and body."

Thankfully, she didn't argue. She took a few moments to collect herself and then nodded.

He started with simple things like images of food, places and animals. Detecting no response, Sean moved on to images of their families.

Again he sensed nothing but a blank wall. He got up, walked around the room, made coffee for both of them while sending her visions of little Sean, the Learned,

Hoffel and scenes from the grimoire. When he recreated the scene of Hoffel attacking her, she flinched.

He sat back down and handed her a cup of coffee. "You've got the pendant, use it."

"Use it how?"

"Caitlin, you used it to call to my dragon when you couldn't reach him. I knew then it was your talisman, your charm."

"I thought it was responding to you."

"What about in my office?"

She shrugged one shoulder. "Again, I thought it was letting me use it to respond to you."

"No. I don't think so." He reminded her, "It doesn't glow for me. When I hold it, it's just a stone."

She turned it over in her hand. The more attention she paid to it, the brighter the pendant glowed. "How much power do you think it has?"

"One way to find out." Without warning, he picked up a spoon and tossed it at her, only to have it bounce off an unseen wall, sending it right back toward him.

Caitlin's eyes grew wide. "I'll be damned."

"Don't say that, even in jest."

"I wonder if it would let me defeat Nathan."

"I doubt if it makes you invincible. So I wouldn't advise jumping off a cliff to test it or anything." He slammed her mind with an unexpected vision of the Learned taking their son.

"No!" She dropped the pendant and covered her face with her hands.

Sean cursed his own bungling stupidity and pulled her from the chair over to the couch, scooping up the pendant at the same time. He slung an arm around her trembling shoulder to hold her against his chest.

"That was callous. I'm sorry."

Putting the amethyst dragon in her palm, he closed her fingers around it. "Let your mind think of this."

"Why are you doing this?"

What would be the harm in just telling her the truth? It wouldn't sway her either way, nor would it change anything. "The dragon and I want nothing more than for you to stay so we can take care of you and the baby."

She lifted her head and gave him a strained look filled with pain. "Sean..."

"Shhh." He put a finger over her lips to stop her words then brushed the hair from her face. "I know you're going to take our son and leave. I'm not going to stop you, but I need to know you'll both be okay. Is it too much to ask that you show us you can take care of yourself and a dragon changeling?"

"I was doing fine until I met you."

"Yeah, you did handle those thugs pretty well. But they were human. I'm not concerned about your dealings with humans."

"Seems to me the only other preternatural besides the Learned who I have any trouble dealing with is you."

If she was trying to get a rise out of his temper, it was working. And he'd sworn that wasn't going to happen. He took a minute then asked, "And why do you think that is?"

"Haven't you noticed? Something has been...off... since the day we met. In the alley that night, when I drained the one thug, he was so unhealthy that I knew I'd be sick. But it hit me instantly, completely catching me off guard, and that had never happened before. And for me—me of all people—to wake up, not able to remember taking you to my home and spending three days in bed with you? How does that happen?"

She immediately answered her own question. "It doesn't. Ever." Then she added, "And to end up pregnant? By someone not of my own kind?" She took a breath. "And now it's like we're either ready to jump down each other's throat or fall into bed. There's nothing in between. It's hate or lust with us, no middle ground whatsoever. You can't tell me that's normal."

"Define *normal*. You're a succubus. I'm a dragon changeling—a cursed dragon changeling. How does *normal* even work into our vocabulary?"

"You know what I mean. Normal for us. Yes, I'm a succubus and there's nothing I enjoy more than sex. It feeds me, it gives me energy the fastest way possible and I don't deny I love a man's body. But I can't get enough of you. No matter what we do, it's not enough. You can fill me to the brim, give me life for months in one night's romp and I still want more."

He was supposed to have a problem with that?

She rolled her eyes. Either she'd read his thought, or correctly interpreted his expression. "Never before have I wanted anything else from a man than just sex."

"And that scares you?"

"Scares me? No! It outrages me. I need to be in control of my life. Me. Not my desires or some craving I can't define. Me."

"I haven't tried to control you." The instant the words left his mouth he knew them for a lie.

And she proved that by leaning away to look at him as if he'd just tried to tell her the grass was purple. "No, not at all."

"The dragon and I were in shock from learning I had

a son." He tried to defend his actions upon her arrival at Dragon's Lair.

"Oh, is that what you're going to call that whole bit about mating for life, not seeing my son crap?"

"It wasn't crap. Letting you leave with our son goes against every instinct I have."

"*Letting* me leave? *Letting* me? You don't own me."

This was not going well at all. "That isn't what I meant."

She scooted away from him on the couch. "Then explain what you did mean."

"I meant that I'd realized it would be a mistake to try forcing you to stay, so I wasn't going to fight you on it."

"That's generous of you. Especially considering it's not your decision to make. At all."

Sean stood up to poke absently at the fire. If he kept up at this rate he'd never see her or his son again. "One day, Caitlin, you're going to want someone so badly that you need them. Are you going to walk away because being alone is far more important than anything else?"

"Being alone? No, it's about being independent. People have had control of me and my life since the day I was conceived. Even now they're telling me who to marry, where to live, whether or not I can keep my child. No more. Once little Sean is back in my arms, nobody is going to tell me anything. I'm done following orders. Done having anyone else tell me how to live my life."

Why did it feel as though she'd just kicked him in the gut? Why was his dragon's heart beating so hard and fast? He didn't understand what was going on inside him. If he didn't know better, he'd say that he and dragon were in love. But they hadn't known her long enough for any lasting attachment to have formed. Yes, they were mated, but so what? Throughout the history of man, couples had married without having any feelings for each other. Besides, he was certain that love wasn't this difficult or painful.

Without turning around, Sean asked, "And it doesn't matter what you do to anyone else?"

"Such as who?"

"Our son, for one." *Me, for another.* But he wasn't about to tell her that. It was an admission he wasn't ready to put into words.

"He'll be with me, so it's not like I'm going to be causing him pain or strife."

"Are you going to teach him how to be a dragon changeling? Will you be able to explain the wild emotions rushing through him and how to control them? Or help him cope with the pain during the first few shifts?"

She placed a hand on his shoulder, and it was all he could do not to jump in surprise. "Sean, I'm not going to keep you from our son. I understand that you need to imprint with him so that he'll trust you when the time comes to teach him what he needs to know. If that time ever comes. We don't even know if he's a changeling or not. I promise that you'll have plenty of visits."

*Visits.* He clenched his jaw. He didn't want visits. He wanted more. He wanted to be a full-time father. His stomach churned. They needed to get off this topic. This was not the reason he brought her here.

He placed the poker back in the bucket on the hearth, turned around to grasp her wrist and headed for the door. "Do you have your pendant?"

"Yes, but why?"

She sounded confused at the abrupt change in the

conversation. Right now he didn't much care. "Let's see how powerful it is."

Once outside he said, "Go stand at the other side of the clearing and focus on that pendant."

As she walked away he heard her mutter, "This should be loads of fun."

For him, maybe.

Sean collected a pile of good-sized rocks then shouted, "If this doesn't work, it's going to hurt."

The amethyst dragon hanging around her neck glowed. She shouted back, "Bring it."

He threw the rocks, one right after another, as hard as he could. To his relief the magic surrounding her held fast. The rocks bounced off the invisible shield, protecting her from danger.

Quickly, before he could change his mind, he shifted to solid dragon form. The beast drew in a large breath and let it out as a stream of fire aimed at her.

Caitlin's eyes grew large, but the pendant around her neck glowed brighter.

His breath expelled, he started to draw in another, only to notice she held a fireball in her hand. Smiling at him, she arched an eyebrow right before she threw the fiery ball at him.

To his surprise, not only did the ball make it all the way across the clearing, but her aim was also accurate enough that he had to lean to one side to avoid getting hit. Thankfully, he wasn't standing directly in front of the cabin. Otherwise it'd be a pile of charcoal.

He shifted back to human form. "Not bad. Hang on a second." Sean went back into the cabin and came out with two swords.

"Up for a little swordplay?" He motioned her forward.

Halfway across the clearing, she held out her hand. Ascalon slammed into her ready palm. The spine already glowed, ready for battling a dragon.

"No." Sean stopped and shook his head. "Not on your life."

"Afraid?"

"No." He wasn't. However, his trembling beast felt sick. "I'm just not that stupid."

"You don't trust me." She gave him a mock pout.

"I wouldn't trust anyone with that weapon." He pointed to the ground. "Put it down."

She tossed the sword in the air and it disappeared. Then she reached out to take the blade he offered her. "Fine. Be that way. We'll play with your toys."

They faced off. Back and forth across the clearing, neither of them getting the better of the other. Although Sean quickly realized that she was quite a bit more experienced than he was. The only way he kept up with her faster pace was to have a stronger swing. He essentially wore her down by making her fight with all of her strength to hold back his blade.

"Damn." He swore after mistakenly taking his eyes off her for a split second. She'd lunged in, nicking his arm. Had that been Ascalon, he'd be dead in minutes.

She backed off, gasping. "I'm sorry, I'm sorry."

Sean motioned her to continue, laughing. "I've cut myself worse with a razor."

When she didn't come back at him, he lunged forward and slapped her hip with the side of his blade. "Don't just stand there."

The next thing he knew, Caitlin screamed and raised her sword toward his face. He flinched and then heard the sound of another blade slamming against hers before it bounced away onto the ground.

He looked down to see Ascalon.

She tossed aside the blade she'd been using to see to her sword then sent it back to Mirabilus, before throwing herself against his chest. "I am so sorry. I didn't know it would do that. It could have killed you."

"It's all right, I'm fine. Don't worry about it." Although he wasn't certain his dragon hadn't fainted.

"No, it's not all right."

He put his arms around her to stop her from shaking. "Caitlin, it's okay. I'm alive thanks to your speed."

She rested her forehead against his shoulder and shook her head. "Are we done with this training stuff now?"

"Yeah, I'm pretty sure we can call it quits for the day." He dropped a kiss on the top of her head. "I've got a couple things I need to see to. Why don't you go inside and relax for a while. When I get back we'll see if we can rustle up something to eat."

He watched her walk back into the cabin and close the door before taking off for the other side of the island.

"Where do you think they went?" Braeden looked out the windows of his office for what had to be the hundredth time before turning back to Cam and their aunt.

Danielle set Aelthed's box on the desk. "I don't know. He took off in beast form carrying her with him."

Aelthed offered, *"For all the blood and rough handling, she actually didn't seem too afraid of him."*

"Why would she be? She's not a Drake, so she's probably not on his hit list."

Danielle shook her head at Cam's statement. "You didn't see what he did to her. That poor girl."

Braeden rolled his eyes. "You don't know if what you read in her mind was real or something she made up. I don't see Sean being capable of abusing a woman like that."

What his aunt had described to him earlier was essentially a horrific rape scene. He highly doubted if it was real. Somehow Sean, Caitlin, or the two of them together had put that in her mind to throw them off. And it had worked. They had no clue what Sean was planning.

"What I want to know is why that scene was in her mind."

"We don't know if it's real or not." Cam leaned forward. "Nor do we know how far Sean is under the Learned's spell."

Braeden shrugged. "I'm sure we'll know soon enough."

"So we just sit around and wait until he kills one or more of us?"

"I am not going to kill him without having a solid reason to do so." Braeden stared at his twin. "Neither are you."

"I hadn't planned on it. But he shouldn't be allowed to run free until we know one way or another."

Danielle laughed weakly. "If you have a way of capturing and holding him, perhaps you'll share it with us?"

*"That's the problem with smoke dragons. The beasts are nearly impossible to contain."* Aelthed sighed. *"Although, something like this cube would probably work, if someone could cast the spell."*

"You don't think he'd know what we were up to as soon as he saw the cube?" Braeden asked.

"And then what? We just hold him like that for an eternity?" Cam shook his head and leaned back in his chair. "It'd be more humane to kill him."

Aelthed and his cube disappeared. Danielle looked from one brother to the other. "That was a bit heartless, don't you think?"

Braeden winced. "We were talking about Sean, not Aelthed."

"I know that. But he's been trapped in the cube for over eight hundred years. Should he have simply been put to death instead?"

Cam cleared his throat then reminded her, "Aunt Dani, you do remember that he's already dead, right? It's just his spirit in that box, not the man himself."

Braeden shot Cam a glare as their aunt rose and without another word marched stiffly out of his office.

"Smooth."

"Well, it's the truth, and one day she's going to have to face it."

"Don't you think we have enough to deal with right now?"

Cam shrugged. "Speaking of dealing with things, what are we going to do with Hoffel?"

Braeden sighed. He wasn't certain what to do with the baron. They'd questioned him. Which wasn't as easy as he'd first thought it would be. Hoffel was a coward and a bully, but as a vampire, the man was already dead, so the threat of death held no weight. And the baron was well aware that they weren't going to destroy him. Doing so would only garner the wrath of the council and while neither he nor Cam were afraid of them, they had to think of Lexi, Ariel and the kids.

They had learned that he was working with—or for—

the Learned. He'd been the one who had told Nathan about Caitlin being pregnant with Sean's child, which had started this whole mess.

"Once we have Sean's child, we could give the baron to Caitlin along with the information we learned."

Cam laughed. "That would serve him right."

While the High Council might be angry at his death, they might not seek retaliation from a St. George.

"One thing at a time." Braeden tapped his desk. "First, Sean. We need to find him and see what's going on."

"You're worried about him."

"Of course."

"He's not a kid anymore, Braeden. He hasn't been for a long time."

"But his dragon is. There's no telling what crazy plan the two of them will come up with."

Caitlin paced the cold floor of the cabin. What was he doing? More important, was he coming back?

She couldn't blame Sean if he didn't. Not after what had happened.

Ascalon had never come to her defense like that before. Then again, she'd never been in a match like that before—not sword against sword.

It amazed her that she'd even seen the weapon before it was too late. Thankfully, the flash of amethyst caught her eye just in time for her to throw her blade in its path.

She peered out the window again, searching the clearing for any sign of Sean. The sun was already below the line of trees. Soon it would be too dark to see anything out there. Would he be back by then? Letting the curtain fall back into place, she sighed with disappointment.

Caitlin laughed softly at herself. Just mere hours ago,

she'd claimed to neither want nor need anyone. She'd convinced him of her determination to be independent.

Yet here she was anxiously awaiting his return.

Was she simply on edge because she was in a strange place, and night was getting ready to fall, or was she lying to herself about what she felt for him?

She wasn't sure.

It didn't make sense. They hadn't known each other long enough for her to be so attached to him. And she hadn't lied; their emotions did run either hot or cold. Except today, when he'd been forcing her to learn how to use the pendant.

At first she'd been ticked off about it. But not as outraged as she'd tried to pretend. And then it had been sort of…exciting…fun to see how much power she could channel with the amethyst dragon.

Their time at the cabin could actually be considered the most extended period of *normal* time they'd had together since they'd first met. And it wasn't all that bad.

A swarm of butterflies fluttered in her stomach. She looked out the window again and saw him coming across the clearing.

He looked tired, nearly exhausted.

Caitlin quickly ran into the bedroom and slipped out of her clothes then tossed on an oversize T-shirt before racing back to the cabin door and pulling it open.

# Chapter 15

Sean's expression was priceless. From the widening of his eyes and the half smile twitching at his lips, his surprise was evident. Desire flared to life, lacing the heat surrounding him with want and lust.

She backed away, inviting him in with what she hoped was a smile of welcome, and not the goofy grin of a raving lunatic. "I wasn't sure you were coming back."

He kicked the door closed behind him and kept walking toward her. His seductive half smile deepening to the focused hooded gaze of a beast stalking its prey. Her heart beat faster.

"I'm fairly certain I said I would be back."

Caitlin swallowed a groan at the deep, husky tone of man-beast. She reached behind her to make sure she wasn't going to run into anything as she angled toward the bedroom, still walking backward.

She teased him, staying just out of his reach. When he lengthened his stride, she moved quicker, luring him with pheromones she didn't need judging from the shimmer of his eyes, but couldn't stop producing.

"But you were gone so long that I started to worry." Her own voice had dropped an octave. The lower, whispery tone surprised her.

"Were you afraid I'd left you on the island alone?"

Caitlin shrugged a shoulder, tilted her head and looked up at him from beneath half lowered eyelashes. *Good grief, I'm flirting with him.*

Flirting? She never resorted to such childish games. She either took what she wanted or sent out enough pheromones that the other party did the chasing—or at least they thought they did.

Truth be told, this silly game actually made her feel sort of…giddy. And the fact that he was playing along made her want him that much more.

She backed into the doorjamb. Readjusting her path, she entered the bedroom, with him just inches away.

"You look tired."

"Exhausted."

She motioned to the bed. "Perhaps I should go and let you get some sleep."

Sean shrugged. "If that's what you want."

Caitlin stopped. What had she done? He was actually going to let her leave so he could sleep?

He swept her into his embrace with a low growl, pulling her against his chest and backing her up until her legs hit the edge of the bed, then dropped her onto the mattress, still in his arms.

She sighed. "I thought—"

"Shut up." His tongue slid along her lips, stopping her words. "No talking."

Parting her lips, she didn't think to disagree with him. They'd already proven earlier that talking did nothing but get them in trouble.

*"Can you hear me?"*

His voice drifted into her mind. The tone rumbling in-

side her added more fuel to the fire already burning. She
answered in the same manner, *"You said no talking."*

*"Talking. I said nothing about any other form of com-
municating."*

*"Ah."* But they'd already been communicating without words.

*"If all goes well, and I'm certain it will, this is our
last night together. Tell me what you want."*

She moaned softly, arching her body beneath him,
straining to get impossibly closer. He couldn't tell what
she wanted?

Sean slid his mouth from hers, turning her moan of
growing desire into a whine of loss. *"Come on, darlin'."* He edged down her body, tugging her shirt up as
he inched lower.

The chilly air of the bedroom brought a shiver to her
body, chasing gooseflesh along her belly.

*"Do you want a fast, hard fuck that'll leave us fight-
ing for breath?"*

He closed his teeth around her pebbled nipple hard
enough to send a jolt of electricity to curl her toes and
drawing a gasp of shock from her lips.

*"Or do you want it slow and easy, taking time to
savor every inch of our bodies?"*

His tongue slowly lathed her still-tingling nipple before he closed his lips over it, sucking gently until she
moaned.

He stopped his teasing torment to gaze up at her,
asking, *"Well?"*

Caitlin's heart thudded hard enough inside her chest
that she was certain he could feel it. It was hard to
fathom never sharing a bed with him again, never feeling his hands on her body, his lips against hers. She

drew a hand through his hair, caressing the side of his head. *"Sean, if this is our last night together, I want to remember it and you forever."*

His eyes gleamed as he nodded before moving off her to stretch out alongside and pull her into a warm embrace made warmer still by the return of his lips to hers.

Their kiss was slow, languid, the easy movement of his tongue across hers, brushing the roof of her mouth as tentatively as a first kiss—or perhaps a last one meant to savor the moment.

His taste, his touch so sweet, she wanted to cry at the thought of never again sharing such an exquisite caress.

*"Shhh, baby."* His whisper raced softly against her mind. *"Focus on now, this moment. Let tomorrow go."*

He trailed his lips against her chin, along the side of her face, until he settled on the soft spot beneath her ear. Her toes curled from the attention he paid to that small spot of skin.

How could such light, barely perceptible teasing make her nearly swoon with such longing?

Sean released her long enough to pull his shirt off and toss it to the floor. In the next instant it was joined by hers.

He rolled her over in his arms and eased her back tightly against his chest. One arm slid beneath her head, the bend of his arm forming a pillow. The other he slung around her, his hand resting on her belly.

For a moment or two he didn't move, and she was fine with that, welcomed the chance to savor his warmth against her back. In the silence of the bedroom she could hear his heartbeat as it pulsed strong and steady behind her.

The dragon crooned in the darkness. A soft, sad lament of longing and farewell. The sound, and the emotion it held, touched her deeply, making her long to throw her arms around the beast and promise to never leave him. What was she doing? How could she go? What was she thinking? Her throat tightened with unshed tears, and she parted her lips.

*"No."* Sean silently stopped her vow. *"Leave him be, Caitlin. Make no promises in a moment of lust. It wouldn't be fair to any of us."*

She choked back a sob, fighting to gain control of her jumbled emotions and thoughts as she forced herself to focus on his hand sweeping up to caress her breast.

That was all she needed to concentrate on—the mind-stealing feel of his fingertips stroking, teasing, building the desire to a fevered pitch. And on his mouth, pressed against her flesh where her neck met her shoulder, nipping lightly, sucking, making a mark that would still be there in the morning.

He slid a denim-encased leg between her naked ones, parting her legs, giving him room to rest his wandering hand.

She held her breath in anticipation. Her thighs quivered, waiting, expecting his oh, so expert touch. Her stomach tightened in preparation for the closest thing she would ever come to flying.

She waited, her heart thudding heavy in her chest.

And waited…

Caitlin frowned at his hesitation. He didn't move. He barely breathed. Surely he hadn't fallen asleep, had he? Disappointment flooded her, slowing her racing heart, evening out her breathing.

A soft chuckle vibrated against her shoulder. Before she could think of the words to berate him for teasing her so mercilessly, the touch she'd anticipated took her breath away.

While his fingers danced against her heat, hers curled into the covers beneath them, seeking something more substantial to touch.

He tugged at the gold chain around her neck with his teeth, reminding her of the power at her beck and call.

Caitlin reached up to clasp the brilliant amethyst in her hand and brought his body into view in her mind. He stood before her in all his naked glory, that devastatingly sexy half smile playing at his lips.

She ran her palms across his chest and shoulders, memorizing the feel of his hard muscles beneath his smooth flesh. Her fingertips trailed over the bulge of biceps that he flexed for her benefit, making her smile at his silliness.

That was yet another thing she would miss. Yes, they fought and argued almost constantly. But his patience in the bedroom was beyond comparison to anyone.

He didn't complain about her leisurely exploration of his body. Like now, as she traced the line of muscle protecting his ribs. There wasn't a spare ounce of fat anywhere. He was built as perfectly as the beast who possessed him—lean and strong, every limb, each muscle, created for power, endurance and survival.

Her attention slipped as his touch slid deeper between the folds of her flesh. The roughness of denim brushed against her thighs, parting her legs farther, giving him more room to torment and tease, to slide a seeking finger inside.

Caitlin forced her thoughts back to the pendant, and the man it brought to life in her mind. Unable to stand on shaking legs, she dropped to her knees before him and slid her mouth over the hard length of his cock.

The velvety softness of the skin covering the hardness never failed to amaze her. It was a contradiction she found fascinating. And his ragged groan as she grazed her teeth lightly over the ridge was like a sensual touch against her own skin.

He ran his fingers through her hair, caressing her head. His thumb tracing the rim of her ear sent a shiver zinging down her spine.

Before she could send her mind further along the fantasy she was creating in her mind, he grasped her shoulders and hauled her to her feet, spun her around and pulled her back against his chest.

The sharp bite of teeth on her shoulder jolted her out of the mental fantasy. She dropped the pendant, letting it dangle from her neck. She'd been so lost in the love play of her own making that she hadn't realized he had literally rolled her onto her knees, stripped off his jeans and was now leaning over her, his knees between hers, his teeth sinking into the sensitive flesh of her shoulder.

She sensed the awakening of his dragon. Even if she hadn't, the near-brutal grasp he had on her wrists and the controlling bite would have been enough to enlighten her.

Through no intentional effort, her own fangs, useless as they were, pushed against her lips as they lengthened. She swung her head side to side, trying to break free of the beast's hold.

Drawing in a deep breath, Caitlin forced herself to relax. He wasn't going to hurt her. Once the dragon knew he was completely in charge, he would gentle. She arched her back, supporting his weight, and swayed her hips against him.

The sharp hold on her shoulder lessened until he lathed the area with his tongue, easing the sting of his bite. Her fangs retracted, and he released her wrists to thread his fingers between hers.

His lips were against her ear. "Don't make me wait." His rough whisper, breaking his own request for no talking, sent an unexpected thrill shooting through her. He wanted her so desperately that he'd break his own rules.

"Fuck me." She knew her response was crude, but the words she never said at any other time were the only ones she could think of in the heat of this moment.

He entered her fast and hard, in one steady stroke, drawing a gasp then a moan of pleasure from her. Nothing—absolutely nothing—felt as wonderful or complete as him filling her.

Together like this they were one—her, Sean and yes, even the beast, became one entity without individual beginning or ending. And together they built the magic that carried them higher, breaking the bonds holding them to the earth.

His fingers tightened around hers, she felt him strain against her, his climax building as hers raced to catch up.

Their hearts pounding, their ragged breaths mingling in the otherwise silent room, they reached the pinnacle at the same time and fell onto the bed laughing weakly, fighting to catch their breath.

To her horror, for no reason whatsoever, Caitlin burst into tears. She buried her face in the pillow, not wanting him to see the weakness she wouldn't be able to explain.

Sean rose up enough to turn her onto her back then rested on his forearms atop her. He gazed down at her and slung his arms beneath her shoulders to cradle her head in his hands. "Shh. Caitlin, it's okay."

He kissed her tears away. "Listen to me. You know where to find me. I'm not going anywhere. Take your time, do whatever it is you have to do. But if you need me, for anything, I'm here." He stretched his thumb down and hooked it through the chain of her pendant. "You know how to call me."

All she could think of was how unfair that was. He was going to sit at Dragon's Lair waiting for her? What if she discovered that once she'd taken the time to mourn a relationship that never was, she didn't need him? What then? As determined as she was to explore her own independence, even she wasn't that selfish. Guilt flowed into her, cold and ugly.

He shook his head. "You've nothing to be guilty for. I will wait for you until the day I die. It's not a decision. It's just the way it is. This dragon has chosen his mate, plain and simple. But that doesn't mean I'm not going to live, or that I'm going to live like a monk. I may be a mated beast, but I'm also still a man with my own wants and needs."

Instead of making her feel better, or at least not as guilty, it felt as if someone reached inside her chest and tore her heart free. Caitlin swallowed hard, trying desperately to stop the tears from flowing all over again.

What was wrong with her? Why was she suddenly so emotional?

He covered her lips with his own, sweeping his tongue along hers as he settled between her thighs and entered her, making slow, sweet love to her. Giving her something more to remember and much more to miss.

\* \* \*

Danielle unlocked the door to Sean's suite of rooms, knocking as she pushed the door open. "Sean?"

No sound answered her in return, so she walked in, closing the door behind her. "Aelthed?"

When he and his cube had disappeared from Braeden's office, she'd looked for him in her suite, but he hadn't been there.

"Aelthed, please answer me."

*"In here."*

She followed the sound of his voice into Sean's office and picked the wooden box up from the desk.

"You know that Cam just spoke out of turn, right? He didn't mean anything by it."

*"Perhaps. But he was correct. I am already dead. It's something I seem to forget at times."*

"Don't say that." Danielle sat down behind the desk, holding the cube against her chest. "You are as real to me as the air I breathe."

*"Real or not, I have no physical body. I am nothing more than a voice to you."*

"That isn't true." Danielle frowned. How was she going to explain something to him that she'd yet figured out how to explain to herself?

"Aelthed, I don't care what you are or aren't. You've provided me with more companionship, more advice, comfort and understanding than any human or preternatural I've ever known. I love you dearly. Deeply, with all of my heart. And if it were possible, I would spend eternity in that cube with you."

*"Oh, Danielle, as much as I cherish your words and your love, you deserve someone who can hold you tightly in his arms. Someone made of flesh and bone who can*

*steal your mind away with kisses and drive you wild with touches."*

She smiled at what he'd just unknowingly given away. "So you've thought of these things, too?"

*"Of course I have, woman. What I wouldn't give to run my fingers through your raven tresses, or to hold you naked in my arms, or to wipe that smug smile from your face with a kiss you'd not soon forget."*

Danielle laughed. "Someday, Aelthed, I'll no longer be on this physical plane of existence, and you'll be forced to prove whether those words are true or not. I wonder what you'll do then."

*"You need not fear that I'll run like some frightened boy. I was quite the ladies' man in my day."*

"Hmm. That would have been the twelfth century? Did you ogle them from afar or write songs about their beauty? Or perhaps place chaste kisses on their hand? Things have changed a little since then, my dear."

His laughter filled her mind. *"Trust me, some things have not changed as much as you seem to think they have."*

She found his chortle of amusement interesting. But decided not to delve into the topic any further. Instead, she asked, "Have you discovered where Sean might be hiding?"

*"Coward."* He cleared his throat then answered her question. *"No. He's found himself someplace unknown to us, obviously, and taken the girl with him."*

"What do you think of what we saw in Caitlin's mind?"

Aelthed's snort echoed her own thoughts. *"I think she, or they, figured out how to show us an outright lie."*

"So do I. Which leaves me wondering how I can trust anything I see in either of their minds."

*"You can't."*

"So how are we ever going to know if Sean is under Nathan's control or not?"

*"We aren't, at least not by mining their thoughts. We're all going to have to watch him carefully and guard our backs. If it were up to me, I'd send you, the other women and the children to Dragon's Lair. I certainly wouldn't leave them within such easy reach."*

Danielle nodded. "I agree with sending Alexia, Ariel and the children, but I'm not going anywhere. The boys can use my help with keeping an eye—or a mind— turned on Sean and Caitlin."

*"That just places you in danger."*

"Afraid I'll join you sooner rather than later?"

*"Don't talk like that, woman."*

He only called her *woman* when she'd irritated him or he was worried. Danielle relented. "Sorry. I actually don't think Sean is under Nathan's control. I think he and Caitlin have hidden themselves away somewhere to plan the child's rescue, and that frightens me."

*"Why?"*

"He shouldn't go alone. It's too dangerous. He should be making his plans with his brothers."

*"To some degree, you're right. However, have you thought about putting all of them in danger at once? Isn't that what they'd be doing if all three of them went to the Learned's stronghold at once?"*

Danielle pursed her lips then said, "I actually hadn't thought about that. I wonder if Braeden has."

*"I'm sure the Dragon Lord has considered all angles. He isn't foolish, nor is he stupid."*

"True."

Danielle rose and carried the cube to the linen closet. She opened the door and waited until he levitated his box to the top shelf before closing it. Placing a hand on the door, she whispered, "Be safe, my love."

# Chapter 16

Sean opened his eyes to complete darkness. They'd fallen asleep, which hadn't been his intention, since he'd wanted to fly to the Learned's stronghold and back to Mirabilus before the sun rose. But what was done was done. It wasn't as if he could turn back time.

The warm bundle pressed against his chest sighed in her sleep. He tightened the arm he'd wrapped over her and she groaned in protest, clinging tighter to his forearm.

His other arm was beneath her head, the bend at the elbow acting as her pillow. He wiggled his foot free from between her ankles and stretched his leg out against hers.

Soon he needed to wake her up. There were things to be done tonight. But not yet. Right now he just wanted to stay right here, like this, not moving, savoring the feel of their combined warmth.

How long would it take her to realize her independence was like a shiny new toy that would dull with age? How many months or years would pass before she came to understand that sharing a life with someone didn't necessarily mean she'd have to give up any part of herself?

And how many days or weeks would pass before she

discovered she was carrying not just one more child, but twins?

Two more dragonettes were growing in her womb. Two more Drakes. Two more offspring for him and his dragon to watch over.

He wasn't going to change his mind about her leaving. She could go. But he didn't have to like it, and he'd be damned if she or their children were ever going to be out of his sight.

He hadn't quite formulated a plan to pull that off, but he would. It wasn't as though she left him much choice.

After this event with Nathan, he wasn't about to risk another kidnapping. Especially when there would soon be three little ones to keep safe.

How had Braeden and Cameron convinced their mates to stay? Stupid question when he knew the answer without giving it much thought.

Braeden and Alexia were easy enough to understand since they had still been married when she came to Braeden for help. They cared enough about each other to work through their misunderstanding and to take another chance with their marriage. So far, whatever they were doing seemed to be working for them.

Cameron and Ariel were an interesting couple. She'd been blackmailed into working for the Learned and came to both Mirabilus and the Dragon's Lair essentially as an enemy. But they'd come to trust each other. While the two of them still got into massive arguments, it was obvious to everyone that they loved each other deeply.

How could he attempt to clear up any misunderstanding or begin to build any trust with Caitlin when she wasn't going to be around?

Sean frowned. This line of thought was just going to

fan his anger over the entire situation. He didn't want to spend their last hours together arguing.

He closed his eyes and dragged his chin across her shoulder.

She shrugged, trying to escape the stubble scraping across her skin.

"Caitlin, it's time to get going."

Instead of pulling free of the lingering threads of sleep, she tugged on his forearm, snuggling it beneath her chin.

He once again dragged his chin across her shoulder. His efforts gained him two sets of fingernails seeking to embed themselves in the flesh of his arm. Yeah, she was awake.

Sean flicked his fingers toward the oil lamp, setting it alight.

Caitlin buried her face in the bed. "That's just mean."

He pulled his arms free and sat up. "Get up."

"No."

He ran a hand over her hip, lingering, and then caressed one padded cheek.

She came up on her elbow to look at him over her shoulder. "Don't even think about it."

"I'm pretty sure one sharp slap would have you on your feet in short order."

"You're probably right. But I don't think you really want to go there."

"Someday, I might." He patted her hip, sighing with fake regret. "Just not right now."

She sat up, swinging her legs over the side of the bed. "It's time, isn't it?"

"Yes."

"I should be excited. Relieved that Sean will be back

in my arms." She turned to look at him. "But I'm terrified something will go wrong."

"I have every step planned out. A little faith in me would go far." He looked away, not wanting to admit his own doubts about this rescue.

Sean rolled out of the bed. His feet hit the ice-cold floor, making him want nothing more than to burrow back in the warmth of the bed.

Caitlin tossed him his clothes then asked, "I haven't seen a bathroom."

"There's an outhouse of sorts round back." He reached in the nightstand drawer and pulled out a flashlight that he tossed on the bed. "Use this. It'll be dark."

She stared at him a few seconds before picking up the flashlight. "Ohhhkay. Not exactly an upscale resort."

"Nope. I built it for myself."

She slowly looked around the bedroom. "You built this?"

The shock in her voice was evident. "What surprises you more—that the little rich boy used his hands for manual labor, or that the computer geek can use a saw and hammer?"

"With you? Neither. I'm surprised there's no ultramodern bath."

He didn't follow her comment and just looked at her.

Caitlin shrugged then explained. "You have callouses on your hands, so it's obvious you don't shy away from manual labor. However, your suites—both the one at the Lair and the one at Mirabilus, while sparsely furnished, are done so with no thought given to expense. Everything is quality. And your showers?" She paused to sigh loudly. "They rate such a huge OMG that I want to take one of them with me when I go. I mean, seriously,

Sean, six shower bars with eight adjustable nozzles on each one? An unsuspecting bather could drown from just turning the water on."

"I think in the shower, so I may as well have a good one."

"Good? I'd go with magnificent myself." She headed toward the door. "I'll meet you out front?"

Since he didn't want to take the time to dress when they got back to Mirabilus, he did so now. That was one thing he hadn't been able to figure out—when he shifted, where did his clothes go? If he left human form dressed, he returned dressed. It wasn't that important, so he hadn't made it an issue. It was just odd.

After making certain the oil lamp and the embers in the fireplace were both fully out, he walked out of the cabin. Making the bed could wait until he returned tomorrow or the day after. After making sure Caitlin and their son were safely back at the Lair, he knew he wasn't going to be in any mood to deal with his family, so he'd come here to make his plans for keeping an eye on her without appearing to be some crazed stalker.

The night air was cold. If he wasn't careful, she would freeze on the trip back to Mirabilus.

Caitlin put the flashlight back inside the cabin then joined him. "I'm ready." She brushed her hands up and down her arms. "This isn't going to be pleasant, is it?"

"It'll be fine." He reached out to take her hand as they crossed the clearing. "I'll keep you warm enough."

Once they arrived at the clearing near the cliffs, he turned to her. "When you climb onto my foot, lie down so I can hold you next to my chest without squishing you."

"Ew, I'd hate to get dragon squished." She laughed softly before kissing his cheek. "I'm ready. Let's go."

Caitlin stood back and held her breath. Watching Sean change from man to smoke and then to dragon amazed her. She wondered how it felt. Did it hurt? If so, he didn't give evidence of any pain. Did it just feel…strange?

When he held out his foot, she did as he'd asked and stretched out on the pad. She suffered a moment of panic when he lifted her toward his chest, and the image of being crushed flitted across her mind. Thankfully, her panic subsided as quickly as it had formed.

In fact, between the firm padding of his foot beneath her and the warmth of his chest, she found herself fighting sleep. It was so comfortable and cozy her eyelids kept drifting closed. She couldn't imagine a more pleasant flight.

"Caitlin, wake up."

A blast of cold air rushed across her body, dragging her from sleep. She opened her eyes, startled to find they had already landed on the beach at Mirabilus. A puff of warm air blew her hair across her face, and she looked up into the beast's nostrils.

She patted his nose before rolling up to her knees to climb off his foot. "I'm going, I'm going."

Once he changed back into human form, he took her hand and headed for the castle. "We need to make sure I have everything I need before I head to the Learned's. And you need to get your story of my brothers' deaths set in your mind."

She slowed her steps, hanging back, trying to slow him down. "I'm not so sure this is a wise idea."

"Doesn't matter what you think. I'm going."

"But—"

He stopped and swung around so fast that she ran into him, literally bouncing off his chest.

"I am not going to argue this with you. So you can shut up and either lend me a hand or not. Doesn't matter to me."

"Please don't go there alone." Her legs shook. "I'm afraid."

The anger etched on his face lessened. "You came to me for help. I swore to you that I would get our son back. That vow was from me. I made no promises for my brothers." He grasped her chin and lifted it so she had no choice but to look at him. "Caitlin, this is my battle, not theirs. I am doing this my way. I will not fail you."

She knew she wasn't going to be able to sway him from his path. Grabbing the front of his shirt, she pulled him closer. "If you get yourself killed, I swear to you I will make your afterlife miserable."

That damn sexy, mind-stealing half smile made her wonder if she should kiss him or smack him.

He took the choice away. Lowering his head, he whispered, "Darlin', you do that."

And then kissed away any comment she might have made had she had any control over her ability to think.

Before she could regain any intelligence, they were in his suite. He stood in the living room frowning then dragged her to the bathroom and turned on the shower. "Can you light up that pendant?"

She pulled it free from beneath her sweatshirt and held it in her hand, willing it to come alive. When it shimmered with an amethyst light, she held it up. "Now what?"

"We need to combine our energy to put a shield

around this suite. Once I release Aelthed, I can't have him escaping."

"Afraid he'll go blabbing your plan?"

"Yes."

That wouldn't be such a bad thing from her point of view, but it also probably wouldn't change anything. "What do you want me to do?"

"Instead of trying to secure the entire suite, pick a room to confine him to while I'm gone."

"How about the bedroom? It's small enough to secure, yet it should be large enough for him to roam around in considering he's been trapped in a six-inch cube for so long."

Sean nodded. "All right, now focus on the bedroom and envision a shield around it. An unbreakable barrier for Aelthed."

She closed her eyes and focused. Bringing the bedroom into view wasn't hard, but when she added the shield, the whole thing kept changing color. Caitlin swore silently then looked at Sean to ask, "Any specific color for this shield?"

He shrugged. "I'd go with amethyst."

She rolled her eyes at her own lack of forethought. Of course the obvious would be just out of her reach. Closing her eyes again, she brought the vision of the bedroom into her mind, this time surrounded with an amethyst light shield. That color held steady. Since she had no clue what he really looked like, she pictured Aelthed as an old man in medieval robes trapped in the room. She sent him to the door to ensure he was unable to open it or to go through it if anyone else opened it. And did the same thing with the sliding glass doors to the balcony and the door to the bathroom, just in case.

She inspected every inch, every nook and cranny of the room, making sure there was no escape and that the shield covered everything completely.

Sean turned off the shower. "That should do it."

Caitlin opened her eyes asking, "How do you know if... Never mind." The shimmer of amethyst light seeping in beneath the bathroom door answered her unasked question. Their spell had worked.

"I'm going to go get the grimoire and the other two pendants. You collect the cube and bring him in the bedroom. And, I know you don't like the idea, but I'm going to need your sword."

No, she didn't like the idea, but she also didn't think it would be too big of a threat to him, because if she wasn't using it, the magic wouldn't be there. She held out her hand and called the weapon to her.

Handing it to Sean, she warned, "If it thinks I need it, nothing you do will keep it with you."

"Got it." He placed it on the bed and headed out of the bedroom.

She followed him out the door and while he went to the office, she opened the linen closet and felt around on the top shelf until she was able to wrap her hand around the small box.

*"What are you doing?"*

Caitlin bit her lip to keep from saying anything. Instead, she quickly pulled the box down from the shelf and rushed into the bedroom before Aelthed could levitate himself out of their reach.

Sean was right behind her, and after quickly closing the door, he put his items on the bed, motioning her to do the same. "Now, from what the beast and I could figure, this is going to take two of us."

He picked up the sapphire pendant that currently belonged to Ariel. "We need to put this pendant and yours on opposite sides of the box at the same time."

She sat down on the edge of the bed, holding her dragon pendant, and studied the box. "I don't see any place for them to fit into."

"Humor me." He pulled a piece of chalk from his jeans and sat near her on the bed. "Since this might take a few tries, I'm going to number the sides."

After he'd jotted a number on each of the six sides, he said, "I'll count to three and on three just press your pendant against the center of side two."

They did that three times, with her using the even-numbered sides. Then switched with her using the odd-numbered sides.

On the second try—with her pendant in the center of side three and his in the center of side four—the flat surface mutated. The indented shape of a dragon, the exact size of the pendants, appeared on those sides of the box.

Sean smiled. "I was right. Okay, now, again on three, turn your dragon clockwise."

Nothing happened.

They removed the pendants from the box, and the indentations disappeared. Then they repeated placing and turning, but this time counterclockwise.

Caitlin gasped as they heard a distinct click, immediately followed by tiny pieces of the box shifting, moving like a 3D puzzle working itself, until the top opened and a stream of fog escaped. Sean motioned her to remove her pendant, and she watched as the pieces once again shifted and moved back into a flat-sided cube.

The stream took shape, and to her satisfaction the

shape was of an old man, with a long white beard and hair, wearing medieval-style robes.

Sean rose. "You must be Aelthed."

"What have you done?" The wizard appeared horrified, but his eyes blazed with anger.

"A thank-you will suffice."

"I'll not thank you for using black magic to free me."

"Black magic?" Caitlin broke into the men's conversation. "Wasn't it a dark power that put you there in the first place?"

Aelthed turned a look of disdain in her direction. "You know nothing."

She picked her pendant up from the bed, letting it dangle from the chain. "If its power is dark, then you've no one to blame but yourself, since this came from your own creation."

His eyes widened. He reached out to touch a fingertip to the amethyst. "Where did you get this?"

Sean said, "It fell out of the grimoire."

"That's not possible. This gemstone beast was shattered into dust."

Caitlin blew a warm breath over the small dragon, bringing it to shimmering life. "Doesn't look like any dust I've ever seen."

The old wizard stepped back, his wary gaze on Caitlin. "Be careful with that."

Sean took the pendant from her. "I've wasted enough time." He then gathered up Ascalon, the grimoire, the other two pendants and the now-empty cube.

He stepped closer to the wizard. "Not even a thank-you? Fine. But you owe me."

"What do you want?"

"You stay right here, in this room. When I call, you bring me back here. Got it?"

Caitlin frowned. Why wouldn't he be able to bring himself back here?

Aelthed muttered to himself then said, "You're going to the Learned's."

"Yes, I am. And when I return, I'll have my son."

"A lot of good that'll do once Nathan has everything in his possession."

Adding to Caitlin's confusion, Sean smiled as he headed for the balcony while slipping the gold chain holding her pendant over his head. "He'll be too dead to use any of them."

# Chapter 17

Sean landed on a ledge outside one of the windows lining the Great Hall at the Learned's stronghold and shifted from dragon to human form. He leaned tightly against the wall, widening his stance to ensure he had a good purchase on the ledge, then took a deep steadying breath and removed the pack from his back, setting it on the ledge next to him.

"Ready, buddy? It's time."

Gritting his teeth, he and his beast concentrated, each focusing on their own individual form. Sean clenched his jaw harder to keep from crying out as his dragon tore free of its human bond. The separation felt as if his flesh and muscle were being ripped apart as his body mutated. The burning pain seared through him, leaving him shaking and gasping for breath.

They'd only practiced this twice, and each time it had worked. The painful process wasn't anything he wanted to experience too often, but worse than the pain was the emptiness—a cold, sickly hollowness deep inside that drained him of energy and light. His heart and soul became dark, depressing entities that threatened to consume him.

Once the beast was free and Sean had regained the

ability to stand without trembling and gasping for air, he handed the dragon Caitlin's amethyst pendant, while he took the sapphire one from the pocket of the backpack.

The two of them worked in unison just as he and Caitlin had done to open the box. Once the top opened, the beast changed into smoke and quickly streamed into the box before it closed up again.

Sean grinned. Wouldn't Nathan be surprised when he opened the cube expecting to find his uncle inside?

Once the exchange was made and he left the stronghold, it would be up to the beast to ensure the Learned's death. He didn't doubt his dragon's bravery or strength; what worried him was Nathan's trickery.

Hopefully, he and his dragon managed to outtrick the wizard this time.

Ascalon hung securely from its scabbard at his side. He slipped the small sapphire beast back into the pocket of the backpack along with the emerald one and opened the pack to retrieve a small scrap of leather. After wrapping the amethyst pendant securely in the leather, he slid it into the pocket of his jeans. Hopefully, if for whatever reason, the thing decided to shimmer and glow, the leather would keep the light contained. He didn't want Nathan to know there was a third dragon pendant.

Holding the cube in one hand and the straps to the pack in the other, Sean climbed into the stronghold through the window and jumped down to the floor of the Great Hall. He flicked his fingers toward the torches, setting them afire. Elongated flickers of light danced across the stone floor and up the walls, casting eerie shadows that seemed to reach out for him like the evil, clawing fingers of a demon.

Sean shook off the image and crossed to the altar at

the far side of the hall. The castle was quiet—far too quiet. Not even the sound of mice scurrying across the floor broke the silence. The lack of noise put him on edge. Not a bad thing considering what or who he was up against. He wiped those thoughts from his mind. He had to remember not to think of anything. The Learned would pick up on the slightest thread of a misplaced thought and easily deduce something foul was afoot.

The candles on the altar flickered to life, warning him that the Learned was near.

"Well, well. A Drake who appears to be able to follow orders…eventually. You simply needed a booster of sorts."

Nathan materialized behind the altar. He caught sight of the cube in Sean's grasp and clapped his hands. "The rest?"

Sean placed the cube and backpack on top of the altar. He unstrapped Ascalon from around his waist and placed that next to the other items.

"My son?"

"I beg your pardon?" Nathan sneered. "Is that how you speak to your lord?"

Against every fiber of his being, Sean calmed his churning ego, bowed his head and moderated his tone. "May I have my son, my lord?"

"Not quite yet." Nathan pulled the grimoire from the pack and swept clean a place for it to rest. He opened the family book.

Sean glanced up enough to see that the pages of the grimoire were blank. That wasn't anything he could control. He didn't have the power to create scenes on the pages.

A guttural curse echoed in the hall before Nathan

slammed the ancient tome closed. He glared at Sean before pulling the two pendants out of the pack's pocket.

After inspecting the gemstone dragons closely, he placed them next to their respective dragon statues on the altar. To Sean's surprise both pendants glowed, and a warmth grew against his thigh. The amethyst pendant in his pocket was radiating heat through the leather wrap. Resisting the urge to look down at his pocket to see if the light showed, and giving away its existence to Nathan, Sean focused on the flicking candles atop the altar.

"Ah," Nathan said, turning his attention to the weapon. "This must be the fabled sword of the dragon slayer."

He pulled Ascalon from its scabbard and held it up before him. With an evil smirk, he pointed it toward Sean. "Your brothers?"

"Both dead."

Sean let the image of him using Ascalon to stab Braeden and then Cam form in his mind. He shifted the vision to Alexia and Ariel sobbing and screaming over the two beasts writhing on the floor of Braeden's office in their final death throes. He let the scenes drag out, wanting Nathan to savor every moment of his victory.

"Very good. You make an excellent pet." Nathan raised and lowered the blade a couple times before placing it back on the altar. "I might have a use for you in the future."

The wizard then raised an arm and snapped his fingers. "Take your spawn and go. I will beckon you soon." He pinned Sean with a narrowed eye stare. "And you will answer."

Sean tipped his head forward, nodding once to show

he understood. At the sound of a baby's crying, he turned to see a woman carry the child into the hall.

As calmly and emotionless as possible, he met the woman halfway across the chamber and took his son into his arms for the first time. The boy ceased his cries and stared up at him with eyes the color of emeralds. The searching, curious gaze threatened to destroy Sean's air of calm.

He unbuttoned his shirt and pulled it around the baby to keep him warm then stepped up onto the window ledge and out into the cold night.

*"Caitlin, bring us home."*

Caitlin swung away from the sliding glass doors. "Now! Bring him back, now."

Aelthed grumbled but waved his hands before him, chanting in a language she didn't understand.

Within a matter of seconds, Sean materialized in the bedroom.

She held her breath. His back was to her so it was impossible to tell if he had their son or if he'd been injured.

Taking a hesitant step toward him, she reached out, whispering in a voice that shook as much as her hand, "Sean?"

He turned to face her, unbuttoning his shirt as he did so.

Relief, joy and a surge of love overwhelmed her, leaving her lightheaded and trembling. She took another step forward and dropped to her knees.

"Shh, Caitlin, he is safe." Sean knelt in front of her. He held the baby between them. "See, he's fine."

He *was* fine. He was more than fine—he was here. Caitlin brushed her thumb across a soft, plump cheek and leaned closer to kiss his forehead. "Oh, sweetheart, Mommy has missed you."

He turned to look at her with eyes so like his father's and reached up to tangle his little fingers in her hair.

Sean untangled the grasping fingers from her hair. "He's missed you, too."

Little Sean turned his head to peer up at his father and wrapped his fingers around the chain hanging from Sean's neck then promptly stuck it in his mouth.

Caitlin smiled. "I don't think I mentioned that he's at the hand-to-mouth stage."

She looked up at Sean. Something was…wrong… missing…not quite right. She touched his arm. "Are you all right?"

"Fine."

She scooted around to sit on the floor with her back against the bed. "How did it go?"

He handed her the baby then did the same, sitting next to her. "Easier than I thought. Time will tell."

Caitlin held her son close. "Time will tell what?"

"Excuse me." Aelthed interrupted them. "Is it possible that I might leave now?"

Sean pulled the chain over his head and handed the dragon pendant to Caitlin. "I suppose we can let him go now."

Between the two of them they removed the amethyst shield confining the old wizard to the room.

The instant the glow dissipated, the door to the bedroom opened then slammed closed. Caitlin snorted. "How do you like that? Not even a farewell."

"Oh, I'm sure he'll be back."

"With your family in tow, I suppose."

Sean nodded in agreement.

"So, what did you mean *time will tell*?"

"You never can tell with Nathan."

He was doing it again—holding an odd conversation that left her with more questions than answers.

She drew her brows together and glared at him. "Was he dead or alive when you left?"

"Alive...for a time."

Caitlin clenched her jaw. Her son picked up on her tenseness and started to fuss. She forced herself to relax and bent her legs. Placing the baby along her thighs, she bounced her heels on the floor, quieting him down almost instantly.

"Did he know Aelthed wasn't in the box anymore?"

Sean chuckled. "Nope."

"Why is that amusing? He's going to be livid when he finds out."

"Doubtful."

"Sean."

He leaned his shoulder against hers. "I promise to explain everything in the morning. Right now I am exhausted. Could we maybe make use of the bed?"

"You promise you're going to tell me what happened?"

He stroked the baby's foot. "I vowed to rescue our son and did so, didn't I?"

"Yes."

"Then I'm fairly certain you can believe me now."

She looked closer at him, realizing what was different—what was missing. How foolish of her. He'd needed help getting back here to Mirabilus. She asked, "Where's your dragon?"

Sean rose. "Tomorrow."

He helped her up from the floor.

"You didn't leave him at Nathan's?"

"I said, tomorrow."

She swung the baby over to one hip and grabbed Sean's arm. "Where is he?"

He jerked free of her hold. "Look, I'm exhausted and—"

"Exhausted? You're only half alive. Of course you're exhausted. What the hell did you do?" No wonder he refused to tell her all of his plans. He knew damn well she never would have agreed to this. Never. She would have gone to his brothers in a heartbeat.

He stepped closer and glared down at her. "Our son is safe. I would have done anything to make that happen. Anything for you and the baby. Do you understand me?"

Their son picked that moment to start throwing a fit. He jerked and twisted around in Caitlin's arms, screaming until his tear-streaked face was red.

She was so angry nothing she did soothed him. She wanted to kick Sean for being so foolish and for upsetting her and their son.

He took the baby from her arms, held him close to his chest and paced at the end of the bed. "I'm sorry, little one, hush. It's okay."

Faster than she thought possible, the cries turned to whimpers then to the sound of soft breathing as he fell asleep against his father's chest.

Caitlin stared at the two of them, torn between relief and shock, with a twinge of jealousy and this odd urge to cry from a heart brimming with the warmth of what she knew was love.

Was that all it took to fall in love? The sight of her son resting so comfortably at ease against Sean's chest?

No. There had to be more to it than that. She was just upset and it had her emotions all jumbled.

"We need a crib." Sean's softly spoken statement broke into her thoughts. "Ask one of my brothers."

The last thing she wanted to do right now was to ask another Drake male for anything. She focused instead on Braeden's wife, Alexia. Within a matter of minutes a fully furnished nursery appeared in their bedroom. Complete with a rocking chair that would never get used.

Sean shook his head. "I said a crib."

"So did I."

He laid the baby in the crib then came to stand before her. "Caitlin, I will always do what I think best for my family. We'll talk about it in the morning, when I'm back to my full self. Right now I feel ready to fall on my face."

She pushed him gently toward the bed. "Go to sleep."

Sean hooked two fingers around her wrist. "Are you coming?"

"In a minute or two."

While he got ready for bed and slipped beneath the covers, she stood at the side of the crib, staring down at their son.

Unshed tears burned her eyes. Fear as cold and deadly as a vampire's death bite wrapped around her heart.

This sacrifice of his could all have been for nothing. If his dragon was unable to vanquish the Learned, they would all soon die.

She knew his beast was strong and brave. But he was young, so very young, and Nathan had Ascalon.

She could do nothing except hope for the best. Caitlin choked back a sob, fearing the worst.

Nathan chortled with glee and ran his hands lovingly over the items on his altar. The dragon pendants glowed as brightly as they had centuries ago when they'd been created. And while only blank pages filled the grimoire, he knew that once Aelthed was gone from this plane, the book would work its magic for him.

He reached out to touch the sword. Ascalon. The only weapon he would ever again require. Nathan lifted his arms toward the ceiling and chanted over the sword, taking the spell from the dragon slayer and gifting it to himself. He stopped only when the raised spine running the length of the blade glowed with an amethyst light.

Now he had everything he needed to rid the world of the remaining Drakes—the wives and their spawns along with that aunt of theirs. Then his way would be clear to assume complete control of all. Both the human and preternatural worlds would belong to him alone.

Finally, he would rule in the manner to which he'd been destined—as supreme Hierophant. No other ruler, not a king, emperor or president, would hold as much power as he. His word would be law over them all. Any rights granted would be by his hand alone. All would bow to his whim.

He fought the urge to sob with exquisite joy. How long had he worked for this very moment? How many endless nights had he dreamed of this success?

And how many lives had been lost in order for him to realize his goal?

Drakes and his own sons alike had suffered and in the end he had won, not the Drakes.

Nathan picked up the wooden puzzle cube he'd manifested so many centuries ago. He held it up to eye level, admiring his handiwork.

"Well, dearest uncle, the time has finally come for you to go free and be on your way." He laughed before adding, "Right after I exhume any bit of energy you might have left."

With trembling fingers, Nathan worked the cube, moving unseen pieces into place, twisting and flipping bits here, then there, until finally he heard the distinct click of the lock.

He set the wooden box atop his altar and pressed lightly on the top. "Come, greet me, Uncle Aelthed."

The instant he raised his finger, the top sprung up, opening the box to the daylight.

Nathan stepped back and waved one hand over the now-open box. "Come."

A stream of smoke rose from the box. Nathan frowned at the unexpected display. "My, my, Uncle. It seems you have plenty of energy left to provide me."

The smoke swirled then took shape.

Nathan's legs began to tremble; his heart pounded heavy in his chest. Something wasn't right. This was not the shape of a man.

It was the shape of a dragon.

He blindly reached out to retrieve Ascalon.

The beast towered over him. Thrashing in rage it knocked down walls. Pillars supporting the floor above crashed to the ground at their feet.

Roars of anger shook the remaining walls, sending centuries-old stones and bricks crashing down around him, smashing onto the altar, destroying it and all it held.

Oil and torch material from the wall sconces collided with the lit candles. Flames leaped to ancient wall hangings and rugs, fanning the inferno higher and hotter.

In one still partially standing corner of the castle, the ghost of the gypsy mage laughed uproariously.

She shouted over the maelstrom, asking, *"Is this the power you sought, wizard?"*

A chunk of stone, large enough to kill a mortal man, tumbled from the ceiling, knocking Nathan down onto the rubble. He reached out to catch himself, releasing Ascalon in his haste.

The sword clattered across the Great Hall, skipping over cracks in the floor and bouncing over broken hunks of masonry.

Scrambling for purchase on the shattered floor, he lunged for the sword. It was the only weapon that could defeat the beast threatening his life.

It wouldn't require great strength or skill, just one small cut from the blade to bring the dragon down. But first Nathan had to get his hands on the sword.

He crawled on his hands and knees, but he could already feel the beast's hot breath rushing against his back.

One talon hooked into the flesh of his leg, ripping through skin and muscle. A scream tore from Nathan's throat.

The instinct to survive pushed him forward. Dragging his useless bloody limb behind, he bolted over a broken statue and wrapped one hand around the hilt of the sword.

Quickly, before he lost all courage and his life, he flipped over onto his back.

The dragon clawed at his chest, sharp talons outstretched, intent on nothing less than ending his life.

Nathan screamed again as the instrument of his certain death found its mark, crushing and tearing the life from his body.

With his final breath, Nathan the Learned raised the sword, nicking a single scale on the beast's chest.

The sword fell from the dead hand holding it and clattered to the floor.

*"Oh, beastie, this is not what I envisioned for you."* The gypsy mage floated out of the shadows, coming to rest before the now-calm dragon.

She placed her hand on his side, and he looked down at her, a frown of confusion furrowing his brow. Stroking the injured scale, she coaxed, *"Come rest with me a while. I'll not leave you."*

When he fell heavily to the floor, she sat beside him to offer comfort and encouragement in his final moments. "You were brave and strong, my pet."

# Chapter 18

"No!"

Caitlin struggled to awaken from the nightmare that held her fast in its grip. She knew it was a nightmare, just a dream, but it was like a movie playing over and over in her head that would never end.

She knelt over Sean lying among the rubble at what could only be the Learned's castle. He was dead. Killed by her own sword.

Nathan stood on the other side of the ruined room holding Ascalon. The weapon glowed with a bright line of amethyst, and he laughed.

His maniacal laugh threatened to drive her mad. Couldn't he see what he'd done? Didn't it matter that he'd killed her mate, or that their son was now left without a father?

Stupid questions. Of course it didn't matter. That had been his intention all along. He'd only wanted the items he needed to become all powerful.

Well, now he had them.

She turned back to Sean's body and stroked his cheek. He was so pale, so cold.

Caitlin bowed her head over him and gasped for

breath. The pain was unbearable. It was a struggle to breathe, an insurmountable effort to focus, to even think.

"Wake up, wake up. Not real. Just a dream."

The sound of a baby crying dragged her from the clutches of the nightmare. Bolting upright on the bed, Caitlin fumbled around on the nightstand for the bedside lamp. A pale glow lit the room, enabling her to see Sean sleeping next to her on the bed.

She heaved a sigh of relief then rose to see what was troubling their son. He was dry, and she'd fed him just a few hours earlier, so it wasn't yet time to eat again. But from the sound of his broken sobs, he was upset about something.

Caitlin held him close, his warm body plastered to hers, crooning to him in that odd singsong dragon cry. The beast had used it on her, she had used it on Sean and now she sang the song to their son. True to past experience, it performed the same magic.

Perhaps he'd had a nightmare, too. Or something had frightened him. Regardless, the crooning calmed him, and that was all that mattered. He rested his head against her shoulder, stuck his thumb in his mouth and soon his body went slack in her arms. He'd fallen back to sleep.

She put him back in his crib and stared down at him. He'd been gone less than two weeks, but it had felt like a lifetime to her. Unable to resist, she traced a finger along his petal-soft check. Sometimes she had to touch him to remind herself that he was indeed back where he belonged.

Gratitude and relief didn't begin to describe what she still felt about his return. It was more like an overwhelming rush of warmth, of love that wrapped around her when she held him or gently touched him.

She couldn't help but wonder if her parents had ever felt this way about her. Had they, at any time in her life, felt any warmth for her?

*"Don't be silly, child. Of course we did."*

"Mother?"

*"Right here."*

Caitlin felt a breeze brush against her arm.

"What are you doing here?"

*"Watching you. Realizing how wrong I'd been."*

"About what?" Her mother had been wrong about a lot of things. Which one was she talking about?

*"This child. It would be against nature to take him away from you."*

"It's not like I was going to let you."

*"Rest easy, Caitlin Anna Marie St. George, that is not why I've come."*

She rolled her eyes at her mother's use of her full given name. It was such a time-honored, foolproof way of getting someone's attention. "Then why have you?"

Her mother slowly materialized beside her. "I've come here to try making amends. I know you aren't going to spread your arms and welcome me, but I do not like us being estranged. You are my daughter, and I miss you."

"All I ever wanted was my son."

"And not to be married to Hoffel."

Caitlin laughed softly so as not to awaken Sean or little Sean. "Well, that's not even a consideration any-more. I understand he met with an…accident yesterday."

"Yes, we know. The Dragon Lord called to explain."

That was nice, especially since no one had yet taken the time to explain what had happened to her. Not that it really mattered; it wasn't as if his death bothered her in the least. She was mostly just curious. "It was his own fault for working with the Learned."

Her mother rested a hand on her arm. "I don't disagree with you. Neither does your father."

"So who does he have in store for me now?"

"I couldn't tell you." Her mother turned her head to cast a brief glance toward the bed. "But I'd say that decision is out of his hands, wouldn't you?"

Caitlin shrugged. "We aren't married."

"I see."

She doubted if her mother saw anything. But it wasn't a point she wanted to argue. "What do you mean, you couldn't tell me?"

"Your father and I…" Her mother shrugged and looked away. "We aren't…he's moved on."

"Oh, is that how that works?"

"Well, darling, I am dead."

Really? Her mother was going to split hairs over the degree of *dead* between a ghost and a vampire? The day had been far too long for this conversation to happen. So Caitlin simply pointed out, "So is he."

"Yes, but he has a solid form." The woman waved a hand down her body. "And I no longer do."

Caitlin rubbed her temples.

"You've had a long day. I just wanted to see if you were willing to allow me to make amends—or at least try."

"Yes, Mother, of course I'm willing." What was she going to do? Say no? She was angry at what her parents had done, but as insane as it was, she didn't hate them. Would never trust them again, but they were her parents.

"Good. Thank you. I'll leave you to your sleep."

Caitlin waved goodbye then went and sat on the edge

of the bed to hold her throbbing head in her hands. She'd thought the sudden pounding was due to her mother's conversation, but now she wasn't so certain.

Her head was threatening to kill her. She was strangely dizzy and sick to her stomach. Something was wrong.

She reached behind her to pat the bed. "Sean?"

When he didn't respond, she leaned back groaning at the stabbing pain in her head and grasped his leg to shake it. She opened her eyes and ran her hand down his leg then spun around.

"Sean?"

He was cold—an inhuman sort of cold—more like a corpse than a cold body.

She scrambled across the bed to his side and shook him. "Sean!"

This couldn't be happening.

"Mother!"

Instantly, her mother was back at her side. "What's wrong?"

"I can't wake him."

Her mother looked around the room then closed her eyes for a brief second. "He isn't dead."

Caitlin put her ear to his chest and the palm of her hand in front of his lips. "His heart is barely beating, and his breathing isn't much better." Worse, his dragon hadn't yet returned. Without the beast's strength, whatever ailed him could kill him.

At that moment her son awoke and started crying. She climbed off the bed to pick up little Sean and waved one hand at her mother. "Get the Dragon Lord. Get someone, now."

After the longest few minutes of her life, Braeden,

followed by Cameron and their Aunt Danielle, appeared in the bedroom. Her mother was close behind.

"What's going on?" Braeden bent over Sean, doing the same things she'd just done.

The look on his face when he stood up took her breath away. She slid the baby to one hip and grasped the front of Braeden's shirt with her free hand. "What is happening?"

Braeden shook his head. "I'm not sure."

Another form appeared in the crowd around Sean's bed. "I think I might know."

The Drakes all stared at the newcomer in shock, except for little Sean, who reached out in delight toward Aelthed's long white beard.

The old wizard smiled at the child, asking, "May I?"

Caitlin handed him the baby.

Danielle kept poking Aelthed's arm. "How did this happen? When did this happen?"

Cameron cleared his throat. "Focus, please."

"I believe the younger Drake and the dragon figured out a way to separate."

Caitlin had already figured that much out, but she kept her mouth shut.

Braeden groaned. "Not a wise idea."

Aelthed nodded in agreement. "Wise or not, it's the best possible explanation." He nodded toward Caitlin. "She and Sean released me from my cube. Then he left with it."

Before she could get him to shut up, he added, "Along with the dragon pendants, the grimoire and Ascalon."

Everyone stared at her.

"He told me not to say anything. He was certain his plan would work."

Braeden fisted his hands at his sides. "And what exactly was his plan?"

"I don't know all of it. From what I could gather, he gave Nathan the items he'd demanded, rescuing our son, and at some point the dragon inhabited the cube, intending to kill Nathan."

Her mother vanished, only to return right away. "That much of it obviously succeeded. Nathan is dead."

"And the dragon?"

She put a hand on Caitlin's shoulder. "I'm sorry, child, but I don't think he'll survive. It was Ascalon."

Caitlin slowly sank down onto the edge of the bed. At once, everyone started closing in, offering condolences, telling her how sorry they were and how they'd find someone to help Sean.

Her head hurt so bad she could barely see. But their noise—their clanging din of noise would drive her insane. "Stop!"

She reached up to touch the dragon pendant hanging around her neck, rose and took little Sean from Aelthed then turned to Braeden. "Get us there."

"But—"

She glared at him and repeated, "Get us there."

He nodded, but added, "You aren't going alone."

"I don't care."

In the next instant, she was standing in the rubble that used to be the Learned's stronghold, next to the prone body of Sean's beast. He was still alive; she could see the rise and fall of his chest.

With her foot she cleared the rubble from a space near his head and sat down, holding her son on her lap. She rested a hand on the beast's snout. Stroking gently, she crooned to him. The dragon opened his eyes slightly and stared at her then the child.

Little Sean's eyes were huge, but he didn't cry. Fearlessly, he reached out his little hands and patted the dragon's nose.

The soft rumble started low and soft in the beast's chest, but Caitlin heard it, and the sweetness of the dragon's song was enough to make her sob.

Her son wouldn't understand, nor would he remember, but she scooted closer to the dragon and said, "This is your father's beast. This is the bravest and strongest part of him."

She removed her pendant and draped the fine chain around one of his ears. The amethyst sparkled in the light from the torch Braeden had lit and perched in the crack of a boulder. "We will remember you always, and little Sean here will know of you, I promise you that."

Caitlin shuddered then said, "Thank you for saving us all. We can never repay you for so great a sacrifice except with our love." She leaned over and kissed him between the eyes. "Oh, I will miss you so."

The dragon's song faded away. His chest rose and fell one last time. Caitlin rested her head against his larger one and cried.

She heard Braeden approach. He leaned down to take the baby, whispering, "Come on, buddy, give your mother a minute or two."

When her arms were free, she wrapped them around the beast. "You brave fool. We could have found another way."

A few minutes later Braeden cleared his throat, and she knew it was time to get back to Mirabilus. She had to see to Sean, hoping that she didn't have to go through this same thing again with him. She didn't know if she could bear it.

She dropped one last kiss on the dragon's head and turned away. Braeden handed her little Sean, picked up a backpack and pointed at Ascalon. "Take that with you."

She picked up her sword and looked back at the dragon as Braeden spelled them back to Mirabilus.

The gypsy mage moved out of the shadows with a sigh to caress the beastie's ear. *"Yes, you were strong and brave. And, my sweet, you are well and truly loved. More than I ever could have hoped for you."*

She frowned and then slipped the chain holding the amethyst pendant from his ear. The mage studied the pendant before she looked around the ruined chamber. *"A love like that should never go unrewarded. You should never be without that love. You should never be alone."*

Using a broken piece of lumber, she cleared a circle around the unmoving beast then tossed the wood aside. After placing the pendant on the floor next to her beastie, she surveyed her handiwork and nodded in approval. *"And some morons need spells, blood, pain and death. The fool only needed to dance."*

She stepped inside the circle and began to do just that. Feet tapping, body swaying, she spun around and around dancing inside the circle's edge. Her swirling skirts brushing the dragon.

*"Not a dragon born."*

She clapped while spinning another round.

*"Yet a dragon you shall be."*

She turned, so her back faced the outer edge of the circle.

*"Once this beast has taken form."*

This time she danced so her back faced the dragon.

*"It will answer only to thee."*

She shrugged at her bad rhyme, but kept dancing, turning back and forth, facing the dragon then facing the outside of the circle.

*"St. George will set you free."*

Her magic spun, she continued to chant and dance faster and faster until her feet would carry her no more, then she fell laughing inside the empty circle.

The second her feet hit the floor of her bedroom, Caitlin headed to Sean's side. On the way she tossed Ascalon to her mother. "Tell Father we need to respell that."

Danielle reached out and took the baby. Heading for the bedroom door, she said, "Your mother and I will see to him for now."

Her mother followed, adding, "We'll manage just fine."

Caitlin sat on the edge of the bed and motioned to the door. "If there's nothing you can do, could the rest of you just go? I'll call you if I need you."

Cameron blustered something about being there for brothers, but Braeden pushed him through the open bedroom door and waved Aelthed to join them. "We'll be in the living room."

She nodded absently and leaned down to place her lips over Sean's. Uncertain whether sharing her life force would work or not, she exhaled a long breath.

After a couple tries, she sat up and felt his cheeks. The coldness beneath her fingers drew a cry from her. "Sean, don't you dare die. Do you hear me?"

She leaned down again. Summoning all the energy

she had, she exhaled again, her tears dropping onto his face.

When his lips remained icy and lifeless, she stopped. Stretching out next to him, she rested her head on his shoulder and wrapped an arm around him. "Sean, please, move. Say something. Stay. Don't leave us."

She didn't try to stop her tears; it wouldn't have done any good, anyway. They fell freely onto his shoulder, to seep beneath her cheek.

With a shuddering breath she closed her eyes, determined to commit every moment they'd had together to memory. Every argument, each kiss, every glare, each laugh—she wanted them all engraved in granite. Even though she knew that time would try its best to soften the memories, she didn't ever want to forget even one tiny detail.

A brisk wind blew through the sliding glass doors, sending a chill across her. Caitlin reached behind her to pull the edge of the quilt over them and froze.

Above the bed a smoky mist swirled.

She held her breath. It couldn't be. She'd watched him die.

From nowhere she heard a familiar voice chanting a familiar curse.

*Not a dragon born, yet a dragon you shall be. Once this beast has taken form, it will answer only to thee. St. George will set you free.*

The mist lowered. She moved aside to give it room. It flowed over and around Sean's body, enveloping him, pulsing with life, and then seeped into his body.

He jerked, his face contorted with pain. His arms flailed as if trying to fight off an invisible opponent.

Caitlin hesitated. Should she call for his brothers? Or was this normal when the beast and man became one?

As quickly as it had started, he calmed, easing back into a restful slumber.

She moved back to his side and placed her ear against his chest.

This time the tears that fell from her eyes were tears of happiness.

The beast crooned to her, erasing her fears, reassuring her that all was well.

Sean's arm came around her, holding her tightly against him in his sleep.

# Chapter 19

Caitlin tossed the last of her clothes into the suitcase. She couldn't believe he was making her leave.

She glared at his back. He was standing in front of the sliding door in the bedroom, holding their son, not saying a word. Right now she was fairly certain he was using the baby as a shield against her outrage. He knew damn well that she wasn't going to start anything with little Sean right here in the room.

What was wrong with him? Less than twelve hours ago he had been at death's door. Today, with the rising of the sun, he acted as if nothing had happened.

Since the moment he'd woken up this morning he had treated her politely, like he would a guest at the Lair, or some stranger he'd met on the street.

Over breakfast, he'd informed her that the jet would be here to take her back to the States before noon.

She'd been speechless. He wasn't even going to give her a choice? Or a chance to change her mind?

Fine. She'd leave. But if he thought she was going to come running if he changed his mind later, he needed to think again. She was not a puppet to manipulate at whim.

Jerk.

A knock at the bedroom door tore her away from her fuming. "What?"

Danielle Drake entered. "I was wondering if I could have a little time with the baby before the plane arrives?"

Wonderful. He'd told the entire family she was leaving? Caitlin took a deep breath. Her anger wasn't at Danielle. She nodded. "Sure."

Once Danielle left the bedroom with little Sean, and Caitlin heard the outer door to the apartment close, she turned to stare at Sean.

He wouldn't even look at her.

She crossed the distance between them and tapped him on the shoulder. "You want to tell me what's going on?"

"I told you I wasn't going to stop you from leaving."

"You never mentioned throwing me out."

"I'm giving you what you want."

"Oh, really? You are, are you? Tossing me and my son out is what I want?"

"*Our* son."

"Fine." She corrected herself. "Our son. This is how you treat *our* son?"

"I'm not doing anything you didn't want."

"How do you know what I want? Are you suddenly all-knowing?"

"Have you changed your mind? Do you want something else first? The cabin wasn't enough, so you want another fuck before you go?"

A haze of pure red clouded her sight and mind. She raised her arm, palm open, and swung toward him.

Faster than she knew was possible, he spun around and backed her toward the bed. Before she could so much as gasp, they were naked on the bed, with him on top of her.

"Is this what you wanted? Do you need some energy to tide you over until you can find someone else to supply it?"

She didn't know what was wrong with him. But she did know something was. Not only wasn't this normal, it wasn't even rational.

She knew better than to physically fight him. There was no way she could win, and in his current state of mind she didn't know if he'd be able to stop himself from killing her.

So she wrapped her arms tightly around him and whispered, "Sean, where are you? What happened? Talk to me."

The rage in his eyes made his glare as hard and sharp as any cut gemstone. He hadn't heard her.

Caitlin closed her eyes and crooned to the beast inside. To her relief, the dragon listened and crooned back.

The man holding himself so tense atop her slowly relaxed. He buried his face against her shoulder. "Forgive me. I'm sorry."

"What happened? Where did you go?"

"A changeling isn't meant to separate from his beast. When I was by myself, I was filled with a rage I couldn't control. A cold fury that threatened to consume me."

She ran her fingers through his hair. "I noticed."

"I was trying so hard to get you out of here before it broke free."

Caitlin sighed. "And of course I just egged it on."

"I was acting like an ass. What else were you going to do?"

"Yeah, well, from now on, you don't ever—and I mean ever, ever, never—separate from your beast again."

"No fears there since I have no intention of doing that again."

"Good."

Sean rolled off her and spelled their clothes back on. "There's time for a walk before the jet arrives. We have a few things to discuss."

"Yes, we do."

He took her hand and led her out of the bedroom, down to the main floor and out of the castle. The entire Drake clan was gathered in front of the castle. But he didn't stop to chat, just nodded and kept walking to the beach.

Once there, he turned to her and took both of her hands in his. "You're pregnant."

Caitlin stared at him. "Beg pardon?"

"I said you're pregnant. With twins."

While that probably explained her emotional highs and lows these last few days, this wasn't exactly the way she wanted to discover the news. In fact, wasn't it usually the woman telling the man?

"And how long have you known this?"

"When we were at the cabin."

"Oh."

"So, are you going to marry me?"

She looked up at him. "No."

Before she could say anything else, like explaining why, he released her hands, turned away, shifted into a smoky dragon and took off.

Caitlin wanted to scream. If she did nothing else in this lifetime, she was going to break him from this habit of running away.

She took three steps to chase after him and felt the wind rush through her skin. She frowned. Something was happening. Her body suddenly felt as light as air. She looked down at the beach, shocked to find it a good twenty feet below her.

She shifted her attention to her body, which was no longer there. No arms, no legs, no nothing.

Caitlin headed toward the water and glanced down at her reflection. If her eyes weren't playing tricks on her, she was the most gorgeous amethyst-hued smoky dragon alive.

She was lighter than a feather. Not just her body, but her heart. This was impossible, but it was fabulous. She was happy.

The cool breeze flowed through her; the colors of the earth and sea were more brilliant than she'd ever seen, brighter than she could ever have envisioned.

She flew over the castle, circled the people staring at her from the lawn.

Danielle Drake pointed to the left, shouting, "Go get him."

Caitlin wanted to laugh. Oh, she'd get him all right. If her mate thought for one minute he was going to escape his fate, he was sadly mistaken.

She veered to the left and instantly spotted him soaring over the ocean.

It took little effort to catch up with him, and she fell into line next to him.

He looked at her, surprise evident in the way he slowed down to study the form next to him.

Caitlin smiled to herself and then flew straight into him, her form and his blending into one.

"I'm not going to marry you because you haven't ever asked me to."

He welcomed her, filled her with warmth, cocooning her within the expanse of his misty wings. "And if I did?"

She snuggled into his warmth, breathing her life force into him and accepting the energy he returned. "If you did, you would never be able to get rid of me."

"Well, so tell me Caitlin St. George, milady Dragon Slayer, will you marry this beast who loves you dearly?"

She sighed at his words. "Yes, my love, I will marry you."

He took control of their flight, swirling, rising and dipping before he brought them both to a gentle landing on the beach.

Once they both returned to human form, he dropped down on one knee and took her hands between his. "I am honored. I swear to you that I will always love you, always care for you and keep you safe."

"Of course you will. You haven't broken a vow yet, why would you in the future?"

He kissed her hand. "I have to warn you of something, though."

"And what might that be?"

He rose to envelop her in an embrace and whispered against her ear, "Dragons mate for life."

# Chapter 20

*Mirabilus Island—Six months later*

Caitlin lowered her oversize form down onto the lawn chair on the beach. She was fairly certain she'd be giving birth to hippos, not babies. Pulling a folding fan from the beach bag Sean had provided, she snapped it open and waved it in front of her face. Not that it helped; the summer heat was sweltering.

Alexia, sitting in the chair next to her, patted her hand. "It'll get better."

"Yeah, in three to four months?"

"That sounds about right."

Caitlin sighed. "So, is everything ready for the wedding?"

"Everything except for the bride."

Sean came up behind them. He handed Caitlin a glass of iced tea and massaged her shoulders. "What's Danielle's problem now?"

"Her veil was delivered this morning, and she doesn't like it."

Braeden dropped onto the sand at his wife's feet. "And she thinks Aelthed will care what veil she wears?"

"She just wants everything to be perfect." Caitlin tried to explain the woman's reasoning.

"Speaking of the happy couple." Braeden nodded toward the other end of the beach.

Aelthed and Danielle were walking hand in hand at the edge of the water.

Ariel snatched one of her children out of the water and joined them. "What do you think of Aelthed's new look?"

He'd shaved off his beard and cut his hair. The cleaner look made him appear younger than his nine hundred or so years. The blue jeans and sneakers helped with the overall look.

Caitlin mused out loud. "How long do you think he'll be here?"

Cameron shook water all over his wife, before sitting in the chair next to her. "Who knows? Does it matter?"

Sean answered, "Since none of us knows how long we'll live, I suppose not."

"Are your parents coming for the wedding?" Alexia asked.

"My mother says yes. My father just snarls."

Ariel laughed. "He's still not happy about that whole being married for an eternity concept the High Council imposed on him?"

"Considering he just bought my mother the house of her dreams and let her furnish it to her exacting tastes, he's obviously fine with it." Caitlin shook her head. "He just likes to kvetch, to hear himself talk."

"When are they bringing Sean back?" Braeden's tone was a little on the sharp side. He still wasn't used to being related to the St. Georges and even though Caitlin had made her peace with both of her parents, he didn't trust them.

"They'll fly in tomorrow."

The babies decided to fight for space in her womb. Caitlin groaned and rubbed her hand over them.

Sean took the tea from her. "Come on, we're going in. You need to rest."

"That's all I do is rest."

"Now."

He helped her to her feet and looked at Braeden. "A little assist?"

In the next instant they were in their cool, air-conditioned bedroom. Sean pulled the curtains closed over the sliding doors to block out the sun.

He then helped her onto the bed and took her shoes off before stretching out next to her.

She had to admit, she was much more comfortable out of the heat, and the dragonettes seemed to like it better when she stretched out. Maybe it gave them more room.

Sean rolled onto his side and caressed the bulge that encased their babies. "Are you happy, Mrs. Drake?"

She placed her hand over his. "Very, Mr. Drake."

"Do you regret anything?"

No, she didn't. Not one single second of their time together. Not their first three days together, or coming to him for help when their son had been kidnapped, or their fights, or disagreements, or even their whirlwind justice of the peace wedding. "Yes."

His eyes widened. "What?"

"That we still haven't put any utilities in at the cabin."

"Woman, you'll drive me out of my mind." He dropped a kiss on the tip of her nose. "But, darlin', I love you, anyway."

"That's good."

"Oh? And why is that?"

She reached up to cup his face and bring him down for a slow, leisurely kiss. Then she whispered against his lips, "Because, my love, dragons mate for life."

\* \* \* \* \*

# THE WORLD IS BETTER WITH

## Romance

Harlequin has everything from contemporary, passionate and heartwarming to suspenseful and inspirational stories.

Whatever your mood,
we have a romance just for you!

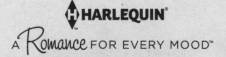

# Turn your love of reading into rewards you'll love with
# Harlequin My Rewards

# Love the Harlequin book you just read?

Your opinion matters.

Review this book on your favorite
book site, review site, blog or your own
social media properties and share
your opinion with other readers!

**Be sure to connect with us at:**
Harlequin.com/Newsletters
Facebook.com/HarlequinBooks
Twitter.com/HarlequinBooks

**HARLEQUIN®**

A *Romance* FOR EVERY MOOD™

# JUST CAN'T GET ENOUGH?

Join our social communities
and talk to us online.

You will have access to the latest
news on upcoming titles and special
promotions, but most importantly,
you can talk to other fans about your
favorite Harlequin reads.

Harlequin.com/Community

Facebook.com/HarlequinBooks

Twitter.com/HarlequinBooks

Pinterest.com/HarlequinBooks

**HARLEQUIN®**

A *Romance* FOR EVERY MOOD™

Stay up-to-date on all your
romance-reading news with the
***Harlequin Shopping Guide,***
featuring bestselling authors, exciting new
miniseries, books to watch and more!

The newest issue will be delivered right to you
with our compliments! There are 4 each year.

Signing up is easy.

## EMAIL

ShoppingGuide@Harlequin.ca

## WRITE TO US

HARLEQUIN BOOKS
Attention: Customer Service Department
P.O. Box 9057, Buffalo, NY 14269-9057

## OR PHONE

1-800-873-8635 in the United States
1-888-343-9777 in Canada

Please allow 4-6 weeks for delivery of the first issue by mail.